Smoke Gets in Your Eyes

British Library Cataloguing in Publication Data:
A catalogue record for this book is available from the British Library
ISBN 978-1-904109-174

Published 2007
Reprinted 2008, 2010

The Hastings Press
www.hastingspress.co.uk
hastings.press@gmail.com

Set in Garamond
Cover design by Bill Citrine
Printed by Printondemand-worldwide, Peterborough

SMOKE GETS IN YOUR EYES

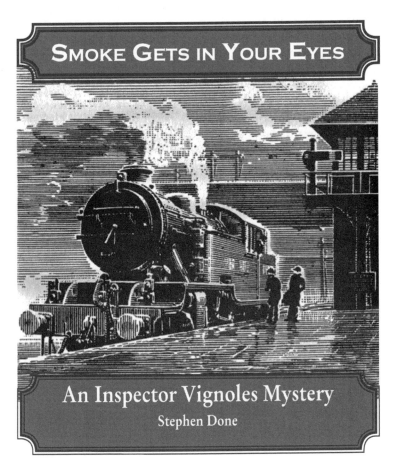

An Inspector Vignoles Mystery

Stephen Done

~ ACKNOWLEDGEMENTS ~

I would like to thank those who have helped, advised and encouraged me along the way.

Mum and Dad especially, for they, from my earliest days, developed my love of books, reading, words and writing and gave a wealth of helpful advice for this story and its creation (that hot June day in the garden, a glass of wine, and thoughts of 1946). My only regret, however, is that it was not completed in time for Dad to read how it ended.

Adrian for his informative and valuable annotations, Helena Wojtczak and Adrian Hancock, Nina (Viva Violet!), Rachel and Dave, Bill for the lovely cover design, Melita, Carl (Black Sheep and The Modernaires) and of course Irena, for her enthusiastic encouragement, support and love throughout.

A number of books have helped in the research for this novel, but particular mention needs to be made of *Railwaywomen* by Helena Wojtczak, and *The Making of a Railway* by R. T. C. Rolt.

Thanks,

Stephen.

~ AUTHOR'S NOTE ~

The Great Central Railway really did run between Marylebone, Leicester and the North via Woodford Halse, later operated by the London & North Eastern Railway and British Railways, until closure in 1967–8.

The actual line bears only a passing resemblance to that described within this book and many liberties have been taken. I am unaware of any detective department within a British railway company, and any similarity to persons living or dead is unintentional.

Stephen Done was born in August 1960. On his eight birthday he declared that he wanted to be a steam engine driver, only to be told they were going out of service a few days later. He took up writing about them instead.

A museum curator by profession, he has worked at the Bristol Industrial Museum, Cyfarthfa Castle Museum, and overseen the Liverpool Football Club Museum since 1997.

He volunteers on the Llangollen, and the Welshpool & Llanfair railways, likes real English ale and enjoys bird-watching.

Copies of his books can be obtained by contacting him at Stephen.done@googlemail.com

Dedicated to Dad, with love

Harry Done

1932~2006

Turning and turning in the widening gyre
The falcon cannot hear the falconer;
Things fall apart; the centre cannot hold;
Mere anarchy is loosed upon the world.

W. B. Yeats, *The Second Coming.*

Contents

Chapter One

'Blue Skies Are around the corner'

Sam Browne with Jack Hylton & his Orchestra

'Oh, what a waste of time — and money!'

Violet McIntyre was cursing silently to herself as she walked down Baker Street, past its shabby shops and sooty trees. Her spirits were low and, despite the early morning sunlight, London looked tired and unwashed. The pale sun seemed only to accentuate the yellowing net curtains, cobwebby windows and faded paintwork. As she looked above the shops that offered little but empty promises, the stucco and brickwork were scarred and shattered. Wounds suffered in the Blitz, still startlingly clean against the smoke-stained walls.

'But what on earth should I do now?'

Violet was aware that whatever she decided, it would lead inevitably to further decisions and actions, each sending a ripple through her life. And she was all too aware that, sometimes, taking what seemed like a perfectly reasonable course of action could lead to unexpected, and perhaps unwelcome, results. Violet knew all about that. Her life had already been permanently altered by a choice she had made, carelessly, if also wilfully, eighteen years earlier. In many ways it had been a mistaken one, and had created more of a tidal wave than a ripple as it turned out. But, with the passing of the years, she had come to view this as her 'brilliant mistake'.

So Violet took decision-making seriously. But no matter how carefully she considered the matter in hand, she could not have foreseen that events unfolding that same bright, April morning, in a marshalling yard near Nottingham, were to have such terrible repercussions. All she knew was that her mind was agitated, filled as it was with questions and doubts.

The genteel air of Marylebone Station soothed her, however. The grim bustle and fuss of London were stilled within moments of walking through the stone-arched entrance, into the modest, but airy, train-shed. A big express locomotive gently panted its steamy breath at the platform end, like an eager dog on a leash, but otherwise the station seemed untroubled by much activity.

Violet settled down with a copy of *The Leader* magazine she had purchased from W. H. Smith's stall in the entrance lobby. It was a threepenny indulgence, but her heart was heavy and needed distraction. The pretty model on the cover was smiling, whilst kneeling, rather ludicrously, Violet thought, in a flower bed. She was wearing a large bow knotted at the top of her head, which made Violet think of Easter bunnies. Glancing at the contents list, she began to wonder if she really wanted to learn 'Where the Rumba comes from'.

The compartment was comfortable, though dusty and unswept. The seat springs were a bit saggy and the windows were covered in a film of rain-streaked coal dust. Picture frames, on either side of the small rectangular mirrors on the compartment walls, displayed sepia scenes of Holy Island, the Avon at Stratford and a rural idyll near Amersham. The fourth frame, however, displayed a poster that nagged at her conscience: 'Is your journey really necessary?' She pondered this question and sighed. Yes, it was really necessary, thank you. Well, it had seemed necessary the day before, but now she was unsure how fruitful it had actually been.

A frosty interview at the War Pensions Fund the afternoon before had irritated and saddened her, rather than reassured. Her father had been killed five years before in the Blitz, whilst on duty with the Civil Defence Corps. If that had not been bad enough, they had lost their house a few weeks later in another raid. Her mother had tried to make some kind of a home for Violet and her younger sister Jenny, but it had become increasingly obvious that their mother had been seriously affected by these events and was failing to cope.

Life really was a struggle now and money was tight. The war pension had been a long shot, but Violet had hoped her father's service and subsequent death was worth something. After all, the government had been banging on about giving service to the country for long enough. The prospects, however, did not look promising. She had been advised that her father had volunteered for the CDC, and whilst his 'selfless act of courage in the face of enemy action' was 'much appreciated', the uppity little man had otherwise been, frankly, dismissive. He had spent more time cleaning his glasses with a silken handkerchief than actually speaking and, when he did so, he made it explicit that he felt others were 'far more deserving causes'. So it looked like Violet needed another solution to her problems. It was this matter that she was churning over in her mind.

As the train slowly heaved its way into motion and the creaking carriages gathered speed, Violet watched the cramped house-backs and occasional gaping bombsite roll by. She was thankful for the distraction, and continued to look out of the window. She saw fragrant buddleia and rosebay willowherb growing where destruction had rained down only a few years before. Their own house in Leicester was now similarly transformed into a strange garden of tumbled bricks, abandoned junk and flowery weeds. Soon, the scene outside of the carriage window changed into a neat, utopian Metroland of matching semis and tidy roads. She caught glimpses of leafy avenues leading to modern lending libraries and go-ahead shops in concrete, glass and brick. Odeon and Gaumont cinemas, swimming baths and recreational grounds, all sped past as the train rolled through the London suburbs.

The soporific, clickity-clacks of the wheels started to make her eyes feel heavy, temporarily lulling the worries of her life. She now watched an England glide past that seemed unaltered by war, for this was a railway that appeared to avoid cities and factories, collieries and coal wharves, choosing instead to pass through verdant fields and meadows and over reedy rivers, whilst stands of trees strode across the horizon. The engine shovelled white steam over its shoulder sending billowing patterns across the gently-rolling land. She was riding on what was once the Great Central Railway; but to Violet, who knew nothing of its history, it was just a pleasing, if now rather shabby, railway serving farmers and landowners, day-trippers and London shoppers, and much-frequented, in her experience, by the commuters from the new estates springing up around Nottingham and Leicester.

She dozed, with her head against the dusty moquette, the magazine open on her lap. A succession of stations with comforting names passed by, with just the sound of an occasional carriage door slamming shut, a peep on the guard's whistle and a repeat from the engine. Princes Risborough and Bicester, Calvert and Finmere slipped away as the train carried her north.

Violet's mind was again filled with worries and doubts. She and her sister had moved out of Leicester a year ago, renting a tatty little shop in Woodford Halse. They lived above this, in two damp rooms, whilst she eked out a living dressmaking, or more often than not just making alterations. There was plenty of this work, for the austerity measures in force made people creative and inventive. The simple lines of the fashions she found easy enough to re-create, but their debts were crippling, and this work paid poorly, so she never seemed to make ends meet. It was lucky that they both had ration books, as this at least guaranteed some food each week.

Her mother was now sharing a flat in Leicester with an ageing aunt, unwilling to join them even though she was clearly suffering from the traumatic events of the past years. Bills had been left unpaid and now needed to be settled urgently. Added to this, Violet felt deeply protective towards young Jennifer. She had become in effect the head of the family, a role she had never imagined for herself, nor wanted. It had not been easy moving away, but Violet believed that they needed a fresh start, and had somehow made the decision to up sticks and move, and was now determined to make it the correct decision.

'Oh dear, but I do so need a lucky break. I need something to happen, and soon … I just wonder …' Violet looked again at the small, printed flyer that had been posted through their door a few days earlier. 'The Super Fast Loan Company' offered 'an instant decision and cash in hand — the same day'. Violet appreciated that thirty percent was a terrible rate of interest, but she also knew that there would be no further assistance from the bank — they had been anything but sympathetic. If she could just clear all the debts, improve the place they were living in, invest in some more stock … well, it might give them all a chance. She knew she had to get this right. A mistake now and they could face ruin.

Violet nodded asleep again through the movement of the carriages and the rhythmic drumming of the wheels on the rail joints, then jolted awake and stared through blinking eyes, just as the land suddenly fell away. Her train was crossing a tall, curving, brick viaduct over the almost imperceptible Great Ouse as it slowed to a halt at Brackley. She knew to look out for the other viaduct at Helmdon, then she would be nearly home. Violet collected together her small case, hat and gloves, placed the flyer in her handbag, looked at the magazine and then decided to leave it on the seat cushions for someone else. The train slowed as the green, cow-filled pastures suddenly gave way to accommodate the curving tracks of junctions and sidings filled with massed rows of wagons and huffing shunting engines.

The station at Woodford Halse was situated on an elevated island between two small hills dotted with houses, a church and a row of shops. It consisted of a series of small, red-brick buildings in a row down the centre of the platform, with ornate canopies extending either side to offer shelter. The composition was rather spoilt by a narrow, rickety, wooden platform that lay to one side, linked to the main platform by a metal latticework footbridge, and it was this bridge that now pushed the steam from the locomotive's chimney down past the carriage windows in great balls of soft cotton wool, as the train came to a halt.

'Woodford and Hinton! Woodford and Hinton! Change for Banbury and Stratford-Upon-Avon!' The guard was already calling out as the train's brakes squealed. Violet descended onto the platform and looked around. Jenny was not waiting for her. Looking up at the station clock she noticed it was just after 8 am, and realised that her sister was probably just getting ready to start work in the station refreshment room. As Violet's mood was confused, she decided to wait until later to talk, hoping that time and decisive action would lighten her heart. She headed for the steps down onto Station Road as the train started to pull away. As it did so, Violet almost bumped into her sister, who was bounding up the steps, breathless and flushed.

'Oh Vi! I nearly missed you — I saw your train arrive. Oh, but gosh, I'm late as well.' She hugged her startled sister, who wavered for a second on one of the steps under the force of the warm embrace. Violet then returned it, having managed to first place her case on a step. Violet held Jenny close for a few seconds.

'We can talk tonight. But you are hot — have you been running?' She looked quizzically at Jennifer.

'Probably.' With that the younger woman continued bounding up the stairs, calling 'Tell me all about it tonight.' and was gone.

Violet smiled to herself and walked down the steps into the cool gloom of the station exit, located beneath the massive, twin railway bridges that spanned the road. A young man was striding purposefully up the incline of Station Road, whistling cheerfully.

'Somebody is happy today. That makes two of them. Well, well, well,' Violet thought, and smiled knowingly, tilting her head slightly to one side in thought for a moment, then set off in the same direction, realising that seeing Jennifer had already lightened her mood a little.

She had also made up her mind.

Chapter Two

'MARCH WINDS AND APRIL SHOWERS'
Teddy Joyce & his Orchestra

Sergeant Trinder was feeling the chill of a keen wind, despite it being a sunny morning. As white clouds scudded overhead he stepped behind the shunter's hut and pressed himself flat against a creosoted wall. He took out a small box of Moreland's Glory from his jacket pocket and with one hand deftly opened it, extracted a match and struck it on the rough edge of the box, but needed to cup it with both hands as he struggled to light a cigarette. Once alight though, he straightened up, tossed the match to the ground and carefully readjusted his cap, trying not to disturb his immaculately brilliantined hair, which he liked to wear with a perfect side parting. The cap was greasy, dirty and too small, but it was the best he could do under the circumstances. He had found it lying behind one of the benches in the hut and borrowed it to try and help him look more like one of the many railwaymen working in the yard.

The poor little building he was standing beside was not much more than a shed, being rather like those built by pigeon fanciers in allotment gardens. However, this one had a brick-built chimney which was belching a yellowy smoke from the small, pot-bellied iron stove being stoked to a scorching fury by the men and women who were crammed inside for their rest break. The rusting, corrugated-iron roof was patched with felt and washes of treacly black tar, smothered by great swathes of bindweed that was encroaching with its curling tendrils from the hedgerow that bordered the yard.

Trinder had tried sitting inside, but the filth upon the floor plus the stench of oily rags, sour milk and stale cigarette smoke, all stewed in the fearsome heat from the stove, combined to make him prefer the bracing wind whipping across the goods' yards. Anyway, Trinder had a far better view from outside of the engineman's mess room, where his quarry was presently holed-up. This was little better than the shed he was currently standing beside, but the powerful social demarcations of the railway forbade gangers and shunters to mix with the more elevated ranks of footplate crew. So for now Sergeant Trinder was careful to adopt the classic pose of the resting workman, leaning against the wall with cigarette in hand, whilst remaining vigilant for when his men left the other building.

Sergeant John Trinder worked for the London and North Eastern Railway police (Southern Division), based in Leicester Central Station. He was part of the recently-formed detective branch, and as such had the privilege of undercover work such as this. This was a far better option, in Sergeant Trinder's mind anyway, than just dealing with drunken servicemen on late night trains, and recapturing escaped cattle from the running tracks, although he still was required to do such duties at times.

He was a patient, quiet man, able to spend long hours watching and waiting, occasionally allowing himself a glance at a recent copy of *The British Songwriter & Dance Band Journal* or, when this was not appropriate, amusing himself by recalling the lyrics of his favourite songs, or by quietly humming their melodies. In this way he could find the reserves of energy and concentration required for jobs that often involved long hours, filled only by the expectation that something may, just possibly, happen.

The sergeant had already put in many hours, having first travelled up in the early hours of Friday morning — it seemed like an age ago now — following a call to his digs from his superior, Detective Inspector Charles Vignoles. Trinder's landlady never seemed to get used to the fact that such calls were all part of the policeman's lot, and whilst annoying when they disturbed a much-needed night's sleep, they were also important. They needed to be handled without her fussing and 'tut-tutting' around the hallway in her grubby, floral housecoat whilst he fielded the call. One day he might be able to convince her to have the telephone placed outside his bedroom door, but she had so far rejected this sensible suggestion. Trinder had then cycled to the goods' yard from his digs, where he met up with the immaculately turned-out D. I. Vignoles, who had managed to cadge a lift from Belgrave & Birstall station, just to the north of Leicester, on a newspaper train.

As soon as they made the rendezvous, Vignoles had proceeded to pass on to Trinder what he knew about the incident whilst they walked beside long rows of wagons and across a tangle of rails. A line of wooden vans, parked in a little-used siding on the far edge of the vast fan of lines, had caught fire. A firetender and some railway employees had successfully contained the blaze, but not before two of the vans had been burned down to their metal frames.

Upon arrival at the crime scene, their nostrils were filled with the acrid smell of burnt wood, and they observed the slow drift of steam rising from water pumped from a nearby stream onto the hot embers. Groups of railwaymen were talking and smoking and three firemen were laughing at a joke, relaxed in their work as they packed away their equipment. Vignoles had immediately called everyone as far away from the smouldering wreckage as possible, whilst he tried to assess the heavily disturbed area around the crime scene with his torch, carefully walking around with head bent, often peering into the bushes that bordered the yard perimeter. Trinder, meanwhile, had set to work obtaining statements from the railwaymen who had sounded the alarm, and the chief fire officer. It was these statements, together with the astute observations made by Inspector Vignoles, which Trinder was now running over in his mind as he stood sheltering from the wind that sunny Saturday morning. He decided that he could be more productive by reminding himself of the exact details, so opened his little black notebook in order to re-read his notes.

The fire had been reported at 3.04 am, on the morning of Friday, 26th April 1946. (Trinder liked to be very clear about times and dates, even, rather unecessarily, to the year.) A shunter by the name of Dougan had seen a flickering glow and smoke rising from one of vans. He had called to his mate (a man called Allday) and they had run over to investigate. They pulled open the van's sliding door and a huge fireball of flame had then engulfed it. The fire officer had later confirmed that that was a very plausible scenario, caused by the increased oxygen flooding into the enclosed space. They had not called the fire brigade themselves, because by the time they had crossed the yard to find a telephone, they were informed by the Leicester South signalman that he had already done so, having already observed the conflagration (Trinder felt quite pleased with this word). The blaze was too fierce to fight without an appliance, so they had, instead, concentrated their efforts upon uncoupling the burning wagon and the one adjacent to it that was already smouldering, and which subsequently caught fire. A locomotive had hauled the remaining train some distance away, to safety.

The fire officer, an Irishman called Docherty, had fairly easily controlled the blaze once on site, particularly as the vans were empty, but raised questions about how the fire had started. Vignoles and Docherty had both been most interested in this matter and some discussion had followed. Both believed that they detected a slight odour of petrol in the vicinity, and for the fire to burn so furiously,

Fire Officer Docherty observed that 'an accelerant' would be needed. Trinder had written 'Petrol?' beside this.

However, it was Vignoles who then turned their attention as to why the vans were deliberately set alight — for surely this was the case. Trinder had underlined this bit. Both vans appeared to have been empty. But the remainder of the train was extremely full — full of clothing and blankets, according to the little cards clipped into the rectangular panels on the sides of the undamaged wagons, and all destined for London.

'Why would empty vehicles travel with a full train, sergeant?'

'Returning empties back to their destination?'

'Perhaps, but somehow that seems odd. Just the two empty vans in a train composed of identical vans, but all of which are full. Most odd, don't you think? And notice that the fire is in the two wagons that are empty … why set fire to empty space?' It was a rhetorical question, as Vignoles had continued after just the shortest of pauses, 'There again, perhaps what was inside has been removed, and whoever did this wanted to ensure that they erased any traces of them having being here. We can't have a hope of finding fingerprints, for example.'

'So if they stole the blankets, clothes, and the other stores that the train is carrying, then perhaps we are looking at black-marketeers.'

'Looks that way, sergeant. Make a note: we need to get the train diagram number, its point of origin, its destination, and see if we can't get a full description of the contents of these vans. And this Dougan fellow, he said they "pulled the van door open" as soon as they arrived on the scene. This suggests to me that the two vans were unlocked. The others, however, are all padlocked.'

'Good point.'

At that moment Vignoles had produced from his pocket, wrapped in a handkerchief, a padlock that had evidently been sheared through, the breaks in the metal still bright and shiny. 'I found this in the long grass over there and I feel certain the second one will be there also. It is hard to search in this light. It looks like bolt cutters have been used. It might be too early to say for certain that this was the lock on one of the vans, but it looks that way.'

Sergeant Trinder looked up from his notebook, drifting out of his recollections, and took a long drag on his cigarette. He surveyed the great lines of railway wagons and the billowing clouds of steam which constantly obscured his view, confusing his perception of the complex yard. It was a bewilderingly busy place and the huge, overarching sky was filled, despite the wind, with the clang of buffers, the squealing of brakes pinned against steel wheels and the barking, whistling clamour of at least half a dozen engines. It was daring to raid a train in such a location, but there again he thought, the size of the yard and the relentless comings and goings, perhaps might make the perfect cover, if you had the nerve.

He must be careful to not lose sight in this confusion of the two men he was tailing. He studied the distant hut, but the door remained closed. He brought his tired mind back to the events that had then unfolded early that Friday morning, whilst he and Vignoles stood beside the charred wagons. Trinder found visualising a scene repeatedly helped him keep it vivid and fresh in his mind, and sometimes he recalled a detail previously overlooked.

A man in scruffy overalls and a full-length coat that billowed behind him had approached them on a bicycle, frantically ringing its bell to draw attention. As they turned to watch, he freewheeled at speed, his bike tyres scrunching and bouncing over the cinders between the railway tracks. Trinder had stepped forward and commanded him to 'Halt!' for fear that he would speed past them and onto the crime scene.

'Sir! Excuse me, sir!' and at that, the cycling worker doffed his grubby flat cap and dismounted at the same time, with the ease of someone who had made the same action all his working life. Placing his bicycle against a signal post and adjusting his knapsack, which he wore diagonally across one shoulder, he strode purposefully towards the uniformed fire officer. 'I saw something, it might be nothing, but well, it's better to say it rather than not, eh, guvnor?' He then looked between Docherty and Vignoles, perhaps sensing the unspoken authority of the inspector, in his smartly tailored suit.

'Yes? I am Detective Inspector Vignoles, of the L.N.E.R police. Sergeant Trinder, of the same, is beside you. What is it that you saw?'

'Ah, inspector, detective … Um. Well, you see, I was on my way to work here — I'm a ganger, working on the permanent way — so I was on my way to work, unexpected like, as I had been woken by the knock-up lass, tellin' me to get down here extra early like, as we have a big problem down the line. Well, as I was heading towards the yard, what happens? Two blinkin' great lorries come thundering right out of the back access road — that one over there.' He waved in a vague direction beyond the burnt vehicles, 'Nearly knocked me clean off me bike, they did! I tell you, I was cursing somethin' rotten, an' I gave them a really good look, thinkin' that if I saw the likes of them again I would give 'em a right piece of my mind, know what I mean?' He nodded in a knowing manner, looking first at Vignoles and then Docherty.

'Can you describe the vehicles?' Vignoles was looking intently at the railwayman.

'Oh yes. Bedford trucks, both the same, with canvas covers at the back, and both brand new. Typical army issue.'

'Why do you say they were new?'

'Ah well, you see, they had that olive green paint that the army use, but with like a slight sheen to the paint, caught by the moonlight it was. But that sheen, it soon fades in service. I know, I've seen enough of them around 'ere in the last few years. And the wheels — well, I got a close look didn't I? Right past me bloody face they were! Really clean tyres, and all the nuts for the wheels, painted like the army want them. Oh, they were new, no doubt.'

'So you are sure that they were British Army vehicles?' Trinder had asked this question whilst writing notes.

'Well, they were painted like army, but with no insignia on the sides, so I reckon as they could be army surplus. There's loads of the stuff being sold off at the moment.'

'Very true,' added Vignoles, 'I don't suppose you got the registration numbers, or a good look at the drivers.'

The ganger looked crestfallen at this point. He was enjoying the limelight with the police officers, who were taking careful note of all he said, but now he was disappointed to not have the information they needed.

'Well, it was hard to get a really good look, and it was a surprise, and dark, despite the moon. But, I think one of them had 887 or maybe was it 778 on it. But I can't remember anymore. Oh, but wait. Yeah, but I do remember that both plates looked handpainted. Nice job, but clearly painted on wood — like they never had time to fit proper ones.'

'Did they, now? That is most useful. And the drivers?'

'I'm sorry, that's all I could get. I'm lucky to still be here to tell you this much. It was only when I clocked on for work here and the other lads said there was an incident, and I got talkin' to 'em, that I had the idea maybe this was of some use.'

Inspector Vignoles had thanked the man for his quick thinking and then Trinder had taken a full statement. Meanwhile the inspector had looked again at some tyre tracks that had initially attracted his attention beside the smouldering wagons. They certainly looked to have been made by a pair of heavy trucks. They were scuffed, damaged and drenched in water, but there was enough to suggest that perhaps these tracks and the ganger's mystery vehicles were the same. Vignoles had decided that, as this was the only lead they had to work upon, it might be useful to waste no further time in alerting the Leicestershire civilian police force and telegraphing all the stations along the line, to put out an alert for these vehicles. The morning local paper might even be able to run a stop-press story. So Vignoles had drafted a brief statement, then he and Trinder had made their way to the yard foreman's office and spent a frantic half an hour telegraphing and telephoning.

Only after this work was completed did they draw a breath, and drink a gratefully received mug of sweetened tea, eat a round of dry toast, and take stock.

Chapter Three

'PAINTING THE CLOUDS WITH SUNSHINE'
Al Bowlly with Jack Hylton & his Orchestra

Whilst Vignoles and Trinder were taking their meagre, early breakfast in the yard foreman's office, Edward Earnshaw was starting his morning's work at not long after 5.30 am. So it was with relief that Edward saw the clock hands move towards eight. It was time to scrub the last of the flour and sugar from his hands and fingernails, and sort out the deliveries.

His mother had already assembled a mound of fresh bread rolls with their variety of fillings that ranged all the way from ham to cheese to ham and mustard. Rationing had curbed any aspirations to expand beyond this narrow range. These rolls needed counting and placing into the voluminous, brown paper bags that Edward thought always smelled a bit funny. As the already-warming sun streamed through the display windows, creating shafts of light that swirled with fine particles of flour and dusty caster sugar, he carefully placed a dozen iced buns into white cardboard boxes that bore the legend 'Earnshaw's Family Bakery — Church Street, Woodford Halse' in royal blue ink. He then tied them closed with dark green raffia string. The brown parcels and bun boxes were then nestled into the hefty wicker basket that would soon be placed snugly into the tubular frame at the front of the delivery bike.

Edward's father walked past humming, with a tray of freshly baked bread. He glanced across and said, 'Don't forget the "Special Delight" cakes.' James Earnshaw was a large — though not overly tall — man, who clearly enjoyed the products of the family bakery. He also had an enthusiasm for amateur dramatics, and was currently learning the songs from the 'The Mikado', practising them whilst he worked.

Edward had spent the better part of that morning, and too many others to count, filling cakes with this 'Special Delight', an artificial concoction that he was not especially enthusiastic about, as real cream clearly beat the stuff into a cocked hat. Still, there had been a war on and this formed one of the Earnshaw's patriotic drives to save scarce resources. So it was with great care that he placed these in yet more of the white confectionary boxes that his mother had earlier folded up from flat. He tied them again with green raffia bows and then laid them on the basket upon the buns and rolls. The basket was not weighed down by the contents, but was bulky to manoeuvre across the shop floor to the bicycle propped on its stand outside the door. As he swung the basket in front of him, one edge caught a piece of card tacked to one of the display units and it fluttered to the scrubbed wooden floor. Edward knew that he would now have to go back and pin it up as soon as he put the basket in the bike carrier. The interior of the bakery had numerous other such pieces of card, cut in all manner of shapes, some more elegant than others. All had been written out by Edward in red ink with some expressive use of coloured chalk by his young sister Annie, proclaiming (according to his father's dictation); 'Our customers once they taste Earnshaw's Special Delight never forget it!' and 'Go on try it — it may surprise you!' Edward was just in a hurry to mount his bike and escape the confines of the bakery for an equally aromatic place. If he could just pin the card back up and get on his way, he would arrive in time to see the train from Marylebone pull into Woodford & Hinton.

He mounted the heavy delivery bike and pushed it off its stand with both feet, got the measure of the basket that made the handlebars want to swing to either side, and then he was off. Freewheeling down Station Road, rapidly gaining momentum by the moment, just gently resting his fingers in the metal brake handles ready to ease down the speed.

'A good driver must read the road and be ready to anticipate adverse signals and bringing the train to a controlled halt, if needed.' Today Edward was driving a heavy mineral engine with thirty wagons behind. 'Control, not speed, was essential.' Mr Turner's coal lorry was grinding its way noisily up the hill towards him, black exhaust trailing and collecting in the dark tunnel formed by the two over-bridges that supported Woodford & Hinton Station above the dip in the road. His fireman will have to work hard on the steep incline, I hope he's got a good head of steam. Edward freewheeled faster, but today he was not going to dip under the bridges, past the subterranean entrance to the platform and then on towards the tiny hamlet of Hinton; instead he leaned into the corner, eased back the regulator with a gentle touch of brakes, and took the swinging left-hand turn to send his train up the delivery road to the station. His momentum took him nearly to the crest of the rise, requiring just a couple of pushes on the pedals to reach track level. He eased his train to a smooth halt, preserving his delicate cargo for the station refreshment room, and just had time to plant his feet firmly on the ground when he heard a distant bell, the twang of wires and the clang of signals that set the road for the Manchester train.

Edward could already hear the exhaust beat in the distance, and see a plume of white steam marking its progress as it came huffing around the bend. Anticipation was a big part of the thrill — what would be the engine today?

'Excellent. A B3 …' Edward exclaimed under his breath. These were amongst his favourites. Despite its dull name, it was a beautifully sleek machine with a long boiler set high in the frames, and an elegant splasher over the top of the three big driving wheels. The cab had two wooden-framed windows on each side, making it look like a little summerhouse. The rearmost window was fully lowered and he could clearly see the head of the driver leaning out, a black, shiny-topped cap set far back on his head in a jaunty style. A brief plume of white steam jetted from near the cab roof and a piercing whistle announced its hissing, sighing arrival.

The engine was in a dreadful condition though. The drab wartime livery of black was itself masked by layers of oil, coal dust and track dirt. Dribbles of white limescale ran down from the washout plugs. Despite this there were touches of colour, in the shape of big, golden letters forming 'N.E.' upon the tender and the number on the cab side. A wet brush looked to have been wiped over them earlier in the day, revealing both, but now leaving rivulets of sun-dried water upon the surface. Edward's attention, however, was drawn to the nameplate: 'Valour'. The same cleaner who had sloshed water over the number and insignia had clearly made an effort to give this a wipe with a cloth so that the raised letters glinted in the sunlight.

Edward reached into the back pocket of his shorts and pulled out his penny notebook and stub of pencil, licked the point and wrote down the name and number on a fresh page, together with the date. Another locomotive added to his long, carefully compiled lists. Edward's little notebooks were filled not only with the names and numbers of his beloved steam locomotives, but with observations about the weather, the time of day and questions about things that he felt needed answers. He always seemed to have more questions than answers.

The guard's whistle sounded shrill. The engine made a soft 'whoof!' and the coaches gave a gentle groaning sound in response, as the powerful engine strained them into motion. Whoof! Shoo … Whoof! Shoo … Whoof! Shoo… Exhaust blasted into the sky as the train gathered pace, the beats increasing, then the sound diminished slightly as the heavy train pulled away. The carriage windows, nearly opaque with grime, dimly revealed a clutch of passengers; mainly service boys in uniform, with kit bags piled in the luggage racks or others in what looked like standard, ill-fitting, Government issue, demob suits.

Edward watched the train accelerate north then put his notebook away. He approached the barrow way that allowed him to wheel his bike across the rails and then up on to the island platform. He scooted along to the station refreshment room, standing one-footed on the left pedal, using his free leg to propel himself. He glanced towards the huge array of locomotives simmering in the far distance outside Woodford engine shed. Steam, smoke and a slight morning mistiness mingling to create a soft, dreamy vision of the place that Edward was soon about to join. He felt a thrill. Just this weekend to go, and then he could walk over to that distant Promised Land. It was a land of noise and clamour, sulphurous odours and great, powerful machines with their heroic crews. He would become a railwayman. Well, a cleaner actually. But one thing leads to another, and eventually he hoped to become a 'top link' driver. That was his dream.

'Morning, Edward. How are you today?' It was the cheerful voice of Kathleen Jones, one of the two young waitresses in the station's refreshment rooms. She was busy mopping the linoleum floor with hot water and some pungent disinfectant that stung the eyes. The water steamed gently, adding to the sense of the whole of Woodford Halse being alive with steam and smoke and smell.

'Good morning, Miss Jones. Did you see the engine just now? What a beauty!'

'If you say so, Edward.' With an indulgent smile she returned to her mopping.

'They're just noisy, mucky things that ruin my refreshment room and make my husband's shirts black, if you ask me.' Barbara Walsh, the proprietress, came out of the back kitchen and walked across to Edward.

'Any ways, let's be having them rolls, and I'll get Jenny to sort out the coupons — where is she, come to think of it?' She took the wicker basket from Edward, who had carried it inside whilst stepping carefully around the mop bucket and pools of water.

As Barbara inspected the day's supplies and started placing them in the glass display cases, Edward stole a glance across towards Kathleen and rather enjoyed the way her light, floral print dress moved as she worked, and how the strong sunlight outlined her legs. There was something attractive about the way her dress moulded to her body. He looked hurriedly away, but then could not resist a second glance. This time it was just as she stood upright and stretched. Kathleen looked across at Edward, their eyes met and she immediately reacted:

'Hey, cheeky!' She made to flick the mop at him and he turned away hurriedly, cheeks burning. The two women laughed.

'Want a cuppa, Master Earnshaw?' and before he could answer, Barbara had lifted the truly gigantic aluminium teapot that could in her words, 'refresh a whole through-carriage in one mashing,' and deftly wielded it to pour three treacly-brown teas into white mugs with L.N.E.R. on their sides.

'Thank you,' he mumbled and took it quickly outside to get some air. Still, he couldn't help but feel it had been worth the look.

'Where's that McIntyre girl got to? She's late again. Really, does she know how lucky she is? It's not like work grows on trees, you know.' It was Mrs Walsh speaking aloud to whoever was listening. As if on cue, the young waitress in question came running up the stairs from the station entrance and breathlessly arrived at the café with a flush of colour to her cheeks and neck.

'I am so sorry, Mrs Walsh, I got a bit delayed: I just bumped into Vi.'

'You did? That's all right then. Did she just arrive on the Manchester train? How did she get on, my dear?'

'We didn't have time to talk just now, what with me not wanting to be late.'

'Eh, she should have come in for a cup of tea with us.' Her mood changed in an instant, 'You'll be wanting one, I'm sure. I do hope she's got some good news. Heaven knows, you two deserve a break.' Barbara poured another tea whilst she was speaking. 'Here you go. Right then, you can sort out the coupons for Eddie here … well, he's hereabouts somewhere.'

'Yes of course, Mrs Walsh, right away.'

'So?' Kathleen had picked up the mop bucket and was about to leave the room.

'What?' Jenny smiled, coyly.

'What was the *real* reason you were late? A certain lad called Tom, if I am not mistaken.' Alison followed Edward outside and started to hum along to 'Painting the Clouds with Sunshine' playing on the wireless behind the counter, as she walked towards the ladies' to empty the dirty water from the bucket.

Taking his mug of tea, Edward walked a little way down the platform and sat on a barrow in the sun, which even this early was taking the chill from the air. A porter strolled towards him with a couple of large parcels wrapped in brown paper, one under his arm, the other swinging by its string from his hand whilst he held a carefully folded newspaper in the other. He was reading the sports page at the back. He looked up as he approached.

'What you reckon then? Derby or Athletic for the Cup?'

'Not sure. Derby I think. Though Charlton are supposed to be a pretty decent side.' Edward knew the porter from around the village; he had been in the year above Edward in school. He was daft about football.

'Could be. Will be a close game, I reckon. We got a lot of specials coming through today on account. The Midland line needs some relief so they're sending a few our way.'

'Really? Oh, that's great news.' Edward was interested, because football specials brought in all kinds of unusual engines. Interesting 'foreign' ones from the London, Midland and Scottish Railway, or older locomotives revived from the back of a shed somewhere. He was planning to meet his best friend Simon in the early afternoon and they were to go for a cycle ride. If they found a good spot to watch the trains go by, they might look out for those returning with Derby County fans from Wembley.

Two women porters were moving tall metal milk churns into neat rows along one side of the platform ready for collection. A lad from the dairy was rolling empties onto the back of a delivery cart and seemed to be making cheeky comments about their appearance, which judging by their reactions, neither porteress seemed to mind very much. Whilst Edward looked on, the signals cleared for the train to London, so he turned to watch for its arrival. As it steamed into view he saw that the locomotive was one of Sir Nigel Gresley's Pacifics. These were the most powerful express engines on the line, and to see one was always an event. It was called 'Solario', a first for Edward. He fished out his notebook again. Just like 'Valour' the engine was black all over, but the elegant lines of the engine were undiminished. It was lean and athletic, suiting the name of the racehorse that it carried. The obligatory, solitary carriage door then slammed, the guard whistled, and the big engine eased the train into motion, seemingly with little effort.

*　　*　　*　　*

Detective Inspector Vignoles walked into the refreshment room at Woodford & Hinton Station. He was gasping for a coffee and hungry as well. He had been working, with just a few hours' hurried sleep, since the early hours of Friday morning, and couldn't recall the last time he had eaten a proper meal. He crossed over to the counter and eagerly inspected the meagre selection of rolls being placed on display.

'Good morning, inspector. What can we do for you today?'

'Good morning, Mrs Walsh. A coffee, please. Correction, a "real" coffee, if you have any. What's in these rolls?'

'Coffee?' she laughed pleasantly, '"Yes, we have no bananas", more like. I'm sorry, we're all out, I just can't get hold of it anymore, but I can give you a nice cuppa tea, though. The rolls? Just the normal "wide selection".'

'You know what, Mrs Walsh? I am so hungry, I'm not sure why I'm asking. I'll take two of whatever — but with mustard. And plenty of it. It is English, isn't it?'

'Sorry, is what English?'

'The mustard — I like it really fiery. I *need* it really fiery — to wake me up.' he grinned.

'It's Colman's, which is English. We don't have any other kind', interjected a young lad, who Vignoles reckoned to be about fourteen or so years old. 'Sir,' the lad added, rather hurriedly. He had just entered the refreshment room from the platform.

'Ah, good.' Vignoles paused a moment to look at him. 'At least that's something they haven't rationed yet,' and after sifting through some change placed a couple of shillings on the counter then crossed over to a table by the door. It was drenched in sunlight, and the inspector carefully placed his coat on a chair, put his hat on top and, after he had taken a seat, took his police notebook out of his jacket, together with a small, slim booklet, which he placed on the table. Opening the notebook, he read through the two pages of notes he had written in his neat, meticulous handwriting, then having reminded himself of the facts of the case as he so far understood them, placed it upon the table, leaned back in the chair and closed his eyes. He started to run over all the events of the last forty-eight hours or so. In particular he was interested in what his sergeant was going to report back to him from the Leicester goods' yard. For Sergeant Trinder had spent the previous afternoon, and night, observing a warehouse, following a useful tip-off. The telegraphed alert they had issued in the early hours of Friday morning had delivered a result that exceeded their wildest expectations.

A telephone call had come in at noon, when he and Trinder were back in the office, compiling their initial reports. A policeman with the Leicestershire civvies had been walking his beat, which covered an industrial and manufacturing quarter of the city, an area now terribly run down and bomb-damaged. Significantly however, the area lay between the main line and goods' yards of Leicester, and the River Soar. Many of the empty premises attracted the attention of vagrants and drunks, so the policeman took particular care to give the 'once over' to most of the buildings each day. What attracted him to a particular warehouse in Water Street however, were two brand new Bedford trucks parked just inside the partially opened wooden gates. His brother was recently home, having been an army driver in Germany, and was looking to get into the haulage trade. He was seeking a vehicle at a good price. The police constable immediately thought that these were just the ticket, and wanted to enquire where they had been obtained. However, his friendly salutations to the two men unloading boxes from one of the vehicles drew only strangely evasive and frosty replies. The men had seemed nervous and defensive, immediately arousing the constable's suspicions. Memorising the number plates, he had returned to his police station at lunchtime, where he read the telegraphed alert pinned to the notice board. Minutes later, this astute constable had earned the well-deserved praise of Inspector Vignoles for the valuable information gained.

A pretty waitress placing a plate with the two rolls onto the table interrupted Vignoles's thoughts. He smiled at her and took a grateful bite into one, just as his stomach rumbled.

Food will help me think more clearly, he thought. He sipped the strong tea, and its warmth, together with that of the sun, immediately restored some of his energy. What I wouldn't give for a big, slap-up breakfast right now. He shook his head and tried to banish the thought, then took another bite into the roll. Vignoles then returned to considering the case. Sergeant Trinder had been sent off to pay a discreet visit to the Water Street premises. 'Strictly observation, sergeant. Under no circumstances intervene — we are some way off our territory and have no warrant. *And*, they may be perfectly innocent. So remember this is "hush hush"; observe and use your initiative, just as long as you don't challenge anyone, or look too much like a policeman.'

Trinder was an intelligent officer, so Vignoles knew he could trust him to fulfil the command with discretion. Trinder had later telephoned the office at six o'clock from a nearby pub, reporting that the suspicious Bedford trucks were still there, and that the various comings and goings to the premises were 'intriguing'. Trinder's suspicions were aroused, and he said that he would like to stake out the place through the night. Vignoles had heard nothing else from his sergeant until very early that morning, when he had telephoned Vignoles at his home. Trinder, it seems, was now back at the Leicester South goods' yard, watching two railwaymen who had paid a nocturnal visit to Water Street.

'Any ideas why they did this?'

'None at all, sir, but they have clearly come down from the loco depot, which is only fifteen or so minutes walk away, and are now apparently having breakfast.'

'Where are you at the moment?' Vignoles had asked, immediately fully alert despite being suddenly awakened from sleep.

'Using a telephone out in the yard. I've managed to borrow a cap and a filthy rotten jacket, so hopefully I look like a railway worker. The men in question are in the loco crew mess rooms. Two of them definitely came to Water Street at 2 a.m. I would like to see what they do next.'

'You did well. How are you going to proceed?'

'Watch, try to see what train they take out, and see if that offers any clues to what they are about. I have a good description of them.'

'Good. I've found out a bit more about the train — and more specifically, its cargo. We are not talking about knock-off coats, sergeant. That particular freight diagram is shrouded in some mystery, to say the least, and it has taken a lot of time to discover exactly what it was transporting. A deliberate cloud of ... ambiguity, has been created to make it very hard for anyone to know what those two vans contained. They originated from a specialist paper mill near Blackburn, and were transporting perfectly watermarked, paper blanks — for five-pound notes. Enough for a cool million pounds.'

'Ho ho, very interesting!'

'Indeed. And I can tell you that the Royal Mint is going spare about its missing cargo. The stakes are potentially very high. Be extremely careful, sergeant. I fear the people behind this might stop at nothing. I shall shortly travel to Woodford Halse, as it was from there that the locomotive that hauled the train originated. I shall see if I can identify the crew. We should aim to meet up back at the office by early afternoon.'

'Understood. I just hope I don't lose these men. It's a crazily busy place here, I can tell you,' and with that, Trinder had then rung off.

Vignoles opened his eyes, and brought himself back to the present moment, looking out of the open doorway towards the gently steaming locomotive depot. The lad who knew about mustard seemed to share his fascination with the locomotive yard. 'Somebody over there knows something about this, and I am going to find him,' Vignoles mused to himself. He was thinking in particular about the locomotive crew that had abandoned the freight train in Leicester Yard, complaining that their engine was in mechanical trouble. The crew had taken an age to travel from Blackburn and repeatedly advised the signalmen along the way that they were losing steam. Vignoles suspected that this was a ruse to allow them to stable the train overnight in a location of their own choosing, one conveniently close to Water Street, rather then deliver it the same day, as booked, to its London destination. Vignoles had already obtained the train reporting number and established that Woodford Halse supplied the crew and locomotive. He needed now to identify the engine, its crew and the guard. They had some questions to answer. He felt hopeful that this matter might be resolved fairly quickly, as the case, such as it was, had started briskly with some promising leads.

Chapter Four

'American Patrol'
Glenn Miller & his Orchestra

Mickey Rollo was not a man who liked to be kept waiting. He liked to get things done, get on, and get the job finished. His years in the British 8th Army had drilled into him a certain discipline and resourcefulness. He had not been a bad soldier, albeit at times he'd been a touch confrontational to his superiors. In some ways he had shown himself to be, whilst not exactly heroic, at least able to assess a situation, and then find a strategy for survival for himself and his mates. He could tackle most problems thrown at him and find solutions. And that included how to make money. His experiences in North Africa had hardened him. Knocked the edges off, so to speak. It had made him someone who knew what he wanted and was willing to go for it, and blow the consequences to anyone else. Living on the edge of death for over five years made a man forget the niceties of life and live for the present. Well, that was his thinking anyway, and in peacetime he was trying to make the most of whatever opportunities came to hand. And there were plenty of those if you were prepared to stick your neck out.

So why the hell was he waiting? He looked angrily across the railway yard and drew sharply upon his cigarette. Pulled so hard he got strands of tobacco in his mouth from the Navy Cut. Phaw! He spat bits out, his mood darkening by the moment, and flung the smoking fag to the ground. He glanced at his watch. He knew it was correct, for the watch was a perfect timekeeper. A beautifully engineered Swiss mechanism set in a simple, functional and yet elegant case. The emblem of a Swastika held in the claws of the German eagle above the number six betrayed its origin. He'd pulled it off the wrist of a dead German officer near Tobruk. It was a good watch, so why let it go to waste? The watch couldn't lie and Rollo couldn't ignore the fact that they were running late, so he was nervous.

He trusted the engine driver, though. This was vital in order to do the job well. A driver and fireman who could work well together, could coax the best out of the poorly maintained engines, the inferior coal and the endless speed restrictions. Unlike a driver who flogged the engine hard and used the steam wastefully and who could make the job very hard for the poor fireman, no matter how hard he worked.

Rollo had doubts about the others. The guard — phaw! He was just a long streak of piss, always worrying and whingeing. Rollo didn't know how far he could trust *him*. And in this operation a weakness could ruin them all. He didn't know the link-up man who was making the drop. That was part of the operation: each person only knew those he dealt with directly. That way they couldn't grass-up the top men, and the so-called Top Link himself. But Rollo knew the man they were passing the stuff onto, and he didn't trust *him* as far as he could fling him, either.

Rollo looked towards the rear of the long train and the guard pacing the ground, glancing also at his watch. Their link-man was late, and they needed to keep to time. 'Jesus. What is wrong?' he spoke under his breath. 'We should've taken the stuff when we were there.' Their long train of empty wooden wagons was destined for the London Brick Company at Calvert, and it was ready for the off. His driver had finished oiling around the locomotive and was now leaning out of the cab, a pipe jutting out of his mouth, teeth clenched. Kenno was a cool customer. He wouldn't show it, but Rollo knew that Kenno was nervous as well. He could tell by the angle of his pipe and the shape of his jaw muscles.

There was a metallic clang as the signal dropped. 'The board's set, we've got the road. Got to get going.' As if to emphasise the urgency in the driver's tone, the safety valves lifted with a loud 'pop' as a huge, roaring jet of steam streamed skywards. The noise fizzled in their ears, making them ring. The guard's whistle peeped peevishly.

'Yeah, yeah, we know. Jesus, Joseph and Mary, we're in trouble now ... he's given us the off.' Rollo was glaring towards the guard, who was, in turn, nervously scanning the yard, holding a furled green flag ready to start the train into motion. 'Hold on! Hold on!' Rollo was hissing the words out under his breath, but he understood the dilemma. His frustration was directed towards the man whose arrival they all anxiously awaited. At that very moment a delivery truck roared its way down the cinder-covered yard, oily smoke pouring out of its exhaust pipe, clouds of steam from the radiator, whilst barrels of paraffin bouncing noisily on its flatbed. It shuddered to a halt opposite the guard's van, the driver stepping out of the cab without so much as a glance, leaving the door wide open. He was cursing, and immediately opened the long bonnet that formed a nose to the vehicle. As he did so, the guard darted forward and in a move that took just seconds, lifted a leather bag from the driver's seat. He swivelled and jumped aboard the veranda of his guard's van, waving the flag and giving an extra, shrill blast on his whistle. The train was already starting into motion as he did so, with slow, heavy beats and long jets of steam pouring out front from the cylinders with a roar like a geyser. The engine leaked steam like a sieve, and threw a column of grey smoke and ash high into the air, which was then whipped by the wind across the yard, in great dancing billows of dirty grey, that weaved around lines of wagons filling the adjacent sidings.

'Too bloody close, that was.' Rollo was throwing coal into the fire with angry thrusts of his shovel.

'Ay, it was. I couldn't hold her any longer. We'd have had the signalman doing his nut.' The driver shouted this over his shoulder as he leaned out of the cab to check the line.

'Yeah. And Top Link would have gone even crazier if we'd missed this ...' Rollo shovelled more coal into the hungry firebox. 'I just hope we haven't got in with a bunch of amateurs.' Rollo slammed the steel doors closed with his shovel.

Sergeant Trinder did not miss what had happened. Although in truth he very nearly did so, distracted as he was by the cursing van driver. The steam issuing from the radiator had attracted Trinder's gaze away from the train crew, towards the van and its attractive livery of navy blue with cream letters, proclaiming 'The Anglo-Empire Oil Co'. Strangely, just such a flatbed truck had been parked in the Water Street yard the night before. Stranger still, in Trinder's mind, was that the vehicle was clearly ailing and in poor health, but sported a gleaming, freshly applied livery. His instincts were aroused that all was not quite what it seemed. Fortunately the sergeant was also alert enough to turn his attention away from the vehicle and the antics of its driver, back to the railway guard, just in time to catch a fleeting glimpse of a bulging, dark-coloured bag thrown into the guard's van. Trinder smiled to himself. Well, I wonder what that could be about. He was intrigued. It was strange also, that the train departed the very moment that this bag was collected.

Somehow, I don't see them waiting for a bag of dirty laundry, he muttered under his breath. He checked the registration of the Anglo-Empire Oil Co vehicle, and it was the same as that he had noted a few hours earlier. The driver was also familiar to him following his surveillance operation.

He had plenty to report back to the detective inspector, and feeling satisfied that he had done enough for the time being Trinder discarded the ancient donkey jacket and cap, leaving them hanging on a metal post for someone else to claim, and collecting his trusty Rudge Whitworth he cycled toward the city centre whilst whistling the uplifting melody of 'American Patrol'. It was time to find a decent breakfast.

Chapter 5

'WISHING WILL MAKE IT SO.'
Vera Lynn, Ambrose & his Orchestra

The man's accent was definitely educated and he was wearing a smart navy suit that fitted far too well to be 'demob' issue. A matching hat, pale blue shirt and a striped tie in red and silver finished the effect, whilst the heavy military style overcoat, slung over a chair back, hinted that perhaps he had recently been in the services. He had close-cropped hair, was clean-shaven and wore spectacles with narrow, rectangular silver frames that suited him well. They looked more modern than those worn by the booking clerks, whose circular horn-rimmed affairs had the effect of making them look like a pair of owls.

The man was looking at a small notebook and appeared to be engrossed in something serious, so Edward lost interest in him and went back to looking across at the distant, hazy image of the engine shed and the indistinct shapes of the many engines formed up into lines outside. Some were slowly moving their way towards the concrete coaling tower that loomed over the shed buildings. He could see a loaded coal truck being winched up its side; soon it would be tipped over at the top, and empty its load into the hoppers below, with a sickening rumble like distant shelling. Each engine would wait its turn beneath this concrete monster, the deafening noise and huge palls of black dust indicating that its tender had been filled with steam coal. The racket continued day after day almost without end. Edward's Auntie Maud had told him that this sound disturbed her because it reminded her of lying awake in a flooded Anderson shelter, during the blitz on Leicester, back in 1940. It certainly was an infernal place to work; the men permanently moving around in clouds of choking black dust with the crash of tumbling coal making their ears ring long after their shifts had ended.

'You seem fascinated by the engines.' It was the man at the table, addressing Edward.

'Oh yes, sir. I like them very much.' The man smiled back and placed his closed notebook on the table. As he did so, Edward noticed that underneath there lay a small, slim booklet with a cover design in orange and blue. 'Oh, I have that book, it's the latest ABC, isn't it?' Edward nodded towards the table, and the man looked the same way.

'You mean this?' He reached for the booklet, and offered it to Edward, inviting him to take it. Edward did so and started to turn the pages carefully, looking at the neat under linings in blue ink.

'You take the numbers, then? They are great books, aren't they? Are you in the Ian Allan Locospotters' Club?'

'Whoa! Slow down, young man, too many questions. But, to answer your enquires in order. I do indeed make a note of the numbers — I was, in an idle moment, thinking I might have had time just now. And yes, these little ABC books are most useful. I have most of them since they started production — and for all the regions, not just the L.N.E.R. — however, despite that I feel I might be a little too old for the Locospotters' Club.'

'I'm starting work here on Monday. One day I'm going to be an engine driver, in the top link!'

'Really? I thought you were looking rather wistfully, at the depot. Well, congratulations are the order of the day then. Of course, it's hard work you know.'

'Yes, I know. My father — he's a baker actually — in fact he made that roll.' They both looked down at it sitting on the plate. 'Well, he's tried to talk me out of it, saying that I'd spend hours each day on my feet and getting awfully hot and dirty, but I reminded him that this was not so unlike being a baker really, and ...'

'Did you, now? Well, I am sure he was just sorry to see you leave, and not help with the family business.'

'Maybe ...' Edward suddenly felt a pang of remorse. His father had been disappointed. However, he had finally come around to accepting the idea, and they had agreed that Edward would start as a cleaner and call-up boy — which meant knocking at the doors and windows of enginemen at all kinds of strange hours to get them into work — but if this did not suit, then Earnshaw's Bakery would always be waiting. His mother, meanwhile, had wanted him to stay on at school and maybe go to college. 'But it is what I have always wanted to do,' Edward's face lit up as he spoke, 'and I feel that I should at least give it my best shot and make a go of it.'

'I see. Well, one should follow one's calling,' agreed the man, 'and the railway certainly needs more cleaners,' he continued. 'So I won't dissuade you. It's not the most attractive job, so I hope you stick to it, young man.' He stood up and looked at his watch. 'Excuse me. I must be going. It was nice to talk with you'. He picked up his coat, pocketed the uneaten roll then took back the ABC, putting it in his jacket pocket; whilst doing so, he asked, 'What's your name?'

'Edward. Edward Earnshaw, sir.'

'Well, Edward, I hope you enjoy working for the railway and that we meet again — but maybe not professionally.' He raised an eyebrow, whilst Edward looked at him quizzically. He extended his arm, although it was weighed down with the overcoat. 'Detective Inspector Charles Vignoles of the L.N.E.R police,' and winked. Both were aware that whilst they were speaking, the station pilot engine had drawn up at the platform and the driver had stepped out.

'Your taxi, sir!' The engine driver clearly knew the detective inspector, who had in turn been expecting him. The policeman turned, acknowledged the driver, gave a 'thank you' to the women behind the counter, and put his hat on. He walked across the platform, stepped in the cab and then, with a short 'peep' on the whistle; the little engine trundled off towards the sheds.

※　※　※　※

'Morning, William.' Charles Vignoles greeted the driver cheerfully. William Hoggart was in his late fifties and had served on the railways during the war. He had become positively rotund despite the best efforts of rationing, and had eyes rather too small for his face, all of which did nothing to stop the unfortunate nickname of 'Piggy' that he had gained when he had first started as a cleaner. He was, however, a kindly, cheerful man, and Vignoles thought him one of the more likeable drivers based at the depot.

They exchanged a few words about the afternoon's cup final. Driver Hoggart was excited about the game, hailing as he did from London, and Charlton Athletic being his team. Vignoles was content to make conversation, just as he had done with the young lad in the station, as a way of diverting his mind from what might be happening further down the line.

Within a minute or so, the engine jolted its way over the poorly maintained track of the depot and drew to a halt. After wishing his team good luck, Vignoles swung himself off the footplate, down the steps onto the grey and grimy surface of the huge locomotive yard, after first nodding goodbye towards the fireman, a young man he had not met before.

He started to pick his way carefully over the uneven wooden sleepers and rails, around pools of oily water and mounds of ash and clinker. The air was sulphurous and it caught at the back of his throat. He was careful to mind the deep, ashy pits cut between many of the tracks: these were where locomotives dropped their fires when cleaned out at the end of their working day. Long lines of engines stood swathed in gentle curls of smoke. From one side came the regular clang of something metal upon metal as a fitter coaxed something loose. The boom and crump of the coal hoist shook the ground. A large, heavy workbench was placed outside the shed entrance in the full sunlight, surrounded by oil lamps. Two women in overalls sat at the bench, their hair tied up in scarves knotted at the top of their heads in the fashion of the time, chatting quietly as they trimmed the wicks and topped up the reservoirs with paraffin.

A gleaming, elegant locomotive standing beside them took Vignoles's attention. She was clearly sporting a freshly applied coat of apple-green paint that made her sparkle like a jewel amongst the monochromatic surroundings. As he drew closer, Vignoles could read the nameplate that identified the engine as 'Queen Mary' and a beautiful sight she made in the warm morning air. He could not resist taking out his police notebook and noting the number, name and date at the top of a fresh page. As he did so, a voice called out to him

'Detective Inspector Vignoles I presume. Caught in the act!' It was the shedmaster, Timothy Saunders, who strode confidently across to him, hand extended. 'Good to see you, Vignoles. She's a looker, eh? Bit like that lovely wife of yours,' and he winked in a manner that clearly did not completely amuse Vignoles. Vignoles restricted his reaction to just giving a look that implied that the comments would stop there, but shook the offered hand warmly, none the less.

'The Central only ever built two of them, you know. We managed to convince head office to take the old Queen in for a visit to the works, certainly for the last time. After that it's —'

'— time for her to abdicate?' The word coming immediately to mind, as only the night before, Vignoles had been listening to his wife talking about the possibility of King Victor Emmanuel stepping down in Italy. As Anna was half Italian, this was quite understandable, but as Saunders was not, his comment was met with a quizzical look. They both laughed however, and after one last admiring look at the splendid engine, they then walked towards the shedmaster's office. This had an elegant bay window and the remains of what once had been a small lawn outside. But this was now extremely threadbare through neglect and the daily assault by ash and grime that landed upon it.

The shedmaster was the reason for Vignoles's visit; however, the detective had been able to mask his real reason for coming there, owing to the fact that Tim Saunders had the day before reported the worrying news that a box of fog signals had been stolen. These small but potent explosives were always being taken (or lost) in small numbers, but the theft of a whole box of twenty-four was unusual. It was also potentially extremely dangerous. But whilst the theft was a genuine cause for concern, it also gave Vignoles an opportunity to veil his real motive for visiting.

'Take a seat, Charles. I'll get us both a mug of tea.' A few moments later Saunders returned with two large, and almost clean, mugs of steaming brown liquid. The shedmaster took a gulp, and pulled a face 'Hmm... Could do with more sugar. Do you miss sugar?'

'All the time.'

'Me too.' The shedmaster shook his head thoughtfully, 'We're all out. No one seems to have any coupons either, worse luck.' He sighed and sat down behind his desk littered with papers weighted down by a hefty, maroon-covered book with the title *General Appendix to the Rules and Regulations and Working Time Tables and Sectional Appendix (Southern Region)*. Vignoles recognised this, as he had just been given one himself the day before. There might be paper shortages, but not as far as the L.N.E.R. was concerned. It issued these massive volumes with a surprising regularity. Vignoles used three of them to prop open his office door when it was warm. The majority of the desk, however, was filled by small rectangles of paper with names written on them, formed into ragged columns. The shedmaster caught Vignoles looking at them and replied to his silent question.

'Bloody rosters. They're the bane of my life. Driver so-and-so wants to work with fireman what's-his-name, but not with fireman whoever, and then, when you get 'em happy with that, they get all fussy and Bolshie about what guard they want to be with. I ask you.'

'I can sympathise, it's a bit like that in the force. After a while I just give them the roster and then tell them to get on with it.' Vignoles was watching Saunders carefully.

'Well I tried that, but with morale low, the engines knackered, the coal of poor quality …' He blew air out of his cheeks and suddenly looked tired. 'I think in a way they deserve to at least half like the man they are paired with, so when everything breaks down — as it does all the bloody time — it helps 'em cope. And then there is always one who won't work with a woman guard. I tell you, it'll be easier when they send 'em back to being housewives.'

'You don't really mean that.'

'Aw, not really, but they do cause problems, in their own way, like. Some of the men are so stuck in their ways.' He stopped and thought for a moment. 'Thinking on, I suppose that means it's the men that's causing the problems with the girls …' He stopped his train of thought and picked up his mug of tea.

'So, apart from the eternal battle of the sexes, are any of the lads really giving you a problem?' Vignoles kept his tone conversational. He was also glancing down at the card rectangles, trying to read them, upside down.

'Nah, not really,' Tim sipped more tea. 'Not problems as such,' he added.

'Well maybe "problem" was a touch strong.' Vignoles moved his hands in a conciliatory manner, encouraging the shedmaster to continue.

'You know, it's the guards that give me grief. Well, not the guards themselves, but the rostering of them with certain footplate crew. Obviously we get the standard hullabaloo if a gal gets the job from some of 'em — especially the freight lads — oh Lord! But it's not just the girls; I give one of the new lads a run out, or ring the changes a bit, next thing I know I've got a cheesed-off driver giving me earache.'

'Yes.' Vignoles ventured another sympathetic smile, 'So, they like to keep together then, footplate crew and guards, cosy little threesomes, eh?'

'Something like that.'

'Looking at all these cards and everything, it's a complex operation, Tim.'

'You can say that again. Endless paper work, endless filing. It's hard to keep up at times.'

'So you keep a record of every train, every crewman, what engine they were driving?'

'And when they departed, returned, coal used, breakdowns

— oh and we get breakdowns — overtime worked, you name it, we log it, Vignoles.'

Vignoles drank the rest of his tea before continuing. 'So, if I was to ask you about this,' he offered the shedmaster an open page of his notebook, blank except for a series of numbers and digits that formed a train reporting number, 'you could tell me the locomotive and its crew?' Saunders looked at the number, frowned for a moment, then he looked at Vignoles.

'Yes, I should think so, assuming of course that we supplied the engine for that particular turn. What day?'

'Thursday last, the 25th. But this one got stopped along the way. Engine broke down, apparently.'

'Yeah. No surprise there then. Why do you want to know?'

'A couple of wagons caught fire, and we are just checking out the details, background stuff, you know how it is with us detectives. Nothing serious. And in a way it all helps me understand the way the railway works, in all its complexities.'

'Hmm, a wagon fire. Probably an axlebox running hot — they can spark a fire very easily in dry weather. So, the loco returned home without the train. Okey dokey, let me see ...' Saunders got up and quickly walked into the adjacent office, where his assistant, an Irishman called Reed, normally worked maintaining the rosters and planning the other work routines for the railway shed. Saunders returned with a hefty ledger and placed this on the only empty space on his desk, resting the bulk of it on top of the clutter.

'OK; let's see. Thursday 25th ... ah, here we go. What the hell. Look at this. Ink spilt on the sodding page. It's ruined. What was he doing?' Saunders seemed genuinely angry and surprised, whilst Vignoles maintained an aloof calm, observing the shedmaster carefully whilst inspecting the page in question. 'Well, maybe I can make something out. Here is the working, I think, and it was an Austerity 2-8-0, but the number? I don't believe this! It's completely obliterated, the names of the crew as well. Idiot. Ah, but wait, I might pick up the number of the locomotive by establishing the outward, northern-bound trip.' Saunders was now flicking back through a few pages of neatly completed entries. Vignoles noted that tea rings and oily thumbprints stained many of the pages. 'Got it. Number 3152, now that's one of ours, went out on the Wednesday. Well, at least Reedy hasn't poured ink all over that one, though he has managed to smudge the number. He really is careless.' Saunders pointed to the relevant entry, so that Vignoles could read it. The neat handiwork was indeed marked by a huge oily thumbprint over the locomotive number. But far more importantly, as far as Vignoles was concerned, was the fact that the crew names were not so obscured as to be illegible. Vignoles memorised them, not wanting to attract undue attention at this stage. They were recorded as a 'K. Price' and 'M. Rollo'. The guard was listed, as one 'J. Cresswell'.

'So could these have been the same crew as returned with the train on the Friday'

'Not necessarily, but possibly. To be honest I am not sure who were the crew from this mess, but my guess is that they're the same. I shall have to speak to Reed about this. He's not here yet; he's got a half-day because he worked late last night. We can find out, but it will take a bit of time, cross-checking the overtime records, guards' log books, and so on. If you really want it, that is.' Saunders looked at Vignoles with little enthusiasm, fearing that he was going to be lumbered with what he believed to be a pointless task.

'Do please confirm the names. Perhaps I could trouble you to telephone them through to me as soon as you have them? Do the same crew always work this diagram?'

'The same? Couldn't say. Would need to go through all these pages trying to find the same diagram. Take forever, you know. Your best bet is to ask your lovely wife in goods' despatch — she could far more easily find the particular working. And it's likely that the guard will be identified beside the goods' working, and his report filed — somewhere.'

Vignoles smiled and wondered why he had not thought of doing that himself. 'Good idea. And Tim, could I ask that only you look into this matter?'

'Oh? Well, yes, of course. Is there something wrong?'

'No, no …' Vignoles deliberately played down his interest, 'but I can appreciate that working men get uncomfortable if they hear that the police are asking questions, even if just routine — no need to alarm them. And you know how people like to gossip in the mess rooms.'

'That's a fair point, Vignoles.'

'And another thing, the locomotive, the "Ossie", did it need much repair?'

'Repair? Why do you say that?' Saunders looked surprised then immediately returned to the log book, looking at the later entries. 'There's no report of failure that I can see … look, here it is. It "worked light engine from Leicester South", but no report of a defect.'

'It was reported as being in trouble, the crew were forced to abandon their train in Leicester, and limp on, light engine.'

'Really? That just makes no sense. Leicester Shed is part of the goods' complex, literally minutes away. Hang on …' Saunders picked up his telephone and dialled a couple of numbers and waited. 'Yes John. Have you got an "Ossie" booked in for repair — number 3152, came in yesterday? No? No 2-8-0's at all? Well, thanks for that.' He replaced the handset and looked at Vignoles. 'You heard the answer, and in fact if the number is correct, then that engine is at this moment on its way to Wath, with some coal empties.' He shrugged and made a face, 'Maybe it was nothing. Sticking injector or something. A few minutes whacking it with a lump hammer can sometimes sort that out.'

'Probably.' Vignoles smiled in agreement. He was content to now deflect the conversation away from the subject. Saunder's face also brightened into a broad smile.

'What the hell. So how's the world treating you, Charles? Marriage still suiting you? Hope the wife's OK.'

'Yes, Anna is very well, thanks. How about yourself and the family? Any news from Paul recently?'

'Oh, we are fine and dandy really. Mind you, Mary is playing merry hell over the rationing, and I have to say she has a point. I mean, how are you supposed to live on what they give us? I thought it was going to get better once we won the bloody war.'

'It's not getting any easier, that's for sure.'

'And did you read the suggestion that we all start eating squirrel pie? I'm not eating squirrels. It's too much!'

'I can't say I am very eager myself.' They both laughed.

'But you asked after Paul. We've not heard a lot, he's still in Palestine, you know. He says things are very tense. Lots of problems with terrorist threats and that but no actual fighting, thank goodness. Still, he says the food is great and the weather wonderful. Been swimming in the Red Sea, apparently.'

'That sounds nice.' Vignoles sipped some more of the treacly tea.

'I don't know, Charles; but they're strange times, eh? I'll tell you something for nothing: some of the lads here are getting a bit fired up with all this talk of socialisation. They spend their time in the mess and up at Hinton Gorse — you know, the company's social club — talking all manner of stuff, the union reps in particular.'

'Yes?'

'Oh, you know. How they want the railways socialised now and want to demand more "free collective bargaining" —— whatever the hell that is. Some of them want to really shake things up, want the workers to take more control. "Fair shares for all" or something — I can't say exactly, but that kind of revolutionary stuff.'

'I am not sure state ownership by an elected government can be called a revolution, Tim.'

'Well, I'm no politician. And maybe some of this is a good thing. But some of these lads are really agitating. Maybe this is how trouble starts. I'm not saying there's anything actually wrong of course. I'm just mentioning it.' As he was speaking, the shedmaster pulled his pipe from the breast pocket of his jacket and started to fill it from a leather pouch on the desk, nodding to Vignoles, inviting him to do the same.

'Things are changing, there's little doubt about that,' Vignoles conceded. 'This Labour government is certainly making bold plans. Perhaps you're right, where it will all end?' Vignoles emptied his mug and fell silent for a few moments, taking the tobacco pouch offered him, and starting to fill his own pipe. Tim filled the office with aromatic smoke and continued, 'Of course, you are really here about those fog signals stolen yesterday.'

'The detonators? Indeed I am. How were they lost? Taken from the trackside?'

'Not this time. It was yesterday afternoon, one of the lamp men came to see me, about three-ish, and reported that a box had been lifted from a stores' van parked in the yard.'

'A locked van?'

The shedmaster winced. 'No. Someone left the door slid wide open. Yes, I know, bloody stupid thing to do. No excuses.'

'No doubt you'll offer me one.' Vignoles looked over his glasses at Saunders, pipe in mouth, as he started to make notes.

'Well, we got word that the signal box down at Charwelton was running low on stock. They use them to warn of signals and blockages on the lines and such, in times of poor visibility.'

'I know.'

'Well we'd sent down for more supplies and were putting

the new boxes in the stores. Others were being divvied out for Charwelton, and anyone else who had put in a requisition chit. So then the men on the job got called away. They'd all but finished. The last box was tucked right in the corner of the van in the dark. Somehow they just lost count, and it got overlooked. It was human error.'

Vignoles raised his eyebrows and looked over the top of his glasses. 'So how did you know you are a box short, if they lost count?'

'Ah, yes, well, a bit later when things quietened down the head lengthman sat down and checked everything over, realised there had been a cock-up and we discovered that someone had nicked them. No one had been issued too many boxes, so I am pretty sure they have been lifted — probably by local lads.'

'Unfortunately, you are probably right.' Vignoles closed his notebook and sighed. 'OK, let's have a look at where the van was parked. I'll send an officer down, they can ask around the village and hope to God that some poor kid doesn't get his arm blown off.' They walked back into the sunlight and crossed the many tracks heading towards the yard set furthest away from the main line. A row of small, solidly-built store sheds were located there. Beyond the sidings lay open fields behind a leafy hedgerow and a well-trodden path that many of the depot workers used to get to work. 'It would be a work of just a few moments to cut across these lines and duck behind the hedge.' Vignoles was surveying the scene and assessing if it warranted a full search. 'I suppose you had a look around the area.'

'Yeah, we had a good poke around, but the detonators are long gone.'

As if to illustrate their thoughts, another loaded coal wagon emptied its contents into the hopper with a noise like an explosion. The two men exchanged glances and then walked back towards the shed.

Chapter Six

'FOOLS RUSH IN'

Frank Sinatra with Tommy Dorsey & his Orchestra

Edward and Simon met up not long after St Mary's had chimed noon. Simon had been on the early shift, but with the promise of a gloriously hot afternoon, free from work, he had agreed to make the most of it and meet up with Edward to go cycling. The Earnshaw Bakery delivery bike had been commandeered, complete with basket, so that they could pile it full of sandwiches, locally grown apples, a couple of 'Special Delight Horns' and a rare treat, a bottle of dandelion and burdock bought from Cullen's corner store. Simon's haversack had also found its way there, and this clinked intriguingly every time Edward pedalled over a bump in the road.

Both of them were now hungry and decided to cycle directly to one of their favourite, and also secret, places: Culworth station. This had been built to serve — it would appear — no obvious place, though it lay fairly close to the tiny village of Moreton Pinkney, whose residents already had a station on another railway line. Culworth was also within striking distance of yet another — equally lonely — station, at Eydon Road on the Banbury Line, so anyone living in the farms and scattered cottages that formed its catchment area were puzzled to find they had more stations to choose from than the cities of Northampton or Leicester. This also meant that Culworth never really had any passengers to speak of. And so, it quietly passed into disuse. The railway lines still carried trains that thundered through frequently, but now they never stopped.

The lads found this a fascinating place. It was a ghost station, and one that looked so very like their own Woodford & Hinton in many ways, but which now seemed to be haunted only by shadows of the departed station staff. The booking office still had many unused tickets in its racks; others were strewn on the floor. Official books of rules and regulations and numerous old newspapers lay mouldering on the dirty floor together with broken glass, a chair with no seat, a few empty bottles and a solitary sock. The clock on the wall declared that it would forever be 3.34 at Culworth. Yellow ragwort was now growing through cracks in the platform and the pink roses planted years ago around the station sign had run wild, but added a charming touch of romantic melancholy to the place.

They pushed their bikes into a hedge that abutted the brick wall of the road overbridge that supported a covered stairway, and descended onto the platform, mooching around the small buildings, noting that few vandals had as yet invaded and further damaged the place. A small lizard darted into a crevice. As the day was still sunny, they sat on the hot tarmac platform surface, with their backs against the smooth red brick of the ladies' waiting room wall, and munched a sandwich each.

'So Eddie, fancy a beer?'

'A what? A beer?'

'Oh yes — look!' And with that Simon brought out two brown bottles from his military-style rucksack.

'I managed to talk Ivy, who works at the staff social, to let me have 'em — always pays to be nice to people who serve food and drink, Eddie.' Edward was holding the bottle in both hands and reading the label.

'India Pale Ale. Wow, well done, Si. Wonder what it tastes like. I can't say I have ever had this, though Dad did let me have a half-pint on my last birthday. Sneakily like, without telling Mum.'

'Well, better knock the tops off and find out I reckon'. As he said this, Simon started to try to remove the metal cap by bringing the bottle down vertically to strike a glancing blow on the stone window sill. The first two attempts were unsuccessful although he did graze his knuckles and blood started to flow. Upon the third attempt however, the top flew off and foaming beer started to fizz out of the top. He greedily placed the neck to his mouth to catch the foam.

Edward, having seen the technique, did the same with similar results and then got the first taste of the bitter foamy head. The bubbles went up his nose and he spluttered for a moment, drew breath and then took a deeper draught, finally tasting the warm, hoppy liquid. It was bitter but malty, just slightly warm and fizzy on the tongue.

'Oh my, that's good.' Simon was licking his lips.

'Mmm… yeah, it is,' remarked Edward, adjusting his taste buds to the new sensations by sloshing the beer around his mouth, exploring the flavour. His second, longer and deeper draught gained his nodded approval.

They grinned at each other and then both tipped the bottles again.

'Cigarette?' Simon was reaching deeper into the bag.

'Blinkin' 'eck, Simon, what have you got in there? I didn't know you'd taken up smoking. Since when?'

'About yesterday lunchtime. One of the firemen offered me a smoke and I thought, 'yeah OK'. Well, it would have been rude to refuse.'

'Phaw! And?'

'Well, go on, then.'

Edward looked at the small packet of ten Churchmans and shook his head. 'Nah, it's all right, think I get enough smoke as it is.'

'Okay, suit yourself. It's not like engine smoke, you know. Just shout if you change your mind.' With that, Simon lit up whilst giving Edward a sly smile, and lay back against the wall, a picture of contentment. Almost immediately he suddenly leaned forward in a fit of coughing and spluttering that shattered the illusion. A fast train of empty ore wagons sped past at the very same time, scattering tiny pieces of grit on the platform and throwing filthy grey smoke in their faces, doing nothing to help Simon regain his composure. Edward was laughing so much his eyes watered, but he managed to pat his friend on the back. Eventually Simon sat back against the wall, face flushed and eyes streaming, tousled red hair completing a picture that was a study in red and orange. But he was laughing as well.

'Well, it takes a...' he coughed, 'bit of practice...'

'I can see that. Anyway, we missed that one, thanks to you.'

'Yeah, well, I couldn't see a darned thing,' and Simon coughed yet again, inducing further tears.

'Sounds like another on the way though — listen.'

Sure enough a train could be heard approaching on the opposite line, and it would soon pass behind them. Simon stood up and leaned on the corner of the building, still wiping away the last of the tears, and peered around so he could catch a glimpse of the engine as it passed. Edward also got to his feet and looked through the cracked and stained windows of the waiting room.

The train approached. It consisted of a long line of open wooden wagons, and was rattling along at a fair speed. Both lads readied themselves to 'cop' the number of the locomotive as it passed. But then it became clear that it was unexpectedly slowing down. Simon and Edward glanced at each other. Was the train really about to stop? This would be most peculiar, bringing such a long train to a halt was wasteful of both time and coal. But then, just as the train looked like it would actually halt, it produced a series of sharp 'barks', threw a filthy grey ball of smoke out of the chimney, and began to regain speed, rumbling away past them. The guard's van at the tail of the train trailed smoke from its stovepipe chimney. The guard was clearly brewing tea, despite the warmth of the day. They glimpsed his back as he stepped from the veranda at the rear of the vehicle, into the covered part.

'Why did he slow down?' asked Simon.

'Strange thing to do.'

'A temporary speed restriction, maybe?'

'But there's no sign of maintenance work,' Edward was looking around him as he spoke, 'and the line is dead straight just here. A speed restriction for what?'

'You're right. That other train went through at a fair lick and was certainly not slowing.'

'Although that was the other line.'

'Maybe the driver thought he saw something on the line, a horse or something.' Simon was looking into the distance along the parallel railway lines, trying to see any sign of livestock or other animals.

'Yeah, that's true. That's probably it.'

Whilst they were talking, both of them walked from behind the waiting room over onto the platform that the train had just passed to have a better look at the line. But it was then that they saw it.

The platform was no longer empty.

There was a bag.

A leather holdall, to be precise, with a big, heavy zip along the top and two looped handles, also in leather. It was lying on its side not far from the wall of the booking office.

'What the...?'

'Where did that come from?' Edward was slowly walking towards it. 'This was not here before, I am sure of it. We would have seen it'.

'It must have fallen off the train,' added Simon.

Both of them stopped a short distance from the bag and surveyed it. The station seemed very still, somehow emptier and more desolate. A black crow croaked as it landed in the field opposite.

'I am getting an odd feeling about this, Simon.'

'It's just a bag, Eddie.' Simon's voice, however, did not sound totally confident.

'I know, but why is it here all of a sudden? It's weird.'

'As I said, it must have fallen off the train.'

They were now kneeling beside the bag. It looked full to bursting; stretching the leather into shape despite being clearly quite old and worn. The leather in places was dry and abraded.

'Bit careless to lose a bag off a train, but I guess it could have got kicked off the footplate.'

'Yeah, but surely you would notice. I mean, it looks heavy.'

'It does, stuffed full of somebody's clothes, I reckon. He'll be a bit sick when he wants to change after his shift. Should we open it?' Edward had righted the bag and had a hand on the leather tab that pulled the zip.

'I think so. Yes, we should. As you say it could have clothes and things inside that might help us get it back to whoever lost it.'

Edward looked at Simon and agreed. 'Good point. If one of the crew have lost it, it's possible they are Woodford men and we can get it back to them.'

'But how would you kick this off the engine and not notice?' Simon was frowning; something in his voice halted Edward, as he was about to open it up.

'And why did the train slow down at the same moment? Oh well, here goes ...' Edward took hold of the leather fob on the zip and tugged it open, the contents forcing it wide as the pressure was released.

'Oh my God.'

'Bloody hell!'

The bag was completely full of perfectly brand new, neatly-sorted five pound notes. The bundles had a dark-blue wrapper branded 'Bank of England' and indicating that they each held £200. Both of them were motionless for a moment or two. A skylark's song hung in the air; a motorbike spluttered in a distant lane. Simon reached forward and picked up a wad of the crisp, white notes.

'How much money must there be? Thousands and thousands and thousands of pounds.' His voice was slow and breathless.

'Oh, I don't like this. This is not right, no way does a railwayman have money like this. It cannot have come from the train.' Edward glanced around, suddenly feeling very uneasy. 'Put it back, Simon.' He was speaking under his breath, feeling his pulse quicken. 'This is not ours and I am sure it's wrong. I think we should leave this where it is.'

'Are you kidding? We could be millionaires, Eddie. We *are* millionaires!' Despite the passion and enthusiasm of his words,

Simon spoke in a hushed, breathless voice. 'We can't just leave it here.' Simon had extracted one of the notes and was inspecting it lovingly. The scent of newly-printed banknote wafted under his nose.

A kind of silence fell as the two were mesmerised by the sheer, overwhelming wealth before them. A sheep bleated quietly in a nearby field. They gazed at the bright-white, pristine rectangles of good fortune.

'Are you kidding, Si? We can't keep this, but what should we do with it?' Edward was feeling agitated. He had a knot in his stomach and kept glancing around as if a ghostly stationmaster would suddenly step out of his office and give them a roasting.

'Oh, come off it. We found it, Eddie; I mean, if someone's stupid enough to lose this much money then —'

'— they will come back to look for it.'

They were both suddenly conscious that the sound of the motorbike had stopped and that it had been very close only a few seconds earlier. They looked towards the bridge, but the station awning and the roof to the covered stairway blocked their view of the road. However, they could hear slow, heavy footsteps.

'Oh Jesus, someone's coming.' hissed Simon, stuffing the bundle back in the bag, but not having time to fully zip it closed.

'Leave it! We've got to hide.' Edward grabbed his friend's arm and rapidly looking around, they ran just a few steps, stooped low to the ground and ducked into the open door of the stationmaster's office. Once inside they pressed themselves hard against the wall and took deep breaths, trying to hold the air in, to prevent their breathing from betraying them.

The crunch of heavy boots could clearly be heard, then the squeak of a leather jacket and trousers. The motorcyclist was immediately outside the open door, probably standing beside the holdall. Simon's unfinished Churchman smoked accusingly on the dirty floor of the office where it had fallen, just a tiny wisp of smoke, but it seemed to scream: 'look at me'.

'Bloody idiots! Are you stupid, or what?' The hard voice was almost in their ears, sending jolts of fear through the two lads. He must have seen them hide and was letting them know they were going to get it. They heard his breathing, and then the sound of the zip being tugged closed, his leathers creaking as he stood, a soft thump as he swung the holdall over his shoulder and walked away. Moments later the motorbike roared into life and raced noisily away.

'Jesus, that was too scary for words.' Edward was holding his hands to his chest. He almost never swore, but now found it helped him release the tension. 'Bugger!'

'It's gone. He's taken it. He's taken the whole lot!' Simon had peered around the door, trying to look calm, but his breathing and a livid red around his neck betrayed that he was not feeling as cool as he was trying to appear.

'Good riddance! What was that about? Actually, I don't want to know.' Edward was looking pale. 'Look, Simon. Let's just forget we were here today and go home. I don't think we should hang around, it feels too dangerous'.

'Well, we can't completely forget it, can we, Eddie?'

'Why on earth not?' He was getting irritated with Simon's clearly fake nonchalance.

'Because of this.' Simon was holding up the big bright white fiver he had extracted.

'Oh no. You idiot! What do you think you're doing? He'll be back looking for it!'

'He won't miss one — I mean he had plenty, after all. What's one fiver out of thousands? Anyway, he doesn't know that we are here, so he can't know that we took it… Oh, but wait a minute — the rucksack! Our bikes!' Simon suddenly looked very white: 'if he saw them, and then finds money missing …'

'… and with Earnshaw's Bakery — Woodford-bleedin-Halse written on the side of my bike — oh, great.'

They both fell silent.

'Right, I agree with you, let's get out of here and cycle like hell back home.' Suddenly Simon had lost his bravado, so they quickly collected the haversack and ran up the stairs, forgetting the unfinished bottles of beer. They then checked the road, which was thankfully deserted, and pulled their bikes from the hedge.

'They are quite well hidden,' Edward spoke aloud in an encouraging tone of voice as he mounted the heavy delivery bike, aware that he would be hard-pressed to outrun his aunt's elderly Jack Russell, let alone have a cat's chance in hell against a motorbike.

'Yep. He would never have seen the bikes,' Simon sounded relieved.

Nonetheless, they cycled like possessed men. With each yard they put between Culworth and themselves, they felt the fear of what had happened slowly lessen.

But it was far from forgotten.

Chapter Seven

'ZING! WENT THE STRINGS OF MY HEART'
Lew Stone and his band

After his fruitful visit to Woodford Halse, Vignoles returned to his office, eager to hear from Sergeant Trinder. The office was situated inside the big trainshed at Leicester Central and was a rather plain room with very high, unadorned walls. These were tinged with a yellowy-cream paint and were now rather grubby from engine and pipe smoke. Above was a large skylight that was part of the overall canopy covering the station concourse. Through this streamed dusty bands of sunlight, slanting across the walls and pooling on the brown linoleum floor. It was good to see daylight in the office again. The roof glazing had only recently been scrubbed clear of blackout paint. Electric lights with small, dark-blue enamelled shades dangled from metal tubes carrying the power across the roof space. These cast extra — and, until recently, the only illumination — upon two heavy desks and a table that took up much of the floor space. One wall was lined with shelves that held manila folders and box files, bundles of papers, books and odd items that seemed to find their own, uninvited way there.

The opposite wall had a window that opened out onto the 'down' platform that hosted trains travelling north, towards Nottingham Victoria and Manchester Central. Vignoles had a desk set just back from this window. He could sit in his wooden swivel chair, turn to rest his feet on the heating pipes, tip the chair back slightly and keep an eye on the world passing by. He loved the continual ebb and flow of the station and would often observe the way people behaved during the endless comings-and-goings: the tearful embraces, joyful hugs and sad, solitary departures, all wrapped in wisps of intangible white steam around the bodies of the travellers. He watched the groups of uniformed men and women sitting on kit bags, encumbered by the mountains of equipment and clutter of warfare, and wondered how many had never returned. Then there were the impatient men, for they were always men, strutting and pirouetting across the platform irritated by their surroundings, just eager to get the experience of travelling over and done with.

Vignoles was looking out of his office window now, deep in thought. He had turned away for a few moments from his Remington typewriter, which held the notes he had been writing up about the day's events. He was holding a cup of Camp Coffee. The sunlight rendered the scene before him like something out of a painting. Thick diagonals of pale, straw-coloured light scything through the palls of swirling steam curling towards a sky, which was darkening with purple thunderclouds. Shiny metal, oily paintwork and varnished wood were brought alive by the touch of the sun. It was a wonderful palette of earthy russets and greens, ochres and browns. A Pacific locomotive across the platform before him especially took his eye. It shone with the colour of a fresh cooking apple.

He spun himself back around to face his desk, then pulled a heavy cord with a knot at its end, which dangled beside his chair. The cord was connected to a brass arm that protruded through the brown, match-boarded party wall running the length of his office to his left. The arm jangled a bell in the office on the other side of the partition. Vignoles had been requesting an intercom for years, but first 'financial resources', then 'the war' and now 'austerity restrictions' had been used as excuses to delay the installation of this vital piece of equipment. Improvisation however had served him quite well. He glanced once more at his notes, and then looked up as his sergeant entered the room through a door in the panelled wall.

'Ah, Trinder, take a seat.'

His sergeant saluted casually, crossed the room and sat in one of the two wooden chairs with curved backs and arms in front of the inspector's wooden desk.

'So. Tell me about your adventures. You must be dreadfully tired. Did you get any sleep?'

Trinder still retained a hint of oil and coal dust about his person, having had no time to return home and wash, and his chin was darkened by stubble. His hair was however slicked into place. He looked briefly out of the window whilst measuring his reply.

'Not a lot of sleep, sir, but it is all part of the job and worth the effort. I feel sure that there is now a clear link between the burnt wagons, the Water Street yard and the Bedford vans. They also have a delivery truck in the name of the Anglo-Empire Oil Co, and it was this that I observed this morning, making what appeared to be a surreptitious delivery of some kind to the guard of a train.'

Sergeant Trinder then explained in detail what he had seen, in particular how he had observed the late-night arrival of two railwaymen at the Water Street premises, and how he had decided to tail the two men, who turned out to be a guard and fireman.

'Interesting. So these people, we know, have their hands upon a lot of paper, perfect for making counterfeit banknotes of superior quality. I suspect that inside that warehouse there is a printing press. I also suspect that the train crew you followed this morning are one and the same as those who claimed that their engine was in trouble and abandoned their valuable cargo in an overcrowded yard, pushed to a conveniently distant siding. A train abandoned by a locomotive allegedly in trouble, but which then steamed all the way back home. So, could we make a mental leap, and say that the bag you saw exchanged, contained something of value?' Vignoles paused, and both men considered this point for a few moments.

'Newly printed banknotes perhaps?' Trinder suggested.

'My thoughts exactly. So, if this really was the case, then we must establish where it went. Maybe they will repeat the exercise. A million pounds in fivers fills up a darn sight more than one holdall.'

Trinder pulled a thoughtful face. 'Where are they sending the money, and to whom? And then they need to find a way of using this hot money, maybe exchanging it for goods, or even "real" money in some way. There is a lot we still don't know.'

'Indeed. Indeed, but that is the challenge of good detective work, sergeant. But actually this lot have already given away quite a lot of information,' and then Vignoles proceeded to tell Trinder about his investigations at Woodford. He mentioned the possibly coincidental spilling of ink upon the entry for that train movement, and how he was asking Anna to run a few checks on which guards had been booked onto the same train in previous months. 'So you see, we have quite a lot to work with. But I think we might have to pay a nocturnal visit to Water Street. We may find a door fortuitously unlocked, enabling us to take a little peek inside.' Vignoles raised an eyebrow towards Trinder.

'But we have no warrant to search. Are you suggesting that we enter the premises, ah, hum, without permission, sir?' There was a glint in the sergeant's eye.

'Well, according to this Leicester Trade Directory,' he lifted a small, chubby, soft-backed book from his desk, 'it is an abandoned building. Blitzed. So it would not be at all surprising if we found a door to be open ... encouraged to open, if necessary, by your considerable abilities with a lock pick, and we would be merely entering a shut-down business. Of course this would be strictly off the record. But it could prove extremely useful.' Vignoles held his unlit pipe in his left hand and swivelled his chair so that he could stretch his legs to one side of his desk and grinned.

'Extremely.'

'I am interested also in that oil delivery vehicle...' Vignoles picked up the trade directory lying on his desk and started to leaf through it whilst he was speaking, 'and it appears that the Anglo-Empire Oil Company does not exist, although a company with a very similar name does. Get P.C. Blencowe to run checks on who delivers paraffin oil to the railway in the Nottingham area. I suspect that they are bogus.' Vignoles was filling his pipe whilst talking. 'A smoke?' Vignoles indicated to Trinder that he might join him. The sergeant fished a packet of Player's from his jacket pocket in answer to Vignoles's invitation.

They talked a while longer about what might be their strategy for taking the investigation to the next stage. Both men agreed that after a good night's sleep they would call into the Water Street warehouse on the Sunday night.

'Oh and another interesting thing, sir. They had a fair line up of vehicles tucked away in that yard. Under wraps. I counted seven, all looked ex-army and brand new — strange really, as their delivery vehicle was on its last legs.'

'Did they, now? Hmm... buying and selling stock — it's a good way to convert quantities of freshly printed money.' Vignoles was using his pipe to punctuate what he was saying. 'Take the registration numbers of the Bedfords and that oil truck, and chase them up with the Leicester City Licensing Office. Do try and chivvy them along, they can drag their heels terribly. The names and addresses will probably be spurious, but even if you can get the place they were purchased from, it may prove useful. Ask P.C. Blencowe to plot, where the owners are alleged to come from, on one of his marvellous charts — you never know what it will show us.' The two men fell silent, whilst Trinder jotted a few quick notes.

Vignoles thought back to the shedmaster at Woodford and his problems rostering crews. This was part of the scheme, he felt sure of it. Keeping certain crews together. But could Tim really be in on the scam? Vignoles took another puff on his pipe, discovered that it had gone out, but left it in his mouth, and the two men fell again into a thoughtful silence for a few moments, punctuated only by the clack of their secretary's typewriter. Vignoles then broke his reverie and spoke. 'OK sergeant, we shall meet here again tomorrow, 10 p.m. Come prepared for a night visit. Good work today, by the way.'

Sergeant Trinder nodded in acknowledgement, stood up, stubbed his cigarette out and started to turn to leave, but then stopped. 'Oh sir, one thing: we have an item of lost property you might like to see.' He smiled, raising an eyebrow.

'Really? Well as long as it is not another walking stick.' Leicester Central collected hundreds of these items a year, adding to the staggering forest of sticks accumulating at Marylebone HQ.

'Not exactly. See for yourself.' At that Trinder dived back through the door into his office. Vignoles frowned and looked on with little real interest, but then opened his mouth and leaned forward:'What the Dickens?'

A foot, with a black leather shoe and fawn sock, started to appear around the door, inching slowly into the room. Then it suddenly rose up into the air, wiggling and jiggling, and then thrust out parallel to the floor as far as the knee. The leg was a most peculiar colour and shape. It was wooden.

'Da dah.' The sergeant stepped into the room and brandished the leg like a sword.

Vignoles was left momentarily speechless, whilst the sound of giggling could be heard from over the party wall. 'Where on earth did you get that?'

'Found by the cleaners in the empty coaching stock early this morning, apparently. Can you believe it? I mean, who forgets their false leg as they get out of a railway carriage?' Trinder was now holding the leg with both hands, the shoe and sock lending it a most surreal air.

'Yeees. So we are looking for a one-legged gentleman in a black shoe with a terrible case of amnesia.' Vignoles was now smiling, although more at the oddness of the vision than with real humour. The giggling had stopped, and the smiling faces of W.P.C. Jane Benson and Mavis Green, the department secretary, peered around the door frame.

'It's quite a rum thing sir, isn't it? I know I am always saying that one day I'll forget my own head, but this takes the biscuit!' Mavis was barely concealing her laughter.

'Quite a mystery. One for Sherlock Holmes I should say, sir,' W.P.C. Benson chipped in.

'We are searching the line for a man who was last seen leaving Leicester Station — and he was hopping.' Sergeant Trinder was now holding one of his legs up behind his back whilst steadying himself with the false leg.

'Enough! This is indeed a strange one. However despite the peculiar circumstances, I don't think that a false leg is really a laughing matter. What sad story lies behind this? There's something rather pathetic about this lost leg.'

Vignoles looked hard at the object, with his pipe in the corner of his mouth. The others fell silent, although without much conviction. Vignoles was remembering a night not long after D Day, when he and W.P.C. Benson stood for long silent hours beside a train of newspaper vans in one of the bays at Central. They had been telegraphed earlier about the train and its 'special cargo' and the necessity of 'keeping Mum' over its presence. When he accepted the train from the railway guard, a Londoner, Vignoles had briefly opened one of the van doors and played a yellow beam from his hooded lamp across the contents, revealing rows of plain wooden coffins, each draped with the Union Flag, one or two with the Stars and Stripes, stacked three high.

'Terrible sight sir, ain'it? Fair makes me skin crawl.' The guard shook his head slowly.

'Oh dear God.'

'Sorry to say, but this is nuffink to what some of the lahds 'ave bin dealin' wiv dahn Dover way. Christ knows what it's like over in Frahnce...'

W.P.C. Benson had joined them as they fell silent for a few moments in contemplation of the gloomy sight, made more so by the pale shaft of light from the flashlight.

'Worst of all, some of 'em ain't got much inside — if yer catch me drift?

'I.D. badge —"dog tag" the Yankees call 'em — an' what bits and pieces they can recover. No weight to some of them boxes, see.'

Vignoles broke himself away from the memory. 'So, it's a matter for Holmes eh, Benson? I don't think we need a fictional detective when we have the mighty combined force of yourself and the sergeant on the case.' He smiled at the young uniformed officer. 'I feel sure that there is a perfectly logical explanation. So, I await your findings with interest.'

'Yes sir.' The W.P.C. blushed.

'Oh do take it away, and for heaven's sake put it somewhere other than in here.' He glanced at the shelves on the opposite wall, with their accumulation of detritus picked up from the station waiting rooms and carriages. Most of it ended up going to the corporation tip, especially the forests of sticks and umbrellas, or given to charity organisations, which seemed to have an endless appetite for coats.

Calm returned to his office and he could hear Mavis tapping away again on her typewriter. He spent another hour going through reports on various incidents of theft, a few cases of drunk and disorderly, and an insurance claim for a racing pigeon that had not returned home. Maybe it just wanted to leave home, he mused as he closed the file and tossed it onto the pile accumulating on his desk. He checked the time, stood up and collected his hat and coat: it was time to go and meet his wife.

Anna Vignoles worked in the goods' despatch department, located in a large, square building that looked rather marooned in the centre of the island platform. Her husband still vividly remembered the day he first set eyes upon her, walking along the platform towards this building, just days after she started work there. Anna joined up in January 1940. Her cheerful and vivacious approach to life, Italian looks and winning smile had made even the most gruesome day seem better. She, like thousands of other women, had signed up to work for the Railway Executive soon after war was declared. The railway had almost ground to a halt through a desperate lack of manpower. It was a tough, harsh environment to work in, so Anna considered herself lucky landing a desk job. It was about as civilised as it could get.

Anna, however, had caused a bigger transformation in Vignoles's life than the war. The long-term bachelor, holed up in his pokey digs, with a complaining landlady, a gas fire that never seemed to work and a hot water geyser that unnerved him, had found himself married by the spring of 1944. It had been the briefest of ceremonies, followed by just two photographs on the church steps in fine drizzle and then celebrations afterwards, in the remarkably drab Great Central Hotel, adjacent to the station. A small group of friends who had been able to arrange leave had toasted the happy couple with bottled beer. His parents-in-law had provided mountains of very welcome home-made pasta and an enormous carrot cake, despite the rationing. It had been a perfect day.

'Charles! How was your day?' Anna was walking briskly towards him across the covered station concourse, and then kissed him gently on the cheek. He returned it gratefully. Her ebullient nature had finally overcome his typical British reticence about public displays of affection, much to the amusement — and undoubted envy — of the other station staff.

'Quite successful, I think. And you? Did you have any luck with that information I asked you to look into?'

'Yes! But it takes time, and so far I 've just traced the last three trips, and I have the names of the men. But it is very slow work. And it is very a strange train,' she looked up at him, 'there's something odd about it. Not quite "right", if you know what I mean?'

'There is indeed! And my guess is, that if you have managed to deduce that, then so did someone else — and hence the robbery. But I shall tell you exactly why it is so strange, when we are away from listening walls and ears. But the train crews and guards, were they always the same ones?'

'Yes. I wrote them down for you.' She passed him a small slip of paper, folded over.

'Excellent work, Anna.' He quickly glanced at the names and all three matched those he had noted at Woodford Halse. 'Well, well, well. Good work!' he folded the note and put it away in his jacket, then smiled. 'Guess what? On a different matter, we are also on the hunt for a man who inadvertently forgot his false leg whilst on a train.' He smiled.

'Crazy! I will let you know if he turns up.'

'What would you like to do? Go home, or maybe we could see a film in town first. We could do with some food, though.'

Anna thought for a few seconds and then replied. 'It's a good plan. The girls in the office said we must go and see the new film that's showing. So, I have an idea. We can call in to see my parents. Mama will give us some pasta, without a doubt.'

Vignoles agreed enthusiastically. He was feeling very hungry suddenly and didn't fancy waiting until they got the train back to their new house on the outskirts of the city. Carelli's Ice Cream Parlour was only ten minutes away. It had been some years since it had sold ice cream of course, if one discounted the dreadful experimental stuff made from powdered milk that Beppe Carelli had tried last summer. But they served excellent food, no matter how scarce it allegedly was, and were currently experimenting with the blessedly un-rationed fish and chips. Vignoles's father-in-law insisted that this most British of institutions was actually an Italian invention. Whatever, Vignoles knew that 'Mama' Carelli would feed them so well he would almost certainly fall asleep during the film.

'What's the film?'

'I don't know. Except that it is a-new, it's a-British, and is a-very romantic.' She put on an Italian accent, as she liked to do when eager to convince Vignoles to follow one of her suggestions. It invariably had the right effect. She looked up at him, smiled at his unspoken assent, and linked her arm through his as they walked out onto Great Central Street.

The long façade of the station lay behind them in all its terracotta glory. It was an elegant, mock-Elizabethan construction, with decorative gable ends that lent it something of the air of a country house. Miraculously it had survived the war unscathed. The clock tower with its copper, onion-shaped dome glowed orange as it caught the early evening sun dipping behind angry thunder clouds boiling in the distance as the Vignoleses made their way into town, side-stepping the jingling trams.

* * * *

Whilst Vignoles and Anna were walking through Leicester, Violet and her sister were talking at home, in the rented shop premises on Station Road in Woodford Halse.

The shop was located at the lower end of the hilly road, close to a motor garage and the railway bridge. The White Hart Hotel dominated the view from the shop window, although a bank of allotment gardens and the gentle rise of the good access road to the station softened the effect. It was not thought a desirable location, so the landlord had struggled to let the place, hence the modest rent. The premises were also shabby and poorly maintained. No matter how hard the two sisters scrubbed the wooden floors or mopped the ugly, brown linoleum of the back kitchen or beat the living daylights out of the rugs, it still stubbornly refused to give up its tatty appearance. The shop had previously been a seed merchant's, and the decoration had an earthy bias, favouring glossy brown and dark green paint, enlivened only by cream on the walls. The musty odour of hessian sacks and smells evocative of a warm garden shed permeated the rooms, despite the copious use of carbolic and hot water.

The two sisters were sitting behind an old and highly polished dining-room table placed towards the rear of the shop floor. Violet used this for her sewing work. Behind them was a huge range of built-in drawers that once held seed packets. These now contained all manner of buttons and fastenings, tapes and elastic, trimmings, needles and thread, and whatever else that they had been able to acquire. Great bolts of precious austerity cloth, branded 'CC41', were leaning against the shelves in one corner, mainly in shades of navy and faun, brown and olive green. Through the shop window, which still retained a strip of translucent advertising for seed corn, they could catch a glimpse of the evening sun through a gap between the two big houses opposite. It was gilding the fields and trees far beyond the village, the colour made all the more intense, by dark bronze thunderclouds as a backcloth.

'So as you see Jenny, the outlook is really not so good with regard to a pension from the State.'

'How beastly of them.'

'Yes, I thought so too. Hardly a flicker of emotion from that awful …' she paused, looking for a suitable word, '… that awful, jobsworth of a man.'

'I could think of something stronger than that.'

'Well mind you don't.' and Violet gave her sister a look, tempered, however, by a glint in her eye. 'As I was saying. I am not at all hopeful of a result from that stuffy little man, and anyway we really cannot wait any longer for our luck to change. So, Jenny, that is why this afternoon, I met with a gentleman from this loan company.' She moved her hand towards the flyer on the table. 'And if we are very careful with how we use this £50, and try to keep a closer watch on mother, then we should pull through this crisis.'

'Oh yes, Vi, I think it will be fine. You did the right thing, I am sure,' and Jenny replaced the pile of crisp, white notes that she had been inspecting, on the table.

'I do hope so. It is really quite a worry. It's hard to be sure I have made the right decision. So very much money … and why did he insist on giving me these things? Somehow they are intimidating. Single pounds seem more friendly and familiar.' Violet looked intently at the big, white five-pound notes, then closed her eyes briefly and sighed. Jenny leaned across and put her arm around Violet's shoulder.

'I've never even seen one before,' Jenny giggled. 'Anyway, I think you did right. We can get things sorted out now, sis. Just think how nice it will be with this place all clean and bright. It will be such fun doing it up.' She smiled with genuine pleasure. Violet, seeing the look on Jenny's face, smiled in return, whilst trying to hold back tears welling in her eyes.

'Thank you for saying so.' Violet dabbed her eyes with a handkerchief. 'Its nice to see you excited about the idea. That does help. However, Jenny dear, I can't help but think that you are in particularly high spirits today. Any particular reason?'

'What do you mean, Vi?' Jenny answered in mock surprise.

'Ah. You see. You can't hide anything from me. Including being delayed for work by a certain young man.'

'Who? Outrageous! He was just passing on his way to work. He said hello.'

Violet smiled at her sister, 'Hmm … and?'

'And nothing. I was merely being polite, and I wished him a good morning, of course. Well, it would have been terribly bad form not to have done so.' Jenny added, with unconvincing indignation, her eyes glinting.

'On the way to work, was he? But if I am not mistaken, Jenny, this particular young man lives above his parents' ironmongery shop at the top of this street. A jolly funny way of going to work.' Violet grinned. 'Well, he had better treat you well, or I shall be after him,' she added, with a tone that whilst light, had a hint of something else behind it.

'Oh, but he's very nice, Vi. Actually he's quite a sweetheart.'

'You see, I was right! Sweetheart, eh?'

'No. I mean, yes, well maybe. OK. So we have met just a few times and passed the time of day.'

'But you do like him?'

Jenny smiled before answering. 'Ye-es. He's perhaps a touch shy, maybe.'

'I'm sure he isn't, it's just that he never gets a word in edgeways when you get up to speed.'

'Charming!'

'Admit it, you like to talk.' Violet was still smiling.

'It's jolly well better than being a wallflower, hiding in the corner.'

'Of course. I'm only pulling your leg. But … but do be careful, Jenny. Don't rush things, will you? Get to know him a bit better.'

'Whatever do you mean, Vi?' Jenny's eyes were sparkling and her cheeks flushed, but she looked intently at her elder sister with some confusion.

'Nothing. Sorry. Oh, it's just that I ... I just don't want you to get hurt.'

'Hurt? Who said anything about getting hurt? I only wished him a "good day". Don't get carried away, Vi.'

'Sorry. That was silly thing to say, and unkind. Forget it, please. Really, I am delighted. It's so nice to see you happy at last.' Violet paused, then added, 'I don't suppose he is any good with a paintbrush, is he?' and Violet laughed, shrugging off her doubts, and responding positively to her sister's obvious excitement.

'I should think he's very practical, what with being in the hardware business.' Jenny still seemed a bit put out.

'Only joking. OK, enough. Let's be practical now. Let's start making a list of what debts we must settle, and what we need to buy to get this place ship-shape. But before that, I'll put the kettle on, and we can listen to Tommy Handley on the wireless, because it's time for "that man again".'

Chapter Eight

'I COULDN'T SLEEP A WINK LAST NIGHT'
Vera Lynn

That night Edward had gone to bed early, feeling increasingly preoccupied with the afternoon's turn of events. His parents, if they had noticed, certainly did not show it. His father had been similarly preoccupied, having just landed the title role in the Mikado, in the Woodford Amateur Dramatics' summer production. As a result he had spent the evening enthusiastically studying the score. His mother had been busy with cooking and washing and looking after his sister, and now, as Edward lay on the bed in his room, he could hear her listening to her favourite 78s on the wind-up gramophone. Vera Lynn's soothing tones drifted up the stairs, declaring that she 'couldn't sleep a wink last night'. The song was appropriate. Edward was finding that sleep also evaded him.

Oh that stupid song. Don't keep reminding me. He just could not get comfortable in his little bed. He had the sash window open to let in the night air, as it was hot and muggy, hinting at a break in the weather. The sound of wagons clattering in the distant shunting yards carried clearly on the still air and started to jangle in his head. Ordinarily he loved these sounds; the domino effect of one wagon clunking into the other as they were pushed and pulled into order. It was something he had grown up with, and he found it lulled him to sleep knowing that the railway was getting on with its business. Like a familiar ticking clock, he found it actually disturbed him when it stopped.

But tonight his mind was racing, turning over and over the events of the afternoon. He just could not arrange the facts into any comforting order, or find some kind of logical sequence that satisfied him and which would allow sleep to still his aching head. No matter how he looked at it, there was something wrong about the incident of the bag, the goods train and the motorcyclist.

His mind kept asking him the same questions; had the bag been there when they arrived? If so, how had they missed it? And even if it had been, why was it there? If it had fallen off the train by accident, how did the motorbike man know to arrive at the abandoned station and pick it up? If he was a friend of the railway men, why not get there a few minutes earlier and take it from them?

And then there was the matter of the money.

So much money. Edward spoke the words softly to himself, needing to form the words in order to express his feelings. So new and so perfect. No railwayman ever earned this kind of money. Surely no one could just lose money like this?

The wagons continued to bang and reverberate in his head; the wheels squealing on the sidings like fingers down a blackboard. He got up angrily and pushed the sash window up and locked it shut despite the mugginess of the night. The sound diminished, but still troubled him. He turned over and re-lit the candle beside his bed and reached for his little notebook. He had noted down the place, the time and date, as well as the number of the locomotive they had observed. It was what he and Simon called an 'Ossie'. These were huge, ungainly machines, built quickly under austerity measures, hence their nickname. There were many of them at Woodford Depot and he was familiar with their appearance. Edward stared at the pencilled number on the page. This had definitely been the engine on the train that slowed down. He had seen it clearly and there was no doubt that it was correct.

Edward heard the sound of the mail train thunder through the village, almost level with his bedroom window as it traversed the high embankment, the note of its hardworking engine shifting as it drew level then sped past. If you were still awake when the mail passed through, then it was deep into the morning. Far too late to still be awake, but more questions kept crowding into his mind. Where was the engine based? If it were a Woodford engine then likely as not it would have been crewed by Woodford men. If he could work out the service number of the goods train he might be able to find out the identities of the men.

But then what? What to do with this information?

He carefully wrote a list of questions in his neat hand, but before he had finished, he finally fell asleep with the stub of the candle still burning.

It started to rain in big, heavy drops that cooled the air and released a gentle scent, whilst the first rumbles of thunder could be heard far in the distance over the fields.

Chapter Nine

'BEI MIR BIST DU SCHON'

The Andrews Sisters

The following day, Sunday, the weather was still unusually warm. Thunder had rolled and crashed around the sky in the early hours of morning and it had rained for a few hours, but the day had dawned clear and the sun soon burned off much of the dampness.

Edward, like most fifteen-year-olds, was not the most attentive churchgoer, although he always accompanied his mother each Sunday. But this morning he awakened early, still filled by nagging doubts gnawing away inside him. He had a sense of having somehow crossed a line between right and wrong, or maybe it was a strange feeling of foreboding. So that morning he gave special attention to his confession prior to taking communion, speaking clearly and earnestly, rather than with the almost inaudible mumble he usually managed. The communion wine warmed his blood, and he felt a sense of calm trickle through his veins, although it might just have been the excessively large draught of wine that he took. His mother restricted her observations of Edward's sudden and curiously devout behaviour to a half smile and a slightly raised eyebrow.

After church, and after changing out of their Sunday best, Edward and Simon spent a few hours gently cycling along the narrow lanes around Woodford. They were lined with hedgerows and they breathed the welcome scent of the many wild flowers, the drying earth and grass of the fields. Now they were stretched out in the long grass that formed the crest of a steep embankment leading up to the running lines just north of Woodford goods' yards. His conscience salved for the time being, Edward felt more able to enjoy himself after his troubled night. They had a great low-level vantage point of the railway. Peering over clover flowers that tickled their chins, and through taller grasses that hissed as they swayed, they looked across the grey and brown stone ballast to the rails. The sun burnt hot through their shirts and, as they both wore shorts, it made the backs of their legs and knees feel like they would be sore that evening. The creosoted wooden sleepers oozed a pungent warm smell mingled with that of oil and cinders. The goods' yards were full of lines of brown and grey wagons awaiting the early morning shift the next day that would start to drag them across the country to places such as Sheffield, Manchester, Immingham and Birkenhead. Until then, the little station pilot engine was chuffing about, banging and clanging them into order.

A bottle of dandelion and burdock lay in the grass between the two lads and they both had notebooks and pencils to hand.

'It was a great game by all accounts.' Simon was talking about the F. A. Cup Final the previous afternoon, and studiously avoiding the subject of the bag of money.

'What was the score? I just know that Derby County won it.'

'4-1. But only after extra time. At the end of the ninety minutes it was tied at one each. It was anybody's call. The game really came alive then; Docherty and Stamps got three goals between them and really finished Athletic off.'

'I bet the Charlton fans were pretty sick at the end. What a game. Did you listen to it?'

'A bit. I was ashing out a loco at the time, but they had the wireless on as loud as they could in the shed and I could hear bits of it. Then when we got to extra time a gang of us made a brew and sat and listened. Even Mr Saunders joined us, so it was all right.' Simon reached for the bottle but stopped before taking a drink, 'OK, next swig of D and B goes to the one who guesses what the next loco it is from the sound alone'.

'Ouch, that's hard. But, all right then.' Edward turned to lay on his back with one hand shielding his eyes from the sun. 'I can't cheat like this. Come on Simon, do the same. You've got a grandstand view there.'

The gentle breeze continued to rustle the grasses, the lowing of some cows impatient for milking and the endless, distant rumble of coal being tippled into the hopper were the only sounds to disturb the tall heat of the day. Time passed.

'Hey ... listen.'

The distant rhythm of a locomotive could just be heard. Both boys concentrated on the beat, trying to decide how big the engine was, how many cylinders it might have, any clue to its identity.

'Two...'

'Nah, it's gotta be three – I reckon it's a V2.'

Edward lay back and looked into the clear azure blue and listened. 'I reckon it's a goods' engine because it sounds like it's got a load of wagons behind, you can hear them rattle.' The sound was far more distinct now, the syncopated chuff and hiss growing louder with the rattle and rumble of a long, heavy goods' train in tow.

'Not necessarily; but I do think you're right. It's definitely three cylinders, and that means I stick with a V2,' said Simon.

'I think it's one of Robinson's O4's. I think I mean an O4, the ones with the eight coupled wheels.' In truth, Edward was stalling for time as he was really not sure, and then he rolled over on to his front to look over the tracks at the approaching engine, which was now almost upon them.

'You see, I was right.' Simon smiled triumphantly as the elegant form of the engine trundled past, spewing steam from leaking glands. It was, as usual, a near-uniform black-brown colour, caked in grime and filth and devoid of any sparkle or glimmer. Only the cab side had been partially wiped clear to reveal her number. They looked on and tried to identify the crew, but they were not Woodford men.

'What a wreck.'

'Poor old thing.' Simon was swigging greedily his prized taste of the warm, flat pop then wiped his mouth. 'Sad. They say these engines won the war, you know. What a way to treat a war hero.'

'How did they win the war, exactly? I mean I thought it was Spitfires, tanks, guns, the atom bomb and a hell of a lot of Yankees that won it.' Edward was unconcerned about losing the bet, and was, as usual, wondering and asking questions, as much to himself as anyone.

'Funny you should say that. I dunno, really. Probably because, well, because without engines to pull all the trains of troops and tanks and war stuff we would never have had D-Day and everything ...' Simon tailed off. 'Well, what the heck, they helped win the war and that sounds all right to me, and that one there needs some help right now, if you ask me, else it won't even get home. I tell you, Eddie, when you start tomorrow, you'd best not fall out with Mr Saunders or he'll give you a filthy beast like that to look after, and it'll near kill you trying just to get the muck off, let alone fire her up.'

'She'd look great afterwards, though.' Edward was concentrating on writing in his small neat handwriting not only the number of the engine, but a note to himself saying 'How did the V2 engines win the war *exactly*?' He remembered that the policeman had made notes in a similar way.

'Don't think you'll feel that way after seven or eight hours hard graft.'

'So will I see you at the shed tomorrow?'

'Of course. It's a big place though, and there's lots of us there, so we may not be working together all the time. But I reckon as we will. And then there's the mess rooms for lunch, though they are a bit disgusting.'

'It's funny, but I'm glad you're working there, Simon. Now it's come down to it, I'm sort of a bit nervous. Is that stupid?' Edward looked across at his friend.

'Oh you'll be fine. But I know what you mean. I felt the same. Takes a bit of getting used to, like anything, I s'pose. All I would say is — be careful about the drivers. Don't go and start talking to 'em unless you've really good cause.'

'Yeah.'

'The top link drivers in particular. They keep themselves to themselves, and until you've passed as fireman you don't even register in their world. You must know your place.'

'At the bottom.'

'Yep. You've got it, Eddie. That's us cleaners. Here, finish this — it's got a bit boiled, though;' and Simon handed Edward the bottle of pop. Silence fell for a few moments, punctuated only by the distant rumbling. Finally Edward felt it was time to broach the subject that still preoccupied his mind.

'So. Have you still got that fiver?'

'Of course. What d'you think I'd do with it?'

'Not sure. But what should we do with it, actually? And what about that bag?'

Simon looked across the railway tracks and pondered Edward's questions. 'First off, let's spend the money.'

'No, Si! It's not ours.'

'So, whose is it then? I mean we can't exactly give it back, can we?' Edward remained silent. 'No. Whatever you think about it, we have it, and we might as well turn it to good advantage. Once we break into it, we can forget how we got it.'

'How you got it.'

'Oh that's not fair, Eddie; — we were both there.'

'Hmm.'

'Then we can forget how we got it, and enjoy having some real money at last.'

'Put it like that, and I am coming to your way of thinking'.

'So, what shall we buy?'

'Dunno.' Edward was, however, already beginning to think about just what this money could mean for them, and that just, perhaps, it might be all right to spend it. But another voice in his head was telling him to wash his hands of the whole matter. He moved the conversation along. 'But apart from this five pounds, Si, what about that bag? It was ever so weird what happened. Look, I was thinking about it last night, like a detective might, and I've made a list of things we should investigate,' and he turned to the page he was writing the night before.

Simon read through the list and nodded. 'Yes. We could be like real detectives — better still, like British agents. Tell you what, the first thing we can do — tomorrow — we can both easily see if the "Ossie" is on shed, maybe even ask one of the shed crew if it is a Woodford engine. No one would think anything of us asking.'

'Especially if we make it look like we are just collecting numbers and stuff.'

'To throw them off the scent.' Simon grinned and continued, excitement growing in his voice, 'And my father, being signalman here, he would know the goods' train routes, times, and all that jazz. I'm not sure, but I think that was an empty brick train. Narrows it down a bit. Once we have that, we could watch out again for them.'

'You mean the same train? Are you thinking to go back?'

'Why not? We could hide ourselves like proper spies, and observe what happens. Maybe even follow the bloke with the money.'

'The man on the motorbike? Fat chance on bicycles.'

'Well, OK, no.' Simon was thoughtful for a few moments. 'But if we managed to get the registration number we could. Well, I'm not sure what we could do then. Better still we could get in first, and take all the money.' Simon looked mischievously at Edward, who was feeling a mixture of mounting excitement and complete dread.

'I don't know about that, Simon. It sounds a bit scary. Although I must admit I do at least want to know more.'

'That's the spirit — spot on. Agreed then?' The lads fell silent again, thinking about what they were planning, both of them subject to a curious tug-of-war between fear and excitement playing out in their minds and in the pit of their stomachs. What were they doing? Was it better to forget the whole affair and throw the stolen five pounds away?

But excitement and curiosity won out.

Looking around at the great, burning sun low over the trees and hedges, the still air starting to fill with clouds of midges, and the lowing cattle, they could tell it was after seven, at least. They listened out for the bell in St Mary the Virgin, but it was silent.

'Head back?' Simon was already walking slowly down the side of the embankment, towards their bicycles lying in the field below.

'Si, how did you know it was a V2, by the way?'

'It's all in the rhythm, in the beat. With three cylinders you get a kind of swing beat.'

'Yeah. I think I know what you mean.'

'You know that Andrews Sisters song your mum is always playing? "Beer Mister Shane", or something funny like that.'

'"Bei mir bist du schon".'

'Yeah, whatever, some blinkin' Gerry stuff. Well, that sort of has the beat — da ta-da-da, da ta-da-da, da ta-da-da…'

Edward looked at Simon then nodded, picking up the rhythm with his head. The two lads joined together humming the song, exaggerating the rhythm. Edward attempted the trumpet solo using his lips and free hand to mimic the instrument. They ended in fits of laughter by which time they had wheeled the bicycles across the now-dampening grass, occasionally slapping a bare arm or leg as the insects bit them.

Then they were pedalling home along the Byfield Road, back to Edward's house for some Earnshaw's home-baked bread with a smear of butter, a thick, oozing layer of honey and a pot of tea. Both had agreed on the ride home to say no more that evening about the spying operation, and most definitely nothing about the fiver.

Afterwards they sat at the big kitchen table whilst the clock ticked gently, and they carefully underlined the day's 'cops' in their *ABC of L.N.E.R. Locomotives.* It was a pleasant feeling, that of making order and sense of the world, that descended as each neat red line helped complete the columns of letters and numbers that crossed the pages. The anticipation of comparing the numbers taken down in their notebooks during the day with those underlined and those not, was something hard to explain. The leap in the heart as a new sighting was revealed. The curious, inexplicable pleasure of looking at the freshly-inked lines, looking at the patterns and sequences, the rhythms in the play of black columns of type, cream paper and red highlights. Looking for a sense of order. Everything in its place and a place for everything.

The only dissonant note in their evening's work was that struck by the number of the Austerity locomotive. Edward placed a double line beneath this. It spoiled the symmetry, but somehow it needed doing.

Chapter Ten

'OPUS NO.1'

Tommy Dorsey & his Orchestra

Charles Vignoles and John Trinder had eaten some greasy fish and chips out of the paper whilst sitting on a wooden bench beside a bus stop. Vignoles could taste the sour flavour of old chip fat in his mouth, and his hands had a slight sheen from the fat, in the pale gaslight. He reached into one of the pockets of his heavy, R.A.F. overcoat and extracted a neatly folded and ironed handkerchief, and started to rub his hands clean. 'It filled a hole. We were fortunate, I suppose, to have even found a chip van still serving. I hate to be hungry on a job like this.' Vignoles stood up, and handed the handkerchief to Trinder. 'Here — it helps remove the grease a little. I could do with a beer to wash that down.'

'Thanks. At least the government haven't rationed fish and chips. I know what you mean about a drink though. These might do the trick — Victory V's,' Trinder was proffering a small paper packet of lozenges, after first popping one in his own mouth. 'They'll strip the chip fat away.' he grinned.

'Take the roof of your mouth as well.' Vignoles took one and started to pull on a pair of black leather gloves. Trinder, after wiping his hands, did the same. It was still far too warm and muggy for heavy overcoats and gloves, but a storm was threatening, and both men had need of the deep pockets their overcoats provided. They started walking along the dimly-lit street, sucking on the fiery sweets, enjoying the clean, spacious feeling it brought to their nervous breathing.

A towering brick wall ran for many yards to their left, forming the side of a great warehouse. A steam lorry clattered past on the granite sets of the road, its canvas covering quivering as the poorly-sprung wheels jolted over the surface. They made a series of turns to the left and right and the streets narrowed at each successive turn, appearing to be overpowered by tall, brick chimneys and banks of warehouses in ever-denser groups, all with small, mean windows. Chains swung menacingly from protruding hoists, like gallows in the eaves, making the innocent repositories look like prisons. The street lamps had ceased to be lit, or even exist once they stepped into an area clearly less prosperous than before. Many of the premises were bomb-damaged, some were completely burnt out; the open spaces where once had been roofs clearly visible even in the deep, cobalt blue of the night. Other buildings had been destroyed; heaps of rubble lay where once a business had thrived. Strange, shadowy figures flitted in the dark, amongst these weed-filled bombsites, betrayed by the sound of a brick tumbling or the scrunch of broken glass, as they tried to move out of sight. These were the forgotten homeless, the lost and the dispossessed, scratching a grubby life amidst the ruins. There was an ugly, acrid smell of burnt wood, damp cinders and rotting rubbish permeating the air as the policemen passed by.

'Ugh, gives me the creeps. It did even in daylight, when I staked the place out.'

'Agreed. It's my first time around here, but I suspect familiarity does not make it any the nicer.'

In truth Vignoles was also surprised at just how menacing night had rendered the scene. He knew it was just the effect of darkness, and the depressing after-effects of the Blitz, but it was unnerving all the same. A fox stood and stared at them, its eyes like bright brassy disks, reflecting what little light there was. It turned and briskly darted through an open doorway to be swallowed up by the darkness.

'Nearly there...'

They stopped, and both reached for their hefty torches, stowed in the deep pockets of their overcoats. Each torch had little metal covers screwed in front of the lens, reducing the beam to a narrow, concentrated spot of yellow light, for use during the blackout. After years of working with these, both men had adapted to the tiny glimmers of light the torches produced, and tonight they were perfect for the job in hand, so had been retrieved from a desk drawer and replaced on each torch. A curious by-product of the Blitz, thought Vignoles, as he briefly checked his was working. 'Speaking to a minimum from now on. Retreat immediately if we meet anyone, act dumb and stupid if caught. However...' Vignoles reached inside his coat and hefted a service revolver in his hand. 'If it gets really hairy... I do have this.'

If the sight of the D.I. carrying a revolver surprised Sergeant Trinder, he didn't show it, he just nodded. Vignoles replaced the gun inside his coat and touched Trinder on the shoulder to indicate that they should advance towards the Water Street premises. The double wooden gates leading to the yard were pulled shut tight against the arched opening in the high perimeter wall. Trinder placed a hand on one of the gates and started to slowly but firmly push against it, testing that it was bolted shut. There was almost no give in the door, and he gently reduced the pressure so that the door would not rattle. Let into one of the big gates was a small pass-door, and now Trinder turned his attention to this. It was locked, but after briefly flashing a pool of light upon the keyhole, he extracted from a pocket a set of skeleton keys and with a few deft turns they heard the lock open. The sound seemed to echo across the street. Both men held their breath and waited to see if the sound caused any reaction. Trinder had an ear pressed close to the door, his nostrils filled by the smell of the flaking blue paint and the wood of the door, still slightly warm from the day's sun and now releasing the scent of the oils within. He nodded and slowly pushed the little door open.

Both stepped into the yard, and Vignoles carefully pushed the door closed behind him. They were immediately confronted by the bulk of three trucks, pulled up close to the gates. They were rendered colourless by the night, and the two Bedfords with their tall radiator grilles and the downward curve of the windscreens looked like strange, unhappy faces with their mouths gaping open in a silent cry. To their left beyond the farthest vehicle, they could just discern a row of big dark shapes under a low roof that ran like a porch along the side of the yard. These were the other vehicles Trinder had reported seeing last Friday.

To their right was a door, and then beyond that a raised loading bay covered by a small roof to protect an unloading lorry. The building towered above them with a good five storeys as indicated by rows of yet more tiny windows. The building was clearly designed to allow in only minimal light.

They stood stock still for a few moments, listening, but apart from a few distant city noises and the far-off whistle of a train, all seemed quiet inside the warehouse. No lights were showing from any visible window, but neither man took much comfort from that. Years of the A.R.P. barking orders to 'put that light out' had made everyone able to prevent any stray light leakage. There was no reason to think that the gang, who clearly had something to hide, would so quickly lose this habit in peacetime.

Vignoles again softly touched Trinder's upper arm, and as his sergeant glanced at him he indicated that they would start by looking at the covered vehicles. They crossed over to them and, glancing around to see if they were still undetected, Trinder knelt down and peered closely at the nearest vehicle's registration plate. Vignoles, meanwhile, was trying to identify the type of lorry by lifting the heavy tarpaulin thrown over it. He fished out his police notebook, flipped it open and started to make notes. It only took a minute or two for them to be satisfied that they had enough information, then they turned and quietly walked over towards the main building. The rain had held off so far; this was fortunate, as wet footprints would potentially betray them. But there were occasional and ominous deep rumblings of thunder in the far distance.

An aeroplane buzzed overhead, its propeller engines throbbing behind the clouds. Using this as a useful mask, Trinder darted forward and, flattening himself against the brickwork, slowly tried the handle of the door to the right of the gates. It turned and he opened the door; any sound it made was drowned in the aircraft's reverberating noise. The door revealed a passageway that ran deep into the heart of the building, with other doors opening off it. There was no light and no sound other than the dying hum of the plane, so Trinder risked a quick sweep with his torch to get their bearings. They exchanged glances, then walked down the corridor, playing light onto each door, trying to assess what was behind them.

Suddenly Vignoles stopped: a jolt like electricity ran though his jangling nerves. What was that? He managed to stop himself speaking aloud, but his quick tap against Trinder's arm was enough to immediately stop him dead in his tracks. A strange cry rang out, and then the sound of a bottle skidding and rolling over stone. A second drunken shout from the street outside was this time followed by the sound of glass shattering. They exhaled slowly and exchanged relieved glances.

They decided to enter a small office located beside the loading dock. It was filled with rows of dark metal filing cabinets, many with their drawers only partially closed. A small desk was littered with papers and the chair in front of it had the seat ripped open and was leaking its stuffing. The room was a shambles. They played their torches over the room and Vignoles inspected some of the papers on the desk. A fine film of dirt caked them, and the uppermost was a despatch note dating from 1942, issued by Walsh & Co, Secure Repositories, Water Street, Leicester. Vignoles knew already that they had ceased trading, having previously checked the trade directories. The office was clearly abandoned and held no obvious interest, so they walked out and into the huge holding area inside the loading bay. Sliding doors were drawn shut against the yard, but Trinder's torch quickly picked out the recent oil on the runners and wheels, and a new padlock shining on the hasp. They exchanged knowing glances. What attracted their attention now however, were cardboard boxes stacked to one side of the bay. Most were sealed, but some lay clearly discarded, scattered randomly upon the floor, whilst one was open, but still partially full, of neat rectangles of white paper.

Trinder knelt down and played his torch beam upon these. He lifted a ream out of the box and looked at the paper wrapper. It was hard to read the printing, which was black on a deep maroon, but he knew already that it would say in bold letters: 'Bank of England'.

Vignoles stood nearby, but kept his eyes sweeping the area, observing the considerable scuff marks in the layers of dust on the floor. He then looked back, and his enquiring glance was met by Trinder nodding. This was surely the paper stolen from Annesley Yard. Vignoles saw that the dust covering the ground was a perfect indicator of activity, of which there had been a lot, and as he played the beam on the floor it became obvious that an area towards the rear of the room had even been swept almost clean. Small mounds of fluff and dust lay in drifts to either side of an area roughly five yards wide. Sitting squarely in the centre of this was a wall of wooden packing crates, forming a crude barrier. Vignoles was sure that behind this would be the printing press they were looking for. The two men approached and walked around the cases and, sure enough, there it sat, in all its heavy, cast-iron solidity. The press was squat, and in the pitch black of the room appeared as random components of oiled metal, assembled in a seemingly meaningless jumble of angles and planes. Trinder was already trying to locate the printing plates, his face bent close to the machine as his pale yellow torch beam sought out the highly polished metal sheets, engraved with the design of the five pound note.

'Sir!' He used a stage whisper, but it was enough to bring Vignoles over to look. They played their torch beams over the plates for a few moments, and then stood up.

'We need to find a sample of money,' whispered Vignoles as softly as he could. Trinder nodded. They moved over to a long bench set behind the press. This was an untidy mess of bottles of what might be inks and solvents, rags, a paper guillotine, boxes, dirty plates with the remains of food, three glasses that had not been washed for a while, empty beer bottles and quarter-full bottle of Scotch. All this was in stark contrast to the neat piles of white notes that lay in the centre. It was immediately obvious that these were freshly printed five pound notes. Vignoles carefully lifted up a pile, extracted a note from the bottom, held the pristine rectangle of paper in one gloved hand for a few moments, then folded it, put it in his overcoat's inside pocket, then stood thoughtfully contemplating the bench. He took a pre-printed paper wrapper lying nearby and slipped it around the stack of notes he had moved, and placed the apparently complete bundle of £200 on top of three similar bundles already prepared nearby. He hoped that no one would realise what he had done and recount the bundles, at least not for a few days.

'Names,' he whispered, 'anything with a name.'

They scanned the desk, and Trinder flicked the beam of his torch onto some small boxes lying on the floor, tucked just under the bench. He inhaled sharply and knelt down, Vignoles saw his reaction and joined him. The first box held a stack of at least ten dark blue British passports, and a manila envelope pushed down to one side. The other box contained a number of driving licences.

'Phew.' Trinder's expression of surprise was barely audible, but still full of feeling. Vignoles was flicking through the passports. They were all blank, but looked high quality and, once completed, would probably fetch a small fortune on the black market. The driving licences were complete, however, and Trinder rested his notebook on one knee, his torch jammed between his body and arm, as he noted the names and addresses in the tiny, red cloth-covered books. Vignoles, meanwhile, replaced the passport blanks in the box and turned his attention to the envelope. He immediately realised that this might be the jackpot. Inside was a jumble of passport-sized photographs and a few sheets of paper with pencilled names, addresses and sums of money beside them. It was obvious that there was no time now to study these, so Vignoles had to make a quick decision. He emptied the contents into the inside pocket of his R.A.F. coat and stood up. He located an old newspaper on the bench and extracting a few pages, he folded them and placed these inside the envelope so that it looked full when replaced in the box. Vignoles knew that this was a risky strategy, but he needed a breakthrough. He had hoped for names and now he and Trinder had some to work with.

But had it perhaps been too easy? Vignoles felt suddenly apprehensive. It had been very simple to find the press, and the other evidence to boot. Was he surprised that what looked to be a well-organised gang had left the place unguarded? As if in answer to his silent question, they were both suddenly aware of the sound of footsteps approaching down what clanged and reverberated like a metal stairway. There were voices talking as well. At least that meant they had not been discovered — yet. They both clicked their torches off instantly and stood stock still, pondering what their next move should be. It was clearly two men, in conversation, and approaching fast. One of them had evidently cracked a joke, as there was brief laughter. Vignoles was desperately trying to visualise the room in its entirety, not an easy task when they had had only the dim torchlight to work with and only a few moments to take it all in. The men were approaching from the opposite side from that in which he and Trinder had entered. This was good news, as Vignoles reckoned their exit route was free.

An electric light was switched on in a corridor and there was now just enough light for Vignoles and Trinder to make each other out and exchange glances. They took a few steps away from the approaching footsteps, and ducked behind the wall of crates, hoping that they were concealed from view. It was too late to make it across the room, into the corridor and out to safety. Vignoles felt for his revolver and eased it slowly out of his pocket, feeling for the safety catch. This was very awkward. They had no warrant to search the premises, and were well off the radar with regard to their area of jurisdiction. They were, in effect, the intruders at that moment. Chief Superintendent Badger would throw the book at them if he knew, although that might just possibly be the least of their worries.

'Drink?' One of the voices was now very close. 'There's some Scotch around here, I think…'

'Scotch, sir? I don't mind if I do.' Both men laughed at the reference to Tommy Handley. The speaker continued, but without the upper class accent, 'You need to ask? I could murder for one.'

'Yep, there it is.'

The footsteps were now just a few yards away from the two intruders, crouched behind the makeshift wall of boxes. A set of overhead lights suddenly drenched the room in light, as they heard one of the men throw a contact switch.

'That's better. What's that? Rats! Ugh, get away, yer little bleeders!' and there was the sound of something heavy crashing against the far wall behind the concealed policemen, both of whom forced themselves not to react. Trinder, however, had another problem. He could feel dust getting up his nose, and was now holding it closed with one hand in a desperate attempt to stop a sneeze, a look of alarm in his eyes.

'I hate rats, really can't stick em.'

The other man laughed. 'Are you gonna spend all night chasing rats, or d'you want a drink? Say, let's get a breath of air, it stinks of flippin' ink and stuff in here.'

'Yeah. Don't want to hang around if there are rats, any road. So, what's with the lorry? You said it was playing up last time.'

The two men were now walking across the loading bay towards the corridor and the yard. Vignoles was able to see their backs clearly, and realised that if the men turned around, they would be discovered. He hefted the gun, ready to make his move if needed, and felt his throat go dry.

'Oh that heap of junk — blinking steam everywhere, clouds of it. Bloody useless. Time to get shot of it, if you ask me.'

The voices faded away, and Vignoles and Trinder allowed themselves to stand, then they quickly crossed the room in the same direction as the departing voices, but stopped with their backs against the wall, beside the door into the corridor. Trinder finally made a muffled sneeze, and they both froze. Nothing happened though, and they breathed again.

'Into the corridor, last room before the yard.' Vignoles moved first, glancing quickly down the corridor, and then, with the pistol raised, he moved with long, light steps, hoping that any loose change he was carrying wouldn't betray him. Trinder was close behind as they ducked into what turned out to be a filthy washroom. Their noses told them so, and they were thankful that it was so dark. It had evidently not had the attention of cleaners in years. The smell of urine — and worse — stung their eyes. The humid night air was not helping reduce the fetid stench. Long, narrow windows with frosted glass were open above the urinals, and through these they could hear the two men continuing to discuss one of the vehicles, although they were out of sight. There was a slight glow of light, probably from a torch, and it sounded like they were now lifting the bonnet of the vehicle in question and looking inside.

'I reckon it's just the radiator hose. Not more than that. Yeah, look here, it's split right down. No wonder it was steaming.'

'You're not kidding. Like a blinkin' kettle, it was.'

'Easy. I can soon fix that. Too dark now, but I'll have a look when it gets light. Anyway, give us some more of that whiskey.' Their conversation carried on for a few minutes in a desultory manner, mainly about horses and betting. Vignoles was assessing the situation. He was fairly sure that the men were standing beside the truck furthest away from where they were, so he and Trinder might just be able to leave the stinking toilet and take cover at the rear of the nearest Bedford truck. It was almost pitch black outside, heavy cloud obscuring any moonlight. The truck was high enough off the ground to offer some kind of refuge. He whispered his plan to the sergeant, who nodded, then immediately moved out of the washroom and stood poised at the open doorway, weighing up the challenge. Then he was gone, running whilst bent low to the ground into the inky dark. Vignoles could hardly see him. Trinder's long dark overcoat helping him blend into the night. Vignoles followed with awkward, crabbed steps, anxious not to make any noise. As he ducked under the chunky metal chassis of the truck his head collided with the spare tyre slung underneath, and his hat rolled off and back into the yard. As he came to this sudden and unexpected halt, a few tiny pieces of gravel, that had probably dropped from the tyres of the truck, pinged on the flagstones from under his shoes. They sounded loud to their ears, and it might not have been coincidence that one of the men inspecting the damaged radiator hose stopped in mid sentence.

'What was that? You heard something?'

'No. Probably the rats.'

Oh heck, thought Vignoles, now we've blown it, but just as he was thinking this, there was a sudden hissing sound filling their ears and a rush of cooler air. Great droplets of rain started to patter all around them in noisy splashes, making a sound just like that of the gravel. Then the whole yard was brilliantly illuminated for a fraction of a second with a cold blue light, followed by a terrific, rumbling bang of a thunderclap. Rain was driving down in torrents now, splashing water onto the faces of Vignoles and Trinder, soaking their shoes and the deep turn-ups of their trousers.

'Bloody hell! Run for it!'

It was clear that the two men had abandoned the broken lorry and they could be heard running back into the building and slamming the door closed behind.

'That was a piece of luck. Now, where is my poor hat?' Vignoles eased his way from under the truck, and scooped his sodden hat from the stone floor, gave it a shake, decided that it was still preferable to the rain that pounded upon his head like small marbles, and pulled it down hard and low. 'Let's get out of here,' said Vignoles and strode over to the still-unlocked pass door and stepped through, buttoning up his greatcoat to protect the photographs and papers he had taken, and then set the safety catch back on his revolver. Trinder was striding along beside him. They both set their hats low at the front, like they had seen gangsters do in films, turned their collars up and, with hands pushed deep into their pockets, walked purposefully back towards the town centre and the station.

Neither man spoke until they reached Leicester Central, a walk that seemed to take forever in the drenching rain. They entered the echoing, cavernous station past a few tired railway workers moving newspapers along one of the platforms, just as an impossibly long and slow overnight train rumbled its laborious way northwards. The carriages had curtains pulled across the windows, some hanging loose from the curtain rails, others imperfectly drawn across. Where the compartments were left exposed they could make out the hunched shapes of many people uncomfortably crammed onto the seats, heads lolling and thrown back in sleep. The locomotive was slipping on the greasy rails, belching great columns of smoke into the night sky. Its percussive barks, like machine-gun fire, ricocheted around the glass canopies of the station. Hellish flickers of red and yellow fire inside the locomotive cab were refracting around the steam that enveloped it, whilst the blurred outlines of the crew looked menacingly Satanic in this vision of an inferno. Rain bounced off the roof and boiler and poured in torrents onto the track, adding to the powerful sense of elements in collision. Finally the creaking, rumbling coaches gathered speed, a few bleary-eyed heads leaned out of the windows, cigarettes burning in their mouths, looking but without really seeing the nocturnal station slide by, whilst swathed in steam and noise the train trundled into the driving rain and thunder.

The two policemen found an empty, but deliciously dry, waiting room. They could have used their own offices but, as P.C. Blencowe was on night duty, they had no wish to attract his obvious questions as to what they were doing. Better to incriminate as few of the team as possible at this stage. At least until they knew they had something that made their illegal trip worthwhile.

The waiting room still had the last embers of a fire burning, and whilst the night was not really cold, their damp clothing made them feel it keenly. So Trinder immediately commenced rattling the coals about in the grate with a poker, and emptied the last handful of coal granules and dust onto them from a bucket beside the fire. In so doing, he managed to coax some welcome warmth into the room, beefed up by a couple of yesterday's newspapers. Their heavy coats steamed lazily and gave off a smell like that of a wet Labrador dog. Vignoles looked at his soaked trousers then removed his shoes, placing them near the cheerful blaze. 'Yuch! Still, the rain was a blessing really, so better not complain too much.'

'Saved our bacon, I reckon, sir.'

'Yes. But it was a productive night. Let's have a look at what we have.'

Vignoles removed the now rather damp contents of his overcoat pocket, placing the typewritten sheets on the wooden bench beside him, and started by looking at the photographs. There were five sets of portraits, all passport sized, in groups of four identical pictures, although some of them had had one or two photos cut out of the sheets. Clearly they had already been used on false documents — passports, Vignoles presumed. They were all men, one of whom had been photographed twice, once in Navy uniform, another in civvies. The others were all wearing suits, but without a hat, as required by the Passport Office.

'What do you reckon? Any of these look like your train crew?'

Trinder took the photographs offered, and looked hard at them. One set, which had three remaining images after one had been neatly cut away, showed a thin-faced man with a good suntan, hair worn in a short, forces' style. He had a moustache, which at first threw him, but on looking closer, and after masking the moustache with a finger, agreed.

'Hmm. Could that be the fireman? Yes, I think it could be. The one they called Roland.'

'Not Roland, but Rollo: Mr M. Rollo. We must get his Christian name.'

'This is quite a lead. Hmm ... and this guy looks a bit like the Anglo-Empire Oil Co van driver. I am sure of it. I don't immediately recognise the others, although this chap here ...' Trinder passed all the pictures back to Vignoles, but indicated one in particular, 'his beard … if you take it away, he might just be the guard.' Trinder squinted at the picture in question as he spoke, and pulled a few faces as he tried to make the identification.

'We can have a better look in daytime.' With that, Vignoles set the pictures aside, turning to the sheets of foolscap that had been with the photographs. Lists of names and addresses, sums of money beside some of them, the odd telephone number, and then a series of numbers and letters like a code. He knew that this was probably going to prove extremely useful, but he felt his eyes itch with tiredness and the letters started to swim on the pages. He rubbed his eyes, yawned and folded the papers and the pictures together and slid them back into his jacket. He looked at his watch: it was nearly 3 a.m. Vignoles tried to find a position that was moderately less uncomfortable than the one he was currently in, tipped his hat over his eyes to shield them from the pale gaslight, and folded his arms. 'Anything interesting, sergeant?' Trinder had been trying to decipher his notes made whilst in the warehouse, of the names on the bogus driving licences.

'Well … aha. Yes! Oh, very clever. These names on the licences are obviously false.'

'It was always going to be a possibility, but how can you be so sure?' Vignoles was speaking from under his hat, eyes still closed.

'It took me a few minutes to make the connection, but whoever was in charge of this operation — creating the false I.D.s that is — well, he likes his music, of that I am quite sure. In dreaming up the names, he's borrowed from what he knows about, with just a few tweaks to try to throw one off the scent. So we have an "Alex Shaw", "John Hylton", "George Miller", "Lawrence Stone" and "Reginald Fox."'

'I am not quite with you.'

'Well "Alex Shaw" is really Artie Shaw, then "John" is really Jack Hylton, and of course "George Miller" is …?'

'Glenn?'

'Exactly, sir. And so on. Trying to make up names they just took inspiration from what they knew.'

'Good Lord, John. How did you crack that little code?' Vignoles pushed the brim of his hat back upon his forehead and squinted across at his sergeant.

'When you see them all together like this, in a list, I just felt there was something familiar about the names, then it jumped out at me. I must say I rather like their taste in music.'

'So we have a bunch of crooks that like a big band sound. Not the strongest suit to make an arrest, but I suppose even the criminal element must have its virtues as well as vices. I didn't know you were so into your music, John.'

'Not half! I spend nearly every spare shilling I earn on records. I know I shouldn't, but I just love music. And as there is no Mrs Trinder at present to look after, it's a good way to relax after a long day at work.'

'Well you certainly deserve a good dose of the Glenn Miller Band after tonight's good work.'

'Thank you, sir. Actually my reward is already planned: tomorrow, I shall collect a new record I have placed on order. I had to send away to Liverpool especially — they get all the newest sounds from America, brought over on the ships. Can't wait to hear it. With a bit of luck,' Trinder glanced at Vignoles, 'tomorrow evening, I shall pour a glass of beer, crank up the player, sit back and lose myself in the music.' The sergeant stretched his legs out before him and put his arms behind his head to illustrate. Vignoles smiled. It was good that he had such a man as Trinder working with him, able to find something to enjoy even when tired and soaked to the skin.

'What is it?'

'The record? A new one, hot from the U.S.A. Tommy Dorsey — he's cut this new track, "Opus Number One". Cracking rhythm and some smooth clarinet playing. I heard it last week on the radio. He has a real lightness of touch to his sound.' Trinder was now sitting up and leaning slightly forward. He looked across at Vignoles, eyes bright with enthusiasm, despite his obvious tiredness.

'I must listen out for it. You've got me quite intrigued. I like a big band myself. Geraldo for instance, and of course I always liked Al Bowlly.'

'Ah, pure genius. What a terrible tragedy to lose him. A V2 rocket got him, of all things.' Trinder shook his head slowly, and they fell silent.

Vignoles yawned, and rubbed his eyes again. 'We can continue this another day. If I am not mistaken,' he looked up at the big circular clock in its mahogany frame on the wall, 'I should be able to hop on the down milk train to Belgrave & Birstall in a few minutes. Get yourself off home as well, John. See you later. Good night.'

Chapter Eleven

'A LITTLE ON THE LONELY SIDE'
Guy Lombardo & his Royal Canadians

April had been unseasonably warm, but at 5.30 a.m. it certainly did not feel like it. Dawn was breaking, although the sun was hidden behind a hill and a dark layer of clouds. The heat of the past few days and nights had mysteriously evaporated, to be replaced by a biting chill. The pale dawn light picked out Edward's breath as he trudged, sleepily, up Station Road.

His heart was beating fast, which helped override his tiredness. He had a brand new pair of stout boots on his feet that felt stiff as he walked. He was already wearing his blue cotton drill dungarees that were a size too large, with turn-ups to the legs. Only the top button fastened his matching blue drill jacket, in the manner many loco crew adopted. With a red-and-white spotted scarf around his neck and white shirt beneath, he felt quite grown up. Glancing down at his attire it helped to boost his confidence believing that he really looked the part. The clothes had been issued to him the week before, following a bit of wrangling by Simon's father who had used his influence to get clothes that came close to fitting.

His father had donated a couple of shirts to the cause and, after some assiduous coupon-collecting, his parents had got him the new boots, as well as his pride and joy — a railwayman's cap. He reached up and adjusted it yet again, as he made his way into Church Street, past the church and his old school, and then down the narrow footpath which cut across fields and on towards the locomotive yard.

Despite the early hour he was not alone. Silent figures were walking towards the same point from both directions along the road, a red glow occasionally signalling a first cigarette of the day. Quiet 'hullos' were exchanged. It was too early and chill for conversation. Edward looked out for Simon, but he failed to make him out. He must remember to agree a meeting place tomorrow, perhaps at the narrow bridge that spanned the winding river. He would be sure not to miss him there, as it was so narrow. Edward had hoped for Simon's guidance in the first moments of arrival, but that was not to be.

The engine shed was starting to gather a pale wreath of smoke as the first fires were lit. These were acrid, throat-burning fires of wood kindling, cotton waste and oily rags. The still air was holding the smoke a few yards above the ground in a thin layer that spread outwards across the fields, mingling with a loamy dampness that created its own pockets of mist. The outline of the engine shed with its saw-toothed roof-line of northlights and forest of chimneys, and the towering presence of the coaling tower, loomed ever closer. The yellow glow of lights inside looked welcoming, however, offsetting the oppressive bulk of the carriage sheds to his right. Everywhere the dark forms of locomotives were hunched together against the night. Long rows of mineral engines towered above Edward, creating deep alleyways between. Their metal bodies were covered in droplets of condensation and even touches of frost. A few engines were already stirring, breath issuing from their iron lungs in pale drifts, just as it was from the people filing past. Shadowy figures could be seen around these breathing forms, clattering and banging them into life as firedoors swung open and the first red glow of fire licked around the cab interiors.

Edward stubbed his toe on a rail and then lost his balance as he trod on something lying in the muck of the depot floor. He wondered how they had managed in the blackout, without even the pale yard lamps to shed some light. He made a mental note to eat extra carrots. His shoulder was jabbed into by the hard edge of a buffer beam.

Edward did at least know where the booking-in office was, as he had explored the shed numerous times before, either by invitation or not. The shed foreman was sitting behind a huge desk with a thick ledger open before him. A massive blackboard with painted panels in columns hung on one wall, covering nearly every inch of the painted brickwork. The board declared in bold letters the word 'Roster', and in a box below that 'Date', with the day's date chalked in. Below the date, were columns of what looked like locomotive numbers, crew names, and curious associations of numbers and letters, which Edward took to represent train workings, but were unintelligible to him.

This was what Simon had referred to yesterday. He stared at the board, trying to make sense of it, hoping to miraculously discover the information they needed, but he knew it would take more experienced eyes. Two lamps in grimy, metal shades dangling from the ceiling illuminated the room. Behind the foreman were olive-green metal cupboards that reached from floor to ceiling, and on the wall a cabinet with a great array of keys on display through a glass window in the door. There were a few battered, wooden chairs pressed against the wall and everywhere were lying bundles of what looked like discarded clothing. Jackets and work trousers hopelessly stained to a filthy brown-black lay in crumpled balls. Odd gloves, a boot, and lumps of heavy metal that looked like a piston or valve rod and bits of tubing lay propped against the wall beside the door. The floor was apparently wooden, but looked more like a cinder path. The room smelt of stale smoke, sulphur and oil.

To the left of the desk was another door, slightly ajar, with 'Mr Timothy Saunders, Shedmaster' painted in neat, cream lettering on the brown paintwork. The whole office was patinated with shades of grubbiness that reached a depth and maturity of colour around the Bakelite lamp switches, door handles and any area of wall convenient for a shoulder to lean against. About a dozen men were crowding into the office, briefly talking with the foreman, nodding, or just silently taking slips of paper from him, sometimes making notes in a pocket book of their own, and looking across at the roster board. Some were smiling, others muttering oaths as they identified their day's work. They quickly dispersed, with the easy assurance of people who knew their place. Edward felt his heart sink. He stared again at the roster board trying again to make some sense of it, but was then aware that he was being spoken to.

'You don't need to worry yourself about that. Now't to do with lads like you.' It was the foreman, Mr Reed, looking across the desk at him. 'Who are you?'

'The new cleaner, sir. Edward Earnshaw, sir.'

'New boy, eh? Well you can start trimming the lamps. Hey, Mary…' he looked across at two women who had just entered the room, 'you can have Sunny Jim here with you, this morning. Show him what's what.'

'Of course, Mr Reed. Lamps again then, is it?' It was clearly a rhetorical question, as already the two women were turning to leave the office, whilst the foreman turned his attention to marking off something in his ledger.

'What's your name?' It was the woman called Mary. She had a headscarf knotted in the manner everyone was wearing at the time, and blue overalls that had clearly been far too large, but with careful shortening and the use of a belt, had been made to look almost attractive on her. Edward thought she was probably about thirty years old. She had a kindly smile and bright lipstick that cut a welcome flash of brilliant colour in the gloomy surroundings.

They were walking through the shed interior, down a long line of engines. Edward was glancing from side to side, trying to take it all in. Trying to accept that he was now part of this huge, noisy confusion of steam, which suddenly seemed far more alien than when he had illegally sneaked in with Simon a few weeks back. It had just been a huge adrenaline thrill then, to dart along the engines, scribble their numbers and duck out of sight as someone walked past.

The other woman was called Margi, and she seemed a bit older. In fact he recognised her from the village, and she certainly knew his face. This made him feel a bit calmer. He had two friendly faces to look out for. The women asked him a few questions but soon fell into talking about other matters that held no interest to Edward, and he was silent.

The work consisted of checking and preparing what seemed like hundreds of oil lamps, used on the front of the engines, not to illuminate the way but as markers to indicate the type of train. Or there were others, with red lenses, which were suspended from the guards' vans at the rear, and those that the guards carried as signalling lamps. All of these needed their wicks trimmed or replaced, paraffin oil needed collecting in big, conical cans, and the lamp reservoirs topped up. Soon Edward's hands were black, and he stank of paraffin and track dirt.

The two women showed him how to do the job though, and smiled at him whenever their eyes met. But mainly they talked about what was in the latest magazine they had read or film they had seen. Edward's taste in films was very different from theirs and he felt he couldn't join in. Men came along at regular intervals and collected lamps, many of them stopping to share a word with the two women, often flirting and exchanging cheeky comments. Almost none of them even noticed Edward, despite his new cap and jacket, which was already becoming authentically grubby.

He was beginning to realise just how very far he had to go before ever becoming a top link driver. He had not so much as seen a driver except at a distance, on the footplate of a locomotive. The firemen were more visible, but seemed no more inclined to notice him. However, as the sun rose, it brought a welcome warmth to the yard, and his spirits lifted with it. He was sitting at the heavy table outside the shed entrance, his back catching the warmth, and he was polishing lamp lenses that sparkled in the light.

Margi had brought him a mug of tea and he had just eaten what he reckoned was a well-deserved sandwich. Before him, three magnificent passenger locomotives were being prepared. All were being given an extra scrub and polish by a gang of cleaners. Edward realised that Simon was sitting astride the boiler of one engine, polishing the dome. Simon upon catching sight of Edward waved and grinned widely. It was nice to see his friend at last, and he wished he could go and help him out, but guessed that as a 'new boy' he had better stick with the task in hand. Suddenly, to his surprise, the two women, downed their rags and stood up. Mary said to Edward, 'Come on lad, let's muck in and help get these sorted out,' and with that, the women strode off towards the engines. He was surprised by this and unsure if he should follow, despite their invitation for him to do so. He glanced nervously across at the bay window of the shedmasters office, but couldn't see anyone inside. 'Well, they did ask me to help,' and with that, he walked briskly across to join them.

There were about ten cleaners in total, a mixture of men and women of differing ages. They were assaulting the engines from all angles. With long-handled brushes some were applying soapy water, others rubbing and scrubbing with rags or small stiff bristled brushes. A man was using a steam lance, directing a powerful jet of boiling water onto the grimiest areas. Others wielded strange metal scrapers and literally carved layers of muck off the link-motion and wheels.

One engine, sporting the odd name of 'Purdon Vicars', was looking the best. As the muck had been removed the original green paintwork was revealed, like an Old Master at a picture restorers. Two women were now applying a finishing sheen of light oil to the paintwork. Both were standing on the running plate and rubbing the oil on with rags, their caps set at saucy angles, and they were singing. It was upon this engine that Simon was sitting astride, applying oil to the steam dome. Edward climbed up to join him, sat on the cab roof and set to work on the brass whistle. 'Oh yes, this is more like it.' Edward surveyed his surroundings from the high vantage point.

Simon grinned. 'It's great high up like this, isn't it? Fantastic view. So how has it been so far?'

'Oh, OK. Lamps mainly, but OK. This is better, though.

What's all the fuss suddenly over these? Any special reason?'

'Apparently head office has said that we've got to pull our fingers out and get the railway looking better. They are getting pretty fed up of the state of the engines, it seems.'

'They have a point.'

'Too right! It's bad for morale. They are set to try and get as many as they can repainted. But guess what? I've heard the company is broke. No money left.' Simon shrugged.

'Really? Who'd have thought that?'

'Anyway, it's not our problem, Eddie. I've also heard the government are thinking of taking the railways over.'

'Get over! You mean buy them?'

'Well, it's only what father told me, but he said the new prime minister wants the people to own all the big industries and things called monopolies — but I'm not too sure what those are — but that includes us, it seems.'

'You're joking!' Edward looked across the rows of engines towards the station shimmering with the heat haze in the distance, and the curves of the green pastures and fields beyond. He shrugged his shoulders: 'I wonder what that will mean for us. Oh well. Hey, Simon, who is "Purdon Vicars"? Weird name for an engine.'

Simon smiled as Edward reached for his ever-handy notebook. 'Eddie, never mind that, I have important information for you.' He paused, waiting for Edward to look up; 'I found number 3152. She was out the back there, on the coal lines. Went out up north about eight this morning. The point is, she was the one from Saturday, and she is one of ours.'

'Woah...'

'Look, I've been thinking about this. We need to get back and see if we can't catch them dropping off another bag. Of course we don't really know if they will, but if we go back at the same time for the same train...' he looked at Edward, who was open-mouthed, 'And I was talking to my Dad last night, he reckons we saw the Calvert Brick train — an empty return working. I've got an idea of the timings.'

' Yes, it's got to be worth a try, I guess. And also we need to try and find out who the crew were. Woodford men, you reckon?'

'Stands to reason. Mr Reed has all that information in those big books of his. All we need to do is find the entry and there will be the names.'

'Just like that?'

'Well of course, Eddie, we can't just have a look, he'd box our ears, no messing. But he must go for lunch breaks and what-not. We'll have to spend the next few days carefully spying out the lie of the land.'

'Important documents needed for British HQ! Another spying mission, deep into enemy territory.' Edward was rising to the challenge, beginning to see the attraction of Simon's plan.

'That's the spirit, Officer Earnshaw. And there's a big fat five pounds — well a half share actually — waiting for you, if successful.'

'That damn fiver. Where is it?'

'In a cocoa tin on my window sill. With two marbles, a headless dragoon guard and that bit of shrapnel the "Vac" gave me. You remember? The East Ender?'

'How could I forget? But how are we going to spend it? It's just too much, if you know what I mean. No one in Woodford will believe us if we turn up with that. Even my Dad hardly ever gets them. Just from "his Lordship" up in the big house once a year when they settle the account. Stupid really … so much money and we can't spend it. And if we do take the bag with all the millions in it — not that I am absolutely sure that we should – we'll just have even more money we can't spend.'

The two lads looked wistfully into the smoky distance and fell into a silent reverie as a driver walked below them, his black leather bag swinging as he whistled the curiously cheerful melody to 'A Little on the Lonely Side'.

✵ ✵ ✵ ✵

Inspector Vignoles gave his wife a peck on the cheek then turned to walk down the platform towards his office. 'Ciao Carlo! See you for lunch in the station refreshment room.' Anna called to him and he turned, 'You never know, I might get a speck of dust in my eye.' Anna smiled at him over her shoulder, in a way that made him remember exactly why he had married her, then walked quickly towards the goods' despatching offices.

'I do hope so.' He laughed and watched her leave. She looked elegant in a chocolate brown dress that fitted perfectly, with a light woollen coat worn open, and thrown across her shoulders. No one would have guessed that it had been run up from a blanket. Her hat was small and angled over her wavy, chestnut hair, which clasped at the back of her head, spilling down over the collar of her coat. No wonder she had such an effect on him when he first set eyes on her.

It was her parting comment however, that made him smile. She was referring to the film they had seen on that Saturday night. *Brief Encounter* had turned out to be exactly as promised: English, romantic and rather well made. But the joke was that most of the action took place on a railway station. They had both seen the funny side of sitting for an hour and half watching a film about the very thing they were 'escaping' from. The railway certainly took up the greater part of their lives. But it also had another special connection. It was the location, if not exactly the reason, for their meeting, just as it was for the celluloid Celia Johnson and Trevor Howard. No wonder the girls in Anna's office had begged her to go with him before they had time to read the reviews. He just hoped they had not spoilt the story of the unrequited love affair for the rest of the audience, with their barely suppressed laughter.

Vignoles entered the railway police offices and walked into a crowded entrance vestibule — and a heated debate. Mavis was seated behind her desk, whilst W.P.C. Lansdowne was seated on one corner of the desk, her navy coat still in her arms. W.P.C. Benson was standing in front of them and speaking passionately, but stopped hurriedly as Vignoles entered.

'Oh, good morning, sir!' She immediately recovered her composure and drew to attention, Lansdowne quickly slipping off the desk and doing the same. Mavis had long since declared that she was far 'too old' to be involved with 'all that saluting business', so just looked up at him, her arms folded. Vignoles valued her service too much to argue the point, but knew it raised a few eyebrows in head office.

'Morning, ladies. Do carry on … don't let me stop you,' he raised a quizzical eyebrow, then made to enter his office. However, Benson stopped him.

'I'm sorry, sir. We probably sounded awfully like a bunch of shop stewards, but it's just that we were talking about the dismissals. I wonder if you might know more about them.' She smiled weakly.

'Dismissals? Which ones?'

'The women, sir. It seems the company want to get rid of us. Send us back —'

'— to women's work, back to just being housewives, rather than managing to be that and do a full week's work.' said Mavis with a contemptuous snort.

'I … er, sorry, but I have not heard anything about this.' Vignoles furrowed his brow and pulled a face. 'I suppose the Railway Executive is bringing essential war work conditions to a close. Could that be it?' Vignoles looked from one face to another, in some confusion.

'Looks like it, sir. I suppose with the call for more Land Army girls, they are hoping to shunt some of us all onto the farms — or back to domestic bliss.' There was a snort from Mavis, but Lansdowne continued, 'But do you really think it will include us here?' She was nervously touching one of the bright chrome numbers fixed to the collar of her uniform.

'I jolly well hope not. I need you — and I mean all of you. It would be plain ridiculous to lose you now. It's not like we have a queue of male police officers returning from overseas, is it?'

'Indeed not, sir. We know that some of us were taken on with the understanding that we must move over one day and let the men get their jobs back. But the horrid truth is, many of the men didn't come back, did they? Not alive, anyway.'

'Yes Jane, sadly you are right enough.' Vignoles made a mirthless grin, and looked at the floor. He knew that they were both thinking of the night they had spent beside the travelling morgue.

'Added to that,' said Mavis, 'even after five years hard and dangerous work, many of the girls still really love it here. They don't want to leave. And they can do the job as well as anyone.' She added this almost under her breath, but still audible to all. 'Things change,' she continued in a more level tone, 'it's not the same world like it was before. Maybe it seemed right enough back at the start of the war to say we had to stand down, but it's not like that now. We've proved our worth.' As if to make a final point on the matter, she slipped some typing paper with a carbon sheet between into her Remington and started to pound the keys.

Vignoles considered his response. 'There is much merit in what you say, Mavis. But I admit you've rather caught me on the hop, so all I can say right now, is that I know nothing of redundancies amongst the railway police, and I will strongly resist them if there are any such ideas. And…' he was conscious of thinking personally, '…I am sure that office grades will be totally unaffected.' I sincerely hope so for Anna's sake, he thought. 'So what makes you think that this is going to happen? Where did you hear of this?' Vignoles continued.

Sergeant Trinder who had been at the back of the office, but within earshot throughout, spoke up. 'It was from me, sir. I have a colleague in head office; he's something pretty big in salaries and welfare. Reckons that the company are going to dismiss a sizeable number of women workers.' He shrugged his shoulders and pulled a wry face, then went back to inspecting a 78 rpm record encased in a plain-brown, cardboard wrapper, that he was holding. 'I only hope he's wrong. They look so much better in the uniform.' Trinder spoke this last sentence more quietly, but still audible to all, a cheeky smile playing over his face, although whether from the meaning of what he had said, or pleasure in the record he was contemplating, was ambiguous.

Lansdowne rolled her eyes and groaned, but instinctively smoothed her uniform jacket. Vignoles knew that it was because Lansdowne, like many other railwaywomen, was proud of her uniform and the responsibilities it carried, rather than the effect it had upon her male colleagues.

Vignoles turned and entered his office, asking Sergeant Trinder to follow him in. Placing his hat and coat on a peg near the door, he walked over to his desk and sat down behind it, eyeing a pile of fresh letters and papers placed neatly on the blotter in the centre. They seemed to grow overnight, like mushrooms.

'Yes, sir.'

'I have been thinking about our next move in this Water Street case. We need to build up some background on our train crew. I've already had personnel look at the Woodford employees, and it looks like we can identify the driver as a man called Kenneth Price, the fireman is one Michael Rollo, and the guard Jimmy Cresswell. We must gather some background on them. Where do they live, where do they drink, who do they socialise with? Did they know each other previously? How might they have become involved in this gang? And what might have driven them to get in with counterfeiters?'

'The chance to earn serious money is a terrible temptation. Especially in these times.'

'True enough. But even so, most of us resist it.'

'Yes, so what tipped them over the edge? We could call them in for questioning. I feel sure we can get this lot bang to rights in no time.'

'I'm not so sure I share your optimism. Question them about what, exactly? Remember, we were not officially inside the warehouse and so officially we know nothing at all about the press and the forgeries. As far as the law is concerned, this bunch has merely collected a bag — which could still turn out to be full of dirty washing — and abandoned their train in a busy marshalling yard, where somebody else appears to have stolen the contents and set fire to it. About the best we have on these men at the moment is that they seem to have overplayed the problem with their locomotive, which subsequently returned to shed in good order.'

'I see what you mean.'

'We have to be a bit canny and very patient. We must not frighten them off their purpose just now. In fact, we positively need them to do at least a couple more runs, so we can have a chance of finding where they drop the stuff off. Until then, it will be hard to catch the other part of this operation: the persons who exchange or trade with this money.'

'How the devil will we manage to establish the drop-off point? We can hardly tail a moving goods' train.'

'It's a ticklish matter indeed, sergeant. We will need to exercise our minds and think of a strategy. And when will they next make a run? That's another burning question. For all we know they are doing so right now.' Vignoles leaned forward in his chair and picked up his fountain pen, idly removing and replacing the cap. 'But, it is my thinking, sergeant, that they will release the money in batches — after all it does need printing, drying, sorting and so on. It's only a hunch, but let's start by assuming that they will do this every week, on the same goods' diagram. We need to gain access to prior information about what trains these three are rostered on, and watch out for any instances when they are on this particular train.'

'Woodford Depot can supply this.'

'They can. But I have a few reservations about a direct approach,' Vignoles tossed the pen onto the blotter and reached for his pipe, with which he gesticulated as he spoke. He found that this helped him focus his thoughts. 'I know Tim Saunders, the depot manager, and I find it hard to suspect him of knowingly participating in a crime. He's a true railwayman, old school, you would say. Dyed-in-the-wool railwaymen would never do anything to compromise the company, let alone their position. He might huff and puff and moan a bit, but that's not the issue. Perhaps I am being romantic, but

I don't think so. He seemed innocent to me. Having said all that...'

'We should avoid revealing our cards too soon. Play them close to our chest.'

'Exactly. I have a feeling that Saunders is the unwitting participant in a little bit of deliberate manipulation of the rosters, to ensure our three stooges are in the right place and on the right train.'

'The shed foreman — is this his influence?'

'I think it might be. He's a Mr Reed. A burly, rough sort of chap, but we can't hold that against him. But perhaps it is more direct than even that. I felt Saunders was being given earache by some of the more vociferous crew, and was relenting — to keep them happy, and give himself an easier life. So in effect they bully him into giving them the runs they want.'

'Who? Price, Rollo and Cresswell?'

'Seems likely.' Vignoles spun his chair around slightly, so that he could look out upon the station platforms, and removed his glasses for a moment, rubbed his eyes, then replaced them. A long, rattling train of wooden vans passed by, reminding them both of the fire in the goods' yard. Vignoles, who had put his unlit pipe in his mouth whilst rubbing his eyes, spoke with it lodged to one side. 'I have an idea. We have a matter of some stolen detonators; a box of twenty-four of them, to be precise. Taken last Wednesday from a van in Woodford depot. Probably opportunistic, and probably by foolish kids, though I suppose we should not rule out deliberate theft.' He waved his pipe stem gently toward the sergeant, 'I'd like you to look into it.'

'Of course.'

'The pertinent details are all in this report,' Vignoles pulled the paper from the typewriter as he spoke and handed his sergeant the carbon copy, who started to read them. 'My guess is, it's just local lads. However, that could still have most unfortunate consequences if they start playing around with them, so we need to recover them. I want you to start by going down to Woodford Halse and asking around. Take W.P.C. Benson with you. Try the shopkeepers, knock on a few doors — it's a small place, as you know. Make contact with the local constabulary. If I remember there is just the one chap on duty as a rule, but he might have a few ideas of the local tearaways.'

'Two officers on this matter when there's the Water Street gang?'

'Rather over-egging the pudding, eh? These detonators are a blasted nuisance, Trinder, but my real motive for sending you both down there is to see if you can sniff some more info on our suspects. We know they are based at Woodford, we know their names, and you even have a good idea of what they look like. But you and Benson could ask around a little. No need to remind you to use extreme caution and tact. The theft of the detonators can be an excuse to hang around the shed, and the men. The mess rooms especially may prove productive. Have tea and some lunch with them.' As he was speaking, Vignoles turned back towards his desk, and after glancing at it, leaned forward and advanced the date on his desktop calendar. This was a small, free-standing wooden box with little knurled metal knobs on each side which turned a roller blind printed with the day, date and month, revealing each in little glass windows.

'Got it. We can use this as a chance to match up the passport photos to actual persons — hopefully, confirming what we already suspect.' This was just the sort of operation Sergeant Trinder enjoyed.

'I think you both should go in full uniform. Be very visible. Just two bobbies asking about some stupid kids stealing railway property. Act the plodding policeman, but the whole time keeping your wits about you.'

'Excellent. A kind of double bluff.' The sergeant glanced at his watch. 'If my memory of the timetable is correct, we can get a train in thirty minutes.'

Chapter Twelve

'DOWN SUNNYSIDE LANE'
Jack Payne & his BBC Dance Orchestra

'But this is impossible! Are you absolutely sure? Violet felt her stomach turn over and a hot and cold shiver roll down her body.

'Well I admit that I could be wrong. I am a baker, not a banker after all, but all my instincts tell me that this is ... that this,' he spoke slowly, 'just does not feel right. I am sorry, Miss McIntyre, really I am.' James Earnshaw smiled weakly, and handed the note back to Violet's shaking hand.

'James, are you really sure? Miss McIntyre — Violet — would never do anything ... odd, I just know it.' His wife Joyce, looked at James with some disbelief, then gave a sympathetic look to Violet. She was rubbing her hands with her apron, initially to remove some flour that had fallen from the loaf she had selected for Violet, but now she continued the motion in a nervous manner. The wireless was turned up loud out in the back bakery, the sound drifting out into the shop. *Workers' Playtime* was in full swing in a factory canteen. Somewhere in Britain, a few hundred workers were spending their lunch break singing enthusiastically along with Anne Shelton, whilst the BBC's pianists pounded out a ragged version of 'Down Sunnyside Lane'. It was painfully incongruous.

'It's hard to say exactly why, but it just feels — wrong. I'm dreadfully sorry about this, but five pounds is an awful lot of money, and I just can't take the risk. But, look, we are quite happy to hold the account over for another week.'

'Oh, of course,' Joyce added, with another sympathetic smile, her hands still working the apron, 'Whilst you sort it out, dear. I'm sure it's nothing.'

Joyce's words were sympathetic and Violet knew that she meant well. But they failed to convince her that everything would be all right. What exactly was she supposed to 'sort out'? Violet was leaning against the glass counter looking at the floor. She saw flickers of red at the corners of her eyes and small silver stars started to flash before her. The sound of the radio started to distort in her ears, jangling at her nerves. Her skin felt clammy and she hoped that she would not add to the already-intense humiliation by fainting. Thank goodness there were no other customers.

'No it's … it's quite all right. Really it is.' She tried to smile and forced tears back. She needed some fresh air. 'I am sure it is just some silly mistake …'

'But where did you get it, dear?' asked Joyce.

'Oh … I … from my bank.' Violet was not sure why she lied. Somehow she had already compounded the problem by telling an untruth. Perhaps she did not want to share with the world the fact that she had been forced to borrow money. One was supposed to live on what means one had. Borrowing seemed shameful somehow. Her head was spinning now.

'Ah, well there you go. If it's from a bank, then I am sure it's fine. That's why it is so new and white. You see, James? You are not used to seeing them so clean like this.'

Her husband coloured and looked flustered. 'I suppose so. I guess you could be right, Joyce.' He still looked uncertain however. 'Oh dear. This is a bit of a rum thing. So it really is from a bank?' The bakers voice was gentle and he hoped, without a trace of accusation, but the words still stung Violet like a slap in the face.

'Of course it is. You don't believe me?' But even as Violet spoke, her voice coloured with righteous indignation, her conscience was nagging away inside, reminding her that she was digging herself deeper into the lie. Her voice faltered and cracked, 'I'm sorry. I'll come back … and settle up everything.' With that she hurried out of the shop, face burning, forgetting the precious loaf and her ration book. Tears welled in Violet's eyes and she gulped in the hot, clear air of the High Street. She took a few steps, then stopped and took a few slow, deep breaths to regain her equilibrium. Only then did she start to walk down the hill, back to her shop.

Her mind was spinning with the realisation that she had, in all probability, borrowed fake money on awful terms from a dreadful crook. And now she was lying for some reason to those kind people in the shop. The bundle of apparently useless white paper, stuffed into her purse, looked like it would cost her everything she had. As it was, Violet had already spent nearly £20 on paying off her mother's debts and her own back rent. She suddenly felt sick at the thought of the humiliation and the problems ahead when the landlord found out — as surely he must.

Violet slowed and dabbed her eyes with her handkerchief, then turned and started to walk. She had no wish to return to her shop at that moment, and so turned down Parson's Street, which she noticed was almost deserted. Only the coal merchant's cart and his ancient horse were to be seen, its tail flicking flies. She walked slowly along the quiet, winding street with its rows of neat cottages, all glowing a deep, golden ochre in the sunlight. The high stone wall that bordered the massive vicarage was to her left, radiating a pleasing warmth, whilst swathes of flowers filled the tiny front gardens opposite, too small to have been dug up for victory vegetable planting. The peaceful beauty of the street calmed her nerves. It seemed impossible that anything bad could happen in such a place. This had been part of her thinking when she had sought to escape the trauma of the bombing in Leicester and the death of her father. Violet started to think more logically about the matter. Maybe Mr Earnshaw was wrong? After all, she had rarely seen such a five-pound note before and had no more idea of a good one from a bad. Neither the baker nor his wife seemed that familiar with one either, so how could he be so sure?

And then there was Mr Attercliffe, the landlord. Well, he had taken the money all too greedily that morning. (Ugh, horrid, grasping little man that he was.) He had seen no fault in her money. Violet stopped and sighed deeply. She closed her eyes for a moment and lifted her head. The sun really was pleasantly warm on her face, the trees were alive with birdsong, she thought she caught the distant rattle of a woodpecker. Perhaps things were not so awful. Violet tucked her handkerchief back in the sleeve of her jacket and took out a compact, shaped like a silver clamshell, and quickly checked her makeup.

'No,' she said to herself, 'this was just Mr Earnshaw being … being careful. That was all. Nothing so very wrong with being careful, I suppose. But it was just so awfully embarrassing.'

Chapter Thirteen

'RUM AND COLA'
The Andrews Sister

Sergeant Trinder and W.P.C. Benson were sitting in the refreshment room at Woodford & Hinton Station, each with a cup of Barbara Walsh's fearsomely strong tea. The doors and windows were wide open to allow some air into the room, but there was almost no wind to offer relief. The smell of coal and sulphurous smoke hung oppressively in the air, exacerbated by a brace of 'Fish' engines, which were waiting in the platform ready to move away onto the engine shed and be refuelled for another high-speed dash to London with a cargo of valuable North Sea fish. The hissing of the engines mirrored that of Mrs Walsh's geyser, which leaked steam alarmingly and made ominous banging noises at intervals, causing Benson to cast it a few questioning glances. The radio was playing as usual, and one of the two waitresses was quietly singing along to 'Rum and Cola', harmonising with the Andrews Sisters. The mood of the song seemed to suit the sultry late afternoon.

'I like this song, it's got a nice sound to it.'

'Me too. Superb trumpet playing. It's done with a mute, you know? Gives it that slightly distant sound. Makes you think of a hot night on a tropical beach.'

'Hard to imagine one of those, sitting here. D'you know, sergeant? I've only ever been to Mablethorpe, and it was jolly cold, I can tell you. Ruddington Water on a Bank Holiday isn't quite the same.' They both laughed. Benson put her head to one side as she listened. 'I like the way they sing. It's clever. The way they say "situ-a-sharn", is that to sound West Indian, do you suppose?'

'I presume so. They are certainly fabulous singers. But, much as I would love to pass the time of day discussing the "Three Jive Bombers", I think we should review what we made of this afternoon's work.' Trinder took a deep draught of his tea then fished his notebook from his uniform breast pocket. 'We got nowhere with the enquiries about the detonators.'

'No, but we did get a lovely piece of seed-cake. That was really quite a treat. I can't even remember the last time I had cake that was made with butter — lots of butter — and real eggs. Oh, heaven.'

'That's living in the country for you. They can side-step

rationing more easily. It made the somewhat futile, door-to-door worthwhile, I agree with you there. Mrs Green was quite a dear. I began to think we would never be allowed to leave until we had eaten her out of house and home.'

'It was certainly tempting to try. When did I last eat until I was full? But, yes sergeant, much as we guessed, little really gained by that exercise,' Benson was also reviewing her notes as she was speaking, 'but I think D.I. Vignoles might find something of use in our little visit to the engine shed.'

'Agreed. What did you make of that Reed fellow? Do you think he was dealing straight with us?' The sergeant looked across the small table at Benson in her trim, black uniform. Her cap was lying beside her teacup, allowing the sunlight to infuse her rich auburn hair with vivid reds and browns. Trinder was struck by what an attractive sight his fellow officer made.

'He was a rum one for sure. Not exactly Mr Personality. He didn't take kindly to me, that's for sure,' and Benson pulled a face with a wry smile, 'I get the feeling that Mr Reed has not quite adapted to the idea that women can wear a uniform and do more than look nice.' She raised her eyes to the sky in despair. Trinder felt a touch of guilt for having just thought about how Benson's uniform suited her, so looked at his notebook with particular concentration.

'Yes. He practically ignored you.'

'But that meant I could observe him, and take a good look around his office, whilst you and he were in conversation. His loss, my gain.' she gave a knowing look at her sergeant.

'And?'

'And, I think he is hiding something. He seemed very brusque, very dismissive of everything you said. You were just talking about the fog signal theft and what-not, but he really wasn't interested. Kept steering the conversation away — did you notice? And then when you tried a few opening gambits on the subject of rosters — ho ho, Mr Reed did not like that, did he?'

'No. He was a bit evasive.'

'Then when I started to flick through the log book…'

'He was, frankly, aggressive. Took it off you double quick. He didn't care a hoot that we were police, did he? Why do you think he did that?'

'Well, we know that some of the entries have been damaged, perhaps deliberately. But he was not to know, that we know, that. If you catch my meaning.'

'Indeed.'

'Did you notice the betting slips tucked into the pages of the log book? Four or five of them. Just slipped there for safekeeping I'd say — bottom edges poking out. I only got a quick glance, but he placed a lot of money today.'

'Really? That was a good move. How much are we talking about here?'

'I saw three bets on one slip, all of two pounds each.'

'Phew. That is either a very confident man — or a very rich one.'

'Or a very foolish one, addicted to gambling. I've heard stories of people who cannot stop themselves, no matter what.'

'What would he earn a week? Maybe seven or eight pounds? Nine with overtime, at best, I would say. So he gambled at least six pounds in a day.'

'I just glanced at three slips, maybe there were more. Of course they could be for other persons. Still, it's most of one's weekly wage in a day. I tell you, if I earned that sort of money I wouldn't be throwing it at horses.'

'No. So, Mr Reed just might have a gambling problem and could be running short on funds, or...'

The two officers' eyes met each others. 'He has suddenly come into a windfall.' Benson spoke the words slowly and quietly. Her eyes were wide with excitement.

'This could be through some luck on the horses, or someone is helping him earn some extra money.'

'By manipulating the rosters, perhaps?'

'Uh huh, for a little back-hander. He could even be right in on something bigger. OK. This is nothing more than speculation. We may be making dangerous assumptions about an innocent man, but I share your feeling that he might be up to something. We should certainly pass this on to the D.I. And so, onto the footplate crew.' Trinder grinned.

'What an infernal place their mess room was, sergeant. What a stinking hole. I know we don't have the smartest of offices, with just one tiny gas ring and a kettle, but really, I had no idea what conditions they have to work under.' Benson shook her head in disbelief, her hair appearing to catch fire in the low evening sun. 'I've been up and down this line over the last few years, but never had call to go in there. It was like the Black Hole of Calcutta.'

'Not that I really know what that looks like, but yes, it took some getting used to.'

Both officers, during their studiously relaxed visit to the shed, had tried to give the impression that they were simply pursuing rather pointless enquiries about a theft that they had little real hope of ever solving. Their act was clearly successful, as it was not long before a particularly gregarious driver had invited them to take some tea. He had escorted them into the drivers' lobby, opening a door in the small, brick lean-to, a door that defied identification of its colour. Possibly it was once a mid-green but had layers upon layers of oil, coal dust and grime caked over it, rubbed to a high sheen where countless hands had polished it with use.

However, the door was the very least of the lobby's problems. As the door was pulled open and Driver Wellbeck gallantly ushered W.P.C. Benson through, to be closely followed by Sergeant Trinder, they were immediately stopped in their tracks. At first they had not even been able to properly see inside the dark, smoky room, as the contrast between the sun-filled yard and the intense black of the room was too extreme. It was the wall of heat carrying the odour of sweaty men, oil and coal dust, tobacco and mildew that initially prevented Benson from taking no more than two steps inside. She then became aware of the presence of a great many men, all looking at her, the whites of their eyes flashing in the dark, and teeth forming into rows of cheerful and sometimes leery grins. It was impossible to know how many were crammed into the room, but it was extremely full. The men squeezed together tightly on long benches that lined the walls. A huge table took up the space left in the middle, and to one side a cast-iron range and metal chimney radiated a searing heat, topped by two mammoth kettles. As if that was not enough to render the place claustrophobic, from the ceiling hung many jackets, coats, shirt and overalls in a grimy disarray. Benson had thought the place was like some strange mixture of a laundry and a place to smoke kippers. The windows were still painted with blackout paint, the need for light apparently considered so unimportant that all anyone had done was scratch a few initials into the paint, which glowed luminously. Just two small quarter-lights were pushed open, allowing thick beams like that of searchlights through cloud cover, to illuminate two groups of men in their white shirts, so they shone like a vision.

Driver Wellbeck had introduced the two of them with a touching formality, at odds with the overpoweringly intimate camaraderie of the place. The elderly driver clearly commanded respect however, and the hubbub of conversation soon dwindled whilst he spoke. When he had told some of the younger drivers to 'shove up! Show some respect for our guests,' they actually attempted to do so, despite the fact that the there was clearly no more room. Three men eventually stood up and leaned sulkily against the table.

Once ensconced in this unappealing place, and handed grimy mugs of boiled tea with only a splash of sour milk, the two officers did nonetheless appreciate that they had managed to strike a rich coal-seam of information. Benson, in particular, attracted all the men's attention; each one trying to outdo the others in courtesy and engaging conversation. In the main it had been respectful, but a few had made saucy comments that Benson studiously ignored. She had made it clear to them that she was 'off duty' and this had let the men feel relaxed. It was their private sanctuary after all, no matter how squalid.

Driver Wellbeck had proved, unwittingly, to be most useful, being more than willing to talk at length on any subject, and frequently bringing others within the room into the conversation. He was clearly a man at ease with himself and his work. Open and trusting, heading for retirement age, and quite possibly, already past it. Apart from a belly that showed that he liked 'a drop', he looked sprightly, despite his years. Sporting a walrus moustache and a head of straggly hair, he wore his shirt buttoned tight at the collar, despite the ferocious heat encountered on the footplate, and a company tie worn in a Windsor knot — a nice touch, Trinder had noted with some envy, for he had never exactly mastered the art. So, with Benson's female charms clearly upsetting the equilibrium, and the loquacious Driver Wellbeck steering the conversation for Trinder, they had learnt an awful lot about the day-to-day life of the shed. It was almost a small town in itself, with all its intrigues, jokes, pranks and tragedies. Trying to untangle and recall the wealth of information they heard, would not be easy.

Sergeant Trinder, looking at the clock on the wall and realising that their train was still some way off, suggested another tea might be needed. He really wanted a pint of Hook Norton, perhaps even two, but felt that he couldn't really drag Benson to the 'Fleur de Lys' and then have to wait for a much later train. 'So, Benson, apart from a few offers to escort you to the next dance,' he raised an eyebrow, 'what did you get from the afternoon?'

'Thanks, sarge. Well I turned down all the offers, I can tell you. There were a lot of stories of men doing this, and men doing that, and the japes they like to get up to. And the language was a bit colourful at times, I must say. Still I heard the name "Rollo" a few times. I sensed that he is not the most popular man on the shed. It seems he got the job as fireman very quickly. Rapid promotion because of the war, and the older lads don't like it.'

'Yes. It can take fourteen, fifteen years to make the grade, so to do it in just a handful — you can see why it rankles.'

'But Rollo is also known for following the horses, and he collects and places bets for some of the others. They like him well enough for that. Not a lot to go on, but I couldn't push the matter too hard.'

'I heard that this Rollo was hanging out with a Kenneth Price — "Kenno" to everyone. Driver Wellbeck considers this Price to be real a real gent, a former Great Central man, soon to retire. He can't see why he's taken such a shine to this upstart Rollo. They go everywhere together in recent months. Even to the pub.'

'Is there a clue in there somewhere?' Benson furrowed her brow in concentration. 'We have an older gentleman, suddenly hanging around a much younger man, who seems a bit of a firebrand. Hard gambler, drinker, loud and aggressive. I wonder what this all means — if anything at all.'

'Indeed, Jane; Wellbeck told me that Price has had some tragedy and hard times recently. He lost his wife to T.B. last year, and his only daughter was killed two years before that on active service. She was a W.A.A.F., I think he said. Anyway, Wellbeck used to be close to Price, worked their way up the railway together, from cleaners to drivers. Both of them regularly topping the company performance charts, and both were regarded very highly by the other men. But recently Wellbeck has found himself a bit estranged from Price. Things seem to have taken a real turn for the worse, when Price's long-term fireman got promotion and a transfer to King Cross.'

'And he got in with Rollo at this point?'

'Looks that way. Wellbeck hinted that Price seems out of sorts, hanging about with a different crowd. But also that he seems to have let things go a touch … his driving performance has slipped. Not that he isn't still a good driver, but he's gone off the boil so to speak.'

'Might be nothing. Just gossipy tittle-tattle.'

'Agreed. And my, those men can tell some tales. They're worse than women. Oh, sorry.'

Benson shook her head slowly. She knew what he meant, even if not sensitively expressed.

'Wellbeck hinted that Price was letting things slip out of work as well, not looking after the home budget.'

'Falling into debt?'

'I think that is what Wellbeck was implying. On top of, or because of, losing his wife, only child and trusted workmate. It's a sad story.'

'Gosh yes. I can really feel for him. Are we looking at someone who just might be tempted — lured — by the promise of unimaginable riches? A means to escape to a whole new life? To some tropical paradise, sipping rum and cola?'

'Well, if he is involved in the Water Street gang, then he's going to have one heck of a lot to live on. Better than anything we could ever dream of, that's for sure. A possible motive for Price, then? I think we did rather well, even if I say so myself. I just hope the inspector feels the same way.'

'What do you think will be our next move?'

'Good question. And, as that sounds like our train, let's get on it and head back to Leicester, and we can find out.'

Chapter Fourteen

'BEGIN THE BEGUINE'
Artie Shaw & his Orchestra

Hours later, his first day at work on the railway over, dog-tired and arms aching, Edward was walking home with Simon. It was late afternoon and he already felt like going to bed.

'My arms ache with muscles I never knew I had.' Edward was rubbing one of them just below the shoulder, he then wiped perspiration from his brow. 'I need something to drink. Let's call in at Cullen's on the way back.' Edward was almost dragging his feet along the road.

'Good idea. Just wait until you get on the ash pits. Ho ho! You just won't believe how hard that is.'

'I don't even want to think about it.'

They purchased a 3d bottle of pop each, and sat on the wooden bench at the edge of the small plot of grass with an overarching tree that served as the village green. 'But I got some great numbers.' Edward looked a bit refreshed after a long draught of the black, fizzy liquid, and was thumbing through his now coal-blackened notebook.

'Me too. That engine, "Lord Farringdon" was the peach. Did you see her out the back? Went out just before lunch.'

'A real peach.'

'So we are agreed about my plan?' Simon suddenly shifted the conversation.

'I don't know. It's a bit scary, Si. I mean we'll really get it in then neck if we're caught.'

'Then we'd better make sure we're not. Look, it's the only way, Eddie; but it needs to be planned like a military operation. And that's why we need to get a gander at those log books. We need to be sure when that train is next running.'

'I guess so. I'm so tired I'm not sure I will still be awake tonight. If we do find out their train is running, we go back next Saturday, and this time *we* take the bag of money — that's the plan.'

'Yes. Of course we will need to be careful the motorcyclist does not arrive before the train — could be tricky.'

'You can say that again. But look, if we are successful, and we do grab the bag and don't get beaten to jelly by the guy on the bike, what then?'

'We hide the stuff, and start our next phase. Watching and observing. They are going to be pretty damn sick when they find the money's gone, and things will happen I reckon, and as we work in the same depot as the men…'

'We don't know that.'

'No, but somehow I reckon they do. I think we will see things a bit out of the ordinary happening.'

'Are you kidding? If they find out it's us with the money they'll kill us! It's like putting our hands into a wasps' nest. And what are we going to do with all this money? I mean we can't even spend that blasted fiver. Never mind the train driver, Dad would kill me if he found out.'

'Mine too.' Simon grinned ruefully. 'Eddie, you're right though, we can't spend a million pounds — not here — there's nothing to buy! But we could take a few more extra fivers. We could go somewhere else, like Leicester or Rugby to spend the money. Nobody would know us and think anything of us splashing out.'

'But what could we buy? The shops are empty.'

'We could get a camera — we can take photographs of the engines, and in between take secret pictures, like real spies.'

'Brilliant idea! And the rest of the money? We keep it hidden, right? To smoke out the gang, a bit like Farmer Turvey does with the moles.'

'Correct. We use it to force their hand, and when we have a clearer picture, we could, um …' Simon furrowed his brow, 'Well, I suppose we could go to the police and claim a huge reward. And in the meantime we have a cracking good camera as well.'

'It all sounds too neat and simple. You make it sound easy. But as I can't think of any better plan, in fact, I can't even think right now, then we had better do it.'

The late afternoon dozed on. A black-and-white cat walked across the grass, flopped onto its side in the shade of the tree, and commenced washing a paw. They sat for a while, content to just watch people pass along the row of shops, flitting through the shadows cast by the pale canvas sun-blinds pulled out from the walls like sails. A door-to-door salesman in a sharp blue suit and matching hat, a thin black moustache above his top lip, dipped in and out of a few of the doors. He stopped at Cullen's Store for an ice cream, mopping his brow with a gaudy pocket-handkerchief.

'Hey ho, Simon, so that was why she was late to work last Saturday.'

'Who?'

'Jenny what's-her-name. Look, she's walking out with that lad from Rigby's.' Edward spoke very quietly and nodded almost imperceptibly towards two figures walking arm-in-arm down Station Road.

'Oh yeah. She's a cracker.' Both of them watched as the young couple, smiling and glowing with more than the late rays of the sun, walked by. 'So what was that about her being late?'

Edward explained as they watched. He wondered if he would mention the incident of Alison and her dress, and decided against it. Jenny was wearing a navy-blue, knee-length skirt and a tightly fitted cardigan in a wavy pattern of navy, red and cream buttoned up the front to a high collar.

'Nice. Is she the one whose sister is the dressmaker? Moved down from Leicester or something. Got bombed out.' Simon looked at Edward.

'That's it. Bombed out.' he whistled under his breath. 'Some people get all the luck. Just imagine ...'

'Yeah. Must have been great. Huddled down in the shelter, searchlights criss-crossing the sky, Heinkels humming high above.'

'Or Dorniers.'

'Both. A.R.P.s sounding the sirens as the incendiaries fall, the fire engines hosing down, the buildings crumbling as the bombs are exploding everywhere.'

'Yeah. And not a sausage dropped on us all war. Just our rotten luck.' Edward took a swig of pop.

'A few did get dropped that one night.'

'Yeah — in a field. Frightened a few cows, that's about it. Most of 'em didn't even go off.'

'True.' Simon was thoughtful, 'I never even saw a Spitfire. Not one solitary, single Spitfire.' He carefully punctuated the words. 'Never mind a Messerschmitt.'

'Dream on. I did see a Hurricane once, though.'

'You never!'

'I did. When I was in Rugby one time. Straight up. But you're right, it was a pretty boring war, all things considered.'

'Still, we did see train-loads of tanks and Yankees and all that jazz.'

'And they had loads of chewing gum. But it's not the same as Heinkels and bombsites — and shrapnel. Those London kids, phew, the stories they told us.' The two lads shook their heads slowly like two old men putting the world to rights. As if to remind the lads of what they had missed, the coaling tower boomed with an exceptionally noisy load of coal.

'Who's that strange bloke over there?' Edward was watching the dapper salesman who had now finished his ice cream and had removed his jacket, slinging it over his shoulder, hat pulled down slightly at the front and to one side. He looked, however, anything but relaxed.

'Oh him, yeah, very suspicious if you ask me,' Both lads watched him strut past them, making strange, nervous jerks with his head, his eyes flitting across the road the whole time.

'Fifth Columnist, for sure.'

'Nah. Don't have those anymore.'

'Never did.'

'Soviet spy, more like.' Simon glanced at Edward.

'Think you're right there.' It had been a favourite game of theirs since the outbreak of war, watching out for Fifth Columnists and German parachutists. Picking on some innocent person going about their business who had something about them deemed, arbitrarily, 'suspicious'. Anything would do; an odd hat, the carrying of a parcel or ownership of an umbrella on a sunny day. It didn't really matter. A strange look or walk was a certainty. The churchwarden of St Mary the Virgin had been a frequent target.

'He's got the look. He is a spy, I know it.'

Edward was nodding. 'We might have to tail him.' His tiredness seemed to have evaporated.

'OK, we'd better be careful, though. Looks a bit of a hard nut,' Simon spoke out of the corner of his mouth in the manner of John Wayne.

'Come on then, let's walk on the other side, we can make out we are looking at my ABC if he turns around.'

＊　＊　＊　＊

Whilst Edward and Simon were testing out their espionage skills in Woodford Halse High Street, D.I. Vignoles was contemplating some real detective work in his office at Leicester Central.

Vignoles put his hands behind his head and swung his chair around so that he could look out upon the station. A late afternoon stopping train to London had just pulled in. Bustling porter-women were moving luggage to and fro. The mobile tea wagon was manoeuvring into place to offer refreshments to arriving travellers. The stationmaster, in his black morning suit with grey pinstriped trousers and top hat, was strutting onto the station adjacent to the first class carriages, glancing at his silver fob watch. He exchanged a pleasantry with a gentleman in a tweed jacket and trousers who was carrying what looked like fishing rods.

The complex functions of the railways were working together like so many players in an orchestra. The engine crews, guards, ticket sellers, gangers, cleaners, telegraph operators and thousands more, all playing their part together in concert. Then there was the signalman controlling everything, using the printed timetables as an orchestra conductor would a score. Setting it all in motion. Vignoles recalled reading somewhere that a signalman was like a church organist, pulling levers like giant stops. He frowned as he tried to remember the quote. He was thinking about the Water Street gang, and he was struck by how unusual it was for railwaymen to be involved in serious crime. As Vignoles filled his pipe he shook his head gently thinking how it seemed that now someone was pulling all the wrong levers, and the trains were taking the wrong tracks.

It felt stifling in his office, and as it would be a while before Trinder and Benson returned from Woodford, Vignoles decided he needed some air. He walked out of the office, pausing for a moment to decide if he should take his hat, decided that he need not, and even left his jacket over the back of the chair. He allowed hope to override extensive experience, and bought a coffee, a transaction that he immediately regretted, just as he knew he would. As usual, the coffee was tasteless and just the palest shade of brown. He smiled cheerfully anyway at the charming tea lady and, as he did so, thought how hot she must be in her calf-length navy coat, with its double row of silver buttons and matching cap perched above a roll of jet-black hair. He felt a twinge of guilt for discarding his jacket and hat, but then strolled to the far end of one of the island platforms, and stood gazing across to the upper floors and rooftops of the city centre.

The station was elevated upon a wide viaduct that spanned much of Leicester and gave a commanding view across a city largely untroubled by significant hills. The city still showed considerable evidence of the intense battering it had received in the Blitz. A few buildings had new roofs and windows, but a great many were still smoke-blackened, with ugly wounds in the stone and brickwork from bombs and shrapnel. Others remained completely unrestored, with charred roof timbers pointing accusingly towards the sky and windows smashed despite the strips of brown, anti-blast tape. Huge cracks and tears in the fabric of some of the buildings rendered them dangerous and suggested that demolition might be the only option. There were also many gaps in the cityscape from buildings that were already demolished. Vignoles struggled to remember what was missing. Wooden boards were now shuttering the bombsites, but the ever-present buddleia filled these dispiriting places with fragrant purple flowers and clouds of butterflies.

He gazed along the main railway tracks that snaked southwards, looking to see if he could identify the buildings around Water Street, but the jumble of roofs and chimneys was too confusing for him to be sure. Livid thunderclouds were looming ominously on the horizon. It was becoming muggy and humid, and he hoped it might rain, to relieve the pressure and wash away the pungent haze of smoky pollution hanging over the city.

He wanted to clear his head as well and think through the next part of his strategy. He hoped that Trinder and Benson would come back with some useful information. But any such information was not in itself going to help him catch the gang red-handed, nor would it, unless they were very fortunate, lead them to the other parts of what looked to be a complex operation. Someone was collecting this counterfeit money and converting it into genuine money or goods. But who were they?

Then there were the passports and driving licences. He was beginning to suspect that the gang was using forged documents to allow them to purchase high-value goods — motor vehicles for example — under false names. The list of names and sums of money logged beside each, that he had found in the manila envelope, looked suspiciously like a shopping list of forged identities that someone had commissioned. The names and addresses would surely be false. But who were the real people that these new identities were being created for?

Vignoles sat on a wooden bench and rested his chin in his hands. How were they to observe the place where the money was dropped off? This was a vexing issue. Short of smuggling himself on board one of the empty brick trains and trying to watch — an impossibly futile and highly dangerous idea — he was a bit stumped. Vignoles flipped open his notebook and looked at the list of all stations between Leicester and the destination of the train, which in this case was the brickworks at Calvert. The train was not booked to stop anywhere along the route, so logic suggested that Calvert was the obvious place for the drop-off point. But Calvert was literally in the middle of nowhere, atrnnd a long way from the printing press. The known suspects were Woodford men, and Water Street was in Leicester, so these facts — perhaps illogically — suggested to Vignoles that the gang was working closer to home than Calvert.

He exhaled loudly. On one level it looked like they had this case almost wrapped up; but on closer inspection it was far from resolved. He sat upright, removed his glasses and pinched his nose. This was going to be a painstaking investigation, and he was likely to need the help of the civvy police. He was not eager to let the case expand from his department because previous experience showed that the bigger county forces tended to look down upon the railway police, treating them as if they were incompetent amateurs.

As regards a plan, the best he could come up with was to place an officer either in or near every signal box along the way and see what happened. However, as there were considerably more boxes than he had officers, it would take a few attempts at the very least to have a chance of success. A bit like looking for the proverbial needle. He practised running through how he might sell the proposition to Chief Superintendent Badger: 'Think of the long game, sir. More akin to a test match than a football game.' Vignoles imagined that the cricket reference might appeal to Badger. 'Patient information-gathering will be the watchword. Building up a case from a variety of sources, and then we go for the big push. I propose strategically spreading out my force along the suspected route. Each officer placed undercover and we shall all try to observe the actual exchange. Hopefully.' Vignoles contemplated Badger's chilly response. 'Well, no, it's not a plan likely to meet with immediate success, I admit.' 'Oh dear,' he thought, 'this is not going to play out awfully well.' What he really needed was some clue as to how the counterfeit money was being used at the other end of the chain.

Suddenly he had an idea, and briskly returned to the office. As he walked into the entrance lobby, he stopped and addressed Mavis: 'Is Lansdowne here?'

'Yes sir, she's writing up a report, about someone being robbed last night.'

'Ah.' Vignoles lifted up the section of the counter that allowed staff admission and entered the larger office that was shared by the remaining members of his staff. There were three oversized wooden tables in the room, each providing, in theory, ample space for two officers with space to spare, but the piles of papers and box files that invariably cluttered every spare inch made the place feel oppressively cramped. He could see Lansdowne typing something, with a look of total concentration on her face. He smiled. Her reports took an age to be written, but were grammatically perfect and had no corrections upon them. Lansdowne preferred to type extremely slowly, but with careful consideration before every key was pressed. She claimed that in the long run her reports were completed in about the same time as those of Sergeant Trinder, who bashed his out in a fury, then amended and corrected then until they were close to illegible. He cleared his throat to attract her attention, and hoped that he had not caused her to type a wrong letter. She looked up from her typing, and made to immediately stand up.

'No, no, stay seated, Lansdowne. I just wanted to ask if you could look into something for me.'

'Yes, sir?'

'I'd like you to go the library and go through all the local newspapers — in the Leicester area to start with. Go back, let's say, six weeks and try to find any adverts for sales of army or other government surplus stock. Vehicles and high-value equipment, that kind of thing. Place, date and so forth. Also, see if you can find any sales of motor-vehicles — at auctions in particular. When you've done that, let me see what you find.'

'Right away, sir.' She looked at her wristwatch, 'The library stays open until eight, I shall try to have a list by the morning.'

'Thank you.' Vignoles walked back to his office, looking forward to seeing the beautifully-crafted list that he knew Lansdowne would present to him. He had long since stopped advising her that such work need not be a work of art, but her attention to detail was such that she would rather sit up late perfecting her presentation, than 'cut corners', as she would put it. Policing was often about attention to details, and Lucy Lansdowne was above reproach in this respect. He shook his head, suddenly remembering the talk of dismissals. How could anyone seriously think about losing these officers?

Chapter Fifteen

'PENNSYLVANIA 6-5000'
Glenn Miller & his Orchestra

And then Violet saw him.

There was no doubt; it was the same dapper little salesman, the same little 'spiv' of a man, who had fobbed her off with the wad of worthless banknotes. Violet felt a fuming indignation boiling inside of her, a sensation that surprised her with its ferocity. She wanted to shout out to him there and then in the street. Make passers-by stop in their tracks and appreciate just how disgracefully he had treated her. However, she managed to rein in her anger sufficiently to stop herself from making a scene. But she still muttered softly under her breath, 'OK then, Mr Speedy Loans, I want to hear what you have to say for yourself...'

She darted out of the shop door and stepped right into his path, forcing him to stop abruptly. He looked startled and needed a few moments to take in who this furious looking woman was, confronting him. 'Could you step inside please? I would like to have a word with you if I may?'

'What the Devil? Oh ... it's you Mrs ... er ... McKenzie. Ah, what a nice surprise,' he added lamely, briefly lifting his hat in an attempt to remain civil, but his eyes flashed with suspicion.

'McIntyre, and it's Miss, actually. Would you oblige me with a few minutes of your time, and step inside, please?' She held the shop door open, making it hard for him to refuse.

'Well it's most inconvenient, Miss, I am in a hurry, you see,' but he walked inside nonetheless.

'Hopefully this won't take long, then. Do take a seat.' Violet indicated the chair Jenny had been sitting in the other evening.

'No thank you, I really am pressed for time.' The salesman extended a hand to reveal what looked like an expensive wristwatch, and glanced at it to emphasise his point.

'Suit yourself. Look, it's about the money that I, I, er, borrowed from you. I have had a most disturbing experience this morning and I want to hear your explanation.'

'I cannot imagine what you mean. What kind of experience?' He dabbed his brow with a yellow silken handkerchief, spotted with red polka dots.

'I had a five pound note refused as being fraudulent.'

'Oh, impossible!'

'Oh, not impossible. It happened yesterday, right here in Woodford Halse. So what have you to say about that?' Her eyes flashed, and she tried to keep her voice steady.

'Are you accusing the company — a very respectable company, I might add — of trading illegal money? If so then I should advise you that that is a very serious accusation Miss, and you should think carefully,' he emphasised the point, 'before repeating it.' The salesman took a deep breath and puffed his chest out, standing with his feet slightly apart, looking confrontational. He was still perspiring, despite the attentions of the expensive handkerchief. It might have been because the shop was warm from the sun, but Violet also wondered if it could be that he was nervous. Violet certainly was, and began to feel her resolve waver.

'I am not accusing you.'

'It certainly sounds like it. I can assure you, that I take this as very bad form indeed.'

'I didn't mean to cause offence, it's just that I tried to pay some bills this morning and the shopkeeper refused my five pound note. He said it was suspicious.'

'A local shopkeeper?'

'Yes. Mr Earnshaw, the baker.'

'Ah. I understand now. Clearly a simple misunderstanding.' The man had regained his self-composure and confidence. His voice took on the assured, well-oiled tone Violet had encountered when they had first met. 'Miss, I will share with you some of the extensive knowledge I have gathered whilst in this business. Village shopkeepers just don't have the, er, experience of handling serious cash transactions.' He emphasised the word 'serious' in a way that suggested that Violet and he shared an enhanced and substantial experience in the matter of serious cash transactions. 'They are decent enough people, of course, but rather small-minded, used to handling the daily shillings and pence, and collecting little paper coupons, but when it comes to real money, well, they are almost amateurs.' He spoke the last sentence with a barely concealed contempt. 'What would a local baker know about a five pound note or two? No, I am afraid you have met with an all-too-common problem. Of course, we have all heard about counterfeiters these days — an outrage! And we all must be vigilant to avoid being duped by these scoundrels.

But this has nothing at all to do with the integrity of the money we passed over to you. Naturally I could, with my practised eye, spot a fraud a mile off, but to the untutored eye — well, it's just guesswork and suspicion, you see?' He made a wide smile that he held whilst his eyes scanned Violet's face.

'Oh well yes, yes, I suppose you are right.' Violet remembered the doubt in both the baker and his wife's assessment of the note.

'Oh I am. Have you, if I may be so impertinent to enquire, had cause to use any other of the notes in question?'

'Yes. Nearly twenty pounds, actually.' Violet was now regretting being alone in the shop and confessing intimate details of her financial dealings to this oily man in the sharp suit. This had not been her plan at all.

'You have been busy.' His eyes narrowed and openly sized her up, 'And were there any problems, when you handed these over?'

'No.'

'I see.' There was long pause. 'Do you happen to have the note in question to hand? May I see it?'

'I suppose so, I have it here in my handbag.' Violet retrieved it and handed it over.

'As I thought, anyone with a professional eye can see that this is perfectly good.' Violet looked on as he opened out the paper rectangle, the size of a ladies' handkerchief. He was nodding slowly and emphatically, 'But look, as you have had an unpleasant experience with this particular note, and as you are really a most charming customer.' His eyes again made no secret of looking up and down her body, making Violet feel uncomfortable, and she involuntarily placed a hand just below her neck, shielding herself, prompting the salesman in return to form a knowing smile.

'I don't often get such —' he paused a beat, '— lovely customers, so just this once, as you are clearly a woman of honour and integrity,' he stressed the words, 'and as a goodwill gesture ...' He reached into his jacket and pulled out a large, black leather wallet that was packed tightly with money. Violet's eyes widened, despite her best attempts to stop herself. 'I shall replace this particular little rascal, with these five, nicely used, single pound notes. A trifle grubby, I am afraid. Too many people have had their hands all over them,' he winked. 'But I think you will find the local shopkeepers will be only too happy to take these from you.' He sighed in an exaggerated manner as he spoke the last part of the sentence, whilst handing Violet the notes, and re-pocketing the bulging wallet. 'But I am in a hurry, so if you don't mind? Good day. I shall be back to collect the first payment next week. I shall look forward to that.' He tipped his hat briefly and was out of the door before Violet could protest. The shop bell jangled, then stopped. A big, fat fly buzzed noisily past Violet's nose, forcing her to wave it away.

She looked down at the evidently well-used notes and admitted to herself that it had been pretty decent of him to make the change. He was a bit creepy, but then, weren't most salesmen these days? There was little doubt that she could now return to Earnshaw's and settle her dues with no questions being asked. But a little warning bell was ringing somewhere in the back of her mind. Its clear tinkling sound trying to attract her attention, to warn her that all was not as it seemed. Then she smiled to herself, it was just 'Pennsylvania Six-Five Thousand' playing on the radio with its silly telephone bell sound-effect, and she walked into the back kitchen to fill the kettle.

Edward and Simon had observed their imaginary 'Soviet Spy' meeting up with his local informant. They were, however, surprised that this was Miss Violet McIntyre — elder sister of the charming Jenny — and even more surprised that she had practically jumped out of her shop and buttonholed the man.

'Wow!'

'In these strange times, we can trust no one.' Simon was whispering to Edward, 'Everyone is a suspect. But who would ever imagine a dressmaker in Woodford Halse working with the Soviets?'

'Too right. The perfect cover!'

'He's a right dandy, anyway; I bet she did some work on that flash suit of his, and he hasn't paid!' Simon and Eddie continued to whisper as they strolled towards the shop window, but then Eddie deliberately dropped his little A.B.C. booklet on the pavement at the very moment they drew level. He stooped to pick it up, whilst Simon, feigning nonchalance, with his hands in his pockets, turned casually to glance inside. He then looked away with an expression of equally profound disinterest, whilst Edward, in turn, shot a look through the window as he stood up. Both saw the five-pound note, as brilliant as a white flag, being exchanged and examined. Edward signalled with his eyes to Simon that he had seen it.

'Walk!' hissed Simon. They stepped past the window and pressed themselves against the shop wall. 'Next move?'

Edward quickly surveyed the surroundings. 'Let's look at that Austin Seven in the garage over there, we can watch the door easily.'

The lads sauntered over to the little car displayed for sale beside the road, and studied its polished, royal-blue paintwork and dazzling chrome radiator grill. Both made excellent mirrors. They saw the man almost immediately leave the shop, adjusting his hat as he did so and carrying his suit jacket over one arm. He darted glances up and down Station Road, then immediately strode across onto the narrow forecourt of the garage and was upon the two boys before they had time to react. Edward tensed and stopped breathing as he watched the distorted shape of the man rapidly advance towards him in the curves of the radiator. A strange, disturbingly twisted face with bulging eyes loomed over his reflection, and then passed by.

'You're too young for one of those. Anyway, it's overpriced.' And with that their man, bold as brass, walked past the front of the two low, gable-ended garage buildings to where a high, bushy hedge formed a screen between the road that dipped under the railway arches, a patch of grass and a 'Dig for Victory' vegetable plot.

They both turned and watched him, and saw that he had a motorcycle sidecar combination parked on the lawn area. It was clearly ex-army, in olive drab with a canvas cover over the passenger well. Simon nudged Edward and they moved and turned their attention to the interior of the car, but stole glances as the salesman changed his clothes. He carefully folded the suit jacket and placed it in the sidecar, then quickly slipped off both shoes. Next, a pair of waterproof over-trousers were pulled on, followed by pair of heavy boots retrieved out of the sidecar and were soon zipped on. He completed the transformation by shrugging on a heavy flying jacket, and fastening on a black helmet. The whole exchange took no more that a couple of minutes.

He climbed onto the bike and fired it up with a deep, throaty roar, then aggressively revving the throttle the sidecar combination pulled eagerly forward. With just a cursory glance up and down the road, the Soviet agent roared away under the station bridge.

'Woah! Did you get all that, Eddie?'

'That voice ... did it remind you of someone?' Edward was shaking his head, but also writing a series of notes in his little book. 'Registration number, Si? Did you get it? I reckon it was LEC 457.'

'Correct. I take it you did see what I saw in the shop?'

'Too right! I tell you what though, Simon, this is getting seriously strange. That was a fiver, wasn't it? And we have a fiver — from a bag thrown off a train. And the bag was picked up by a man on a motorbike.'

'Of course, the motorbike! I'd not thought of that, Eddie. We might just have walked right past the man behind all this, whatever it is.'

'But also he spoke to us. Our cover is blown.'

'No, we're just two lads who like cars, and he was being friendly.'

'He wasn't that friendly.'

'Well, you know what I mean. Anyway, he had his back to us in the shop, he couldn't have known that we saw him and her with the money.'

'Maybe. But I am still worried about why he spoke to us. Surely it was to let us know he had seen us?'

'But he doesn't know we are British agents — he just saw two kids looking at an Austin. You have to look at it from his side.'

'Guess you could be right. He didn't know we were at the station, either.' Edward looked up and broke into a huge grin. 'Blinkin' heck, Simon. We might just have found a real Fifth Columnist!'

'Soviet Agent.'

'This feels like … like the real thing. Right, that decides it. We should now go back on Saturday and try to grab that bag of money. But how on earth does Miss McIntyre fit into all of this?'

'Good question. Righty-ho, let's get back home, have some grub and rendezvous later as agreed.'

Both Edward and Simon used the excuse that they were needed to 'knock up' some early-shift drivers, to leave their respected houses at midnight. This was one of the tiresome tasks that the more junior shed staff were expected to fulfil and it aroused no suspicion at all, but did prompt a sympathetic cup of cocoa from Simon's mother, and a paper bag with a slightly stale, but gratefully received, bun from Edward's.

They were both dressed in their work clothes, that way they would at least look like they should be at the shed. However, they were gripped with apprehension about what they were going to attempt. To be caught would result, at best, in a severe clout around the ears and a significant loss of wages. Both would hurt; however, it was just as likely that they could be dismissed instantly. The thought terrified them both, and yet despite this, adrenaline was coursing through their veins and the feeling that they were in some way trying to solve a crime, drove them on.

They walked into the dimly-lit yard, skulking along close to the lines of stationary engines, staying in the deep, inky-black pools of shadow that gathered around the wheels. They were ready to duck down close to the oily connecting rods if someone walked past their line of vision. It was easy for them to get up close to the entrance to the engine shed without being seen, but now, as they crouched under the front buffer beam of a V2, they had a sterner test. They could see the darkened bay window of the shedmaster's office, and beside that the doorway leading into the small lobby where Mr Reed presided over his ledgers, checking everyone on and off work. It was late, and unlikely that the foreman was still at work, but they could not be sure. He might have locked the doors, which would ruin their plan rather abruptly, but Simon seemed to think that this was unlikely, as there always seemed to be someone coming and going, even at awful hours in the morning. This of course was the problem.

They had to first cross the more brightly illuminated patch of grass to the door, and then hope that as they entered it that they did not bump into anyone. They had no idea of what excuse they would use, but just decided to give it a go and then try to talk their way out of the mess if it happened. Everywhere looked still and empty. There was the sound of a fire being raked out off to one side of them, and the rhythmic clang of a fitter striking something metal, coming from within the shed itself, but otherwise, it seemed as though they had the place virtually to themselves.

'OK? Here goes.' Edward stood up, took two swift glances to the left and right and then strode quickly and purposefully towards the door, with Simon close on his heels. They forced themselves to stand upright and walk confidently, as if they had every reason to be there, but their palms were sweaty and their hearts beat loudly in their chests. Edward opened the door and stepped inside, but took care to keep the sound of his boots to a minimum on the linoleum floor.

A bare light bulb glowed dimly on a brown flex from the corridor ceiling. A second one was also on in the lobby beyond, but it was immediately obvious that the green-shaded lamp on Mr Reed's desk was turned off. This was a good sign, and Simon was encouraged, urging Edward to move forward. They stepped into the room and sighed in relief as they found it empty. There on the tall desk lay a large book, bound in thick, green, fabric-covered boards, with a leather spine and triangular corner protectors. There was an inscription blocked in gold on the cover, confirming that this was the latest list of daily rosters.

Simon stepped behind the desk and sat on the tall stool, opening the ledger as he did so. Edward stood beside him and they peered at the long lists of numbers, train codes, names and other details. It was bewildering and seemed to be written in some strange, foreign language. They stared at the mass of information spread out before them, but could only begin to make sense of parts of what was there.

'Look, these are loco numbers.'

'And this is the date, here, so each of these pages is for today. But what does that mean?'

'Don't know, Eddie. I think it's a code for the type of train it was to pull.'

'So how can we know which is the one we want?'

'Don't know … oh damn, there is so much to take in. I'm not sure where to start.'

'Me neither.'

Their anxiety made them nervous, and Simon started to rapidly turn the pages, hardly stopping to look at each one, not knowing what was important and what was not.

'Stop, Si, I can't make any sense of it when you keep turning the pages. We have to try and be logical about this.' Edward was running his finger across the wide pages, furrowing his brow in concentration. 'Oh blast this, without the codes telling us what each train is, we're stuck.'

'Are you sure?'

'As sure as I am about anything in this bloody book. It's not easy — if only we had more time to look …'

At that moment Simon jabbed Edward in the ribs, 'Listen. I think there's some people coming.' They could clearly hear voices outside of the door that led into the engine shed. The door handle started to turn and the door inched open, but stopped, almost certainly in response to a shout from further away. The two lads exchanged glances and, not for the first time, dashed away to seek cover. Edward was closest to the office of Mr Saunders, and tried the handle. Finding it unlocked, they tumbled inside, crouching behind the door in the dark. Not a second too late, as a group of men then entered the lobby, chatting loudly and clearly passing cigarettes around. The lads were so close they could hear the rasp of matches striking, and the tiny sounds as the matches landed on the grimy lino.

Edward was able to peer into the room through the gap where the door hung from its hinges. His eye, pressed to the slit, could feel the chill air brought in by the men, but whilst he wanted to pull away and rub it, he couldn't, for he was transfixed by the sight of Mr Reed and two others, standing beside the opened ledger. 'Oh no, we left it open,' he thought, 'heck, we are in for it now,' and felt a chill run down his spine. The foreman had his back to Edward, but he knew it was he, as his broad back and mane of unfashionably long hair, draggling almost to his collar, were unmistakable. The men were all smoking now, a silence briefly falling as they took long drags. A younger, wiry man blew the smoke noisily upwards, towards the ceiling in a jet, and then looked at the foreman. 'So, we all fixed for Saturday?' he said, and sniffed.

'Yep, sorted. Just the same as last time. No worries.'

'Good. You've done us proud so far.' He took another lungful of smoke then started to speak as he exhaled, snorting and frothing the smoke like a dragon, 'Another three, maybe four, and we are off your back, yeah? End of the line, so as to speak. Then you can put us on any blinkin' train you want.'

'I'm mighty glad to hear that, Rollo, I don't mind saying that at all.' The foreman was walking slowly around the back of his desk, glancing down at the open ledger with a brief questioning look, and then carefully closed it shut. 'I have to be careful y'know? Saunders gave me a devil of a ticking off for messing up the log. I don't want to be doing that kind of malarky again, OK?'

'Are you sure he doesn't suspect something?' It was the other man speaking; Edward could just see his profile. He was a tall, skinny youth looking no more than perhaps twenty years old. Edward was also aware that Simon had very slowly re-adjusted his position, so that he was kneeling right up and looking through the same crack between door and frame that Edward was.

'Don't you worry, I told him it was me as was clumsy, that's all. He bought it.'

'We pay you well enough, so take it on the chin, and make sure he keeps his nose out of it. On that note ...' Rollo reached into his blue, railwayman's jacket and pulled out a manila envelope. 'We've got something here. For last week — twenty fresh ones. Don't blow them all at once. Try to be a bit careful how you splash it around, yeah?' He handed the envelope over and Reed quickly took it, peered inside the unsealed flap and, visibly relaxing, tucked it into his back pocket.

'Ta. I will, you don't have to worry about me.'

'Good, keep it that way and we're all happy. Well, I'm off.' And with that, Rollo walked past the watching eyes and out, the younger man dutifully following behind without even being asked. Reed sat heavily upon the stool behind the desk, removed the envelope from his trouser pocket and took out the bank notes, fingering each one carefully as he counted them again. Satisfied, he neatly stacked them together and replaced them, folding the envelope in half and tucking it into the breast pocket of his stained overalls. He then sat still and looked intently at the ledger upon the desk. He touched the cover gently with his fingers, as if this would somehow provide an answer to the question that the two who were watching knew was going through his mind. Had he left the ledger open? If not, then who had been looking at it, and why?

He inhaled the last of his cigarette and stood up, looking around him. Reed then walked across to the door to Mr Saunders's office and in one short movement pulled it closed, making Edward and Simon jump, Edward shutting his eyes tightly as if that would somehow protect him. Then there was the sound of jingling keys and the lock was turned in the door. Other sounds could be heard, of Reed walking across the floor and unlocking a cupboard, as if he was placing the heavy ledger in a cupboard and locking it shut. A few moments later and the door to the engine shed opened and closed, the lights extinguished in the corridor.

'Close shave there, Eddie.'

'At least we are safe for a the time being — we're blinkin' locked in.'

'No problem, Eddie, the windows here reach almost to the ground — we'll climb out.' As Simon was speaking, he was silhouetted against the faint, residual brightness left in the night sky, and the pale, sickly light of a yard lamp. He soon had one of the lower sashes lifted. 'Come on Eddie, we'd better scarper.'

They climbed out of the window with ease, then Simon turned back to the window to pull it shut again. The frame moved a few inches but then jammed in the sash. Simon heaved on it, but it was hard to get a purchase on the frame from such an angle and it stubbornly refused to move.

'Give us a hand. We've got to get this closed'

They both tugged in unison at the stubborn window, which then came unstuck so suddenly that both lads had to pull their hands free at the last moment to avoid getting them crushed. The window banged shut, alarmingly loud in the still, and now chill, night air. They turned and started to cross the threadbare lawn when a voice called out from behind them. 'Oy! What are you two doing?'

'Run!' Simon sprinted away, closely followed by Edward, darting between two lines of engines and into the impenetrable black.

'Come 'ere, you little blighters!' They could hear the sound of heavy feet pounding behind them on the gravel. The two lads ran, not stopping to check where their feet were landing, feeling their boots crunch into piles of ash, and splash into pools of water, slide over bits of pipe and rubber hose, and strike against hard objects; but somehow, despite all this, they both stayed on their feet. The lines of engines were coming to an end, however, and there was a long stretch of open yard to cross before they might consider themselves safe. Their pursuer was still shouting, his voice echoing around the yard, though it sounded as if he were on the far side of one of lines of engines some way behind. His desire to run was perhaps not as strong as Edward and Simon's.

'Into the pit!' Edward stopped, crouched low and then crawled on his belly between the wheels of an engine. He dropped down into the ash pit underneath, which was still warm with ash dropped hours before from the firebox. Simon landed near him, throwing up a choking white cloud. They pulled their neckerchiefs over their faces and closed their eyes as the dust settled. It was surprisingly hot and stifling, and their movements fanned some clinker and un-burnt coals into a dull redness. They crouched low and remained silent, listening to the quiet clicks and ticks of the smouldering ash piles. There were voices talking, as someone else joined the man who had given chase. They were talking loudly and walking closer to where the lads crouched, a beam of a flashlight flicking across the ground and then sweeping around the yard. Simon and Edward peered over the lip of the pit and watched the light dance across the uneven surface, and could just about discern two pairs of booted feet approaching.

The two men stopped and talked for a few moments. It sounded like they were abandoning their desultory search and having a cigarette. Their conversation was quieter now, and then they moved away.

'That was close.'

'Bit too close, but that was really something — and we caught them up to no good as well. That Mr Reed is taking money to fix the trains — I'm sure that was what that was all about.'

'Me too. There's something big going on here. We find money dropped off a train, and now it looks like the train crew are paying to be on the same train next week. We didn't get what we came to find — we went one better. So if we go to the same place, same time, then we can —'

'— Grab the money!'

'Yeah! Gosh, this is wild.' Edward was still feeling the adrenaline course through his veins, and shared Simon's excitement. 'Ow! I need to get out of here, I think I'm smouldering.' Edward patted his elbow, which was very hot, and there was a smell of scorched cloth. 'Oh heck!' Edward crawled from under the locomotive, and lay on his belly, glancing around. There was no sign of the flashlight, so he half-ran, stooping low, a few yards to where there was a pool of water, and plunged his sleeve into it. There was a slight hissing sound. Simon quietly joined him. 'That's better. I think I burned a hole in my new jacket. Mother will go spare when she sees that. Damn. No matter, let's make a dash for the fence over there, and then we can work our way around to the gate, staying in the shadows.'

'Yep. Let's get home to bed. We can discuss the night's spying tomorrow.'

Chapter Sixteen

'RIPTIDE'

Lew Stone & his Band

'What do you mean, you've got a problem?'

Rollo snorted and looked back at the man seated opposite in his sharp, dark-blue, pinstriped suit. 'Look, I don't give a monkey's arse about what sort of a problem you've got. And don't bore me with the details.' He dragged heavily upon his cigarette, then stubbed it out with force in the brimming ashtray. 'I don't really wanna know. But...' He leaned forward and placed his faced just inches away from the other and spoke quietly, but with unmistakable menace, '... get it sorted and keep it sorted. Understand? Because if you've got a problem, then we've all got a problem. And I don't like that kind of situation, it spoils business. So don't mess around, Fancy Dan. Sort it out — *permanently!*' He leaned back. He'd made his point. Got it off his chest.

'I told you, Rollo, everything is tickety-boo, and you know what? I don't like your attitude very much. It's bang out of order. I thought we were all supposed to be in this together. And my name is Peter, in case you have forgotten.' The two men stared at each other, the sour scent of anger perceptible in the muggy air.

'Calm it, lads — and keep it down a bit, will you?' Driver Kenneth Price was leaning back on the bench seat in the Great Central Hotel, puffing on his pipe as if it was one of his locomotives. 'What kind of problem is it, Pete? Does it affect our operation?' he continued, in his soft, rich voice that betrayed years of smoke inhalation.

'It was nothing.'

'Then why bother us about it? Jesus!' Rollo shifted in his chair, shaking his head, 'Kenno, how can you be so patient with him? We need people who can just get on with the job, y'know?' The fireman hurriedly picked up his already empty pint glass, thinking to drain it, paused, looked at it and slammed it back on the table.

'Look, keep your hair on, lads, all right? I'm just trying out a new venture, a new angle, OK? I came up with an interesting one. A slow burner, but it will give a nice turnover. And the best bit — compound interest on top. Serious mark-up, I can tell you.' He grinned, the little moustache that clung to his upper lip accentuating the effect.

'Well, sounds interesting, I agree. But what are you doing exactly?'

Rollo snorted at Ken's words, and stared at the unswept floor.

'Ah well, Mum's the word, you know, Kenno. Can't give too much away — just in case,' and Peter glanced at the other three men around the table. 'But, the problem was that this woman in Woodford —'

'— Woman?' Rollo suddenly sat up and grinned wolfishly. 'Oh yeah? A woman involved. Ah ha … that's more like it, you old devil.' Rollo's mood seemed to lighten suddenly. 'Good looking too, eh, Fancy Dan? So you've been getting down to some "business" with a girl, eh? What she do — rob your wallet in the night? Ha!' He grinned at the others.

'Yeah, very funny. It's not like that. Well, not for the time being.' He grinned also, enjoying the instant thawing in the atmosphere. He allowed himself a moment to bring to mind the image of the attractive dressmaker with the flashing eyes. She was quite a dish.

'So what is it like?' Ken Price asked the question quietly and clearly, but heavy with implication. He was a man in his early sixties, a drooping walrus moustache setting off a face weather-beaten to a light nut colour and creased with lines and wrinkles, all ingrained with a suggestion of coal and oil, the legacy of a life spent on the footplate. His hands were criss-crossed with more lines, the nails cut short and outlined in black, as if etched by an artist, despite his liberal use of paraffin to clean them. His status as a driver conferred gravity to his question, despite the men being off duty. Refusing to answer was not an option for Peter.

'Well she got a bit nervous about a —' and he dropped his voice, '— a fiver. I swapped it of course with, um, legit stuff. Settled her nerves, no problem.'

'What is this? You giving your sweetheart money for dresses or something?'

'No.' Peter glared at Rollo. 'She can make them herself. She's a dressmaker. And a good one, I tell you, that dress she wore, fit in all the right places.' He drew a smile at least from Rollo. 'But seriously, I'm not giving her money. It's a business deal. OK, it's cost me a little bit this time, but ...', he tailed off.

'Seems a rotten way to do business, if you ask me. We need high-value deals, not poxy fivers, and then you give the stuff away.

You sure the top man has approved this?'

Peter ignored the question. 'Anyway, you lot can talk. You nearly lost us everything last time.' Peter glared across the table at the other men, and in particular fixed his gaze upon the tall, skinny one, who so far had remained silent.

'What d'you mean by that?'

'The bag was open, Jimmy. Wide open.'

'It never was!'

'Keep it down, will you?' Ken wagged his pipe at Peter, his brow furrowed with concentration.

Peter dropped his voice, and spoke quietly, suddenly crackling with anger, 'And we're a fiver down on the delivery, as it happens — no thanks to you, Jimmy.'

'What? I don't know what you mean.'

'Well, stands to reason, it must have blown away or something from the open bag. Too damn careless and sloppy, if you ask me. Or did you lift one extra for yourself, eh?' Peter looked more confident as he gained the undivided attention of the other three. The thin, lanky, fresh-faced lad by the name of Jimmy Cresswell flushed red around his neck and cheeks, and leaned backwards in his chair, eyes wide with surprise and flicking nervously between the three men.

'Like hell it was! It was never unzipped? Wh-what d'you mean? You're kidding me. You're winding me up.' His tongue licked his lips and he swallowed.

'What is all this about the money being short? This is something we should know about.' Rollo was suddenly quiet and controlled, his loud, demonstrative actions reined back. He sensed a problem, and his combat experience had taught him that survival depended in these moments, upon keeping a level head and assessing the situation.

'Yes. Five quid down on the pick up.'

'No way! I never touched it 'cept to collect and drop over the side. It was zipped tight. On my mother's life, it was.' Jimmy was glaring at Peter, who looked, by contrast, self-assured. Rollo, however, could sense the young man's deeply felt hurt at the accusation.

'Look, I dunno what your game is Pete, but why would Jimmy do something as stupid as that?' Rollo looked across at the flustered guard, who was biting his lip and breathing hard. He was liable to thump his accuser at any moment. 'After all, if he did do something that stupid we'd wring his bloody neck.' Rollo's eyes fixed on Jimmy's, then returned to Peter. 'So I can't see that being likely. Anyway, he had more than enough time to close the bag if he did take some for himself, so why leave it open?' Peter nodded slowly in agreement. 'So maybe, Fancy Dan, you're the one trying to lift a little extra on top? Strange that you claim to have "lost" a fiver in a bad deal, and now we've all suddenly lost one from the shipment as well? Eh?'

'Not me, Rollo, I'm playing a straight bat here.'

'You better watch that you are.' Rollo was again leaning forward, his face menacingly close to Peter's.

'Bloody hell, Rollo, I'm the one who's had to give a fiver of my hard-earned to one of the punters.' He suddenly stopped, Rollo's logic made his situation look bad. This was playing out all wrong. 'Look, it's not how you say it is. Really. We were five down. That's the truth. And no doubt it'll be me who'll make up the shortfall. That makes me down by a bloody tenner all round. I'm no petty thief, you know.'

'OK, OK, steady on, enough. And will you all keep your voices down!' Ken waved his pipe between the men and spoke with a calm, but firm voice. 'The bag most probably came open as it got dropped. Easily explained. And, well, one fiver under, normally, would be a real blow, but no real harm done, eh? Not in our present circumstances anyway. It's annoying, but we can easily afford to make it up. They can always print us another.' He laughed and then blew a cloud of sweet smoke into the air like a peace pipe, and started to rootle deeply in his heavy-serge trouser pockets. 'Here,' he pulled out a small bundle of grubby pound notes and peeled one off, and added a ten shilling note. 'There's a contribution — no hard feelings.'

Rollo watched, then shrugged and did the same. 'But our glasses are empty and I'm sure if you refilled them for us — since you are suddenly so flush — our mood would improve considerably.' Rollo looked around at the two others sitting around the table, and they all laughed with relief, the tension easing again. Rollo handed his glass to the smartly-suited salesman. Peter's face was blotched with crimson around his neck and cheeks. He was back on the defensive. The two men looked at each other for a few moments, but then Rollo looked away, with a shake of the head. 'Go on. What you waiting for — bloody Christmas?' Rollo allowed a slight smile. Peter paused, returned it, then walked across the sticky lino to the bar, trying to regain some composure.

'Are you really playing us straight, young Jimmy?' Rollo spoke quietly and intently.

'God's truth I am.'

'Scout's honour, eh.' Rollo spoke sarcastically and then flicked ash from his cigarette, 'OK. I believe you. For the time being. You'll need more than Baden bloody Powell to help save your skin if you are pulling a fast one, though.'

'So you've already said. But I'm not. Really Mr Rollo.' He paused, 'But are you sure everything's OK? You know, with the arrangements?'

Jimmy Cresswell had an apology for a moustache, which combined with his pale skin and freckles, made him look considerably younger than his actual age, all of which did little to inspire confidence amongst the others, despite the fact that he was a fully qualified guard, with a good service record.

'You worry too much, that's your problem, Jimmy. Everything's fine with the arrangements, as you so nicely put it. OK, so we cut it a bit fine last week — and mind, you better hold your nerve next time that happens.'

'I had to blow up, we had the signals set. We'd get a right rollicking if we'd sat there much longer.'

'I know. You're right enough there.' It was the conciliatory Ken Price speaking.

'But Kenno, I don't know … what's all this stuff with Pete? Is everything really all right? It sort of makes me wonder about it all. I was sort of thinking … maybe it's time to stop? I mean, we have already made a pretty packet and … well … should we just knock it all on the head?'

Mickey Rollo and Ken Price stared at him. The silence that suddenly fell around the small table was heavy with meaning. Jimmy took a drag on his cigarette, managing to look inept in so doing. His hands shook. Rain could be heard pouring in torrents outside.

'It don't work like that, lad. You don't decide when you stop. Top Link decides that. And he ain't asking for volunteers to take retirement,' Rollo's eyes flicked across to Ken, then back to Jimmy, 'so, if you know what's good for you …' A tray laden with pints of beer arrived at that moment, carried by Pete, and Rollo reached for one mid-sentence. You'll drink your beer with us and hope we forget that you ever said that.'

Chapter Seventeen

'LET'S FACE THE MUSIC AND DANCE'
Fred Astaire

The moment Vignoles walked into the reception he knew something was up, for the office had an unnatural stillness to it. There was none of the gentle buzz of office chit-chat or occasional laughter. Mavis was exuding an air of nervous concentration as she bundled foolscap notes together with ties of green string. She immediately looked up, however, met the D.I.'s gaze, and before he could say a word of greeting she mouthed 'Badger' and pointed to his closed office door.

'Oh Lord. How long?'

'The chief superintendent is awaiting your arrival, sir. He has been here a few minutes. I made him a nice cup of tea,' she winked.

'Ah. Good. Well done,' he said, and then, far more softly, 'Wonder what brings him here. Did he say anything?'

'No, sir. Just that as soon as you arrived he wished to see you on a "matter of some importance".' She left the sentence hanging in the air.

'Ah ...' Vignoles took a breath. He re-straightened his tie, rubbed his hand over his chin and checked his jacket. Chief Superintendent Badger was a stickler for appearances. Vignoles was wearing his favourite R.A.F. overcoat and it had got drenched in a sudden stormy downpour, so he now removed it, handing it to Mavis, who turned her nose up at its doggy odour. He was uncertain what to do now with his hat, hesitated and then left it on the desk beside her typewriter. He steeled himself and walked into his office, feeling as if it were no longer his own.

Chief Superintendent Badger, in full uniform and with a shirt starched and ironed like stiff, white cardboard, was sitting rather primly in one of the chairs beside Vignoles's desk. His legs were exactly parallel, both highly polished black shoes were placed exactly side-by-side as he sat bolt upright, his back not touching that of the chair. There was not a shred of relaxation about his small, compact frame. His exuberantly large cap — which Badger clearly adored wearing — lay upturned upon the desk, a pair of white kid leather gloves placed inside. He was holding a porcelain teacup, the one reserved by Mavis for special guests, in his right hand, and this was poised a few inches above the matching saucer in his left. Vignoles was certain that the pose had been struck as soon as Badger's impeccable hearing detected his arrival in the lobby. He was sure that Badger had been straining to catch his conversation with Mavis.

'Ah! Good morning, Charles.' Badger flashed a cool smile, and waited a few seconds as Vignoles saluted in response. He carefully placed the cup and saucer on the desk beside his cap and in the briefest of movements lifted himself a few inches from his chair as if he was going to stand and formally welcome Vignoles, but promptly sat down again, whilst waving his hand to indicate that Vignoles may take a seat.

'Chief superintendent, how nice to see you. Sorry I was not here to welcome you. I was not aware of your impending visit.' Vignoles was nearly always in the office early, but it was typical that that morning he had taken time to pass the time of day with the stationmaster. 'Worse luck,' he thought.

'Quite all right, quite all right. Your secretary furnished me with a most refreshing cup of tea, so that was not a problem.' Despite the chief superintendent's reassuring words, Vignoles noticed that his eyes darted for a few moments to the clock on the wall in silent reproach. 'I wanted to drop in, Charles,' he made it sound like a social visit, thought Vignoles, 'to look over a couple of things that have cropped up.' Badger paused and sniffed sharply, in a manner that had nothing to do with having a cold. 'It came to my attention that you have commandeered the new police motor-car on a number of occasions in the last month. I see you have done so twice in as many weeks. I trust that this was strictly necessary?' He emphasised the last two words with his clipped, mannered voice.

The new Rover was a source of immense interest — and indeed pride — amongst the Leicester Central station staff. Vignoles had been very surprised when it was, unexpectedly, delivered one morning. The salesman dropping the keys and paperwork on his desk, saying that it was 'from the company, sir. The directors of the L.N.E.R. that is, guvnor.' Sure enough, in an aberration of excessive generosity, the board of the L.N.E.R. had purchased a number of these sleek black saloon cars as surplus ex-government stock. As a company, they were in fact quite eager to be seen as forward-thinking, and it seems this stretched to appreciating that even railway police might need a car occasionally. This was a view not shared by Chief Superintendent Badger, who felt that railway police officers who ranked below him — which neatly encompassed all of them — should stick to using the railway. On top of this, Badger was expected to continue to make use his own Humber. Whilst this was characteristically immaculate, it was distinctly pre-war. Badger had made it quite clear that he envied Vignoles this indulgence.

'I hope that you can justify making use of such a valuable resource?'

'It was required sir, for a number of surveillance operations. Essential in fact. I feel that it advanced our understanding of the situation.'

'Ah yes. Surveillance. That is another matter. I notice that you have spent an awful lot of company time, and money, might I add, on these surveillance operations.' Another sniff.

'Well sir, it is part of the detective's work.'

'Maybe. But you know my views on this: I still think that traditional policing is the best. If a man's broken the law, then jolly well move in and arrest the fellow.'

'It's not always quite that easy, sir.' Vignoles's heart was sinking fast. These had been relatively straightforward operations, and had secured arrests. His plan for the Water Street Gang was riddled with flaws. Badger seemed in no mood to be indulgent.

'Hmm. Maybe not. But I shall expect results, of course, Charles. One should be careful — I say this as a colleague, man to man, you understand? One should be careful of falling into the trap of watching every Tom, Dick and Harry go about his daily life in the belief that this is getting results. All too often I find it leads to very little, or takes one down blind alleys, so to speak.'

'Really?' thought Vignoles. 'And when did you ever undertake any surveillance, particularly down a blind alley?' He set his face, however, into one of rapt concentration upon his chief's pearls of wisdom. 'As I said, we are in the business of getting results. I like to see direct action. "Proper policing", as I like to call it. I don't like too much of this shilly-shallying around. We are the railway police, trying to keep law and order on a railway.'

'Indeed we are, sir,' Vignoles nodded gravely, hoping he was not overdoing the act. 'But, as I said, it is not always that easy to achieve results until we can build a strong enough case.'

'Or perhaps the case is not fundamentally strong enough in the first place?'

'Of course, there is always some risk of that.' Vignoles took a deep breath and plunged in, 'but I do think that we are onto something big at the moment, with this Bank of England robbery, sir. We are talking about a considerable fraud operation.'

'Indeed, I read your report. Well, of course, I shall defer to your judgement for the time being. The Bank of England is getting pretty jumpy about the whole matter. They need an arrest, and they need their valuable paper stock returned. We are under pressure to hand the whole case over to the Met.'

'But they are based in London. How on earth could they work at such distance?'

'Agreed. So I could do with something to show them, pretty sharpish.'

'I will try my best, sir. With or without recourse to use of the Rover.'

'Do so. But remember, petrol is getting awfully hard to come by these days, and we need to keep costs down. This new Labour government of ours ...' Badger sniffed again in disapproval. He stressed the word 'Labour' with some contempt, making no pretence that he was a staunch supporter of Mr Churchill and his Conservatives, '...they seem hell bent on saving every farthing they can. They won't last, of course.' Badger spoke the last words quietly and in a dismissive tone, whilst he shifted his body slightly, adjusting the fall of one of the sleeves on his jacket, and brushing away an invisible speck of dust, as if it were Prime Minister Atlee himself. 'However,' Badger continued, shifting the subject away, 'I am always the first to pay tribute when it's due, and I have to say you and your men have done some pretty decent work in recent months, so I have every confidence that you can bring this matter to a rapid conclusion.'

'Thank you. We shall try our best. Some of my officers are women actually, and rather good as well.' Vignoles wondered whether this was the time to broach the subject of rosters.

'Yes? Well, jolly good. Probably brighten the place up a bit, eh?' Badger smiled with a touch of warmth, and an attempt at a weak joke. The lecture was over.

'Now for the real reason you are here', thought Vignoles, abandoning the idea almost immediately. It would have to wait.

'As you know, I am great one for teamwork. It was teamwork that got us through the war, you know. And so it will through these next, rather trying years. Now, I will do all I can to look after us all, the team.'

Where is this leading? thought Vignoles, who realised that he was in mortal danger of nodding off.

'To that end, as you know we are taking a pretty important part in the city's V-Whitsun Day celebrations, in June. Of course this will be a grand affair and inevitably we shall be somewhat overshadowed by the civvies, but that is right and proper.' Badger sniffed again, 'But I feel we need to blow our own trumpets as well, and since the actual V. E. Day anniversary, on the eight of this month, is being somewhat overlooked, I have taken the liberty of inviting a rather important guest to visit, and run his eye over the outfit we operate here. Decent chap. I was at Harrow with him, you know. Given half a chance he will steer us through the mess these bloody socialists will make of the country.'

'And whom may this be, sir…?'

'Sir Anthony Prazen-Beagle, Permanent Under Secretary to the new Minister of Transport. Can't remember the fellow's name…' he waved a dismissive hand.

'Alfred Barnes?'

'Yes. I suppose that must be the one. Well, Sir Anthony is a tremendously important man, Charles. Knows his stuff. Will do us no harm at all to stay in his good books. Sir Anthony can bring some influence, so what I propose is that I bring him to Leicester Central on the morning of the eighth. We may well secure the services of the railway brass band to lend a little colour to the proceedings. Then he can review you and your men and the … er, women, of course. Full dress uniform. Put on a bit of a show, Charles.' Badger smiled and leaned back in the chair, finally looking almost at ease as he delivered the final part of his speech. Vignoles, meanwhile, was wondering what a 'permanent under secretary' did, and if one worked beside, or under, a permanent over secretary.

'Of course,' continued Badger, 'I shall require exclusive use of the force Rover for the duration. A couple of days should cover it. I shall get my man Pedder to collect it the day before, and he can drive Sir Anthony down from London, then after the review he can take us on to my club for the usual: a round of golf and a spot of lunch.'

'Suddenly, petrol is no longer in short supply, when an under secretary is involved,' thought Vignoles. 'He isn't travelling by rail, sir?'

'Good God, no. It's a disgraceful shambles; Sir Anthony would probably arrive here two days late. No, no, no, we must give him the proper red carpet treatment. And that means the new car.'

'Very good, sir. You can count upon our full support.'

'I knew I could. Pedder will forward on the full details of the itinerary.' Badger finally gave vent to a full smile, albeit only briefly, then stood up, sweeping his cap and gloves from the desk in a deft, practised movement. Vignoles stood also, and whilst he was only six foot himself, still appeared to tower over the chief super. They shook hands, and Vignoles opened the office door for him.

'Good day. My man will be in touch.' With that, he placed his cap on his close-cropped head, gave the smallest of nods to Vignoles, and promptly strode out of the building.

'Well, looks like we have a V.I.P. guest, and all the pomp and circumstance that accompanies it, on our hands.' Vignoles was speaking to Mavis. 'Oh dear. Expect a letter or a wire from the chief super's secretary, Pedder, with all the details.'

With that, Vignoles put the whole visit to the back of his mind and retreated to what was now exclusively his own office and slumped in his swivel chair. Strange, swirling patterns of light were playing upon the walls as a weak ray of sun cut through the rivulets of rainwater flooding over the skylights. He stared up and watched it form first tiny streamlets then suddenly join with another, and then another, to create a river. Sometimes the rivers would, in turn, suddenly diverge as if they had encountered an invisible island and went their own ways, before reaching the edge of the glass. He was struck by the way that the water never took the same course, for it was endlessly altering and changing, but ultimately reaching the same destination. It was bit like the investigation, he realised. So much was already known, but he could put this information together in different ways, and each time that he did it took him down a different course, different choices needing to made with each new route, and yet they all lead to the same conclusion: a gang of counterfeiters, who needed to be caught.

It was still raining at the end of the working day, when Vignoles was standing with Anna on the island platform at Leicester Central. The rain was drumming down in torrents upon the glass roof, pouring in noisy streams out of the drainpipes and through any gaps it could find, of which there were many since numerous panes of glass were still missing following the air raids of a few years ago. Water was splashing into a pool beside them, running across the platform and spilling over the white painted edge onto the running line. 'It's like a very big dog is peeing,' observed Vignoles.

Anna nudged him. 'What a thing to say!' but she laughed. 'I don't want to meet that dog,' she added, and glanced over her shoulder as if expecting the giant animal to be approaching. She sighed, 'Oh, what weather. The sun couldn't last, I suppose.' Anna looked back across the railway to the city rooftops, which seemed blacker and drearier that evening.

'Indeed. Here's our train.' Vignoles watched it approach through the downpour. The rain was like a pale curtain of silver through which the train was tearing its way. The strange daylight rendering the colours not so much as colours, but rather degrees of wetness. He noted that the locomotive was an A5 express tank. Despite its dreary title, it was a handsome machine, with rectangular water tanks that cradled the chunky boiler and formed part of the sides of the enclosed cab, the whole effect giving it a look of solidity and power. The crew could be glimpsed inside the haven of their cab, through the distinctive, triple-arched windows and door. He made a mental note of the number whilst opening a carriage door for Anna, both of them trying to avoid a flow of grubby water that spilled from the carriage roof. The compartment windows were misted up with condensation and the floor had an unattractive, slimy wetness. They sat side by side on the musty seat cushions that were lumpy with long usage. It was impossible to see anything of the world outside, especially for Vignoles as his glasses were steaming up, so Anna delved into her handbag and pulled out the latest copy of *The Illustrated London News*.

'Look at these lovely new designs for interiors.' She had flipped through the pages with the air of someone familiar with the contents, opening a double-page spread across their knees. 'I really like this look for the living room. What do you think?' She glanced across at Vignoles with her most winning smile.

Vignoles groaned, but still smiled indulgently. 'What have you seen now, my dear?' He looked down at the magazine. 'Create a fresh, clean look for our modern homes…,' read the headline, '…and still know that you are doing your bit to save our scarce resources.' Three photographs demonstrating how austerity design furniture could be combined to best effect illustrated the article.

'Hmm. Well, they look pretty smart, I must say.'

'Yes, and the living room appears so much bigger. Fresher, don't you think? Without all that chunky, lumpy stuff we have.' He looked again at the photograph of the 'ideal living room' with its simple, angular but comfy-looking chairs and the sofa with just the slightest curve to the tops of the arms. A low bookshelf was placed under the windowsill. It had four shelves, vertically divided down the centre, the uppermost one with a kind of low retaining wall around three sides to prevent items being knocked off.

'I like the bookshelf,' he said, realising that he was probably about to enter a conversation that would ultimately prove costly.

'Exactly. Simple but elegant. I think your books would look good on them.'

'Oh, steady on girl. I didn't say anything about buying one,' although he knew it was probably already a lost cause.

'And if we throw those great, ugly, heavy things out, imagine how nice our little room will look with these. Much bigger and more "moderno".'

'Well ... that would be no bad thing, as our little house is just that. Little.' He was now studying the pictures of the 'new model kitchen' and the dining room. It had a simple, square table, slender-legged wooden chairs with three slightly-splayed, vertical rods reaching to the curved backs, and a simple sideboard with double doors.

'So you approve?' Anna was squeezing his arm and nestling her head against his shoulder. He could smell her scent and her hair. It was difficult to make a stand under such testing conditions.

'In principle I can see what you are getting at.'

'But?'

'But there are all the blessed coupons we would need.'

'But we have plenty. We've bought almost no furniture and neither have our parents. They've collected heaps of coupons. I know: I have them all at home.'

'What?' His wife continually surprised him. 'You asked my parents for their coupons? Good Lord. What did they say?'

'They were quite amenable. They never say no to me.' She pulled away gently and gave him a broad smile, and then retuned to her position nestling against his shoulder. Vignoles just gently shook his head in response and fished his pipe from the breast pocket of his jacket.

'But, coupons aside, there is still a cost. I have no idea how much all this is, but a pretty penny, I am sure. What with the mortgage, I'm not so sure we can afford it, and then —' he was about to mention the rumour of mass dismissals, but stopped himself,

'Of course not, I was not suggesting we buy all of it at once, but we could make a start. With my job and yours, we don't do so very badly. Anyway, I was thinking, we could maybe even borrow some money. There are so many good offers nowadays. Some of the girls at work have been talking about this.'

'Borrow? Oh no, that's out of the question.'

'Listen. Not so fast. You can borrow anything, £5, £20, maybe even £50'.

'Fifty pounds? Steady on!'

'All right, it was just to illustrate. Anyway, you can pay back a little each a week. We've been looking at some leaflets in work and —'

'— Wait a moment!' Vignoles looked deep in thought, his brow furrowed, then he suddenly sat bolt upright, and Anna was forced to raise her head and look at him. 'Sorry, Anna, but what leaflets are these? Can you show me one?'

'Ho ho! You are eager.'

'No, Anna, no, that's not it. Where did you find them? And when?'

'This week, I think. Geraldine who works with me in the office, she was the one, she had it pushed through her letterbox.'

'Where does she live?'

Anna looked at him, 'There's something wrong?'

'I'm not sure, but something is nagging me about all this.'

'Well, she lives in Charwelton. She lives on a farm — her father being a farmer. But Gerry joined the railways for the war work, and stayed. She can't afford to move nearer. Who can? I suppose she likes to dream, like anyone does, and saw the chance to borrow. Get set up in a little place in town. You know how it is.'

Vignoles nodded, but not in approval of Geraldine's hopes for a small flat in Leicester. He was thinking, chasing elusive thoughts that hinted at connections; like the rivulets of water on his skylight, little oddments of information were passing through his mind, and he knew that if he could just hold enough of them together for long enough, he might be able to see clearly what they were.

Earlier that day, P.C. Blencowe, W.P.C. Lansdowne and he had spent an hour looking at a map, upon which Blencowe had plotted with coloured pins, all the government surplus stock auctions in the last few months that Lansdowne had traced in the local papers, plus the regular car auctions. Leicester had hosted an event, Rugby and

Lutterworth another each. Banbury was marked as well. Lansdowne had stumbled upon the auction of tractors and heavy machinery in Banbury by sheer chance, after reading that week's *Banbury Cake*, discarded on top of the pile of papers the cleaners had removed from a train. Some diligent follow-up work by Vignoles and Trinder, telephoning the auctioneers, armed with Trinder's list of phoney names, had called up some fascinating results. At least three persons with names that matched those of bandleaders had made substantial cash purchases. One auctioneer had listened in mounting disbelief as he realised that he'd accepted £400 from Mr Glenn Miller, for two Bedford trucks, both of which were now being investigated in a major fraud investigation. However, he had also strenuously sought to reassure Vignoles that he had been 'quite satisfied with the cash', and explained that all profits had already been reinvested in more stock. 'He's already spent the money is what he's saying.'

'And so the money filters into the system. Cash changing hands before the banks even see it, and we lose the trail. But the buck always stops somewhere, sir. Along the way, some poor sod gets stung with a wad of fake paper.' Trinder had observed this wryly as they had left the auction rooms. There was something about this comment that was tugging at Vignoles now, as he sat beside his wife in the steamed-up railway carriage.

'Look, about all this ...' he gestured at the magazine, 'It's a nice idea and maybe we can look into how we can afford it. But right now, two things: your friends must not even think about entering into any kind of deal with moneylenders, no matter how professional they might seem. Seriously; they can go to the banks if they really must, one is far safer with them.'

'Safer? What from?'

'These loan sharks. They charge extortionate rates of interest, but also there is something else, even worse. I'd like to see any of these leaflets if you have one?'

Anna rootled around in her handbag and pulled out a neatly folded single sheet, with 'The Super Fast Loan Company' printed in bold red letters on cream paper.

'Have any of the girls contacted them?'

'I think not.'

'Thank goodness.' Vignoles was reading the leaflet, and looking for an address. 'It does not really say very much, just a phone number. Hmm ...' He looked thoughtful, 'I wonder?'

'Is this something to do with the case you are working on?' Anna looked curiously at Vignoles; she could sense that he was being more than just cautious.

'I can't say for sure,' he frowned as he thought about his answer, 'but I have a feeling that perhaps it could be. If these are just beginning to appear in the same week ....' He was speaking quietly, thinking aloud. 'You know, I rather like the idea of getting "Mr Speedy Loans" to come and give us a call.'

'What? I thought you said ...?'

'Don't worry, I have absolutely no intention of borrowing a bent farthing from him, but I would like to hear what he has to say, and get a good look at him. But he may be clever enough to make a few simple checks before he visits a house and, if he did so, then he would soon discover my position in the police force. So, do you think you could ask Geraldine if we may pretend to inhabit her house, whilst she and her family make themselves scarce for ten minutes? We can lure him there under a false name.'

'Ooh yes. I am sure she would a love that. An undercover investigation in her very own front parlour, very exciting!'

'I am not expecting anything terribly thrilling to happen, Anna. Far from it; we must act quite normally — as if we are considering a loan for new furniture, perhaps,' he smiled ruefully at his wife, 'but it would be a useful exercise. If she agrees, let me have her address and I shall arrange a time. Tomorrow evening would be ideal.'

'I shall telephone Geraldine as soon as we get back.'

'And here we are.' Vignoles jumped up: he realised that the train was slowing and entering their station. He pulled down the window and grimaced as he got a face full of rain. His glasses were splattered with water drops and he needed to put one hand on his hat to stop it being whipped away by the wind. As he swung the door open, the woman guard was calling out the station name.

'Belgrave and Birstall! Belgrave and Birstall!'

Chapter Eighteen

'LEANING ON A LAMP POST'
George Formby

Edward was walking towards the mess rooms — the 'hellholes', as he and Simon had christened them — but realised that he was not in the mood to squeeze into this grubby and cramped space, so decided he would just fetch a mug of tea and then sit on one of the benches that were placed along the walls inside the running shed. He was passing a long line of ex-war department heavy freight engines. They were ungainly machines, with little refinement and hard to like — but they demanded a kind of respect in their own brutish way. One of these engines was being attended to by a group of men, who were attacking it with some force: wielding a hammer and the largest spanner Edward had ever seen. It was as if the locomotive's unappealing looks were inviting an aggressive response. He glared at the engines as he passed, unwilling to even check if he had noted their numbers before. He was out of sorts with engines today.

It had been, all told, a trying morning, and yet one that had started with plenty of promise when Reedy had given him the order to be one of the 'fire droppers'. A fire dropper had to set the fires in a number of engines, coaxing heat into the cold water within their boilers. He had to produce a modest amount of steam pressure ready for when the firemen came on duty and took over. Edward had been given two small tank engines and one of these massive Austerity machines to fire. This was his chance, the first real step on the way up.

A cleaner could expect to be introduced to every aspect of the cleaning, preparation and maintenance of an engine. This included setting the fire, starting to get up steam first thing in the morning and the disposal and cleaning of the fires at the end of the working day. If he could become a regular fire dropper, it was a good step towards that of fireman. In practice, however, it had felt like a giant leap backwards.

Everything seemed to go wrong from the start. The kindling he fetched was wet. Thunder during the night had ended in a downpour, and even now a gentle, soaking drizzle was in the air. No matter where Edward searched, he couldn't find any kindling wood stored under cover. He had been forced to collect unsuitably damp sticks and slimy, wet coals. He just knew that this was going to be a struggle. Yet all around him fires were starting to glow, coaxed by experienced hands into flame. He was lagging behind, but this just made him more nervous and liable to make mistakes. He started with the Austerity as this was the biggest challenge, and made a pile of wood deep inside the firebox, which involved climbing right inside through the fire hole used to feed the coals into the fire. It was claustrophobic and unpleasant, taking a lot of wriggling to get inside. Then, whilst reaching back onto the footplate for the kindling, he banged his forehead, and then his elbow. This did nothing for his mood. The dark firebox was oppressive and his candle threw disturbing shadows that confused him. He clambered back out into the relief of the fresher air and realised he had forgotten to fetch the oily cotton waste to start the fire. When finally he threw the burning bundle onto the wood, it just created a vast cloud of a greenish, eye-stinging smoke that filled the cab, forcing him to lean over the side to gulp air. Then it went out. He repeated this exercise a few times to no real effect until, in desperation, he poured paraffin onto the smoke-blackened but still damp, wood. This caused a huge fireball that sent flames licking outside the firebox door and created a terrific stink. He threw a few wet coals into the conflagration but they skidded all over the place, and just scattered the kindling into a pathetic disarray of sticks. To make matters worse, the fireman himself climbed aboard at that moment, placing his white enamel teakettle on the metal shelf above the firedoor, and with a sceptical glance inside, asked, 'What's that?' It was not a question that needed an answer. He shook his head with a look that made Edward wish he were somewhere else, and promptly climbed back out, tossing a parting comment across the cab floor, 'Back in ten. Better get a real fire in there, or else I'll flippin' put you on it.'

Things did not improve, however. After more random coals and the liberal use of paraffin, there was some kind of a glow, but the fire bars were showing through all over the place, and he found that he just could not manage to get the shovel to place the coal anywhere useful. He resorted to throwing lumps on by hand, but scorched his eyebrows as a result of peering too hard into the fire.

'Oh hell. Stupid, stupid bloody fire!' Edward was now running hopelessly late, and despite the fire in the Austerity being inadequate, he really had to commence the whole operation again in one of the tank engines parked behind. This went slightly better, the smaller firebox making the fire easier to control, but he had not even started on the third locomotive. He quickly clambered back into the Austerity to see if he could leave it to its own devices, but the fire was a miserable, smoking affair. He threw some more coal on in desperation and, in a deep gloom, leaned over the cab side and looked to see if a friendly face was to hand. As luck would have it, Margi was passing at that moment.

'Hello Eddie. You all right? You look a bit bothered.'

'Oh, don't ask. Actually I could do with some help.'

'No problem, love.' At which, she climbed up the high cab steps with well-practised ease, glanced at the fire, winced and then set to with the shovel. Her fluid and deft movements rapidly saw the holes filled by an even spread of coal. It looked effortless, and Edward observed how she moved with the minimum of fuss and a gracefulness that he envied.

'How do you make it look so easy?'

'Practice. Lots of it. Look, I'm not supposed to do this, but all of us girls know how to because there's not enough men to light all the fires. Here, you try and I'll give you some coaching.'

As he tried, clumsily, to scoop up the coal, which immediately jumped off the shovel and scattered on the floor, she stepped beside him, grasping his forearms and moving them into a better position. He could feel the shape of her body press against his back, and a trace of scent even above the fumes on the footplate. He liked the sensation of a woman so close and her hands holding him. He was sure his face was burning, along with the now-roaring fire. At that moment the fireman's head popped over the edge of the cab floor as he climbed the steps. Edward's heart sank.

'Blinkin' 'eck. Got a woman in your arms already, 'ave yer? Oh no, sorry, my mistake — it's the other way round.' He shook his head in disbelief and contempt, then peered into the fire and grunted. 'Not bad, for a woman. But put that kid down — he's too flippin' young.' He gave Margi a lingering look and then proceeded to check the gauges, as if neither Margi nor Edward were there. Margi pulled away from Edward and pulled a face towards the back of the grumpy fireman,

'Never you mind him, Eddie. He started at the bottom, just like you,' and in a lower voice, but perfectly loud enough to be overheard, added, 'and he took a mighty long time making the grade, from what I hear.'

He made a noise that sounded like 'humph'.

Things remained tense and uneasy, with Margi staying to help Edward for a few more minutes. He was both relieved and yet embarrassed by this. She really knew her stuff and got the fire into a decent shape, and she was undoubtedly a dab hand at shovelling. At the same time, he was very aware that he had not only failed, but he had lost face. He didn't like the way the man looked and spoke with Margi, but Edward also felt uncomfortable that he had been caught being shown how to shovel with her arms wrapped around him. He knew the unfriendly fireman would soon tell everyone, suitably embellishing the facts, and he was going to get ribbed mercilessly for it. He knew it was stupid and a bit ungrateful of him to think like this, but it was hard not to.

Edward had then, with Margi's help, turned his attention to the two little tank locomotives. Margi had offered to get something going in the as-yet-unlit third engine whilst Edward single-handedly forced the other fire into some semblance of a blaze. He was fortunate that the engine Margi was hurriedly preparing was the relief shed pilot, and its failure to be ready exactly on time was met by its crew with a grin and an excuse for another cup of tea. This was good fortune and he would be lucky to get away with it again. He had very nearly delayed three engines from working that morning.

Following this experience, Edward was relieved to end the morning on lamp preparation. At least he knew how to do this work and so just kept his head down and concentrated on not making any mistakes. So now he was more than ready for his sandwiches as he sat on a rickety bench. As he did so, he noticed that close beside him, sitting at a careworn card table, were two men with a newspaper spread out between them on the faded and ripped green baize. Edward glanced across and guessed that they were footplate men, a driver and fireman by the look of them, as one was much the older. He looked away and stared into his tea feeling lost and rather forlorn.

He began to think that maybe baking bread and piping 'Special Delight' into puff pastry horns was not so very bad after all. Edward needed to recover some confidence and belief in his abilities. He suddenly wished that he could talk to these skilled men, seek some friendly advice from them. Perhaps he could gather a few hints about how to try and make a better job of firing? He looked across at them, but only briefly. It was bad form to talk with engine crew, that's what

Simon had told him. Cleaners were expected to know their place and keep quiet. He looked away but still found himself eavesdropping in on their conversation above the clangs and bangs of the engine shed and the thunderous roar of the coaling stage.

They were talking about horse racing, a subject that Edward had no interest in except for one curious aspect; he knew the names of the Derby and St Leger winners dating back to the 1850s. It was a skill that had so far proved to have no value at all as a conversational aid, and of little obvious importance to anyone. Edward had gained this knowledge through enquiring about the curious assortment of names carried by the L.N.E.R. A3 Pacific locomotives. The company directors were clearly very fond of the Derby and St Leger horse races, and chose the winners as the names for their splendid engines. In working out the significance of the names, Edward had made a long list of each and every winner, compiled with the help of his grandfather, who was dedicating his life to trying (and failing) to make his fortune with a once-a-week shilling bet. Edward had become quite fond of the curious names which tripped off his tongue like a sonorous poem: Fifinella, Pommern, Durbar and Aboyeur; Book Law, Fairway, Trigo and Singapore. He learnt them by heart, carrying the exercise forward each year in anticipation that future engines might be given the names of the more recent winners. It could have proven more useful to master the complexities of long division sums or even how to wield a shovel, but that was Edward.

So, as Edward listened, when he heard the older man mention a horse called Ocean Swell, he butted in, without stopping to think about what he was doing. 'Oh yes, I know that one. Won the Derby in 1944. Was foaled from Blue Peter, the 1939 winner.'

'Eh? Were we talking to you?' It was the younger and distinctly more aggressive looking one, who gave but the merest glance towards Edward as he spoke and then turned back to his paper.

'Hang on, Rollo. How come you know so much then, eh, laddie?' The older man was holding his mug above the paper and looking curiously at Edward. He had a thick, slightly drooping walrus moustache, and kindly, if watery, eyes.

'Oh, well I just do.' Edward immediately regretted opening his mouth. He was also struck by a terrible realisation. The younger of the two men was surely the one he had seen handing money to Mr Reed.

'Bully for you! What are you? An escapee from the blinkin' Brains Trust or something?'

'Not so fast.' It was the driver speaking, 'So, you know your horses, do you? You study form?' He winked at Rollo and continued. 'Would you like to pass on any tips? We like backing winners.' He laughed in a voice that sounded like it came from a lifetime of smoking.

'I just know the Derby and St Leger winners ...' Edward tailed off. This was not going right at all. He wished the ground would just swallow him up.

'Ho ho! We don't mind them at all. I'll test you...'

'Jesus. Give it a break. Don't encourage the brat.' Rollo almost spat the words out.

'... as I was saying before my friend so rudely interrupted,' he grinned at Rollo, 'so: "Spearmint". Give me a date.'

'1906, Epsom Derby. Sired Royal Lancer, St Leger winner 1922.' Edward's learning by rote was saving him for a few more moments. He gulped down his tea. Hands shaking a little.

'Ve-ry good. OK, 1934. Who won the Derby?'

'Windsor Lad, won the St Leger as well. It was the name given to ... oh, nothing.'

The two men exchanged glances. Then Rollo turned to Edward, his voice superficially friendly, but hinting at menace. 'Fancy yourself as a bit of an expert, don't you? So how about something useful for a change? I don't give a monkey's arse who won what in nineteen blinkin' thirty-four. Who's gonna win this afternoon? Any race will do.'

'Oh, I can't say.'

'Or won't?'

'No, sir, it's not like that. Oh dear ... I just know the ones that are ...' he tailed off in dismay.

'Come on, don't be shy now. You're cocky enough to butt in on our conversation, so make yourself useful.'

'No, really ... I just know the past Derby and St Leger's ...'

'They'll do. Tell me, laddie,' this was spoken quietly, and in an encouragingly persuasive tone, 'are you working for someone? Placing a few bets, if you catch my drift? We like a flutter and we can pay you the odd shilling if you tip us a winner, know what I mean?' it was the older man speaking, who winked conspiratorially at Edward.

'I'm sorry. I only know them because,' Edward gulped, 'they're the names of the A3s.' Edward felt his face flush.

'A3s? What, the engines? Oh, I don't believe this. Lad, just drink yer tea and shut up!'

'Yes, sir.' Edward's face burned and he stared at the floor in utter despair. The two men, however, seemed to forget about the matter almost immediately, and apart from one sidelong glance at Eddie, that came with a contemptuous smirk, they resumed their conversation. Edward wanted to get up and leave, but somehow found it felt less embarrassing to just sit there and try to make himself look small.

However, he was increasingly convinced that these were the crew of the train that appeared to have dropped the bag of money. Edward was sure that the one called Rollo was the same. He recalled the way the man had leaned with his elbow on the cab side looking backwards, as the train had moved past. Edward needed to forget about his embarrassment and concentrate. He must listen, observe and try to take in what he could. He tuned into the conversation again then suddenly almost jolted upright. Rollo mentioned the empty brick train for Calvert on Saturday. This was it! They were talking about the very same train. Edward made himself appear engrossed in some litter swirling in a gentle circle on the floor, whilst sharpening his hearing.

'So we are all rostered together, which is good. Reed has done us proud, as ever.'

'Yeah, he's a good man. Hope we get a good run.'

'How many more you reckon?'

'Four, maybe five. Then we cut loose. Top Link likes to change things around. Less risk that way.'

'I'm looking forward to that. I'm not minded to keep on much longer. It's time to hang up my old cap.' The man laughed, but without a lot of mirth.

'There's plenty more steam in you, Ken. But seriously, just another month or so, then that's it.'

'Not long then. Good, I'll be glad.'

Edward stole another furtive glance at the two men, taking a careful note of their appearance, then transferred his gaze to some welding taking place on a locomotive tender close by.

'I'll look out for you in the meantime. I just wonder if Jimmy's still up to it? He was wanting out the other night.'

'He's a professional railwayman. It's ingrained into us, this sense of duty to the railway, Rollo. You know that.'

'But this is not strictly railway business, is it?'

'True. But what I mean is, when he say's he'll do something, he'll see it through. We all feel the nerves a bit. That's all. Well, time to get on: we've got a train waiting.' With that, the two men stood up, Rollo, picking up the newspaper, rolled it up into a tube and made to put it under his arm, but then he stopped.

'Oy! Brains Trust! Have a look — check out the horses and try to choose right. Put your mind to something useful.' He threw the newspaper across to Edward.

'Oh! Thank you.' Edward was startled by the intervention and the well-meaning gesture. Perhaps this angry chap was not so bad after all? Edward was confused by the whole incident and so remained seated for a while longer after they had walked away, thinking through all that he had heard and that had happened. He looked around, wondering where Simon was. He needed to see what he made of it all.

The radio suddenly started to play, amplified through the tannoy system rigged up in the rafters when the war had started. It was blasting out a rather tinny and crackly *Workers' Playtime*, much to the delight of a gang of cleaners, led by none other than his other new friend, Mary. She was leading them to their next job — a locomotive named 'Manchester United' — which was looking typically filthy and careworn, with Mary marching along to the music carrying a metal 'Not to be Moved' sign on a pole. She waved this in time to the music as if it were a flag, whilst her motley crew of young men and women tagged behind, carrying boxes of rags, pumice and brick dust, metal scrapers and other tools of their grimy trade. With their caps and raggedly matching blue uniforms belted around their waists, and knotted neckerchiefs, they looked like some ragtag partisan brigade. This image combined with the sound of 'Leaning on a Lamp Post' being sung by George Formby on the radio, caused Edward to burst into laughter, and in so doing released the tension and frustration of the morning.

Chapter Nineteen

'IT'S A PITY TO SAY GOODNIGHT'
Ella Fitzgerald

Charwelton railway station was a short walk from the tiny clutch of buildings that formed the village. Vignoles and Anna had only to walk past the stone cross of the War Memorial and over the tiny Pack Horse Bridge spanning the narrow river, and they were already at Geraldine's house.

It was a striking building, made of the warm, golden-ochre ironstone so typical of Northamptonshire and, upon first impressions, looked of considerable size. The steeply-pitched, slated roof towered above them, with three tall, brick chimney-stacks adding to the impression of immense height. Nine windows of varying sizes punctuated the long front wall of the house, all placed with a delightful lack of precision that lent the house an informality that was most attractive. All the windows had tiny, leaded panes of glass, a number of which were opened to the cool evening air.

They walked past a green-painted gate that gave a glimpse into a garden filled with rows of vegetables, fruit bushes and swathes of flowers in a glorious jumble. But whilst this side entrance was almost certainly that used by Geraldine and her parents, Anna ushered her husband further along the pavement towards the impressive front door. Two stone pillars were set into the wall supporting a small, flat roof formed by a slab of the same golden stone, barely deep enough to shelter a cat from the rain on the step, but the effect was impressive, nonetheless. The front door was a faded black and in need of some fresh paint, but the heavy brass knocker was clearly recently polished, with traces of Brasso staining the paintwork around the base.

It was unnecessary, however, for either of them to spoil the deep shine of the brasswork by using it, for their approach had been both anticipated and observed by the occupants, and the door opened even as they set eyes upon it. They were greeted by a short, fresh and rosy-faced young woman, dressed in a smart navy skirt set off by a cream-and-maroon cardigan, knitted in a fine wool. She blushed as she introduced herself to Vignoles, then she kissed Anna on the cheek. He realised that he recognised her face from Leicester Central, although he had not spoken with her.

Geraldine was excitable, speaking quickly in a hushed voice, as if in fear of eavesdroppers. There was no doubt that she was enjoying the opportunity to help with Vignoles's investigation. He just hoped that she would curb her enthusiasm sufficiently to not ruin the deception. Geraldine bustled them through into the front parlour, the whole time talking quickly, advising Vignoles that her parents were banished outside onto the farm until she gave them leave to return, and that she would retreat to the back kitchen, staying as 'quiet as a mouse' the whole time. She went on to give Anna instructions about where to find tea and milk in the kitchen and that a seed-cake was ready, finishing her rapid-fire chatter with a question as to whether 'that would be enough?'

'Geraldine, please. We have no intention of offering this man anything other than the vague promise of some business. We don't want him to spend the evening with us.' Vignoles smiled, nonetheless.

'But we simply can't welcome a visitor here and offer nothing, it would be a terribly poor show.'

'I can assure you, you need have no such fears. This is a business meeting taking only a few minutes, not a social call. Indeed, brevity will be required. I have heard how these fellows can conduct themselves, and we will do nothing to encourage him to stay,' Vignoles glanced at his wife and the clearly-excited Geraldine, over the top of his glasses, 'In fact we may have to create a diversion to make him leave.'

They finally managed to encourage their hostess to retreat to the kitchen, only after a promise that, if the salesman threatened to overstay his welcome, Anna would — with a pre-arranged signal — summon her friend to the front door to create a diversion. Vignoles and Anna now had a few moments left to take in the surroundings of what was to be their 'home' for a brief while. The furniture was elderly, and solidly made in a style befitting a farming family. Whilst it lacked refinement, it had a definite charm, suiting perfectly the low ceilings and simple, lime-plastered walls. Everything was also spotless. Scrubbed and polished to within an inch of its life. There were few concessions to modernity, the whole house feeling like something from the last century. Vignoles, however, recalled that the dial of a large radiogram had glowed welcomingly in the kitchen when they arrived, and he had caught the rich, plummy voice of the announcer declaring: 'This is London...' as Geraldine guided them into the front parlour. He could just hear the soft tones of the evening news in the background. The rug on the dark, polished floorboards was very old and a little faded, but again scrupulously clean. Everywhere smelled of beeswax polish. A clock ticked on the mantelshelf, framed by two porcelain figures, one of a shepherd, the other a shepherdess. Both figures had white, glassy faces and pink, rouged cheeks, and were standing beside a lamb, smooth and polished, and not in the least bit woolly.

Anna sat on a high-backed chair beside the fireplace, and Vignoles perched on a small sofa, unwilling to lean back for fear of dislodging the lace antimacassars. A small fire was burning, lit specially for their visit. It was smoking slightly, as it was unlikely that it had seen a match in many months. The cast-iron fire surround was lead-blacked to a depth and richness of colour that only hours of hard work could produce. Small hunting prints were suspended by tiny chains from the picture rail, whilst above that, a narrow shelf ran right around the room, leaving just enough space between it and the low roof beams, to support a variety of gaily-coloured porcelain plates, the work of various English potteries.

Vignoles was listening for the approach of a motor-car, but could hear only a blackbird singing in the garden outside and the slow, heavy beats of a locomotive hauling what sounded like a long goods' train through the station. A few minutes later, however, a motorbike engine buzzed and spluttered, then stopped. It had pulled up in the yard to the side of the Fox and Hounds pub, right next door to the house they were in.

Interesting. Vignoles had not considered the possibility of a motorcycle as the salesman's mode of transport. A few minutes later there was the sound of footsteps outside and a heavy, hollow knock on the front door. Vignoles opened it and saw a dapper man, aged perhaps in his mid thirties, wearing a navy pinstriped suit, a brightly striped silk tie and a yellow and red polka-dotted handkerchief flopped foppishly from the breast pocket. His hair was brilliantined flat to his head and shone in the late evening light as he lifted his hat.

'Good evening. Mr Greenway?'

'Good evening. Indeed, yes. Do come in.'

'And a rather pleasing evening it is too, if I may say so, Mr

Greenway. So much nicer than the rain, don't you think?'

'Quite so, quite so ... after you, Mr ... Mr?' Vignoles indicated the open door into the front parlour, whilst taking care to stand in the corridor leading to the back kitchen that concealed Geraldine. They entered the room and Anna was standing before them, her hand outstretched in greeting.

'Mr Prenton. Pleased to meet you. But please, do call me Peter. I'd rather not stand on ceremony.' He shook Anna's hand. Anna smiled slightly in return.

'Take a seat.' Vignoles indicated a chair opposite the sofa, on the other side of the fireplace to where Anna was now seated. This gave Vignoles an excellent view of his subject.

'So, you have invited me here because you may wish to avail yourselves of one of our loan packages. You made a wise choice with Speedy Loans, as we can offer an instant cash advance, at pretty advantageous rates, all things considering.'

'Indeed? We are considering the possibility. So what, Mr Prenton, are the advantageous rates, exactly?'

'Peter, please. Well, we can make a cash advance in a matter of hours. Perhaps even immediately if the sum is modest, and —'

'— And the repayment terms are what, exactly?'

'Well Mr Greenway, I prefer to not discuss these, ah, um, details,' he cleared his throat slightly, 'until we have looked at the ...', he carefully weighed his words with obvious effect, '... exact measure of the financial deal. You see, I am also authorised by the company to consider special rates for different levels of business, so I would not wish to prejudice any decision you may make at this stage by talking about rates of interest.' He smiled at Vignoles and Anna, but his eyes had a hungry look behind them. In the smallest of gestures, but one not missed by Vignoles, Prenton flicked his tongue to the corner of his mouth, and licked his lower lip. Vignoles was immediately and unpleasantly reminded of the snake in Kipling's *Jungle Book*. He had a vision of the salesman turning his head from side to side, flicking his tongue, whilst hypnotising his prey with his eyes. 'You were looking to secure further funds for what, might I ask?'

Vignoles was shaken out of the image by the question, and was vague in his reply, 'We are thinking of some improvements to the farm.'

'And some new furniture, to make the place a little more contemporary,' added Anna. Vignoles smiled indulgently towards his wife, and then winked conspiratorially towards Prenton.

'Actually, I have my eye on a new diesel tractor, but my wife is more interested in domestic matters.'

'I understand. Perhaps we might be able to accommodate both needs? But,' Prenton turned towards Anna, 'do I detect an accent?' His smile was almost a leer.

'Ah, yes,' Anna gave a faint smile, 'I have Italian parents.'

'So, back to business, Mr Prenton. How long have you been with Speedy Loans?' Vignoles was looking intently at the man opposite.

'A number of years. I am the most senior member of the sales team,' he shifted his position slightly. 'I can make all the relevant decisions in helping advance you funds. So, what level of financial assistance were you considering Mr Greenway?'

But Vignoles returned Prenton's question with another, 'During the war? Surprising? It must have been a hard time for your line of business?'

'We managed. People always need money, Mr Greenway.' Prenton smiled weakly and looked as though the wind had been rather taken from his sails. Vignoles wanted to press the advantage a little more.

'But you look a fit and healthy man, if I may say so, Mr Prenton...'

'Peter.'

'... and surely pushing loans was hardly a reserved occupation? So where did you serve during the war?'

'I ... well ... of course I had to take a bit of a break from this work,' he smiled weakly, 'I was with the R.A.F., radio operator, y'know? What I meant was, that I was with the company since before the war, and now have picked things up where I left off.'

'I see. So it is a well-established company?' Vignoles smiled warmly; he did not wish to frighten him off.

'Oh yes! You can have complete faith in our integrity.'

'Where are you based, exactly?' Vignoles produced the flyer from a pocket, and made a show of studying it, 'I just can't quite place your office from this ...' He looked over his glasses at Prenton.

'The head office is just a small affair, strictly just for admin. You see, we prefer the direct approach, taking time to come to our clients' premises for the more personal angle. A far better service, we find.'

'But surely that takes an awful lot of time?' asked Anna.

'But time well spent. At least in my experience.' Prenton had regained his composure and beamed at the two of them. 'We find it rewards the effort. So, how might we help you?' He leaned forward in his chair, pulling out a silver cigarette case in a deft, confident movement, flipping it open and holding it out, 'Cigarette? They're Moroccan. Strong, but rather fine.'

They accepted one each. Vignoles preferred his pipe, but wanted to appear sociable, and Anna, who almost never smoked, also felt that it might help keep the salesman off his guard. Vignoles noticed how Prenton had managed to side-step the question of the exact location of the office, and was now furthering the distraction, by making a show of lighting Anna's cigarette.

'We have made no decision on the exact level of borrowing, Peter, and you should not expect one this evening. These matters require careful consideration, of course.'

'Of course.'

'But we are thinking of a sum of say ... one hundred pounds?' Anna made a good job of disguising choking with shock at her husband's words, by staring at the cigarette and then coughing as if it were too strong.

'They do pack a punch. Take a little getting used to, I'm afraid,' Prenton was looking at Anna, but Vignoles could see that he had caught the salesman's full attention, hook, line and sinker.

'Would this substantial sum pose a problem for Speedy Loans?'

Prenton carefully composed himself with studied calm, settled back into his chair and took a long drag on the cigarette, 'Not in the slightest. This is well within our means. I could even have the amount in question with you by the morning.'

'That will not be necessary. I shall need to consider your terms before making a final decision. But now you have the scope of the loan perhaps you might like to advise me of these terms, and the securities you require.' It was Vignoles's turn to sit back and take a mouthful of the acrid smoke. Prenton's snake-like eyes flicked across towards Anna and he coughed politely, as if unwilling to discuss financial matters in front of her. Anna read the signal and stood up, 'Tea?' and, without waiting to hear their answer, left the room.

'The terms on one hundred pounds would be most favourable, Mr Greenway. We can look at ...' he made a show of calculating in his mind a percentage rate, '... just twenty-five percent, compound, repayable in weekly instalments. I can make the exact calculations now,' and pulled a pocket book from his jacket.

'No need. You can furnish me with this next week — by post. I prefer everything in writing, so I can see everything is above board.'

'I see.' A flicker of a frown played across Prenton's face, but he recovered quickly. 'I can deliver it by hand ... but look, I could, between you and me, advance the full amount now. We can sort the details out later.'

'No. Absolutely not.' Vignoles was thinking rapidly. It might be useful to take the money now and run some checks upon it, but he stopped himself, realising that it could make things difficult for Geraldine's parents. 'Just put it in writing and send by post. My wife and I shall be away for a few days, so a letter will suffice. And securities?'

'A simple contract between gentlemen is sufficient. We have measures to recover unpaid debts, of course, but with a man of your standing,' he glanced around the room, 'I feel sure we need not touch upon such matters.'

'Indeed not. But if, for example, I was to be so remiss as to miss a payment?' Vignoles forced himself to take a slow, apparently pleasurable, pull upon the sharp, bitter cigarette, and exhaled as he spoke.

'In such a regrettable situation, I would, of course gently remind you of your forgetfulness.'

'I feel sure you would,' thought Vignoles, 'and none too gently, either.' For all the man's expensive appearance, he could tell that below the suit and nicely tailored shirt there was a fit and strong body. Mr Prenton beneath the flashy veneer was a tough customer. 'And if I was, er, forgetful enough to still default? I say this, of course, purely hypothetically, not in expectation of such an un-gentlemanly action, you understand?'

'Indeed, Mr Greenway.' He looked curiously at Vignoles, 'But since you ask, well, we have the right to ... take what reasonable actions are needed to recover the debt. A motor-car, livestock, perhaps? We find a gentle reminder is all that is needed in most cases, however.' Prenton looked long and hard at Vignoles and then stubbed his cigarette out in the silver ashtray beside his armchair, twisting it with slow, forceful turns, the action conveying a hidden menace. The message was not lost on Vignoles, and he was happy to signal this by allowing his eyes to linger on the extinguished butt, and then dart deliberately to Prenton and away again.

'Quite, quite. And of course this will be of no relevance to our particular business at all. Mr Prent ... Peter. You came far this evening?' Vignoles kept his voice light. He calculated that his deliberate implication that they would soon make the deal would override Prenton's guard. He was correct.

'Oh no, no distance, just from Woodford. It's central to my particular area. Not that I would allow distance to get in the way of important business.' He gave an oily smile.

Vignoles stood up, Prenton mirroring his action. 'Well, I await your letter with full details of the deal. However, as I understand it, twenty-five percent interest?'

'Compound'.

'Of course. Repayable weekly, over a term of, shall we say, one year?'

'Most acceptable, Mr Greenway.' The oily smile again.

'Oh, one thing more. The sum would be payable in what form exactly? I would prefer smaller denominations. More workable. Fives for example.'

'My recommendation exactly. Multiples of five pound notes, fresh from our bank.'

'Absolutely what I had in mind, Peter.'

At that moment Anna re-entered the room with a tray laden with a teapot, cups and saucers, milk jug and the cake. 'You are leaving, Mr Prenton?'

'Indeed yes, Anna, Mr Prenton is, we have concluded our business,' added Vignoles quickly.

'Regrettably,' Prenton eyed the cake hungrily, 'I must be on my way. Perhaps another time.'

'Perhaps. Well, thank you for your time. It was most useful.' Vignoles held out his hand and gave a perfect example of the smile he reserved for official occasions when in the presence of Chief Superintendent Badger. Anna, who had placed the tray on a table, briefly shook hands and they watched Prenton leave, turning left out of the house, back towards the Fox and Hounds. Vignoles then stood in the front parlour, slightly back from the window so as to be not immediately obvious, and observed as the so-called Mr Peter Prenton, now attired in a leather jacket and heavy boots, roared past a few minutes later towards Woodford Halse.

Chapter Twenty

'The Chattanooga Choo-Choo'
The Andrews Sisters

'So, how are we going to do this, Simon?' Edward was sitting on the front buffer-beam of a shunting engine he had been ashing out, holding a tin mug of tea. Simon was beside him. The sky was filled with dark rain clouds and a naughty wind was swirling around the yard.

'Firstly, we will have to find a suitable hiding place, somewhere really unlikely for him to look into ...' Simon sipped his tea slowly, '... but also a place one of us can quickly nip out of, collect the bag and duck back into.'

'That's not going to be easy. And what if he catches us?'

'Ah, you see he can only catch one of us, as the other will be outside the station — hidden of course — observing the motorbike, checking the number and getting a description of the man.'

'What?' Edward almost spilled tea down his blue jacket that was buttoned against the chill wind whipping across the yard in gusts.

'Of course. How else can we get the whole picture? And anyway, it's safer to split up: he can't chase two of us in two different places at the same time.' Simon took a quick drag on his Churchman. He was getting the hang of it now.

'No. I suppose not. And then what, Si? One of us gets the money and hides? Along comes the motorbike man, he gets really annoyed, searches, gets even angrier and, and then just rides away?'

'He'll never guess we're even there. He'll think the train never dropped it off. That something went wrong, that's my thinking.'

Fine, grey ash was whisked up by the wind and eddied around, making them narrow their eyes until it subsided. A passenger engine slowly moved past on an adjacent track, making gently rhythmic, sighing sounds, like breathing. They both stopped to watch the apple-green engine and its fireman, who was riding the bottom cab step, shotgun-style, ready to drop down and change the points so it could set back onto the coal road. Edward and Simon had both seen 'Mayflower' a number of times before, so did not reach for their notebooks, but still paused their conversation as the elegant machine completed its manoeuvre.

'I am not sure. There seem to be some problems with this idea. I must be nuts going along with this.' Edward took a deep breath. 'But let's do it. I suppose we had better get away from here pretty smartish — remember the train came past soon after we got there?'

'My dad gave me all the times of these freights. He reckoned it was the Calvert brick empties. So we have the time we should be there by.'

'But there is another thing, Si. If I really was talking with the crew of that train yesterday, then they know what I look like.'

'Well, obviously you're not going to stand on the platform, wave at them and say 'Oy, throw us the money.' We've got to be hidden, then quickly rush out and grab it. Secrecy is everything.'

'But where to hide?'

'That we will have to decide when we get there.'

'Then we had better dart away just as fast as we can. Just a rub of paraffin on the face and hands, and off? Won't bother to change clothes, it'll save time.' Edward grinned. He was nervous but excited as well.

'Oh bother — Mr Saunders — Quick!' Simon nimbly slipped down from the engine and started immediately to polish one of the buffers with a filthy rag that had been tucked in his belt. Edward stood up and started to sweep inside the gaping front of the boiler with a small brush and pan, taking out the last of the dry, grey-and-white ash that had collected there.

'It's a blinkin' shunter, laddie. Don't waste time on polishing that.' The shedmaster did not slacken his pace as he walked past, but made it quite clear to whom he was speaking. 'Go and make yourself useful. Driver Wilkins needs someone on the J94 over there ... his usual lad's late. He's the auxiliary shed pilot. We've got a lot of stuff to move around. Go an' make him some steam, he might even let you help out if you're not completely useless.' And with that Mr Saunders stepped over the rails and disappeared from view.

'Simon! He's just told you to fire.'

'Only make steam...'

'No. You're going to help shunt around the depot. This is it, your big chance.'

'Maybe?'

'Go on. Tell me about it later.'

And with no further word Simon started to cross the rails towards the grimy, black engine, adjusting his cap and trying not to show his considerable trepidation, as the wind lashed the first squall of rain onto his back.

Whilst Edward and Simon were discussing their strategy for the afternoon, Vignoles and most of his team were travelling south from Leicester Central on a stopping train, but they were spread across a number of different compartments. None of them were in their police uniforms. Each would step down at their allotted station and take up suitably discreet vantage points, or attempt to look like passengers or station staff in the perhaps optimistic hope that they might just observe the train crew dropping off a bag of counterfeit money.

P.C. Blencowe was not on the train, for he was already waiting in Leicester goods' yard, hoping to observe the handover of the money. The empty brick train for Calvert was booked to depart that morning, just as it had last week, with Driver Ken Price and Fireman Mickey Rollo rostered on the footplate. Anna Vignoles had confirmed that Jimmy Cresswell was the guard.

So far so good.

Vignoles felt no real conviction that they would meet with much success in actually observing the drop-off. In fact, he had nurtured doubts about his plan the whole time. He really felt that he was clutching at straws in the wind, and had a nagging feeling that perhaps he really was squandering valuable resources. Worse still, he had not exactly laid bare his proposals for the day's operation with Chief Superintendent Badger; instead, he had disguised the scale of the operation by indicating that each officer was pursuing 'individual enquiries' in relation to the case. It could be argued that they were, as they would be very much on their own that afternoon. Badger was unlikely to see it that way though, and Vignoles was apprehensive, because if he didn't get a result soon he was likely to get more than an ear–bashing about the benefits of 'real policing'.

Vignoles was sitting in a second-class compartment opposite W.P.C. Benson, who was dressed as a porter, in order to blend in at Charwelton Station. The previous day Vignoles, pretending to be the assistant stationmaster at Leicester Central, had spun a story about wanting to give a new woman employee some more varied work experience, and was sending her down to the tiny station at Charwelton for the day. It was not the most convincing yarn, particularly if the rumours of mass redundancies amongst female staff were true, but luckily the Charwelton stationmaster seemed so completely unmoved by the idea, that he restricted his replies to a series of grunted sounds that could have been a 'yes', and were certainly taken by Vignoles to mean so.

As no one else was sharing the compartment on what was only a half-full train, they allowed themselves a quiet conversation between stations. Nonetheless they had newspapers open, ready to appear engrossed in their respective reading matter, if anyone was to slide the compartment door open and join them.

'So Benson, no joy with the detonators?'

'I am afraid not, sir. Drawn a bit of a blank. The trail has just gone cold. Failing a full search of the village outbuildings and garages, I am not sure how we will find them now.'

'I feared as much, but at least you and Trinder got some useful information about the other matter. And the wooden leg, Benson? Solved the riddle yet?'

'The leg is still unclaimed in lost property at Central. No one has been in for it. I just can't fathom it.'

'And your thoughts on how this one-legged gentleman managed to forget his leg?'

'I'm thinking maybe it was being transported by a two-legged person — it was being delivered, perhaps?'

'A good idea. But then, why the shoe and sock, both with signs of wear?'

'Ah. True enough, sir. That does rather ruin my theory.'

'Not necessarily. It merely poses an additional question about why a false leg would be carried with a worn shoe attached. There may be a perfectly logical explanation.' Vignoles deliberately spoke the last line as if he were Sherlock Holmes.

'I suppose you are right there, Sir. I just haven't found it yet.'

'Try thinking of every possible, outlandish explanation you can, then analyse each one, to see if any stand up to scrutiny and fit the facts. Failing that, put an ad in the local paper,' he grinned at her look of serious concentration whilst she listened to him, and watched as she realised he was poking fun. 'I mean it. Place an advert. Why not? Otherwise I expect it will just become yet another unsolved mystery. There are plenty of those, after all. One more won't hurt.'

'Wilco, sir. Will get onto it first thing tomorrow.'

Vignoles liked Jane Benson. She was a bright officer who showed considerable aptitude. It was because he thought she had a lot to offer, that he liked to gently rib her at times. Challenging her to push herself further, whilst hopefully showing that he was sympathetic, if she didn't always succeed.

'Do you really think logical thinking will solve all cases, sir?'

'No, Benson, I don't, actually. I think Conan Doyle was a bit unfair really. Poor, hapless Watson: he always seemed to be asked his opinion, invariably after Holmes had already deduced the solution by means of some peculiar insight denied to the doctor.'

They both laughed.

'Having said that, I can't help but feel that I'm failing to make some logical deduction in this Water Street case. Am I overlooking something really obvious? We have gathered a lot of very useful information. We have names and descriptions of some of the suspect train crew, we think we know what train diagram they use to transport the money, and we even know it's a big, dark bag. On top of that, Blencowe and Trinder have been working like students swotting for an exam, searching for links between the names we found on the false driving licences and any large cash sales for road vehicles, and they have met with some success. Those two have been plotting incidences on that chart of Blencowes's.'

'He loves a map, doesn't he?'

'Yes. I have to say it is a useful tool. Gives me a sense of the area, the spread of the gang's influence. The problem is, all the addresses they provided to the auctioneers have proved false, leaving us with Water Street as the only definite location for their operation. We must identify the other part of the gang. Hence the reason why we are staking out locations along the line to just north of Calvert.'

'Why not at Calvert, Sir?'

'Not placing someone in Calvert is a big risk, but my instincts are telling me that that is not the place that they make the change. We are desperately short on manpower, so something has to give, and Calvert feels just a bit too far south of the incidents we have so far tracked. Logic tells me that, but it will be just our luck if Sherlock Holmes is wrong on this one,' Vignoles smiled.

'And the list of names and addresses with the passports?'

'Maybe they have a sideline on false identities? It would be lucrative work. There were six passport blanks in total, and ten names and addresses. It looks like some passports have already been assembled and distributed. Remember, we do have the photographs, and these look like they might be some of the Water Street gang, in particular the train crew. A good view of the crew today would be useful.'

'But why would the train crew need false passports? Even if they do take part in some of the purchases of motor cars, they use false driving licences for that. A passport suggests leaving the country.'

'You have answered your own question, Benson. I can't help thinking that at some point when they have completed their job, their aim is to cut and run overseas. Time is not on our side, especially as at some point they will realise that the photos have been lifted. They won't hang around once they know they've been rumbled.' Vignoles winced, wondering if he had calculated correctly by taking this risk.

'I understand, sir. And until we can watch them exchanging the money, and catch someone passing this money on in a transaction, then we have a case that leaks like a colander full of water.'

'Spot on. And Benson, the information Trinder and I obtained was —' he paused for a beat, '— under circumstances that mean we can never use it in court. So it's useful in one respect, but useless if we hope to bring a conviction. Policing can sometimes be a frustrating business.'

'Agreed. If we cannot bring a legally strong case to court, they get away with it.'

They both fell silent and looked out of the window as the rain snaked across the glass and occasional billows of steam swirled past the carriage. Vignoles watched the wooden telegraph poles flash by, the wires looping in gentle, rhythmic sweeps that threatened to lull him to sleep. A squall of wind rattled rain against the glass and shook Vignoles from his thoughts. Jane Benson was reading her newspaper, or at least appearing to do so. They were nearing Charwelton, trundling past a low cutting on the approach to the station, the squalls of wind moving the long, wet grass in rolling folds, as if made of cloth.

'Good luck, Benson.'

'And to you, sir!'

A short while later Vignoles stepped off the train at Woodford & Hinton and proceeded on foot towards the small wooden signal box situated a couple of hundred yards from the platform end, on the edge of the embankment. He walked up the short flight of steps and stood in the open doorway leading into the hot greenhouse of a room, which smelt of wood polish and lamp oil. The sole occupant was Signalwoman Laura Green.

He tapped lightly upon one of the glass panes in the open door. 'Good morning, may I come in?' Vignoles lifted his damp hat to the young woman, who was in the act of pulling a series of tall, thin, metal levers that formed a row the full length of the box, in front of the multi-paned windows.

'Of course. Be my guest, come in out of that rain … just a tick …' she heaved another lever into place, and then sounded a series of bells using a large and beautifully-polished wooden box on a shelf that ran at eye-level across the windows. These actions completed, she wiped her hands on a cloth flopped over a lever, and then walked over, extending her hand to Vignoles.

'Laura Green. You must be D.I. Vignoles. Pleased to meet you, sir.' She smiled warmly as he shook hands and replied that he was. 'Come in, take off your wet coat — leave it by the stove, it will soon dry. Tea? Help yourself: the pot's on the table,' at which she turned to watch a long, slow train laden with steel tubes pass by, waved to the driver, then immediately resumed pulling and clanking levers into place. 'This railway runs on tea, I'm sure of it, inspector!'

Laura was in her late twenties and dressed in navy trousers, a man's white shirt, company tie, and a peaked cap pushed to the back of her head. Vignoles thought she looked a little like Vera Lynn, but it was probably the combination of her cap worn over blonde curls and the uniform. She was now ringing more bells, and looking through the rain-spattered windows with her head to one side. An engine whistled three times quickly. She nodded to herself and pulled more levers.

'Is it always this busy?' Vignoles ventured.

'Oh gosh, this is nothing. You should be here on when it gets really hectic. And this is a fairly quiet box. Number four. They won't let me work on numbers two and three — they're the domain of Mr Howerth and Mr Roth. Heaven help me if I ever step in those places.' She rolled her eyes dramatically. 'They can be a right pair of grumpy old so-and-sos, I can tell you.' The signalwoman suddenly stopped and looked at the D.I., clearly wondering if she had gone too far. 'But I love it here. Really I do. It's nice, clean work. I have my own cosy signal box, a warm stove …' Vignoles involuntarily glanced across at the iron stove in question that was oozing heat. '… and I can wave at all the engine men, but I don't have to have long, insufferable conversations with anyone who I don't really care that much for. You know — about football and cricket — mainly, they want to talk about football.'

'It's probably because they have been starved of it for so long.'

'I haven't had a decent Sunday roast with Yorkshire puddings, potatoes and gravy for as long as I can remember, but I don't talk about it to everyone all day.'

'That's a fair point. I shall try not to disturb you by talking about Charlton Athletic, Len Hutton or the cup final. And I won't even mention roast beef.'

'Derby won — I know.' Laura pulled another lever forward, the wires and pulleys twanging and clanking into place.

'Indeed they did. I'm here just to observe, and so I shall be as quiet as the proverbial mouse.'

'Oh, I didn't mean it like that. It's nice to have the company. Although it is really rather irregular.' She gave a questioning, and anxious, look at Vignoles.

'Don't worry. It's all squared up with divisional H.Q. And I have special powers to enter railway premises.' Vignoles answered her unspoken question. Laura was now leaning on the levers, looking at Vignoles, an enamelled mug of tea suddenly in her hand, and she shrugged in reponse.

'So you came to watch trains?'

'To observe the operations, yes. It helps further my understanding of the railway. It's a complex beast, and it could prove invaluable,' added Vignoles quickly, deliberately adopting a more formal and professional tone of voice, although his eyes were involuntarily drawn to the view outside the window of a passing train.

'Righty-o; just pull up a chair and make yourself at home. None of my business to ask why or what, but if you need, I can tell you about everything that passes this box. Nothing gets past without my permission.'

Vignoles smiled. 'All those tough men in their engines, and you tell them what to do. Quite a sense of power, I suppose?'

'Rather. I always let them through of course — eventually. But if they annoy me, they might just find themselves diverted into a siding for a while.' She threw another charming smile and turned back to the little tinkling bells and the big, heavy levers. Vignoles took a seat beside the windows facing the station, looked up at the circular clock on the wall, filled his pipe, and settled into watching and waiting.

Chapter Twenty-One

'ALL IN FAVOUR SAY 'AYE''
Geraldo & his Orchestra

Edward and Simon had left their bikes pushed deep into soaking wet nettles behind a hedgerow of hawthorn, a short distance from the road overbridge at Culworth station. They had then spent a frantic time scouting out the derelict station, trying to find a safe hiding place, getting thoroughly damp from the squalls of rain in so doing. Their nerves were beginning to kick in, and each time they heard the distant whistle of a train on the wind they stopped and anxiously looked down the running lines to try and discern if it was the expected Calvert brick empties.

Their task was proving harder than they had imagined. If one of them just hid out of sight in any of the empty rooms, they would be discovered too easily, for they were sure that the motorcyclist would look around for the bag once he saw it was not on the platform. Edward stopped and looked at Simon. 'Why wouldn't he arrive before the train? That'll scupper everything.'

Simon stared back at Eddie, and reluctantly nodded in agreement. 'I'd not thought of that. Maybe he was just late last week?'

'So he might be here any minute now.'

They both looked around anxiously. It was also turning chill, not helped by the rain showers and the mischievous wind, which was raising goosebumps on their arms. Their spirits were starting to slump along with the temperature. The deserted rooms felt cold and ugly today, full of unpleasant smells and swirling drafts that banged a door at odd intervals, making them jump.

'Look, I think that this is the best we can do, Eddie: one of us can hide in this cupboard, the other in the pill box up near the bridge.'

The cupboard in question was in the booking office, and stood easily a foot higher than either of them. It was made of metal, painted dark green and had two doors with a hasp to hold them shut. The padlock was missing, however. It had two metal shelves inside and bundles of pamphlets and leaflets about summer excursions to sunnier places like Filey and Bridlington piled at the bottom.

'Throw this stuff out, remove this shelf and it's perfect to duck into with the bag. And look, I can pull it shut quite easily from the inside …' Simon demonstrated the technique.

'We must be out of time now, Si. If we are going to do it, it has to be now.' Edward swallowed and took a deep breath. 'Who stays here?'

'Flip a coin?' As he was speaking, Simon was wrenching the lower shelf free with a nasty screeching noise that set their teeth on edge.

'OK, I've got one here. Heads or tails?'

'Heads.'

Edward spun the penny into the air and caught it, slapping it down on his wrist. 'It's heads Simon … oh, meaning what? You stay…?'

'Not on your life. I won — I choose — I take the pill box on look out duty.'

'Oh.'

'It'll be fine. Stay quiet, hold your breath. And if he does find you …'

'He'll kill me!'

'Just … yell! Loudly! Shout the place down, and I'll ride for help.' Simon grinned and slapped his friend on the arm. 'Chin up, Eddie — this is the big one. We'll be millionaires after today. Or heroes. Or both. Just imagine.'

'Yeees. I guess so.'

'Good luck, Eddie!'

'Same to you.' Edward, with a pounding heart, watched Simon quickly walk, then run, along the platform and up the steps to the bridge.

The station felt very empty and desolate. Edward had visualised their adventure taking place on a warm, sunny day, with cheerful sunbeams streaming through the open door and a clear blue sky above. He had imagined the two of them both watching from a secure vantage point, and then somehow managing to snatch the bag, without any real threat of danger. But Edward now looked around and saw the room for what it really was. It stank of urine and the wind was flinging a piece of paper around in circles and making a rusty tin-can roll backwards and forwards. The telegraph wires hummed and whined in the stronger gusts. His mind started nagging him, a little voice repeatedly saying, 'What a place to die, what a place to die …'

Then Edward heard the whistle. A long, wavering sound, blown and stretched by the wind. Straining his ears, he picked out the rapid succession of exhaust beats of a swiftly moving, but heavily laden, train. Edward's heart was pounding in his ears with the same rapid beat, and his palms were sticky, despite the chill. Instinctively Edward looked up at the stopped station clock. He then crouched low to the ground and peered around the doorway, hoping to be as small a visible target as possible. He could see the train approaching now with white clouds of steam rolling out of the chimney and being pushed down and along the side of the engine. This sight encouraged him, as the steam would largely obscure the engine crew's view of the platform. The train was still approaching at speed, and looked to be heading to run straight past without slowing.

'Damn! That's blown it.' Edward surprised himself by feeling disappointed.

He listened also for the sound of a motorbike, but the wind and exhaust beats of the engine made it hard for him to be sure. There was a sound, but it seemed to come from the sky, perhaps just an aeroplane. The locomotive changed its sound, as if it was starting to slow down. Despite this, it was clear to Edward that it would still pass at a fair lick. Too fast, surely? He ducked back inside the doorway as the station was suddenly filled by the roar and clatter of the train as it swept past. It flung small pieces of grit and dust into his eyes and great balls of soft smoke and steam obscured his vision. He could see nothing except a blanket of all-enveloping white, filled by the rhythmic banging and clattering of a huge string of wagons, the sounds reverberating around the ruined booking office. Just as suddenly, the noise diminished and the clouds disintegrated into tiny will-o'the-wisps that wrapped themselves around the open door and played around the canopy supports, then vanished.

Edward peeked out and saw the guard's van at the rear being pulled along behind the wagons, with no sign of its occupant. He looked along the platform, but could see nothing. He turned and looked the other way, and there it was. The same battered and scuffed old leather holdall. 'Oh yes. It's now or never, Eddie.' Still bent double, he sprinted the three or four yards to the bag, grabbed it, and tried to turn at the same time. He was caught off balance by the surprising weight. He fell forwards, tangling the cumbersome holdall in his legs and suddenly he was toppled over it, grazing his knees on the wet and gritty surface and landing heavily on one shoulder. 'Ow! Agh!'

He lay there for a few seconds in shock, wanting to hold his bleeding knees, feeling sharp needles of pain in his legs and upper arm. But then, somehow, his senses detected danger. He had not consciously heard the approaching motorbike, and the events of the last minutes had masked any other thoughts, but as he lay there, something told him to get up and move. He scrambled to his feet, feeling rather than hearing the approach of the motorcyclist. He ran back into the booking office, stumbling over the rubbish on the floor, and stepped into the metal cupboard, banging the heavy holdall against the rear wall with a shuddering boom. He pulled the doors closed with sweaty hands, finding it hard to keep a firm grip on the cold metal. He was panting, but tried to gulp air and hold it in, letting it out slowly. Edward could hear nothing other than the rush of wind in the trees, the patter of another rain shower and the 'crack-crack' of crows in the nearby trees.

Simon, meanwhile, in the relative security of the old machine-gun emplacement, heard both the train and the motorbike simultaneously and realised that it was going to be a very close call. It now seemed impossible that Edward would be able to get the bag before the motorcyclist arrived on the platform. He really wished he could communicate with his friend and tell him to stay put. He looked through the gun-slot in the side of the squat, hexagonal, concrete building, and waited with a feeling of dread for the man to arrive, thinking, 'Eddie, stay where you are.'

The train was nearly at the station, and by moving to the opposite gun-slot, Simon could see the train's smoke billowing up around the bridge. At that same moment, a motorcycle sidecar combination roared down the lane and pulled up right outside the station entrance. Simon hardly needed to look, he just knew that the man and the bike would be the same as they had seen at Woodford. Sure enough it was the same jacket and leather trousers, black, peaked helmet and the scruffy, military bike with the canvas cover to the sidecar. The driver dismounted and descended the steps in a matter of moments, just as the train started to accelerate and its towering plume of dirty smoke filled the wet sky. Simon waited, expecting to hear Eddie shout out. Time seemed to stop. Nothing happened. Was Eddie OK? Maybe the man was holding him hostage, waiting for Simon to come to the rescue, and thereby step into the trap? Oh Lord, he hadn't thought about that possibility until now. Should he ride away for help? But by the time help arrived, Edward might be dead, or captured and taken away. Simon was rendered motionless with indecision. Suddenly the whole jaunt had taken on a darker aspect.

This was serious. It wasn't fun anymore.

'Oh what idiots we are!' he spoke under his breath. 'Heck, I got you into this mess, Eddie, the least I can do is see if I can help you get out of it.' Simon darted across the road, but instead of descending the steps onto the platform, he pushed through a thinning section of hedge, getting showered by water as he did so and bramble scratches on his arms and legs. Bees buzzed around his face as he brushed away the scented may-blossom, which stuck to his wet skin and clothes in little white clumps. He half slid down the slimy, grassy embankment beyond, keeping as low as he could to the ground, all the time scanning the platform for signs of the struggle he'd imagined. It was, however, deserted. He crouched and darted across to the bushes that nestled against the wire-and-post fencing beside the 'down' line. He peered through from the relative safety of a dense clump of gorse and cow parsley. Culworth station was silent and empty. Where was the man in black? No, wait a minute, there he was, on the ground, beside the railway track on the far side of the station. But what was he doing? Simon could only see the head and shoulders of the man and an occasionally raised arm, wielding a hefty stick, which he was bringing down over and over again, in wild swings.

Oh my God, he's killing Eddie! Again and again the arm was swinging and bringing down the piece of wood in vicious blows, his mouth distorted in a grimace. But the motorcyclist was also moving around, turning this way and that. It no longer looked like he was thrashing someone on the ground and Simon started to feel some relief. No, he was beating the long grass and bushes near the tracks. You're looking for the bag, which can only mean one thing? Eddie, you clever little devil, you got it! Simon clenched a fist and made a slight punching gesture.

The clearly furious motorcyclist was standing now and looking up and down the tracks, and then straight across the platform into Simon's eyes. Simon knew that any movement would betray him, if he was not already lost. So he stood still as if he were made of stone. The man looked away however, and then climbed back onto the platform. He took a few steps, whilst idly swinging the stick, clearly deep in thought. Then with a loud, ugly curse he threw it straight through the booking-office window, smashing the glass as it passed and noisily clanging against something resonant and metallic, that sounded suspiciously like the cupboard.

'Damn! Damn! You double-crossing bastards!' The man cursed again and strode angrily back up the stairs towards his motorbike. Simon had still not moved and was unsure if he had even ventured a breath of air. The bike started up almost immediately and roared, with a crackling ferocity and a backfire, into the distance.

'Holy cow ... Eddie! Eddie! Come out ... it's all clear!' Simon was clambering through the wires of the fence as he shouted, so intent upon reaching his friend that he only just noticed in time the approach of an express train and pressed himself back against the fence. A long, eerie whistle filled the air and he could see the anxious face of the driver leaning out of his cab, motioning with his hand for Simon to keep back. Simon made a thumbs up sign to show he had heeded the warning, and the drivers face visibly relaxed as the engine thundered past, swishing the grasses and bushes, whipping up rain drops and blossom petals and swirling them all into his face. Brown teak coaches creaked and rumbled by in a blur, and it was gone.

'Simon! Simon!' Edward was standing on the platform waving wildly with one hand, knees scarlet with fresh blood, a smile as wide as that of the Cheshire cat, and a grubby, leather holdall at his feet. 'I got it, Si, I got it.'

A short while later they were pedalling back towards Woodford Halse, their precious prize stowed in the wicker basket more used to carrying Earnshaw's loaves and cakes. Simon's jacket lay over the bulky, leather holdall to conceal it from view. As they cycled, however, their initial euphoria and the tingling thrill of inspecting the huge bundles of perfect banknotes started to evaporate. Their nerves were becoming strained. The initial fears, then joyous excitement of achieving their goal, were being replaced by a dread realisation that they had perhaps a cool million pounds with them and that someone was going to be very eager to get it back. This 'someone' had in all probability already seen and spoken with them, and did not look like the sort of man who was going to ask politely 'May I have my money back, please?' when he caught up with them.

'Oh God, what have we done?' Simon suddenly felt overwhelmed by doubt.

'Yeah, and what the hell are we going to do now?'

'Dunno ... hey, but Eddie,' Simon's mood just a quickly

shifted to the positive, 'We … are … rich,' he emphasised each word for effect, pushing down on the pedals of his bike as he pronounced each word. 'I mean *really* rich. We can do anything we want!'

'It's a bit hard to believe, really. But we can't do just anything, can we?' Edward's words were laboured, as the rise in the road and the weighty bike made itself felt. 'We can't even spend that stupid fiver you've still got. We can't just go and buy a … a castle and live in it, can we?'

'We could sail to America…'

'Yeah? And then what?' Edward was puffing with each push of the pedals. 'What about our families? What would they say?'

'That's true.' Then, changing tack: 'Do you think he's around here still?' Simon glanced behind him, whilst leaning forward, standing slightly up on the pedals to help get up the hill.

'He's bound to be, Si! What the heck are we going to do when we get home? I mean, we can't tell our parents, can we?' Edward was looking red in the face as the heavy bag started to take its toll on his legs, already tired from working on the locomotives.

'No. My dad will go mad, I reckon.' Simon looked thoughtful. 'We can hardly say "Look, we've just found us a million quid!"'

'Oh hell! What have we done? I'm getting a bit scared now. Its bad enough thinking what a stink this will kick up if Mum and Dad find out, but that's nothing to what motorbike man will do.'

They stopped cycling and rested on the handlebars for a breather. The wind was calming down and the rain was holding off, just leaving grey-and-white clouds to scud over and behind the tall stands of trees beyond the hedgerows filled with hawthorn and may--blossom. Edward hung his head down; breathing deeply and feeling the sharp, sore ache of his cut knees. Simon noticed and dismounted his Rudge Whitworth, offering to swap cycles. Edward was happy to oblige. However, they first leaned the bikes against a gate leading into a field of green corn and stood talking.

'Perhaps we had better go to the police?'

'And say what? "Look what we just stole: a huge bag of money"? They will go crazy.'

'But I thought this money was stolen?'

'We think it is. Yes, it must be. But we don't really know that, do we?' Simon was finally starting to properly think through their actions, and finding flaws in the plan.

'I reckon we should let the police deal with this, and if the money is stolen, then we could get a reward — real money, that we can honestly spend.'

'You do have a point there, Eddie. But, but this is millions! We could live like film stars — in Hollywood,' Simon sounded regretful.

'But how, Simon? Come on, let's be realistic about this. Anyway I'm not sure I want to live in Hollywood. Listen, I met a nice policeman, a railway one; well, a detective, plain clothes —'

'— Really? A plain-clothes detective? You never told me!'

'I suppose I forgot. He seemed really nice. Liked steam engines as well. I am sure he wouldn't just go mad at us. I think I have his name in my spotter's book.'

'I'm not sure. I think the police are just going to go mad at us and then go straight around to our parents.'

'But if we are helping solve a crime, surely no one will mind?'

'Stealing a bag of cash! My Dad will go berserk — crime solved or not. He'll say we were meddling in things we shouldn't be.'

'Maybe he's right.' Both lads fell silent for a few moments. 'Look, I'm sure we need the police. The more I think about what we've got here,' Edward felt goosebumps on his arms and looked nervously around, 'I just know that we're involved in something really bad.' A sudden squall made the tall elm quiver in front of them, its leaves shivering, like Edward.

'Hmm. I am coming around to your way of thinking, Eddie. So, how do we find him?'

Edward was taking out his little notebook and turning to the entries for 28th April. 'Yes, here he is. Funny name — that's why I wrote it down — but I have no idea how he spells it. 'Detective Inspector', I got that bit OK, 'Vicknolls' or 'Veenos', something weird like that. But it's so funny, I am sure everyone would know it. He was talking to Mrs Walsh at the station refreshment room — like he knew her.'

'All right, we can find him that way, I suppose. But it's going to take some time. Meanwhile, we need to hide this.' They both looked at the big lump under Simon's jacket in the wicker basket.

'And we need to get back home as well. I am totally bushed, Si. Too much excitement, if you ask me. And I tell you what, this place is beginning to give me the creeps.'

They both looked up and down the lane, empty of everything except the possibility of the returning motorbike. The beautiful, verdant lane and the fields all around; they were part of their familiar territory and they loved it. But now it seemed changed. It was almost as if the bag filled with illicit money was oozing some kind of negativity, layering everything with an invisible but palpable menace. Hedges now seemed to serve only as a means of concealing a threat, and the twists, turns, rises and dips in the road were there to block their view and maybe their way back home. And even home was now rendered dangerous, at least whilst they still had possession of their cargo. They quickly remounted and continued cycling towards Woodford.

'I've an idea. There's an Anderson shelter out the back of the shops near the railway station — it's just full of junk and rubbish, you know the one? We've messed around there before?'

'Yeah, I know the one. But that's at the back of the dressmaker's shop, isn't it? Near the garage, where we saw the motorbike man.'

'True, but no one really ever goes there. And he'd never think to look in that old shelter. Anyway, he doesn't know we even stole the money, remember? And I can't think what else to do.'

'Oh, what the Devil. I don't care if he finds the blinkin' money, I just care about him finding us with it. So let's get a move on.'

As the backyard with the junk-filled air-raid shelter was located at the very southern end of the small village, they were able to approach it without having to pass along the High Street or Station Road where they were bound to meet plenty of people they knew. In particular they wanted to avoid Edward's parents, who were probably wondering where their delivery bike had gone. The shop rented by the McIntyres had a long, thin yard turning into an overgrown garden, bounded by brick walls and the steep embankment up to the railway line. There was a wide wooden gate at the far end of the garden. This had been let into the wall to allow, in years gone past, the former seed merchant access to a poor little stable block and a place to park his delivery cart. Towards the end of his time in business he had used a petrol truck of ancient vintage, which now lay abandoned and rusting in a sea of weeds. It was faded to a pale, greyish-green colour with patches of orange rust. The yard itself was a mass of other clutter as well, all too much for the McIntyre sisters to remove themselves, and awaiting a time when their inattentive landlord might take the initiative to remove it. As a result the gate hung open on dropped hinges whilst the lower reaches of the garden were rarely visited by anyone except occasional children playing. Nearer the back door, however, the backyard was clean and tidy, housing a mangle used on washdays, a big, zinc bath hanging on a nail, a rope washing line and the outdoor toilet.

On the way to the McIntyres the two lads had encountered only Farmer Turvey driving some cows home to be milked and, apart from exchanging 'how do's', this encounter passed without incident. They now parked their bikes against the outside of the McIntyres garden wall, furtively sweeping the area to see if they had been detected. Simon lifted the heavy holdall out and then they slowly advanced towards the open gate. Now that they were back on more familiar territory, and closer to being able to hide the bag of money, they were also back into the groove. They were British secret agents on a mission, and their sense of excitement was creeping back. Shafts of welcome sun were starting to pierce the clouds, and its warmth felt reassuring. They peered around the wall to check the lay of the land. All clear. There was no sign of Violet, and with some regret they admitted, neither was there any sign of Jenny.

'Right, Eddie, there's the Anderson. Just ten yards away, maybe less.'

'Yep. Check it's all clear, we'll make a first dash to the old lorry, then I'll lead off, straight to the door, get it open, and you follow. That way, if someone comes and sees me, I can act like I'm just messing around.'

'Good plan.'

The two lads took another quick glance around, but there was no sign of any movement at the back of the shop, so they quickly ran across to the rusting vehicle, Simon crouching in the ragwort, a few hoverflies disturbed by his arrival hung in the air, inquisitively investigating him. Edward was already opening the small, narrow door of the air-raid shelter. The hinges creaked loudly, but still opened without too much effort. Edward turned and beckoned to his friend, standing aside to leave the entrance clear, whilst Simon scooted across the remaining ground and practically dived inside, the momentum of the heavy holdall carrying him forward with some speed. As he passed the threshold, he immediately banged his shins against a heavy box covered in sacking that was lying across his path. He stumbled, and the bag of money thumped into a pile of wood propped against the narrow twin bunk beds in the shelter.

'Ouch! Bugger!' He clutched his stinging shinbones.

'Shhhh!' Edward hissed, as he leaned into the doorway, whilst nervously looking towards the back of the house as the wooden planks rattled noisily. Simon was now gingerly stepping over the box into a cramped space almost completely filled with odorous, musty stuff. Lumpen sacks of what could be potatoes, old garden implements, various cardboard boxes that seemed to be full of newspapers or empty jam jars, strings of onions and a completely rusted hand mower. He started to sneeze as dust billowed in drifts through the shafts of light spilling in through the door.

'This is perfect!' He looked around, and then hefted the bag onto the lower bunk, which had no mattress, pulling an old overcoat over it. 'No one will ever know it's there. Achoo! But let's get ... achoo! Ugh, let's get out of here!' With one last look around the shelter, the two lads sprinted towards the gate in one quick dash, a sudden and surprising feeling of relief flooding through their veins as they moved away from the money. A heavy coal train, held at the signals for the whole time that they had been at the yard, rumbled into motion above them on the embankment, its safety valves blowing steam in a powerful release of pent-up pressure. It expressed the feelings of Edward and Simon, who leapt on their bikes and with renewed energy cycled out of the back lane onto Station Road.

'Up to ours. Don't know what time it is, but I'm sure we can cadge something to eat.' And with that, Edward sprinted away.

Chapter Twenty-Two

'CHOO CHOO CH-BOOGIE'
Louis Jordan & his Tympani Five

Vignoles was sitting in his office, his officers gathered around. The mood was pensive, even a little sombre. It had not been an outwardly successful afternoon although, as Vignoles had reminded them, surveillance was often about eradicating options and possibilities as much as major breakthroughs.

No one had actually seen anything that could be interpreted as a handover of the counterfeit money. The dark-coloured holdall that Sergeant Trinder had observed the Saturday before, and which P.C. Blencowe believed was handed over earlier that morning at Leicester goods depot, had remained unseen as the train went down the line. This was despite their best efforts to second-guess the gang and watch out at the places they felt were potential handover points. Sergeant Blencowe had only seen the guard, Jimmy Creswell, step over to the Anglo-Empire Oil Co van for a few seconds.

'So, you are pretty sure that it was collected?'

'Well, he did approach the van, but my angle of view was not what I had hoped for.'

'Meaning?' Trinder looked exasperated.

'Why else would he do that? I am sure that he must have collected the money.' Vignoles was trying to stay positive. 'Actually, I am not sure if that fact makes me pleased or dismayed, under the circumstances. If they did collect the bag, then where is the blessed thing now?' Vignoles was lighting his pipe as he spoke, waving the lighted match until it went out, leaving a tiny trail of pungent smoke. 'Well', he continued, 'at least we have narrowed down the options. If only through not seeing anything at the places we were observing.' Vignoles gave a wry smile, and there was a murmur of polite laughter at his comment.

'So, Blencowe. Perhaps with aid of your rather splendidly-annotated map, we could look at what options are left, and see if we can't come up with other strategies to further narrow down this operation? If my initial hunch is correct, we have another week to plan until the next run.'

'That's something, at least,' added Jane Benson.

'It is indeed. I just wonder for how much longer they will keep this particular route open. We cannot afford to let much more time slip by,' replied Sergeant Trinder.

'And Badger will throw a fit if we don't make a breakthrough soon.' Vignoles kept this thought to himself. 'My observations of the man calling himself Peter Prenton were useful. His name will probably be bogus — but we need to focus in on him. I am sure he is based in Woodford Halse or in the immediate vicinity. Woodford is small: someone must know him. Sergeant? Can I ask that this is your task in the next few days? Find out who he really is, where he lives, where he really works?'

'Wilco, sir.'

'We know the identities of the driver and fireman. Again, both are Woodford men, whilst the guard is regularly to be found rostered on the same goods workings as these other two. We need to get home addresses for all three of them. Benson — this needs urgent attention, can I leave it with you?'

'Will get straight on to company personnel and find out.'

'Then we turn to the drop-off point. Any ideas? What are we overlooking?' Vignoles turned to look at the large Ordnance Survey map pinned to the wooden dividing wall of his office. It was decorated by coloured pins, carefully plotted by P.C. Blencowe, each one, depending on the colour, representing the places staked out by railway police, the Water Street premises and the locations of army surplus auctions and other places where counterfeit money had been identified as changing hands. 'Blencowe: any thoughts?'

'Ah, um. I think this map clearly indicates that suspicious activity is concentrated down a corridor that neatly mirrors that of the main line between Leicester and an area just north of Calvert. Woodford does seem to concentrate a large proportion of my coloured pins, and this does, I feel, back up your theory that we should be looking in that area for the transfer point.'

P.C. Blencowe was a large man with a rounded face and a full beard of a rich auburn colour. A devotee of a good pint of bitter and considered handy with the bat with the local cricket team, he was a thoughtful character, who preferred desk-bound research and analysis to anything more dynamic. He was not perhaps blessed with the quickest mind, but he had an enormous appetite for the vital, but painstaking, work that was often the policeman's lot. He was a Godsend to Vignoles, who had long ago discovered that Blencowe would gladly sift through mountains of documents or information in the hope of finding the tiny clue that advanced a case. His research into the time, place and circumstances of all cases of counterfeit money in the area over the last few months was already proving instructive. Vignoles studied the map whilst Blencowe continued in his slow, rich voice: 'I have also started a piece of analysis that I feel might have narrowed down the location of the drop-off point.'

'Really?' Vignoles suddenly turned, as did all the others, to look at the large, bearded officer, as he sat with his arms folded across his wide belly.

'Yes, sir. I was thinking about how we might track the progress of the train in question. Clearly we cannot board the train and observe it — not if it consists of empty brick wagons, at least. We cannot watch the train along its whole route, so if they simply lob the thing over the side into a ditch — at a pre-arranged milepost, for example, then we have, with all due respect, sir, not a cat's chance in hell of identifying this location.' He paused for effect, and Vignoles nodded in agreement.

'But you think otherwise?'

'Yes I do. I actually think that this is a controlled handover. Now, a long, heavy train needs to slow down, and then accelerate quite noticeably, in order to do this, significantly affecting the timings of the train.'

'You're right there. It could take a few miles to slow and restart,' interjected Trinder.

'Are you thinking that other railway employees might have observed an unplanned alteration in the train's progress, arousing suspicion?' It was Lansdowne who now joined in, leaning forward slightly as she sensed that her colleague was about to announce a breakthrough in the case.

'In a way yes, Lucy. But not necessarily in a manner that they are aware of. Let me explain; I believe that very nearly the exact progress of this train has been meticulously recorded, on every run it has made.'

'This would be extremely useful. But how?' It was Vignoles now who was looking at him with eagle-eyed concentration, pipe in one corner of his mouth as he sat back in his swivel chair.

'Every signalman records the passage of every train, to the exact minute. They have a detailed operating timetable with the booked times, so they know what to expect, but are charged with recording these actual movements in a log book.'

'Yes. I observed Miss Green doing just that in the signal box at Woodford,' added Vignoles, already grasping where Blencowe was going with his thinking. 'And better still, so does every guard.' Vignoles's voice started to mount in excitement as he spoke. 'It's an essential part of their duties to record not only every arrival and departure time, but each signal box and block section passed, sometimes even certain mileposts and landmarks. That way the loco crew can be monitored in their performance. They can be penalised in extreme circumstances if they cannot account for poor performance, or rewarded for consistently good performances. So, by taking these log books and cross-referencing them to check that they tally, we can firstly sniff out any discrepancies ...'

'... and we can see if our men are trying to hide an un-timetabled slowing down.' Sergeant Trinder was picking up the thread.

'Precisely. I suspect our guard, young Jimmy Creswell, has had the need for accuracy so drilled into him that he has faithfully recorded the exact performance of the train — the dramatic time loss incurred as well — because his training simply won't allow him to do otherwise.'

'But even if he does try to cover it up,' added Lansdowne, 'the signal box records will still show up the difference.'

'Brilliant!' Sergeant Trinder was sharing the enthusiasm.

'We are still talking about a relatively small loss of time, and there are endless delays and speed restrictions on the railway at the moment,' warned Vignoles, 'so it will be a devil of a job to spot this, Blencowe.'

'Not easy, sir, I agree. But I have taken some of the logbooks for the last month, and the lists of special speed restrictions imposed during that time, and I have started to cross-reference these. It is slow work, it takes care and one has to be darned accurate, but I think I might have spotted three places where their train of empty brick wagons slowed down on Saturdays for two weeks running. It will be interesting to see if the same happened today. I then need to see if I can explain away these slowings-down, but if not, then, hey presto!' He grinned.

'It's a lead, at least. Where are you thinking of?' It was Trinder speaking.

'The place that leaps out at me is Culworth. A noticeable loss of time at this section for the past two weeks, but no speed restrictions imposed, and of course the station is ... closed. Oh, I am so stupid! Why didn't I think of this before? It seems obvious now. An abandoned station, providing them with complete privacy.' Vignoles stood up and was looking through his office window at the bustle of the platforms outside, pipe jutting out of his mouth above a clenched jaw. 'Somehow my mind fixated on operational points along the line. Damn it! How could I be so remiss?'

'Don't be so hard on yourself, sir.' It was Sergeant Trinder speaking, 'We are also guilty of this oversight. But I agree, Culworth just seems the obvious place. Close to Woodford & Hinton and in the middle of nowhere; their train could slow, perhaps even stop, totally unobserved.'

Vignoles turned back and faced his team, 'This is good work, Blencowe. Keep working on this, but I'm sure you've found the location, so let's draw up a battle plan. We need to get the Leicestershire Constabulary on board to move in on the Water Street mob as soon as we're ready to catch the other part of the gang down the line. But, in order to do that, we need to think about how we can follow the pick-up man — this Prenton fellow on his motorcycle combination. We might need to rustle up some petrol coupons for that lovely motor-car of ours. But first, maybe we could make another pot of tea and some biscuits? We're going to be here some time.'

Chapter Twenty-Three

'WE THREE (MY ECHO, MY SHADOW AND ME)'

Anne Shelton & the Bert Ambrose Orchestra

Violet McIntyre had spent the week alternating between quietly enjoying putting her business in order by settling outstanding debts, and worrying deeply about the legality of the money she was handling. Her confrontation with the man from Speedy Loans had initially calmed her fears, but the nagging doubts refused to completely leave. She sensed that something was not right. In a way she was foolish to agonise over the problem, for the majority of the money had already been spent, and furthermore, each transaction had passed without alarm-bells ringing or even the sudden appearance of a policeman to arrest her.

But the incident at Earnshaw's bakery upset her deeply, and Violet still remained ill at ease. Jenny, however, was untroubled by such matters and continued to improve in spirits. Her budding romance with Tom from the ironmonger's was clearly doing her the world of good. Violet was pleased about this and gained considerable pleasure from seeing her sister smiling and laughing. But Violet had a gnawing dread in her stomach that she might have made a terrible decision in borrowing the money, one that would somehow wreck everything, including this still-budding relationship.

Despite her worries, the day had been quite productive. She had taken two orders for summer dresses and a pile of mending and alterations, which would keep her busy for the next week, and help to pay the first instalment on the loan. She had spent the whole day working in the shop, and as the day had started chill and wet, this had been a blessing. But now the sun was starting to peek through, and the air felt a little warmer. Violet decided to take a walk to get some fresh air before preparing some food for them both that evening. She took her red mackintosh from the peg by the door and wore a matching peaked cap at a rakish angle. She hoped that the combination would have a cheery effect, even if it actually concealed her own rather fragile sense of well-being.

Violet walked up Station Road and then decided to take a right turn down Parson's Street, walking beside the tall, ironstone wall that formed the perimeter of the elegant vicarage house and gardens. She continued past the imposing Moravian church on the opposite side of the road, and noticed that the churchwarden was sweeping the front steps, and airing the church by leaving the door wide open. Violet glimpsed the dark interior with its rows of pews and a flash, as the brightly polished altar cross caught some filtered sunlight. Mr Kosice smiled warmly at Violet as she walked by, and they exchanged pleasantries about the evening turning nicer.

Violet walked on, eventually taking the narrow, leafy footpath that cut down to the little, weed-choked stream that was the River Cherwell, then out across Shrimpton's Meadow, that lay beside the huge sprawl of the locomotive sheds. It was a curious contrast in many ways, and Violet rather enjoyed the startling juxtaposition of the rolling fields and verdant hedgerows tumbling away as far as her eye could see, with the smoking, clanging, whistling world of the railway. Standing on the crest of the hill that dipped down to the perimeter fence of the huge locomotive shed, Violet had the sensation of standing in one world and looking over into another. From a largely unchanged and unchanging land, governed by the gentle cycle of the seasons, filled with the scent of flowers, fresh earth and the sound of birdsong, to a land run by timetables and tinkling bells, reeking of smoke and sulphur and the echoing reverberations of the strangely-compelling steam engines. No wonder they were called 'iron horses', she mused to herself, as she watched two black examples rumble along the tracks in Indian file.

Whilst she gazed across the bustling yard, her ears assaulted by the sudden explosive thunder of the coal hopper, she suddenly started, drawing an involuntary short intake of breath, and narrowed her eyes. Was that the moneylender she could see crossing the grimy railway lines? She was sure it was. He was wearing a black leather jacket rather than his flashy suit, but she was sure she recognised his features. He was smoking, and walking fast with aggressively-punctuated steps, suggesting that he had a purpose, but also Violet sensed that he was agitated. She knew instinctively that her hunch was correct, that this man was not all that he appeared to be; there was something unquestionably fishy about him.

Without really thinking why and for what purpose, Violet started to walk briskly towards the railway, trying to see where the man was headed. She soon lost sight of him, however, as the organised chaos of the clamouring yard blocked her view. Once she had stepped through the little wooden picket-gate that swung closed on its heavy spring with a clunk, she was immersed in a world previously unknown to her. The piles of ash and clinker, coal dust and pools of grimy water and oil assaulted her senses and threatened to ruin her shoes. She was aware that in her neat red coat and cap she must stand out like a sore thumb. Violet wanted to try and avoid observation, although was unclear as to why she was acting like this. She walked as close as she could to the oppressive bulk of the many engines, peering down the dark alleyways between them, and sometimes stepping between the buffers if she saw someone. He coat brushed against the brown-grey metal and soon collected streaks of muck.

'Ugh, everywhere is so filthy!' She spoke to herself, whilst brushing a mark on her sleeve in a futile gesture that just spread the stain further. Violet had last seen Mr Speedy Loans heading off past the engine shed in the direction of the huge coaling tower. So she chose a route that took her as far to the back wall of the depot as possible, judging correctly that she had the best chance of evading detection that way. Violet eventually came to a point, where before her lay a wide spread of tracks fanning out into the distance, some leading to the concrete tower that dominated the skyline, with rows of engines awaiting feeding with coal. The other tracks stretched as far as she could see and were either empty or held long rows of railway wagons. A few figures dressed in blue overalls could be seen moving around, but otherwise the place seemed strangely deserted. She scanned the area repeatedly, but could see no sign of the man.

Violet suddenly realised what a futile exercise this was. He could be literally anywhere in this vast complex, and more than likely in an office somewhere out of sight, doing whatever it was that he was so eager to undertake. Violet was angry with herself for wasting time and spoiling her shoes and coat on such a foolish wild goose chase. What was she going to do anyway, if she met the man? She had confronted him once already, and he had even exchanged some of the money without being asked. As Violet considered this fact she realised that he had really been pretty decent to her, even if he was a bit of a spiv, and a creepy one at that. She sighed and realised that skulking around like a criminal was unbecoming and more than a little embarrassing. She decided to try and make the best of the situation and now walked boldly towards the ugly tower, thinking to look at the rows of engines and read their names for a few minutes, acting as if this were a quite normal way to pass an evening. It would do as a route for her evening walk, even if the air were not exactly as fresh as she had planned. She could then continue on towards the bridge carrying the Byfield Road over the tracks, where she believed she might escape the dreary world of the railway. As Violet drew close to the coaling tower, the light grew dimmer and a sudden shower of rain spattered down around her. Oh, great. So much for a nice evening.

She quickly ran forward, underneath the massive opening into the cavernous interior. Violet stood beside a big green engine and watched with a heavy heart as the rain started to pour down in what her mother like to call 'stair rods'. It was just a passing shower, but no less drenching for that. Under the tower it was cold and the place stank pungently of sulphurous coal. The whole building was filled with the echoing sounds of water dripping from an immense height, and strange groans and rumbles as the huge hoppers full of coal, high above her head, settled into place. The locomotive beside her ticked as the metal cooled. Violet sensed that it was like a huge beast at rest. She then felt her feet grow cold and wet, looked down and saw her shoes finally reach a point of no recovery, as they sank into a sticky slurry of fine coal dust and rainwater.

'This is just too much. What am I doing here?' Violet felt stinging tears of frustration start to well in her eyes. She reached into her coat pocket, pulled out a small handkerchief and blew her nose. At that very moment all thoughts about her predicament were brutally wrenched from her mind. At first she could not even be sure of what was happening; all she knew was that there was a dreadful, hellish roar and the sound like that of a hundred bombs falling. It was like the terrible night in Leicester, when the Blitz killed her father. The sound grew in volume and reverberated around the walls in a way that was disorientating, and the ground shook. Then Violet was engulfed in a cloud of choking, grey dust. She coughed and held her handkerchief to her mouth, and ran out into the falling rain, relieved to escape the cacophony of the interior. She glanced back at the tower, and then realised that coal was pouring into the tender of the green locomotive. Violet stopped splashing through the oily puddles. Her heart was beating fast, so she made herself draw a few slow, deep breaths. How stupid was she? It was nothing to be so scared of. She gulped more air. However, she was almost immediately startled again, this time by the sudden appearance through the fog of dust and the curtains of rain, of a man running towards her. He was almost immediately right before her, his eyes wide and staring.

It was questionable as to which of them was the more surprised by the encounter. Violet involuntarily stepped backwards and felt the metal of a locomotive press against her back, and let out a slight sound. He, in turn, stopped in his tracks, staring into her eyes in confusion as if he were searching for something, whilst breathing hard and fast. It was Violet who broke the momentary impasse.

'Oh, hello. Fancy meeting you here.'

'What the devil?' The man narrowed his eyes, and then a look of recognition washed over him, but it did nothing for his manner. Water streamed off his leather jacket. 'Shit, you're just what I need.' He pushed his face unpleasantly close to Violet's, forcing her to recoil, 'You keep your nose out — or else! Now, let me past...' and with no further word of explanation he made a swiping gesture with his arm as if to brush Violet aside, although it barely touched her, and he started to run down the cinder track between the railway lines. He stopped after a short while, glanced around then threw a final ugly look over his shoulder at Violet, then cut across the rows of waiting wagons, through the yard and out of sight.

Well, another unsatisfactory encounter with Mr Speedy Loans, Violet thought to herself. I guess that's what comes from skulking around like a petty thief. You end up getting treated like one. She stood still and pondered the curious incident. There was no doubt about it: the running man had been the same one that she had set out to follow. And now he looked even more agitated than before. Clearly something had annoyed or upset him. The rain stopped as quickly as it had started, for that, at least, Violet was thankful, as a flash of warming sun like a searchlight raked the railway yard.

Violet was deeply puzzled about what had just happened, but also thoroughly sick of standing in a filthy railway yard, and had no thought of trying to discover what had caused the man to look so agitated. She just wanted to get home, make some food, and try to clean her grimy clothes. So, turning up the collar of her mackintosh, she pulled her cap down on her head, and with her hands jammed into her coat pockets, she strode quickly towards the edge of the yard, looking to escape to the normality of the village. Violet was grateful that the far edges of the railway yard seemed empty of people. Hopefully she could get back into the village without being seen.

Violet had been observed, however; and her curious watcher had even made a record of the place and time, in his little notebook.

A book that was steadily filling up with pages of notes, some of which already included Violet and the unpleasant man in the leather jacket. For Edward was standing on the coals that filled a locomotive tender, not two rows away from the coal tower, breaking some of the largest lumps into more manageable pieces with a sledgehammer. It was hard, wet and dirty work, and he had paused to wipe away the sweat, mingled with rain, forming on his brow. His eye had been immediately drawn to the red cap and mackintosh of a pretty woman walking near the coal hoist. This was an unexpected sight, and he could not help but be interested. She was quite close by, and he was able to identify her as Miss McIntyre. But why was she walking there?

She was soon lost behind more locomotives and wagons, but Edward decided to record this unusual incident, and thought to talk to Simon about it later. After seeing Miss McIntyre and the motorbike man appearing to exchange a five-pound note the other day, Edward felt that she was, perhaps, not quite what she seemed. He stood in his commanding position, high above the locomotive chimneys and long lines of wagon roofs, and watched for some minutes afterwards for her to reappear. Scanning the far edges of the shunting yards, he eventually picked out her red coat, at the perimeter fence, flashing like a warning light.

*   *   *   *

Peter was worried. Things were spiralling dangerously out of control. He needed to think carefully about what to do next. He knew he was in a very precarious position and a wrong move would see him either under arrest or, even worse, quite probably dead. Thinking about it, either option was likely to end in the same result, for he would surely hang, if sentenced.

He had telephoned Mickey Rollo from the call box on School Street, and had been able to contact him at 'The Barracks', as the rows of company lodging houses were known. If Rollo was unenthusiastic at being called from his brief rest after a long day on the footplate, this was nothing to his mood when Peter had told him that they, and Ken Price too, needed to meet urgently that night.

'Why the hell do I want to see you tonight?'

'I can't say on the telephone — but it's urgent.'

'Why can't it wait? What about tomorrow?'

'No. Absolutely not.'

'Spending a Saturday night with you is not my idea of fun, so it had better be something good.'

'Good is not the word I would use. Look, I really can't say here, but you and Ken need to meet with me. Back room, The White Hart. In half an hour.'

'Bit bloody eager, aren't you?'

'Yes, I suppose I am. I can't say more. See you in the White Hart, right?'

There was an ominous silence for a few moments, then Rollo sighed heavily. 'OK. I'll swing past and knock Kenno up as well. He won't be best pleased, either. It had better be worth it.' There was a click, and Rollo had hung up.

Peter was now sitting in the pub with a near-empty glass of beer, trying to stay calm and look as if he were enjoying being there. Meeting with Mick and Ken was a risk now, but he gambled that no one would think anything of it on a Saturday night, when the normally sleepy pub came alive with thirsty railway workers.

The two men sauntered in at that moment, looking glum. But once Peter had provided them both with a pint of ale each and their glasses had been half drained in long draughts, they looked more relaxed and settled back into their chairs. Peter just wished that it could remain the convivial evening that it appeared to be to anyone observing them.

'So?'

'Yes, Peter, what is the haste? Why have you called us here, and come to think on, when is young Jimmy joining us? He is coming, isn't he?' Ken Price was fiddling with his pipe as he spoke, looking up and almost through his busy eyebrows.

'Well ... I, we actually, have a problem. A serious problem.'

'Oh blinkin' heck! Another? You're like a bloody scratched seventy-eight, you are. Change it, please. So what is it, another dame turning her nose up at your money again?' Rollo reached for his glass and took a deep gulp.

'No. It's far worse,' Peter gulped, feeling his mouth go dry, his hands shaking slightly. The two men saw the signs, and froze in mid-action. It was almost comical, Mick with a pint glass held to his lips, and Ken with pipe in one hand, a burning Swan Vesta in the other.

'You see it's about Jimmy. He's dead.'

The match continued to burn, until it scorched Ken's fingers and he shook it out with an oath. This broke the dreadful stillness, and Mick slowly placed his pint glass back on the table with measured calmness.

'Dead? In what way, dead?'

'What ways are there? I mean he's just … dead.' Peter was speaking as quietly as he could, his voice in danger of breaking.

'What I mean is, why is he dead? How did he come to find himself dead?'

'He … he fell. He got killed. By falling.'

'Oh good Lord. He fell? Where? How? I don't understand.' Ken was still holding his unlit pipe, but was staring intently at Peter, reading his face with searching intensity.

'We had an argument. Look, it was an accident. We were on the coaling tower. We were arguing, yeah? I was really out of sorts with him. We got a bit angry, he shoved me, and he slipped and fell. Off the tower.'

'You sure he slipped?'

'Yes Mick, he slipped, I swear. Jesus…' Peter looked away at the grubby carpet and shook his head. 'There's no way I'd do something like that.'

Rollo took out a Woodbine and lit it, staring the whole time at Peter, wafting the match out, drawing heavily on the cigarette, and then blowing a cloud of smoke towards the ceiling, never once removing his unblinking gaze. His breathing was slow and measured. 'Why were you arguing? And why on the tower?'

'Why do you think? You lot should know better than me.' Peter looked up angrily and stared across the table, 'Bloody hell!' he banged his glass on the table, causing a few others in the pub to look across at them. Peter, forced himself to stop for a few moments, and then continued with exaggerated quietness and control. 'I think you do know. Now I think of it, are you all in on this or was it just that double-crossing bastard Jimmy?'

'No idea what you are on about. Explain yourself.'

'The bloody money, of course! Where was it, eh? Jimmy never dropped it off.'

'What?' Ken was looking anxiously at first Mick and then Peter, 'Of course we dropped it off.'

'Are you sure about that?' Rollo narrowed his eyes, 'We dropped it all right. I just caught sight of it through the steam, as Jimmy chucked it out. You must have missed it.'

'No!. It was not there. He kept it for himself. Screwed me big time. I mean, without the cash,' he raised his hands in a gesture of despair, 'my life's going to be pretty damn short.'

'For us too,' added Ken. 'Are you sure he did drop it off, Mick?'

'Well, there was a lot smoke, but I was pretty sure he did. You must have missed it, that's all. It's still there, is my guess, surely?'

'No. I searched everywhere, even beside the track. So I called Jimmy, didn't I? Told him to meet me. Somewhere out of the way. When I asked him, he denied it all, didn't he? So, OK, I got a bit annoyed with him, started to push him around. You'd do the same, come on.' Peter's eyes betrayed his fear, as he glanced from one to the other.

'Sounds reasonable, I suppose. And?' Rollo was looking at the floor, intent upon his cigarette, but clearly listening and thinking.

'So, there was a bit of argy-bargy, you know? And — oh Jesus — he fell over the bloody railings into the coal bunker thing. Honest, I never pushed him. I mean, not to make him fall like that.' Peter paused. 'It was a long way down.'

'I can't believe what I am hearing. You're in serious trouble, you know that?' It was Ken speaking. 'You'll have to go to the police. It's the only way.'

'Are you kidding, Kenno? Do that and the whole set-up is blown to pieces. Fancy Dan here won't last ten minutes under examination. And anyway, what's he going to tell them? Even if he does manage to spin them a tale,' he looked contemptuously at Peter, 'Top Link is going to blow his top. One of us dead, another in prison and a half a million or so quid missing. Shit. Our lives really won't be worth living.' Rollo took a deep, urgent drag on his cigarette and blew it out of his nostrils, 'Ken, the police are not our problem; they're just an irritation.' He looked up at them, 'We'll be dead men for sure if he comes looking for us.' Rollo stubbed out his cigarette in the ashtray with a slow, deliberate movement, twisting the cigarette until it was crushed and completely extinguished. 'We had better start making a plan, and we don't have long.'

'No way. No way am I getting involved in any of this business. I never agreed to anything like this. It was just a way to make a few pounds for my old age. No more than that.' Ken was shaking his head defiantly. 'I can't agree to any kind of cover-up to a death. We must inform the police. Hand it over it to the proper authorities.'

'Ken, you're not listening. You are involved. And the police are not going to save your neck even if you get banged up in prison — understand? Look, I don't know if this yarn is right, and if it really was an accident, or if our friend here bumped him off,' Rollo looked across at Peter, then back to Ken, 'It doesn't matter right now. If there is an investigation, we are all in the spotlight. We can't cover up the scam with the money. If Peter ends up hanging, well, that's his look out.' Peter winced and looked up at the ceiling, taking a long, deep breath. 'But do you think we will last more that a week or two with the big man himself after us? No chance. You'll get strangled in your own prison bed.' Rollo was looking earnestly at the older man. 'We can get out of this. Trust me. But we need to think and act quickly.' He turned to Peter. 'So where is Jimmy now?'

'He's hidden,' Peter looked grey, and his hands shook. 'He fell into the coal hopper,' he pulled hard on his cigarette. 'It's a long drop; there was no way I could climb down and rescue him. It was impossible.'

'Are you saying he was still alive when he landed in the coal?' Ken was now smoking his pipe, and spoke very quietly.

'I don't know. No, I can't believe that he was. He'd break his neck for sure, wouldn't he?'

'Maybe.'

'So I emptied the hopper into the locomotive waiting below. He's buried under the coal there.'

'Oh, the poor man,' Ken shook his head in despair.

'He won't remain undiscovered for long. If they'd finished coaling for the day, then someone will have noticed. It's noisy enough for the whole bloody village to hear. But even of we're lucky and no one noticed, well, it's Sunday tomorrow … let's think. Maybe they won't move the engine until evening?'

'Yes, that would buy us some time,' Ken was visibly pale.

'Not a lot. I reckon we have until midday, at best. Did anyone see you?'

'I think so. Yes. I suppose someone might have seen me going there. I mean, I never expected anything like this, but I was quite careful. It was afterwards, I bumped into someone.'

'Oh, now he tells us. So we have even less time.'

'It was strange, now I think about it. What was she doing there?' he furrowed his brow. 'It was the same woman who complained about the fiver. You remember?'

'Your girl, the dressmaker?'

'She's not my girl, Rollo. But it was a hell of a shock. She recognised me, worst luck.'

'Damn. But yeah, why was she there? Could she be in on this with Jimmy?'

'She couldn't have known I was going to be there with him … oh, but of course, she would if he told her. But it just doesn't make sense.' Peter's eyes were flicking from side to side, from Rollo to Ken and back, searching for answers.

'I don't like this at all. It's getting complicated. I smell a rat somewhere. We'll have to do something about her.'

Peter and Ken both looked at Rollo, surprise and concern, in their eyes.

'She's a witness. Once the hue and cry goes up she'll put two and two together and give the police a head start. She might even be more than a witness, she might be in on all this and playing us as the patsy. There's something not adding up in this. Listen, Peter, I need to know you're not playing us for fools here. You seem to be involved with her, not Jimmy — so what's the straight deal? '

'Nothing, really. I don't understand all this. I can't see how she fits into anything.'

'Bloody hell.' Rollo suddenly looked worried. 'This is getting my goat, I don't know what going on here. Right, let's pay her a visit, find out what her game really is,' Rollo pulled a face, 'look, if Jimmy really was setting us up, with this woman, then the money could be at his place, or hers, yeah?'

'So … if we could just recover the lost money, we could square things with Top Link himself?' Ken was grasping at straws, his hands starting to shake.

'It would help save our necks.'

'Her shop is right opposite. I've been there.'

'Is it now? Let's go then.' Rollo stood up and drained his glass.

'I hope we are not just getting in even deeper.' Ken stood up reluctantly and moved slowly, as if lack of speed and enthusiasm would somehow prevent anything happening. Neither Rollo nor Peter answered him, but Peter gave him a gentle nudge towards the door.

The three men walked out of the hotel into the cold night air. It had turned foggy and the gas lamps were forming pale yellow halos and throwing just a weak, diffused light on the ground. The fog was collecting at the lower part of the hill around the railway embankment, forming a dense and impenetrable cloud. They stood on the pavement in a small huddle, wreathed in the chill, cotton-wool of the fog. A match flared as Peter lit a Woodbine. They glanced across at the McIntyres' shop. All was dark, except for a pale glimmer at the back of the shop that seemed to come through a partially opened door. The three men walked across the road and Rollo gently tried the front door handle, but it was locked. There was no sign of movement inside, but the murmur of voices talking could just be heard.

'She's got company.' Rollo pressed his ear briefly to the doorframe. 'Or it's the radio? Go round the back.' They walked down the road towards the gloomy, black portal of the railway overbridge, which gaped menacingly as they drew closer, then turned right into the access lane, halting near the McIntyre's rear gate on its dropped hinges.

'You keep a look-out.' Rollo pointed at Ken, who was clearly relieved not to be entering the building. 'Come on, let's get a closer look at your lady friend.' As he spoke, Rollo pulled a German Luger from his coat pocket.

'Bloody hell, why've you got that?'

'Can't be too careful. I didn't like your phone call, so just in case you were thinking of trying anything on …' Rollo calmly slipped the safety catch off the pistol and then deliberately pointed it at Peter, 'I have the means to dissuade you. Understand?'

'OK, OK, cool it. Put that bloody thing away.' Peter stared angrily at the barrel of the pistol being steadily pointed at him. Rollo winked and then lowered it, turning away at the same time and holding the pistol near his hip as he started to walk across the yard. The two men quietly approached the back door, almost feeling or sensing their way forward in the foggy darkness, aiming for a pool of yellow light spilling out from loosely drawn curtains at the back of the house.

This was an unusual sight after years of blackout restrictions. It was suddenly eerily quiet in the way that only fogbound nights can be. Even the railway seemed to be momentarily sleeping. Rollo listened at the door, and then nodded as he confirmed that it was a wireless playing inside the house. From the sudden bursts of laughter it sounded like *ITMA*. He turned the handle and stepped into a small kitchen, and sniffed. The air smelt strongly of paint. A red mackintosh was suspended by a coat hanger from the top of the open door. Peter stood beside Rollo, and nudged him, nodding towards the coat. Rollo understood the signal: the woman they were looking for was inside.

Rollo then confidently stepped into the rear parlour and rapidly surveyed the scene. It was brightly lit by unshaded electric lights and filled with the sound of the radio comedy show. Most of the furniture had been removed or pulled into the centre of the room and covered in a white dust sheet. The floor was similarly covered. They were not curtains at the window, but another sheet roughly tacked into place, and Rollo saw pots of distemper on the floor beneath the windowsill. A stepladder was erected close to the wall to the left of the door, and a young man was standing high up on this, a broad paintbrush in one hand and a paint kettle in the other. A young woman dressed in an old pair of men's trousers tightly belted around the waist, a paint-flecked shirt tucked inside and wearing a headscarf knotted high on her forehead, was standing near the far wall, paintbrush poised in mid-action.

She turned to look at the two men, her face struggling to comprehend what was happening. A look of confusion played across her face, her eyes opened wide and she made as if to speak, but Rollo didn't wait to hear what she had to say. He quickly grabbed the stepladder and wrenched it first forwards then backwards, hurling the young painter off the steps towards the cluster of furniture; as he did so, the paint kettle flew through the air in a shallow arc, spilling a wash of distemper as it moved until it clattered against the wainscot. The young man had only time to exclaim 'What the hell!' before his back landed heavily against a sharp, protruding corner of a table and he let out a loud scream of pain, his face distorted in agony. 'Aagh! Oh God, Aagh ... agh!' He slumped to the floor, twisting and writhing, trying to reach his back with his hands, clearly in severe distress. There was a burst of laughter from the radio as Colonel Chinstrap cracked a joke.

'What have you done? Oh, Tom! Tom!' The young woman dropped her brush and started to run across the room towards the injured man, but Rollo grabbed her roughly, pulled her close to himself, his left hand clamped over her mouth. She struggled and fought like a cornered cat, biting his hand until it drew blood, but he refused to remove it, and then he placed the muzzle of the Luger to her chest.

'Stop now — don't scream, don't move, and you won't get killed. Understand?' He stared into her frightened eyes, looking for her acknowledgement. She tried to nod her head, but his vice-like grip was so tight she could barely manage even that. Her eyes flicked wildly from side to side, wide with shock. The man was still crying out on the floor. 'Bloody hell Pete, shut that bastard up, will you?' There was sickening thump as Peter struck the man on the base of his neck with the butt of a small pistol. The man fell silent, just as the BBC audience gave a round of applause. Rollo looked at the pistol in Peter's hand, 'Where the hell did you find that?'

'You can't be too careful, can you?' The look in Peter's eyes was angry and sarcastic. 'You think I'm just some dandy pimp; well, I can look after myself. Just remember that.'

'Oh, I won't forget.' Rollo then turned back to the girl, whose eyes were staring down at the motionless body on the floor. 'I'm going to release you now, and you are not going to scream, OK? That would be a stupid thing to do. I'll forget you bit me — for now. But I need you to answer some questions. Remember, this gun is loaded and I'll use it if I have to.' He slowly withdrew his hand from the woman's face and she instantly stepped back from him, raising both hands in front of her.

'What do you want? Why are you doing this? Oh, please, leave us!' tears streamed down her face, as she pressed herself back against the wall.

'The money, where is it? Tell us that, and we'll be gone.'

'Money? What money?'

'Oh, you know what I mean. Come on — what's your part in this scam? Were you and Jimmy in it together?'

'Oh God, what are you talking about? I don't understand. Who's Jimmy? I don't know anyone called Jimmy. If you want money … we've got about ten pounds, take it. Oh, please, take it and go!' She put her head in her hands and sobbed loudly.

'Rollo! This isn't the same one. She's the wrong flipping girl. She's too young, she's her daughter or something.'

Rollo spun around. 'What? What d'you mean we've got the wrong bloody woman? Shit! You never said anything about there being two of 'em!'

'How am I supposed to know? I'm not part of the sodding family. Oh Christ, Rollo, why'd you have to get stuck in like this? We're well buggered now. We seriously have one big problem.'

'Three, more like.' Rollo bit his lower lip, clearly trying to assess the situation. He then suddenly turned back to the girl. 'I'm asking you one last time, where's the money? There was plenty of it, in a big, leather bag, so it's not easy to forget.' The girl shook her head, fear in her eyes.

'I really don't think she's got a clue. You've played this out all wrong.'

'Yeah? So what do you suggest?'

'We all go our own ways. Split. Get out now and fast. Head for the ports, get as far away as we can before all hell breaks out here. We can hide these two somewhere, to buy us a few hours?'

'Is he dead?'

The girl took a sharp intake of breath and clasped her hands to her face.

'Nah. He's breathing.'

Rollo looked at the man on the ground, than back to Peter. 'OK. We passed some sheds out the back. Drag him in there. But we'll keep the girl. She might be useful if we get cornered.' Whilst he was speaking he approached her, and she immediately cowered away from the gun pointing at her. With one hand he pulled her headscarf off, and then pocketing the Luger, quickly grabbed her wrists, pulling them behind her and binding them with the scarf. The Luger was soon in the small of her back. 'Remember, don't be so stupid as to scream, OK?' She nodded. 'What's your name?'

'Jenny.'

'OK, Jenny, don't do anything stupid and you'll be all right. Now, if you choose to remember anything about the money in the next few minutes, we will be gone even quicker, yeah?'

Peter, meanwhile, was hefting the unconscious man out of the room, holding him under the armpits and dragging his feet along the ground. As they reached the back door, Peter whistled a quick, sharp note, hoping that the watching engine driver would hear. Sure enough, a dark form started to emerge from the foggy gloom, the red bowl of his ever-present pipe, acting like a beacon.

'Ken? Quickly, give me a lift.'

'Who's he? What's going on?'

'No time to explain,' he was breathing heavily, 'Come on, man. Lift his legs and get him over to one of the outbuildings.' Ken, with considerable trepidation, took the limp legs of the man and started to walk backwards, stumbling slightly as he tried to find his footing, not helped by his surprise at seeing Rollo guiding a young woman to follow them. After just a few steps, he was forced to let his pipe fall out of his mouth to the ground, where it landed in a shower of sparks and embers, little red spots of light in the chilly enveloping fog. 'Stop!' Ken placed the man's legs on the ground and collected his pipe, quickly knocking out the remaining glowing embers, and stuffed it into a pocket. He heaved the man's legs off the ground and started to move, crab-like across the yard, now half facing Peter. 'What the hell is this all about?'

'Problems, Ken, serious problems. We've got to get out of here, get out the country and then lay low, understand?'

'Jesus. Is he dead?' Ken was breathing hard now.

'No. He'll live. Look, that shed, put him in there.' They shuffled over to an Anderson shelter and pulled door open. 'I can't see a damn thing in here. There's junk all over the entrance.'

'Stop moaning and move it, then. We need to get him in here, he's coming round,' Rollo and the girl were beside them now, the gun still firmly pressed into her back. 'Hey, is your motorbike nearby?'

'Uff, this is heavy.' Peter was dragging a large, wooden crate from the entrance area of the air-raid shelter, making a lot of noise in so doing, 'Yeah, I always leave it out the back of that garage, right next door to here. Hey, what are these?' He had opened the box, and was holding up a small, flattened cylinder, with what looked like a woven belt attached to one side.

'That's a fog signal. A detonator. You can attach it to the rail with that fastening. It's a full box.' Ken was kneeling down and picked one up. 'Stuff a few in your pockets — if we are in this much of a mess then you never know. They could prove useful'

'Good idea — but get a move on, will you!'

A locomotive passing above them on the embankment issued a piercing alarm whistle that cut through the thick, foggy air, followed by two swift retorts like gun-shots as the fog signals exploded beneath the engine's wheels. The train started to rattle past in an apparently endless succession of squeaks and groans.

'You hear that?' Ken half turned to look at Rollo, ignoring his command, 'They're setting them on the lines. It means the fog's worsening.'

'Good. It'll help us.'

Peter, meanwhile, entered the black interior of the shelter, clattering and banging into gardening tools and cursing. 'Bloody hell! Come on, haul him in. There's a bed here. We can tie him up and leave him there.' Peter reappeared at the doorway and started to lift the now gently moaning man, dragging him into the gloom with Ken assisting by lifting his feet. 'Hang on, there's something on the bed, I've got to move it out the way.' Peter dropped Tom roughly onto the lower end of the narrow bed as if he were a sack of potatoes. 'Mind out, Ken, I'll chuck it past you, out of the bloody way,' and with that, Peter heaved a heavy leather bag out of the narrow entrance in one skilful move. It thumped heavily at the feet of Rollo, who looked down at it with a puzzled expression. Despite the thickening fog, he didn't need a flashlight or even to bend down and inspect the contents, to know that this was the missing counterfeit money.

A banking engine at the rear of the heavy goods' train passing above them, started to make its presence felt, snorting and pounding with steady, throbbing beats, just like the blue vein wriggling its way down the side of Rollo's forehead was rhythmically pumping to the beat of his heart. 'Well, well, well. So you don't know anything about the money, eh?' Rollo shoved Jenny roughly away from him so that she stumbled and fell backwards against the corrugated iron of the shelter. She reached behind and steadied herself as best she could with her tied hands against the icily cold metal. A look of shock and anger crossed her brow, and for a brief second it looked as if Jenny was going to rush out at her attacker like an angry bull, but this was just as quickly replaced by a look of fear, when Rollo moved to stand opposite her, pointing the gun directly towards her heart, a scowling sneering grin on his face that filled her with dread.

'Hey, lads! Jenny here has got some explaining to do.'

Chapter Twenty-Four

'DON'T FENCE ME IN'
Bing Crosby

Vignoles was sitting at home with a cup of tea, the pot warming underneath a crocheted cosy of surprising ugliness in regards to both colour and design. It had been bought at a Spitfire Fund event a few years past, and no doubt yellow, purple and fawn were the only colours of wool available to the villager who made it. At least he hoped that that was their excuse. He shook his head. A garish tea cosy was a small price to pay for having survived the war unscathed.

The wireless was playing Bing Crosby singing 'Don't Fence Me in'. Vignoles liked this song, and started to sing along gently to what words he could remember and looked out of the window into their small back garden. It was dripping wet from the sudden fog that had blanketed them all night, and which still hung around in drifts. A blackbird was skittering around the base of the fruit bushes and then pulled a worm from the damp soil. Maybe if the sun burnt off the fog, he and Anna could take a train down the line and have a walk by Swithland Reservoir. It was probably a far cry from the open plains and deserts that Bing was picturing, but it appeared no less romantic to Vignoles, that morning.

Such thoughts were interrupted, however, by the ringing of the telephone. Putting his cup down, he walked into the hall and picked up the receiver, looking at this own reflection in the tall mirror on the wall. It was Tim Saunders, the shedmaster at Woodford Depot.

'Mr Vignoles? Tim Saunders here.' He was curiously formal.

'Oh, good morning. To what may I owe this surprise?'

'Not a surprise, but a shock, Vignoles. You had better get down here — fast. Something nasty has happened.'

'What is it?'

'A body. A dead body. The tension was evident in his voice. 'The doctor isn't here yet to confirm that officially, but he looks pretty darned dead to me.'

'Have you called him?'

'Yes, and I took the liberty of putting a local undertaker on alert, yes, I know, a bit presumptious of me, but believe me, he's not going anywhere.'

'So, where is the body?'

'He's in the coal. On the back of an engine — can you believe it?'

'I can see why it was a shock.' Vignoles paused a moment, 'Have you moved him?'

'No, just uncovered a part. An arm were sticking out; scared the life out of the lad and lassie who found him.'

'Don't touch anything, don't move anything. That's an order. Keep the area clear of everyone. No one goes near the place, except the doctor, of course.'

'Don't worry, nobody wants to.'

'I'll be there as quick as I can, with my sergeant. Tim, what are your first impressions? Does it look like an accident? And do you know who he is?'

'Looks like he fell in the coal — from the coaling tower that is, so it could be an accident. Bloody stupid place to be larking around though if that's the case. Maybe he was drunk?' The shedmaster let out a long sigh, 'He's a bit messed up — what with the coal and that, but I reckon I do recognise him; I think he's a guard, but not one of ours. But I don't really want to look, gives me the creeps.'

'Understood. See you later.'

Vignoles and Trinder walked towards the coaling tower and neither spoke. This was typical of the two of them when first arriving upon the scene of a serious crime. Vignoles had stressed to his sergeant many times how important it was to approach the scene in a focussed frame of mind, trying to take in and observe all manner of details, no matter how trivial they might appear. He had often proved his point in previous cases by being able to recall some overlooked or forgotten detail that had been pivotal in closing a case. Vignoles was now walking with what looked like particular care, stepping over the wet and mucky surface of the yard. He was taking note of any footprints and marks, of which there were a considerable number, but his detective brain was filtering out the majority, and seeking something that might appear out of the ordinary. So far, however, it was just a confusion of marks and endless boot prints, all typical of a type worn by nearly every man in the depot. As they drew closer to the location of the body, he stopped, touched the sergeant on his arm.

'No guessing where the crime scene is, then. I don't believe this. I told Saunders to keep everyone away. This is plain ridiculous — what chance do we have of collecting anything useful from this mess?'

Sergeant Trinder was nodding in agreement, and without waiting for instruction, walked briskly ahead calling to attention the group of twenty or more railway workers gathered in groups around the tender of the unfortunate Pacific locomotive. Trinder shooed these gawpers back from the engine, each man and woman reluctantly walking away, until he had them gathered some distance from the now-disturbed crime scene. Trinder then advised them all not to leave the depot, at least not until he had taken their details and interviewed them. At this point he joined Vignoles beside the cab steps. Vignoles was talking with the shedmaster, and so had not yet climbed up to see the body, preferring to wait for Trinder to join him.

'So the locomotive was underneath the coaling tower all night?'

'That's correct, Vignoles. Today being Sunday, we have about twenty locomotives in steam, but come Monday morning, we'll be looking at forty or fifty, so we prepare many of them in advance. "The White Knight" here, was coaled first thing, then pushed out from under the tower. You can see that she is one of six engines all being made ready. Her fire is not due to be lit until about six.'

'Tomorrow morning?'

'Correct.'

'So the engine was under the coal hopper at what time?'

'At 5 am we sent the men on shift, and she was the next in line — except they noticed that she was already coaled, so they shunted her out, at about 5.10 a.m., and started work, on the B12, you see there behind her,' Saunders pointed. Trinder was making notes as the two men talked, looking around him, noting the positions of each engine and their identification numbers.

'So it would appear the engine was coaled yesterday evening? At what time?'

'Well, they knock off at eight. The noise is disturbing after that. But what is strange, the two men seem to think that they had not yet coaled her.'

'Really? I need their names and want to interview them — sergeant, could you follow that up?'

'Of course.'

'They are sure of this?'

'Not so they would swear under oath, but pretty much. They just pour coal into whatever is below, and the exact I.D. of each probably doesn't stick in the mind.'

'Hmm … interesting.' Vignoles turned again to Trinder. 'We must question them about this matter. I feel it is important.'

'Who found the body?'

'Two cleaners; Simon Howerth and Mary Miller. They were breaking the coals into smaller pieces. Some of the coal is too big to use as it comes down the chute, you see?'

'Are they still here?'

'Yes. I sent them for a cup of sweet tea each. It was an awful shock.'

'I can imagine. Sergeant — names and details again.'

'Wilco, sir.'

'Where is that doctor?' Vignoles looked at his wristwatch, 'We're wasting valuable time here. If the poor bugger wasn't dead, he sure as hell will be by now.' He pulled a thoughtful face for a moment, exchanged knowing glances with Trinder and Saunders, then turned decisively and placed his hands on the shiny, steel cab handrails, hauling himself up the locomotive steps into the cab. 'Come on, let's take a quick look.' He could hear his sergeant making notes about Simon and Mary, and then he heaved himself up in turn. Vignoles looked at the black metal wall of the tender that held back the tons of coal like a dam. The coal door was pinned closed, and the fireman's shovel, polished bright with use, was neatly propped against it. The long fire-irons were leant against one side, ready for the next morning. A row of oil cans stood on a metal shelf, a rag flopped over the long spout of one of them. The air smelled strongly of damp coal and oil. Great lumps of coal, the size of coffee tables, rose in a heap in the tender, a lump hammer could be seen resting on the top of one particularly large slab.

'OK, let's have a look.' Vignoles clambered up the metal wall using a toolbox fixed to the side of the cab and a step, to ease his way up. It took some agility and strength, and he appreciated how fit railway crew needed to be, clambering their way up and around their engines. He found his footing on the pile of coal which shifted and groaned a little under his weight, and looked around. He was very high up and would have had a superb vantage point if it were not for the lingering fog that closed off the middle distance into a white sheet. The engine shed was almost invisible, and the rows of parked locomotives faded away into grey and indistinct shapes. They seemed insubstantial, wreathed as they were in the thick, pale air and steam, reminding him of cattle and other farm beasts in the fields at winter.

He looked down into a small hollow in the coal that had clearly been excavated. There was the head, upper torso and right arm of a young man. His legs were still buried deep in the coal and his position made him look almost as if he was standing upright, though his back was bent rather too painfully and his right arm was stretched out wide. The elbow was twisted unpleasantly, and the man's head was bent hard to the left. It was instantly clear that he could not be alive. His eyes were open and his mouth had an expression of surprise locked into position. Trinder had joined Vignoles, and they both manoeuvred themselves into position on either side, looking down at the man for sometime before speaking. The head of Saunders appeared over the parapet of the tender, but he seemed reluctant to come any further. He just stood there and watched the two detectives. Vignoles, without looking at Saunders, but fully aware that he was there, said, 'Yes, he looks dead all right. Is this as he was found?'

'They moved a bit of coal — to see if he was alive.'

'Uh-huh. And when they first found him? Before they moved the coal?'

'Just the arm sticking out, they said. It was obvious it was a person, so they had to see if he was alive.'

'Yes. So why did they decide not to move him?'

'He was very obviously dead. And then they got a bit scared. It was pretty damn weird to find him here like that. It's fair put the shivers up me as well, I can tell you.' The face of Saunders, his eyes wide open and staring, did nothing to relieve the feeling of creepiness to the muffled, dank atmosphere.

'Are you sure you called a doctor?' It was Trinder asking.

'Yes. He really should be here by now.'

'Don't let on that we've already had a look, OK? Doctors can get a bit sniffy if we're seen to be jumping the gun. Oh, and another thing, we need a photographer. Can you rustle up someone with a camera in the village?'

'A camera? Hmm ...Yes, yes, I think I can actually. One of the lads spends all his money on photographing the trains. Does some work on the side for the *Railway Magazine*.'

'Good. Call him immediately, please?' Trinder turned back to contemplating the death scene.

'OK, that's helpful, Tim. Thank you. You can then go and make us a brew if you like.' Vignoles turned to look at the shedmaster and smiled grimly. Saunders did not need to be given another hint, and was only too happy to step down and leave them to it. 'So? Thoughts?'

'I want to see how tall this chap is, and maybe clean some of this black dirt off his face, before I can be really certain,'

'But?'

'I think this is our guard. The one I watched snatch the bag from the Anglo-Imperial Oil Co wagon.'

'Do you, now? So this death could be linked to our Water Street case.' The two men exchanged glances. 'This changes everything. If he is our guard, then why might he find himself down here?' Vignoles knelt down and carefully started to feel in the exposed pockets of the dead man's shirt and overcoat. The inside pocket of which, contained a brown leather wallet 'Let's see ... ah ha. Jimmy Cresswell, guard, L.N.E.Rly. Based in Nottingham. Started in 1941. So it is him.' Vignoles passed the document card to Trinder as he was speaking. 'Ration cards, in the same name ... oh, and quite a lot of money. I make that a good sixteen pounds. Do guards get paid so well these days? I suspect, though, that this fiver is not what it appears to be.' Vignoles pulled out his notebook and flipped it open at a page and compared the number on the big white note, with those he had jotted down in the Water Street printing press. 'That would be a coincidence beyond belief; this note has the same letters in its code, and just one hundred and three away, from the sequence we found on the freshly printed notes.'

Trinder smiled at Vignoles. 'I hate coincidences. They make me suspicious. This is our man then, for sure.'

'And wait ... look at this.' Vignoles removed a ticket, tucked at the back of the wallet. It was for a ship sailing to Rotterdam, dated 22nd June 1946. It was in the name of Mr G. Miller.   'Our favourite band leader was planning on taking a trip, it seems.' Vignoles also allowed himself a smile as he handed to Trinder.

'Ho ho! What's the betting, that one of those passports was being made up for this man, if not already? A new identity to help him escape the country with his cut of the profits, by the look of it. A drunk larking around on the tower and falling? I'm not getting that feeling now, sir.'

'Neither am I. Who would climb up a coaling tower anyway? We need to wait for the doctor and the photographer before we can move him and find out what really killed him, but from what we can see, he looks basically in one piece. Though there maybe other wounds, concealed. I wonder if he was alive when he fell, or was he placed here when dead?'

'He's messed up, and there's quite a lot of blood, but it looks like coal has caused most of that. The clothes are very torn and ripped.'

'The coal could also have done that, I suspect. So he could have died by falling, either through misadventure or by being pushed. Or, he could have been rendered unconscious, and then thrown into the coal hopper.'

'Or was he alive when he was in the hopper, and died by being crushed?'

'The post mortem can put us on the right track here. A few blows to the head by these huge lumps of coal, and he would be finished.'

'So somehow or other, he was on top of the coal as it was poured into the tender?'

'It's beginning to look that way. Murder or manslaughter.' Vignoles rested his chin on his hand and looked long and hard, whilst thinking. 'But why did he end up dead?'

'Perhaps he just became "surplus to requirements"?'

'That's a rather cynical view.'

'It's a cynical world, sir. I don't buy into this "honour amongst thieves" rubbish. I'm sure the kind of people we are dealing with won't have any hesitation about killing, if they think it necessary.'

'I fear you're right. But it's also a very risky strategy. Now that one of them is dead, they must realise that we, or the civvy constabulary, will investigate. It's a stupid action to take if you wish to remain undetected. Everything has changed with this curious death. Something has shifted since last night.' He looked around at the faded, black-and-white scene that surrounded them. 'I think something has gone seriously wrong within the gang. This young man's death is a puzzle, but I sense that it will cause the gang more problems than it will us.'

'Yes. I think we should get that printing press raided at double-quick time.'

Vignoles nodded in agreement, then he and Trinder climbed back down from the tender, as a man holding an impressive-looking camera and flash unit approached, and after a brief 'hello' they left him to get on with his work. Vignoles sat on the inadequately small seat provided for the locomotive driver, and Trinder perched on the even tinier one for the fireman, and they started to draw up a list of urgent actions that needed processing that morning. Trinder then walked a short way across the yard to a telephone located in what looked rather like a bird-nesting box, fixed upon a telegraph pole and made a series of calls upon the instructions of Vignoles, whilst Vignoles walked slowly and methodically around the locomotive, and then back under the coaling tower, studying the many scuffs, footprints and marks in the ground.

He climbed the metal steps that took him to the uppermost level, looking the whole time for any clues to what might have happened up there. The metal platform was narrow and led to a small, glass-windowed cabin, which held a series of levers. These controlled the flow of coal and operated the winch system that hauled loaded coal wagons up the side of the building and tippled their contents into the huge storage reservoirs. The cabin had a door, but the lock was clearly unusable and had been for quite some time, caked as it was in black gunge. Not a problem for someone to operate the coal hopper, then? The floor of the platform was deep in coal dust, ingrained upon the surface, and it was damp from the rain the day before. There were a multitude of marks and boot prints, some of which seemed to indicate feet sliding and slipping on the surface. Beside the low, metal fence that protected the drop down into the cavernous lower hopper, there were many confused marks. Could they be consistent with a struggle? Vignoles couldn't be sure. He walked to a far corner of the platform that was undisturbed and turned his shoe on the surface, then slid it across the floor. It left a strong and dramatic smear in the dirt, and if he did not know better, he might be tempted to see this as evidence of a struggle. Trying to interpret this confusion of marks on the floor was possibly only going to muddle things, and would be inconclusive.

Just as Vignoles was about to step back down, his eyes caught sight of something bright lying on a metal girder, just to one side of the platform, a foot or two below. He knelt down and looked closer. It was a primrose-yellow silk handkerchief, spotted with red polka dots. It was bright, clean and evidently had not lain there long. Vignoles wrapped his R.A.F. coat around him, placed his hat to one side and lay prone on the floor in order to reach down. The handkerchief was still just out of reach. He strained and stretched, pulling himself dangerously forward over the edge, until his finger tips just managed to get the slightest grip on one edge.

'Got you!' He pulled himself back from the void, stood up and looked at the square of silk. 'If I am not mistaken, I have seen you in the suit pocket of a certain Loan Shark. Now, what might you be doing up here...?'

Vignoles and Trinder met up beside the locomotive, just as the photographer was leaving. 'We need them rather urgently, can you get them to our office by tomorrow morning?'

'I should think so. Photographic paper is jolly hard to come by, and I only have a little in stock, so I'll run off the most essential ones first and pass on the negatives. If you need the full set, then maybe you can find some paper stock in Leicester? It can be darned difficult to get hold of, I can tell you.'

'That will do fine. Let me know what we owe you. Thank you.' Vignoles clambered back up onto the tender, and stood looking around at the surrounding scene, studying the way the railway lines, buildings and possible access points were assembled. The encircling fog forcibly restricted his view to a few hundred yards each way, but it was still a busy and confusing picture. It was going to be hard to reconstruct what might have happened here. Vignoles then showed the polka-dotted handkerchief to Trinder. 'Mr Peter Prenton, spiv, Loan Shark, and generally shady character, had just such a handkerchief in his breast pocket when he visited Anna and myself in Charwelton.'

'Did he, now? Spot on. Of course, if I can play Devil's Advocate, other people carry such handkerchieves.'

'They do. But not many others seem to be connected with money counterfeiting and lending in close proximity to the L.N.E.R. Anyway, sergeant, you said yourself that you don't like coincidences.'

'Put it like that, and we have just cause to have a word with Mr Prenton.'

'Exactly. And losing this suggests a struggle. Could he be the man who helped poor Jimmy here end up in the coal?' Vignoles looked thoughtful. 'We must call in Ken Price and Michael Rollo as well, urgently. Originally I wanted to play a waiting game on this case, but, if this turns out to be murder, or manslaughter, it affects our choices. We can't afford the indulgence of sitting back and building the bigger picture. We must move quickly and strike at as many of the gang as we can. Are Lansdowne and Benson on their way here?'

'Yes, sir. Leaving on a train any time now. Blencowe is holding the fort as instructed, and he's going to liaise with the Leicestershire Constabulary to get them to raid the Water Street premises as soon as they can get the operation arranged.'

'Hopefully, in the next hour or so. I am worried that they might start to cut and run. Damn! But why has this man ended up dead?' Vignoles stared down at the unfortunate man, who looked like he was drowning in coal. 'We must try to understand what is actually going on here — and quickly.'

'That looks like the doctor approaching — at last. Quick, hop back down, and act innocent. He might give us some answers.'

A black Austin Ruby bounced its way along the ash roadway towards them, dipping and rolling across the rutted and potholed surface. They could see the round, moon face of the occupant leaning forward, pressed close to the windscreen peering upwards at the locomotives. His face was just above his gloved hands gripping the steering wheel and fighting to keep the little car in a straight line. The doctor gave a friendly wave as he caught sight of the detectives and turned the car into a trajectory that brought it close up to the engine and it stopped with one shiny, wire-spoked wheel raised up onto a half-buried wooden sleeper. The substantial bulk of the doctor eased its way out of the tiny car. He stood up and stretched, in unison with the car's springs, which visibly raised themselves back into shape as the doctor then gathered up his black leather bag and called up to the watching detectives, 'Detective Inspector Charles Vignoles, I presume?'

'Indeed I am. And you are doctor...?'

'Halliday. Doc Halliday. Sorry to be so awfully late — got caught up in an emergency with a newborn baby — but she's going to be all right. And, I have to say, going on what Mr Saunders rather graphically told me, I felt sure our man up there would understand that life comes before death, eh?' He laughed amiably. 'Is he right up there? Oh, dear me, what a fearsome climb.'

The doctor looked up with considerable trepidation at the mound of coal many feet above him. 'How on earth will I manage that vertiginous climb? I'm not sure I'm built for that kind of thing.'

'It's not so bad, really,' Sergeant Trinder lied. 'Here, I'll give you a hand up.' Trinder was leaning out of the cab, offering his hand.

'Give me your bag.' He took it and slung it up to Vignoles, who had climbed back onto the mound of coal. Trinder then turned back to the considerable bulk of the neatly, if snugly, be-suited doctor, who was huffing his way up the cab steps. 'Here … I'm Sergeant Trinder, by the way.'

'Oh gosh. Quite out of puff. Oh, dear me. Pleased to meet you, and thanks. And now we have to get right up there as well? Oh deary me. I fear I am a little out of condition. Haven't done anything like this since I was knee high to a grasshopper, scrumping apples.'

After more heaving and puffing the rotund form of the doctor was hauled into place alongside Vignoles, and as he regained his breath and mopped his brow he took a few moments to survey the fogbound view, just as Vignoles had done earlier, from the top of the tender. 'You managed it like you've had practice.' He gave Vignoles a look with a glint in his eye. 'Still, I must say we are surprisingly high up.' The affable doctor stood upright and looked around him. 'A shame it's so foggy. I would be able see where all those police cars were so busy rushing to. I can't help thinking I shall be called to accompany them before too long.' The doctor sighed, and then grinned with evident pleasure, 'It was a bit of a fuss getting up, but by golly it's worth it.'

'What police cars?'

'Don't you know? But of course, you are railway, not civvy police. Yes, three or four of them, hareing their way towards Woodford. They overtook me at quite a lick. Dammed careless if you ask me, in this fog. Must be something big going on there as well.'

Vignoles and Trinder exchanged glances and Trinder shrugged, 'Could be a U.X.B? There were a few bombs dropped here one night a few years back, most of them duds.'

'Yes, that's probably it.' The doctor looked down at the body. 'Well, well, well, how on earth did you get yourself in there?' It was a rhetorical question, spoken softly as the doctor knelt down and started gently touching the neck of the dead man without waiting for any answer from the watching detectives. He explored the head, feeling the pale waxy skin. He looked at his eyes, and then moved the exposed arm. Opening his bag, he extracted a thermometer and placed it inside the man's partially open mouth. Whist he waited for the mercury to move, he turned to look up at Vignoles. 'He is certainly dead.' He grinned, with a boyish delight. 'But of course you know that already,' he chuckled to himself, 'and what you want to know now is how and when, and other more useful things, eh?' He turned back, removed the thermometer and looked thoughtful for a few moments. 'If pressed to give an estimation —'

'— You are,' interjected Vignoles.

'— then I would say that he's been here most of the night. Seven hours, eight, maybe more. Now as to how he died. I think it would be unwise to speculate before the post mortem. What I can tell you is that his neck is broken, and he shows visible signs of having been hit very hard in a few places, especially to the back of the skull.'

'Could that be what killed him?'

'Quite possibly, inspector, but until a detailed examination can be made, it would be unwise to say so definitely. However, the broken neck and trauma to the skull suggest a fall from a great height.' As if to illustrate the fact, the doctor's eyes were drawn to the sides of the concrete coaling tower.

'Falling from that would rather fit the bill.' He paused 'Or, he was whacked on the back of the head, and tossed into the coal to try to cover it up.' He raised an eyebrow. 'That, gentleman, is about all I can say at this juncture.'

'Would you favour being hit, or falling, as the reason for death?'

'You see, you detectives are always the same, so impatient. It will need a post mortem before I could even begin to say for sure, but since you wish me to stray into your territory for a moment, I would suggest that he fell.'

'Thank you, Dr Halliday, most useful. We will get the body removed now and taken to Leicester.'

Trinder helped the doctor make an undignified descent from the locomotive tender, which involved him getting coal dust liberally smeared across his suit and freshly starched white shirt. His collar pinged loose, so by the time he was upright on the ground, he resembled Oliver Hardy quite faithfully, forcing the sergeant to affect a fit of coughing to hide his inappropriate amusement. The doctor was surprisingly positive about the whole experience, however, brushing his suit ineffectually, and then gazing up at the locomotive with a broad smile. 'I'm rather partial to these machines in a way. Of course they are a bit messy and somewhat ruin a perfectly good shirt — and utterly useless for my job, so I prefer the little Austin.

But really, one can't help but admire such a piece of engineering!' He gave one last glance over his shoulder and softly voiced the words 'The White Knight', and then commenced to shoehorn himself back into the car, its springs creaking noticeably. Then he was off.

'What a cheerful fellow. Not the normal gloomy type we usually seem to get lumbered with. So perhaps he fell, and was not struck? That was not what I expected to hear. Though this might change once they have a closer look. OK, sergeant, we need that cup of tea. And I need to light up my pipe and get the brain into gear. We'll take stock and review the situation. Benson and Lansdowne should be with us by then. You and Benson can then commence taking statements, Lansdowne can liaise with the undertakers to remove the body — I can see them hovering in the distance like a row of eager vultures.' He nodded his head at a distant group of sombre men in long, black coats standing beside a handcart furnished with overly large diameter wheels and bearing a coffin.

'And you, sir?'

'I want a long hard look at the duty rosters, to place exactly where Guard Jimmy Cresswell, Fireman Michael Rollo, and Driver Kenneth Price have been over the last two weeks, and especially the last two days. I also want to know where the two who are not dead are now. We shall call them both in for questioning by the end of the day. Oh, and I'll put a call into the Northants civvies and see what they are up to. If it is an unexploded bomb, then it could mean an evacuation of the area. Exactly what we don't need right now.'

Simon and Mary were drinking enamelled mugs of sweet tea, the precious sugar had been rustled up from somewhere in the mess rooms. Simon was beginning to think that it was worth finding a dead body if it meant he got the hot, sweet liquid he was drinking. He was so very rarely allowed two heaped spoonfuls at home, so it was an indulgence to be savoured.

Simon was also trying to think things through in his mind, to get some kind of order and perspective on what happened, but the talkative Mary and a host of other workers who found excuses to stop by the mess room would continually ask him to repeat the story of how he had found the body, and fire ghoulish questions at him about how the dead man had looked. When the policewoman finally got around to talking to him, he reckoned he would have his story so perfectly burnished and polished that he would be able to do it almost without thinking. Simon was trying to find time between reliving the events of the morning, in all their shocking and quite stomach-turning ghastliness, to retrieve something buried deep in his memory. It was elusive though, slipping away like a fish through water. Just as he thought he had a grip upon this detail, the thrilling excitement of being 'The Lad Who Found the Dead Man' intervened to push it away into another inaccessible corner of his memory. Simon knew that he would be able to live off his story for months, maybe for years, in sleepy Woodford Halse, but right at this moment he needed to remember something, make a connection.

Oh, how he wished Edward were here now. He would have written it all down in that little book of his. But Edward was at home: it was his Sunday off. By rights, it should also have been so for Simon, but he had been called in for extra hours due to another cleaner being off sick. As a result though, he had the 'luck' of discovering the most thrilling event in the history of the depot, since Fireman Davies had put a Robinson O2 through the wall at the back of the shed and brought part of the roof down.

Mary was now re-telling her version of the story to the policewoman, glancing across at Simon as she spoke, and he agreeing or adding small details as she went along, the officer writing fast in strange, squiggly marks that looked unlike anything Simon had seen before. Mary did a good job of describing how the two of them had been told to go and break up the huge lumps of coal on the tenders of the engines being coaled that morning, in readiness for Monday. It was a desperately back-breaking job, 'not fit for convicts or P.O.W.s,' as Mary had put it. They had collected two heavy, long-handled sledgehammers and a smaller lump hammer, and then climbed up on to the tender of 'The White Knight'. The shed pilot had then gently shunted the engine and the three in front of it, all fully coaled, out into the open air, so that the men could commence filling the empty tenders of other engines waiting behind. Mary and Simon had prepared themselves for a few hours of heavy, hot work, by removing their jackets despite the chilly morning air, tying their trouser legs closed with string, adjusting their neck scarves to try and stop dust getting in their shirts, and positioning themselves at each end of the great mound of coal. They had been at it for about fifteen minutes, pounding the great chunks of shiny black coal, and Simon was just raking the smaller broken pieces forward, when he saw something pale and thin sticking out and upwards. It was the arm of the man.

'What did you do at that moment?' asked Benson.

'Simon shouted something like "Stop! Look at that!" and I came forward to where he was kneeling on the coal. He was moving lumps away with his hands.'

'So, Simon. You knew what it was straight away?'

'No, not really. I knew it was something strange, not right, if you know what I mean? So I started to clear the coal away, and then I could see it was an arm.'

'Were you not frightened?'

'A bit. It was a shock. I didn't really want to touch it.'

'I can understand that, and you, Mary?'

'I must admit at first I almost shouted out, but I stopped myself and then just thought, like, "Oh my God, someone's fallen in", and wanted to rescue him.'

'You thought he was alive?'

'Probably not if I think about it, but I just couldn't imagine, or think that he was dead, you know? So we just quickly pulled the coal away like two crazy things, didn't we, Simon? Blimey, I tell you, we never worked that fast before.'

'And then what, you uncovered his head and body?'

'Yeah. Well, that was awful. It was a terrible sight.' Mary pulled on her cigarette, 'It was obvious he was dead. Holy Mary, he were a sight, quite shook me up. But I've seen worse of course, after the air raids in Coventry. I was living there at the time. I am in a bit of a tizzy now, because it stirred things up again, things I had tried to forget. You know?'

'I understand. That's not surprising, Mary. And Simon, what did you do then?'

'Mary told me to go and fetch Mr Reed or Mr Saunders, so I did. Mr Saunders came back with me, and he had a look. He was taken quite queer, you know? I'm sure he was going to be sick. It was quite funny really. And then we were told to sit and wait here.'

Simon's mind, however, was already somewhere else. When Mary mentioned things being 'stirred up', it instantly brought to mind that something he was trying to remember. He had said to Edward that if they took the bag of money and hid it, they would 'stir things up in the depot', and 'make things happen'. Well, things were certainly happening now. Simon felt a cold chill down his back. Maybe he and Edward had caused this man to die. But how? They didn't even know him. He wasn't a Woodford man. And why?

Simon now started to feel sick inside, and shivered, feeling his arms bristle with goose bumps. His palms were clammy and his stomach knotted tight. Suddenly he wanted to find the bag of money and throw it away, or burn it, or put it back on the abandoned station platform. Anything to get rid of it. Eddie had been right all along. It was wrong. It was bad.

Simon was aware that Mary had her arm around his shoulders, and she was speaking softly to him, as he stared at the floor. He really was feeling sick, seeing dancing silver stars before his eyes and with a strange dizziness. 'There's something I have to tell you … ugh, I don't feel so good.'

'It's OK, Simon, have a drink of this tea, it'll calm your nerves.'

'No, it's not that … I know something that might be why he died.'

'Really? What do you know, Simon?' Benson was looking intently as his bowed head. 'Are you saying that you know why he died?' She looked quizzically across at Mary, who shrugged her shoulders in silent reply.

'I … ugh … think so.' And then, without any further warning, he was sick.

* * * *

Vignoles was walking towards the shedmaster's office, accompanied by Saunders, who at regular intervals shook his head in disbelief and repeated his lack of understanding how such a dreadful affair could have happened in his depot. 'There'll be all hell to pay at head office: they won't like this, oh no, not one bit.'

'I am quite sure the young man's family will be rather more concerned.'

'Ah, well yes, of course, of course. It's a terrible business for them. But to climb around such a place under the influence, is a bloody stupid thing to do, you've got to admit that.' Saunders paused, sensing the inspector's silent reproof. 'He was drunk, wasn't he?'

'Tim, we are not so sure it was an accident.'

'What do you mean? That he … he might have jumped?'

'It's an option we must consider, and then there is the other possibility.'

'Oh no. Surely you don't mean he was killed? Murdered.' Saunders stopped in his tracks. 'Dreadful. Now this really will be such a mess for us all.'

'I would rather just say that there are reasons to keep that avenue of investigation open. As a result, Tim, I need full co-operation in everything. And no questions from you in return, understood? And keep this option under your hat, until I am ready to make a press statement. I shall not be amused if I find that you have been talking to every Tom, Dick and Harry about it.'

'Of course ... oh, dear me, what a shock,' he said, accompanied by more head shaking as they approached his office door.

'Tim, have you heard anything about what the civvies are up to in the area? The doctor said he saw a number of police vehicles heading this way.'

'Oh yes, it's the talk of the village. Have you not heard? There's a woman gone missing. She's been abdicated.'

'Abducted.'

'Yes! That's it, and there's rumours going around that her boyfriend was attacked and left tied up. Can you imagine — in Woodford? And now this. But what's puzzling everyone is why they didn't take anything — well, apart from the girl, that is.' He laughed at his foolish slip. 'Most peculiar. Why would someone do that? She's just a poor dressmaker's sister, for Heaven's sake.'

'Indeed. An abduction and no theft? Very curious.' Vignoles stopped and looked at the ground, deep in thought. 'When was this?'

'I've heard that the alarm was raised about eleven last night, when Miss McIntyre — she's the elder sister — apparently in a real state, knocked up some of her neighbours, saying as her young sister had vanished with her boyfriend. He's the lad from the ironmongers, a nice, sensible sort. So no one thought they would run off together or whatever. But with all that fog last night, they couldn't see anything. So it seems they called the police early this morning.'

Vignoles looked intently towards his friend, but without really seeing him, his mind racing, assimilating this new and surprising information, trying to make any of it fit into what he already knew about the dead man and the Water Street gang. It was as if he were trying a lock with an assortment of unidentified keys, taking each one and seeing if it would release the mechanism, but finding that every attempt met with failure. Yet he knew that a key existed that would fit, and when the door was finally opened, he would be able to see further into the case, and make sense of it all.

He removed his glasses and ran a hand over his eyes and forehead, suddenly aware that he was in danger of becoming distracted by what was in all probability an unrelated incident. He had a lot of work to do that morning, and this was pulling him off course. And yet he was reluctant to completely let the matter drop. 'I need to use your office, for today at least. I want you to get me the roster log books covering the last month, and then get someone to run over to the village and make contact with the investigating officer on this abduction case. Ask him to call me as quickly as he can, here, on your telephone. It's important that I speak with him.'

'Do you think the dead man was involved?'

'I asked you to not question me.' Vignoles then softened his voice, 'I doubt it, Tim. But this is a curious situation and it can do no harm to exchange information. And it would be poor form to not advise the civvies that we had a death on site.'

They entered the shedmaster's office and Saunders made to clear the many cards still laid out in rows upon his desk, but Vignoles stopped him, and stood looking down at the names neatly inked onto each, his eyes soon picking out the names of his suspects. 'Tim, I have to ask you this, and forgive me for so doing, but have you ever been —' he paused for a beat, '— persuaded to ensure that certain train crew work together? Remember we discussed this last time I was here?'

Saunders looked straight at Vignoles, unblinking.

'This might be a murder investigation, so please answer honestly.'

'No. Never. I have never taken a bribe in my life, and I am proud to say so.'

'Good. I would have been surprised if you had. I was however thinking more about what you told me earlier; that certain men moaned a lot, gave you a hard time over their rostering. Complained perhaps? Upon further reflection, do you feel that this could have influenced your decisions?'

'Well … it is so much easier when you keep them happy, isn't it? It's better to stop them whingeing. But I never took anything in return.'

'Keep whom happy? I want names.'

Before Saunders could reply, however, W.P.C. Benson appeared at the half-opened door, her knuckles rapping on the door, her face just visible to Vignoles behind the shedmaster. 'Yes, Benson? Come in.'

'Thank you, sir.' She nodded towards Saunders, immediately turning back to Vignoles. 'Sorry to interrupt, but I've just heard something that I really think you really should know about immediately.'

'Yes? Is it about the death?'

'Yes. And there's more, much more ...' She glanced across at Saunders and hesitated before continuing.

'Could you be so kind as to leave us for a few minutes? Perhaps you could get someone to carry that message, please?' The shedmaster for the second time that morning looked relieved that he was able to leave. For the moment at least, he was spared further questioning and gave an eager smile. 'Of course, right away,' he said, and left the office, closing the door behind him.

'What should I hear?'

'The testimony of the young lad who found the body. Simon Howerth is his name. It's not about how he came to find the body so much, it's what else he has told me. He has some extraordinary tale about how he and his best friend, a lad called Edward —' she glanced at her notebook before continuing, '— Edward Earnshaw; he also works here as a cleaner. Well, he told me the strangest of tales, sir, but despite my initial reservations, I rather think it has something. He seems to think that he and the Earnshaw lad have taken and hidden a bag full of money. A vast quantity of money, all in brand new, five-pound notes.' She stopped and looked at Vignoles, who was holding his breath, 'And — wait for it, this bag of money was dropped off the side of the Calvert brick train, Saturday last.'

There were a few moments of silence between the two of them, which allowed the hissing, roaring, metallic clangour of the shed to intrude. Vignoles sat down slowly behind the desk, and waved to Benson to take one of the others. He pulled his pipe out from his breast pocket and used it to punctuate his speech, pointing the stem slightly towards Benson. 'Where is the Howerth lad?'

'In what goes for a kitchen here, just down the corridor.'

'Why did he tell you this?'

'It was almost a confession. He was becoming agitated, and said that he felt responsible for the man's death. He seems much calmer now he has got it off his chest.'

'Responsible? Why?'

'He thinks that they taking the money has "stirred things up", as he put it. Made things happen.'

'Maybe he has a point. This Edward Earnshaw, a young lad, did you say?'

'Yes sir, He just left school, so Simon says.'

'Do you know where is he now?'

'Day off, so he could be at home in the village. His father is the local baker.'

'A baker? Now that is a coincidence.'

'Sorry? What is?'

'Oh, it's nothing. Get yourself over there and find him immediately and bring him straight here, then we can see if his story tallies with the other. If it does, then we could be onto something most interesting. If not, well, we can discount it as youthful imagination. Oh and Benson, track Sergeant Trinder down and ask him to join me. Quickly.'

After W.P.C. Benson had left the room, Vignoles took out his notebook and leafed through its pages, skipping the notes he had made earlier in the morning, and those that contained his dodgy strategy for catching the counterfeiters red-handed along the line, and then started to read the entries he had made about the missing detonators. He scanned the pages, working backwards, and then briefly smiled as he found in his neatly written hand, the name and number of the beautiful, gleaming locomotive that he and Saunders had admired. Vignoles remembered that the entry he was looking for was just before this. It consisted of just a letter and four words, in tiny script: 'E. Earnshaw. Baker now cleaner.'

'It would seem, Master Earnshaw, the baker's son, that we shall meet again...'

* * * *

Edward was feeling a bit dazed about the sudden and dramatic change to his day. Events were moving so fast that he was struggling to make any sense of them. He was also acutely aware that both he and Simon were very deep into something dreadfully serious and rather frightening. Although there was a part of him that also found it quite thrilling.

He was still dressed in his Sunday best, having been accosted by a railway policewoman just as he was leaving St Mary's, right in front of his parents, many of the villagers and the vicar. It had been unbelievably embarrassing, but it would be a close call as to whether it was he or his mother who was the more so. Of course, she had made a scene and his father had threatened to 'beat the living daylights out of him' if he had committed a crime, which had caused the vicar to pull a pained expression. However, the policewoman had done a good job in calming everyone down and he had been escorted, rather unexpectedly, towards the locomotive sheds and not down to the bottom of the village where, apparently, a large group of police were gathered and in the process of knocking on everyone's door and asking questions. He had asked the policewoman why they were not going there, and had been even more puzzled to learn that she knew nothing at all about that investigation, and in fact she had rather quizzed him on what he had heard that morning about the police enquiries, in a manner that suggested that she was eager to go and find out more herself.

It was all most puzzling.

Edward had even shown her the quicker way back to the depot down Kitchen Lane and across the little wooden footbridge over the Cherwell. They had had plenty of time to talk, and by the time he had been ushered into Mr Saunders's office, Edward had felt quite at ease with her, and he sensed that she was more curious than angry about what Simon and he had been up to. Sadly, once in the office, she had left and he had to face Detective Inspector Vignoles and his sergeant, without her friendly face. Edward had immediately recognised the inspector as the man with the train-spotting books he had spoken with one time in the station refreshment room. This had initially eased the meeting, and he had been greeted with a smile that was warm and might even be considered friendly. Edward felt that they had some kind of understanding, and this made the inspector seem less alarming.

However, he had been immediately jolted out of this naively secure position by being confronted with an accusation that he had stolen a bag of money. Worse luck, they even seemed to know all about Simon as well. They had questioned him in great detail, especially the sergeant, who always interrupted him whilst he was trying to explain, asking why? when? how? Always wanting more and more detail. It had been quite tiring.

There was a break in the questioning now, and he was still seated in the office, nursing a grubby mug of tea, whilst the inspector and the sergeant talked quickly and quietly together about what he had told them. Edward didn't like the way the sergeant kept glancing across at him whilst he spoke in a soft but urgent tone, just too quietly for him to really catch what he saying.

What worried Edward most of all was how they had known that he and Simon had taken the bag of money. They had not told him how they had come upon such information, but they seemed to know so much already, it was as if they had been watching at the time. This made Edward shiver. Perhaps he and Simon had stumbled upon a secret police operation and messed it all up. If they had, then they were certainly in trouble. The other nagging doubt running through his mind was that Simon might have provided the police with this information. But why had Simon done this? Edward wondered if Simon had lost his bottle and called the police, admitting all that they had done, just as Edward had, at times, suggested. But then why had the police not said so?

Whilst Edward was pondering these questions, the telephone rang repeatedly, prompting hurried, curt conversations and the issuing of instructions by the inspector, all these calls interrupting the detailed study that the officers were making of his little notebook.

Fortunately, Edward never left home without this booklet, even to go to church. He had learnt from bitter experience that the very day he couldn't note down a 'cop' was the day four or five prize engines would storm over the embankment above him, before he could commit their numbers to memory. Inspector Vignoles had been most impressed when he had been able to show them the page in which he identified the locomotive, the time and the place when the first bag of money had been dropped at Culworth. Edward watched them now, turning each page and occasionally making notes on a sheet of foolscap on the desk. This encouraged Edward a little, as he felt they were now genuinely more interested in the information contained within than in his theft of the money. They were nodding in agreement over something, and both men stood up. The inspector reached for his pipe and walked over to Edward, then sat on the edge of the cluttered desk, holding his pipe in a manner that Edward sensed was unthreatening.

'Who is Miss McIntyre, Edward?' Vignoles placed his pipe in his mouth and left it there.

'She's the dressmaker. In the village; she has a shop at the bottom of the hill.'

'I see.' Vignoles continued to look at Edward's notebook. 'Why did you make a note of her walking through the railway yard?'

'I don't know really. It was just unusual, I suppose.'

'Why unusual?' It was the sergeant asking one of those nagging questions again.

'It was strange to see a nicely dressed woman in a bright coat walking in the rain in the loco yard. What I mean is, we have lots of women working here, but they are always in work clothes. They never change into their best at work. And it was a really dirty, rainy day. I got soaked.'

'You wrote that she was wearing a red coat?' Vignoles spoke from the side of his mouth, the pipe bobbing up and down in the other.

'Yes. A red coat and hat. It stood out really brightly. I suppose that is why I noticed her.'

'You noticed her doing what exactly?' it was the Sergeant again.

'She was just walking ... quite quickly. Yes, really quite quickly, towards the far side of the depot.'

'Did she seem agitated?'

'Er ... I ... I don't think so, just in a hurry.'

'The edge of the yard? Where do you mean, exactly?' Vignoles narrowed his eyes and looked at Edward intently, then reached for another piece of company notepaper and a pencil, resting this on the corner of the desk close to Edward, and started to roughly sketch a diagram of the locomotive depot. 'Here are the engine sheds, yes? Carriage sheds ... here,' he swiftly drew a series of rectangles to represent the buildings, 'and the station ... here. The coal tower is about here, I think. So, where were you, and where was Miss McIntyre?' He grinned at Edward, with the pipe gripped between his teeth as he leaned on the desk.

'I can show you exactly.' Edward placed his mug of now cold tea on the desk, leaned forward and took the proffered pencil from Vignoles. 'I was on a locomotive. It was an Ivatt Atlantic, a real beauty.' He smiled impishly at Vignoles, who restricted his response to just glancing over his glasses at Edward, suggesting that he should continue. 'The number's written down in my book ... so here is the coaling tower and I saw her about here, walking beside a line of engines waiting to be coaled.' Edward felt the confidence ooze back as was talking, he sensed that they were excited about something and that he was actively assisting them, not just looking and acting rather like a foolish schoolboy. He saw the sergeant nod slowly whilst he was speaking, interested rather than aggressive. 'She walked all the way along the line of engines.' He drew a series of shapes to represent them, 'and then right up to the far edge of the yard ... about here.'

'Not towards the village?'

'No, sir. Towards the Byfield Road Bridge end.'

The two police officers exchanged glances. 'Curious? Why might she do that?'

'Was she walking a dog?' the question was directed at both of them by Sergeant Trinder.

'No, she didn't have a dog.'

'Did you see anyone with her, Edward?'

'No. No one'

'Did she go into the coaling tower?'

'The tower? Not that I saw, but she was quite close to it. I suppose she could have, but why would she want to do that?'

'Why, indeed.' Vignoles was now filling his pipe with tobacco. 'Edward, you know a lot about locomotives, and you note the names and numbers down in quite some detail I see,' Vignoles was turning the pages, 'tell me, can you remember where "The White Knight" was exactly, in relation to the coaling tower?'

'The Gresley Pacific? Yeah, it was right under the tower, and just behind was a "Hunt" locomotive. That was "The Cottesmore", I think, they're in my book. They're both namers, you see. I always note them down, even if I've seen them before.'

Vignoles nodded. 'Can you remember if the engines were moved by the time you clocked off work?'

'No, they stayed where they were. It was right near the end of the shift. They don't coal after that shift, it's too noisy.'

'So what was the last locomotive coaled?'

'That was maybe "The White Knight", the one under the tower. But I remember thinking that they were leaving it a bit late, and that they would get it in the neck from Mr Reed, making such a noise that late. So maybe it wasn't. I'm not sure.'

'So this was at what time?'

'It was gone eight, maybe half-past.'

'Thank you, Edward, that is most useful.'

The telephone rang again and the sergeant answered. 'Yes?

He is? Now? Good, show him in, please.' He replaced the handset and spoke to Vignoles. 'An Inspector Bainbridge is here, he is the investigating officer with the Northants Constabulary, looking into the other incident at Woodford. He is very eager to see us, apparently. He's waiting outside.'

'Good. Show him in, please — just give us a minute to conclude here — for now.' As Trinder left the room, Vignoles looked at Edward. 'I shall not at this stage pass any comment on you and your friend's actions in taking and concealing that bag of money. That can wait. It will not be forgotten, however. But right now there are far more pressing matters to attend to, and you and Simon, have so far proved extremely useful in providing us with some vital information.'

'Simon?' Edward's eyes were wide with surprise.

'Yes, we interviewed him earlier this morning. You will not be aware that he had the unfortunate experience of discovering the body of a dead man today.' Edward's mouth fell open. 'We are as yet unsure if your wild and foolish escapades are connected to this death.'

'Oh my God!'

'Hmm, yes, you might very well say that. You just might have got yourselves into a rather serious pickle. But don't be alarmed. We are on the case now and will ensure your safety. It's just rather regrettable that you did not think to report what you saw right from the start and not take it upon yourselves to get involved. However, be that as it may, W.P.C. Benson will take you to join Simon now, and you can return home. But make sure you stay in the village: we might need to speak to you again. And I would like to keep hold of this,' he held up Edward's spotter's notebook, 'for a while longer. Don't worry, I shall take good care of it.' Vignoles gave an encouraging grin.

'Yes … yes, of course, sir.' Edward stood up and looked shell-shocked as he slowly left the office, passing the sergeant and two uniformed policemen on the way out.

Chapter Twenty-Five

'TAKE THE A TRAIN'
Duke Ellington Orchestra

It had so far been a long, cold, uncomfortable night for all of them, punctuated by indecision and occasional bursts of activity, but in the main consisting of achingly slow periods of tedium. Tempers were fraying and the tension served only to highlight the faultlines, tearing at the thin veneer of comradeship that existed between them. However, the dreadful realisation that they were now men on the run, encumbered by a hostage and hunted down by both the authorities and inevitably, by their gang-master, held them together for the time being.

The continuing fog had at least provided them with the perfect cover and they had no immediate fears of being observed. However, now that the dawn sun was trying to filter its milky light across the world outside, they knew they could not continue to rely upon its continuing effect. They had delayed and dithered for far too long, with endless, cyclical arguments about what next to do, where to run, to which port, or whether they should try to seek out and confront the man behind the whole counterfeiting gang: the mysterious Top Link himself.

It was not that they had been completely idle, or had spent the whole night frozen with indecision like rabbits transfixed by the headlights of a motor car. It had been a tense moment outside the Anderson shelter. Ken had managed to calm down Rollo sufficiently to prevent him from killing the poor girl, but Rollo had still vented his anger and frustration on Jenny, by striking her cruelly across the face with the butt of his pistol. This had sickened Ken, but he reasoned it was at least better than her being killed.

They had then abandoned her unfortunate beau to a night of being bound and gagged on the truckle bed in the shelter, with a sore head and damaged back. With pockets stuffed full of detonators, and Peter carrying the heavy bag of counterfeit money, they had proceeded to make their way along the base of the railway embankment, looking for a way of clambering up the slimy, wet grass until they were level with the running tracks. Rollo had been forced to untie Jenny's hands, as she could not climb the greasy surface without the use of them, and it was still an undignified struggle to make their way to the top, often falling onto their hands and almost clawing their way up.

Jenny took advantage of this confusion, to deliberately leave her headscarf on the grass as she clawed her way up, pushing one corner of the scarf into the wet soil beneath her fingers. This action went unnoticed at the time, and if anyone later realised that she no longer had the scarf, they made no mention of the fact. Rollo seemed to lose interest in retying her hands after their climb, and his attention turned to how to make their escape.

Their initial destination was a small hut beside the railway lines, some distance from signal box number three and the station platform, both of which were almost invisible in the dense fog. Signal lamps glowed dully in the distance, seeming to hang in the air with no obvious support. Detonators cracked and boomed as trains inched their way forward, the ground rumbling under their feet and the sleepers groaning and flexing as the heavy trains passed just yards from the hut. Jumping one of these slow-moving trains would pose little problem and it looked as though they would quickly agree on this strategy, but soon differences of opinion stymied any immediate action, with all three men arguing about where they should travel to, and how best to effect their escape.

'Get ourselves down to London, then onto a boat train. We can exchange some of this junk for francs at one of the currency offices at Waterloo or Dover. We'd be set up then. No worries.'

'Too obvious, Rollo. Once they get on our scent, that's exactly what they would expect us to do. They'll have police crawling all over Marylebone, Waterloo, Charing Cross, everywhere. We'd have no chance.'

'Ken's got a point there, you know? We should maybe head for Harwich, or the Hook, far less obvious.' Peter was opening a packet of Black Cat cigarettes as he spoke.

'London's bigger, we can lose ourselves easier. Who said we get out at Marylebone? We could hop out at an earlier station .'

'All well and good, but then how are we going to get into the City?' Peter took one and proffered the open packet to Rollo.

'Catch a bus. Lift a car? I dunno, we can find a way, all right.' He took a cigarette and sniffed it cautiously. 'Since when did you smoke?'

'But why run, Pete? We've got the fake money back. Couldn't we try and get it back to this Top Link guy, see if can't straighten things out? He could set up a new system somewhere else. Of course, we'd have to split afterwards, but I'm sure he'd help sort something out.'

'But who is he, Kenno? What do you know about him?' Rollo was lighting the cigarette, the Luger lying in his lap with the barrel pointing towards their hostage, who was seated miserably on a heap of sacking the corner. There was a dark bruise across her cheek. 'Where do we find him? Pete, you were our middle man, come on, what do you know?'

'Not a lot. As you know we all were just aware of our immediate links in the chain, so as to speak. I just handed the real stuff over to some guy in a pub.'

'Where?'

'Helmdon way. Not far from here. I reckon the top man hides out in a farm somewhere. There are plenty of these tucked away off the beaten track around here. But I've got no idea where.'

'What were the arrangements for meeting?' Ken was thinking hard.

'I had an initial time and date, then each time we've met, he's given me another different time, date and place. It shifts.'

'When are you due to meet up again?' Rollo took a long drag on his cigarette.

'Well there's the rub; tomorrow lunchtime.' Peter spread his hands in apology.

'So word is going to get back, when you don't show?'

'Yes. Top Link will send his heavies out for us, no doubt of that.'

'So that's why I say we try to get to Top Link as soon as we can, try to calm his nerves. We lay low, then make the rendezvous with this middle man, as planned, and explain what's happened.' Ken was speaking quickly, nervously.

'And what if the area is crawling with police?'

'You're right there, Rollo. There might even be roadblocks around the area by early evening; we wouldn't be safe to make the rendezvous. So we had better cut and run. Like I said before, we should split up and go different ways. It might be easier. I'll take my chance on the motorcycle.'

'Yeah? And since you are the only one with a direct link to Top Link, how do we know you won't go straight there?'

'Rollo, don't be ludicrous. I got us all together earlier this evening remember? The small problem of Jimmy lying dead in a heap of coal, in case you've forgotten.'

Jenny whimpered in the corner. The three men glanced at her, and then continued.

'OK, OK ... I'm getting jumpy, that's all. Sitting here like lame ducks is getting to me.' Rollo stood up and walked to the small, square window and peered out onto the pale glow of the approaching dawn, which was just starting to etch the hazy lines of signal posts and the parallel lines of damp, glistening rails. 'We've got to go, and now. No more debate. Next bloody long-distance train that goes past, we jump it. But southbound.'

'By my reckoning,' Ken was peering closely at his pocket watch by the flare of a lighted match, 'there's a London train due in twenty or so minutes. But with this fog, it could still be hours away.'

'Well we haven't been keeping track, but any number of delayed trains could be coming through and at any time. I'll get out and place some detonators up the line. They'll be stopping anyway, but we might as well get them to pull up opposite. Pete, keep an eye on our lady friend. You can use your gun if she causes trouble.' Rollo walked into the enveloping fog, the tread of his boots audible long after he had ceased to be visible.

'So we take an express train, Pete? We can ride the cushions?'

'Yeah? And what about a ticket? And then there are the passengers, all of whom might remember us. And what about her?'

'I see what you mean.'

'I'm sure Rollo is thinking we need a goods', that way we can jump the guard, tie him up and one of you do his work. Right up front on the engine, with this pea souper outside, they'll never know.'

'Good thinking, Peter. Perhaps we'd better tell Rollo, just to be sure.' Ken was standing by the open door of the hut, wisps of fog curling around him like the fingers of ghosts. 'Blast, but I can't see him.' Ken stepped outside and listened. Two distant booms sounded out, and the faint trace of a muffled whistle. He stared hard into the swirling fog, his eyes playing tricks, creating imaginary shapes and forms. As he stared, a small patch of darkness started to resolve itself into the shape of a figure in a long overcoat and flat cap, swinging a lamp in one of its hands, the beam playing across the rails before it. Ken was about to call out, but stopped himself just in time as he realised that this was not Rollo. The lamp beam played from side to side, sweeping the rails. Then the figure stopped, not twenty yards from Ken, his face still a blur. The sack of detonators slung over one shoulder was dropped to the ground as the fogman knelt to attach a detonator to a rail.

Ken quietly stepped back into the hut, his left arm frantically gesticulating to Peter, quickly looking over his shoulder and placing a finger to his lips. Peter understood immediately and crouched down beside Jenny, 'Not a peep, OK?' he whispered. She nodded in reply and then lowered her eyes towards the small gun that had appeared in his hand. Ken watched from behind the door, which he drew almost closed.

'What is it?' hissed Peter.

'Shhhh.' Ken saw the figure stand up, heft the heavy sack over one shoulder and walk closer, and he realised with a shock that he not only recognised, but knew, the person in front of him. It wasn't a man in the long overcoat and cap, but the tall figure of a woman. Ken voicelessly formed the words 'Annie Winter!'

He had known her since she had been a baby dandled on his knee, when in happier times, long before the war, he and his wife would visit her parents. He'd watched her grow up, he remembered her coming home from school with his own son on many a day. He'd watched her grow into the tall, athletic woman before him, remembered the day she signed up for war work on the railway. Ken looked away into the impenetrable distance as if somewhere, lost in the fog, was an explanation as to how and why he found himself skulking behind a door, on the run from the law, afraid to greet a family friend. He knew that if he were to step outside and walk up to Annie, despite her initial surprise, she would greet him warmly and unquestioningly believe any tall story that he spun her. Her sweet, trusting face would look at him and smile, delighted to see him, and they could exchange a few words about their families. He hadn't seen her to speak with for nearly a year; they had never even spoken about the loss of his wife. He felt a lump in his throat. Suddenly he wished he could join her, discuss the weather, the bone-numbing chill of standing for eight or nine hours on fog-duty, the desire for the warmth of a friendly fire, the impossibility of getting enough butter and a decent meal. Lose himself in the normality of life.

Annie had now stopped walking and was very close to the platelayers' hut, standing on the ballast between the running tracks and the perimeter fence. The wires threaded through the wooden uprights of the fence were beaded with droplets of water. When the beam of her lamp momentarily caught these, they burst into life as if with flashes of fire. Annie was now pouring some tea from her cream-coloured, enamelled can into its lid, which doubled as a cup. She was so close he could hear the liquid as it filled the cup.

He looked back at her, and then was suddenly transfixed by the startling sight of a large barn owl soundlessly gliding into view. Its curiously disturbing, heart-shaped face was pale in contrast to its staring, jet-black eyes. It glided between Annie and the hut, apparently unconcerned by her presence, alighting on one of the fence posts. It sat there imperiously, swivelling its head like some mechanical invention of H.G. Wells, searching with its penetrating gaze. The owl's head turned left and right and then seemed to fix its eyes upon the hut, piercing through the tiny, dark crack left by the door being slightly ajar, and boring into Ken's watching gaze. He felt a shiver down his spine and noticed that Annie had also seen the owl and was standing, comically frozen, with the cup held to her mouth without moving. The owl issued an alarming screech of surprising intensity, and then flapped away with a couple of great wing-beats out of sight and over the fogbound fields.

Ken had a feeling of acute discomfort and dread. He pulled his face back from his narrow viewpoint, rested his forehead on the damp wood of the jamb and closed his eyes. At that moment a solitary locomotive clanked its way past the hut, its motion knocking rhythmically, the wheels exploding the detonators as it approached the home signals protecting the station. Annie and the driver were exchanging comments, a quick conversation, and then with a muffled crow on the whistle it wheezed and banged its way into the gloom. Annie reset the fog signals and then walked slowly forwards beyond the hut and down the line.

A few moments later Rollo, almost soundlessly, like the owl, appeared at the door. 'OK? That was a close thing. Did you see the fogman, Kenno? Nearly stumbled into him, but managed to drop to the ground and keep low.' There was a strange, eager brightness in his eyes, in contrast to those of Ken, whose mood was darkening even as the day was trying to brighten. Rollo seemed to be full of energy, a fever of excitement gripping him. 'Come on, we need to move outside, but keep low. I can hear two train movements — listen — both sound like goods'.' Sure enough, the ricochet of buffers clattering together as a long train started into motion could be heard a short distance away, as well as a muffled 'crump crump' of a heavily-laden engine advancing. 'I've set a sequence of signals so they should pull up right in front of us. I'll jump the van, take the guard out, and you lot get on board. Ken, you know the ropes, take the guard's lamp and do the honours — the engine crew won't even see you, let alone notice. Right?' His eyes flicked from Ken to Peter, who was standing nearby. Jenny was still at the far end of the hut, trying to keep as much distance as she could from the gun.

'You're not going to … hurt the guard, are you?' Ken looked worried. 'We've caused too much distress already. No one else must get hurt.' He glanced back at Jenny.

'Nah. Don't worry. We'll tie him up, shove him in a box-van, if we can. Out of sight, out of mind, OK?' he grinned wolfishly.

'Well, yes, I suppose that is not so bad. He won't come to harm like that. Maybe we can do the same with her? I mean, this hostage thing, it makes me very uneasy.'

'She's protection. For the time being, any road. Until we get near London. We'll get shut of her there.'

'Shot?'

'Shut! A turn of phrase, old man, but come on, let's get moving.'

The approaching train was formed of box-vans being pulled by a very black and work-stained V2. The train was of enormous length, it being impossible to see both the locomotive at the front and guard's van at the rear at the same time, because of the poor visibility. It rumbled slowly past the group who were crouching low beside the rails. The wheels of the wagons squealed painfully, passing as they did just a foot or so from their faces, with their brakes pinned down hard to retard the speed whilst the flashes and sparks of the detonators exploded only yards away. Moving at just a snail's pace, the train almost imperceptibly stopped, and only at the last moment did all the wagons concertina together in a wave of metallic ringing sounds along its length. The little wooden shed of the guard,s van was close by. A warm light radiated from an opened door, and a drift of greenish-yellow smoke curled from the stovepipe chimney and blended into the fog.

Rollo darted forward, staying close to the gloomy darkness of the wagons, the Luger in his left hand. Peter told Ken to look after Jenny and sprinted after Rollo, moving around the back of the train and clambering onto the small veranda at the rear, just as Rollo was doing the same at the front, effectively cutting off any means of escape. The guard was standing inside the van preparing to step down onto the tracks, with his lamp in one hand and in the other a spare detonator that he had just extracted from a wooden box on the floor. He was in his forties, stockily built and wearing a thin line of a moustache above his upper lip. Slicked down hair was just visible beneath his cap, and he wore a pair of round, horn-rimmed spectacles. He was surprised at the sudden appearance of Peter, but quickly collected himself.

'Oh, I say! Are you the fogman? I'm coming down there to take a look, y'know.'

'He's no-one you need worry about. Now shut it, and put your hands up where I can see them.' Rollo jabbed the Luger into the small of the guard's back.

'What the devil do you mean by this? This is an outrage!' The guard spun around with surprising speed and agility, and with well-judged accuracy, brought the metal body of the lamp and its bulbous glass lens against Rollo's chin in a fierce upper cut that sent him sprawling backwards with a sickening crack. Rollo slumped on the floor, the Luger sliding under one of the wooden benches that ran the length of the van. The guard immediately turned back to face Peter, who had watched in shock and surprise, failing to react for a couple of seconds. In that time the guard had regained his balance, and, lunging to one side, grabbed a shunter's pole from the rack on the cabin wall, holding it like a lance, the metal hook pointing menacingly towards Peter.

'Now get out of here, I'll have you arrested for this!' He jabbed the pole towards Peter in short, aggressive stabs. 'Or do you want to fight? Eh?' He lunged the pole close to Peter's face, 'Come on then, you little bugger, come on!' The guard's confidence startled Peter, who was being forced to make movements to avoid the jabbing point of the pole, but after a few moments he regained his composure and stepped a pace backwards, brandishing the little pistol.

'Put it down! Put the pole down!'

The guard's eyes widened at the sight of the pistol, but any fear he felt was changed into fury and he let out a blood-curdling yell that echoed around the tiny cabin, and in three swift, deft movements, the pole had been used to flick upwards and strike Peter's hand holding the gun, lifting it off target. A shot was fired that fizzed its way through the roof of the van, then the pole crashed down on Peter's hand, forcing him to release the gun. The third movement brought the pole sideways, propelled by the full weight of the guard against Peter's upper chest and throat, forcing him backwards against the end wall. The guard leaned on the pole, restricting Peter's breathing, but not sufficiently to prevent him from landing two rabbit-punches swiftly into the guard's stomach, causing him to fall backwards, coughing and spluttering. Peter took advantage and launched a kick at his head, sending him onto his back. Another shot rang out, and the guard lay still. A pool of red blood started to well out of a hole in the centre of his chest. Rollo was half sitting up, the Luger now lying down at his side. Rollo was holding his jaw, sweating profusely and had a look of intense pain mixed with fury, on his face.

'Take that, you bastard! Aagh, he got me! He's broken me bloody jaw!' Rollo's words were slurred and forced out almost without moving his lips, his face already swelling into a ghastly, red mound. Blood was dripping from a cut on his face and from a split lip. 'Aagh!' Rollo slumped back against the wall clutching his face and closed his eyes.

Peter stood and stared at him for a few moments, then looked down at the dead man. He chewed his lower lip in thought, frozen by indecision. Slowly, Peter picked up the still-functioning lamp and the guard's cap from where it had rolled across the floor, and walked back onto the rear veranda. 'Kenno! Here — catch!' He tossed each one down into Ken's hands. 'Help the girl up to me — now go and do whatever guards do. But don't let anyone come aboard.'

'Of course not, that would be completely against regulations.'

'Good, glad to hear it. Well, get on with it, man.'

'Were those shots? They sounded like gunshots. Is someone hurt?'

'Detonators old boy, detonators. Can't you hear them?'

'Well, they sounded different, if you ask me. What's happened?'

'Leave it, will you, and get this bloody train on the move.' Peter was hauling Jenny up the steps onto the van as he spoke. He changed his tone and tried to sound conciliatory. 'Ken, you've got to play the guard now. Rollo's got hurt, he can't do it. OK?'

'Hurt?' Ken looked up at Peter and Jenny, dumb struck for a few moments. He was shaken out of his inactivity by the realisation that the locomotive was sending angry, sharp whistles through the thick, curdled air. He looked along the train and saw that a hand-lamp was signalling to him. It was Annie, calling him to acknowledge so that the driver could restart the train. He put the cap on his head and then flashed the signal back with his lamp. Annie waved again in acknowledgement. Ken then stepped up onto the veranda just as the deep, booming voice of the V2 started up, and the wagons rattled and shook themselves into movement.

He noticed that the door into the van was closed. He was glad of this, as he could delay a little longer seeing what he dreaded lay behind the door. He felt sick and shivery. Ken pulled the cap low down over his brow, turned up the collar of his jacket against his neck and leaned against the back wall of the van so that none of the already poor light caught his face. As the train trundled forwards he looked down at the approaching figure of Annie Winter, her lamp waving gently from side to side as she called them forward. He knew he must acknowledge her, but was fearful that she would recognise him.

'It's even worse out here. I can't promise you'll get very far in this fog,' she called up to him, and gave a broad, friendly smile. 'But at least you're in the warm with a kettle.' Ken watched as she slowly faded away into the enveloping fog. He managed a half-hearted wave, and then turned away. If the trusting Annie Winter had been able to see more clearly, she might have wondered why the guard turned so abruptly away in response to her cheerful salutation and was screwing his eyes closed, his mouth twisted into a pained, tormented, expression. But instead she shrugged her shoulders at the guard's lukewarm wave and then turned her attention back up the line and the next train she needed to guide through into Woodford Halse.

Chapter Twenty-six

'YOU'VE GOT ME CRYING AGAIN'
Ambrose & his Orchestra

Inspector Bainbridge surprised Vignoles by being younger and fresher-faced than he had imagined. He was another legacy of the war years, having been allowed to climb the ranks more quickly than would have been the case in peacetime. Vignoles hoped that Bainbridge would have a greater breadth of experience than his youthful face and demeanour promised.

They shook hands and Vignoles wheeled the chair he had been using around from behind the desk, before inviting Bainbridge and his sergeant, a tall, gaunt figure called Dodson, to take a seat. Vignoles was careful to not, even accidentally, imply any superiority over Bainbridge, as he felt sure he was going to need his full co-operation. Trinder, observant as ever, took the hint and perched on the windowsill with a booted foot resting on a water pipe, notebook and pencil in his hands, allowing Dobson to take the remaining empty chair.

'Glad to make your acquaintance, Vignoles. Not related by any chance to the illustrious engineer? He helped build part of this line, you know. But of course I am sure you are aware of that.' Bainbridge grinned.

'Yes, indeed I am. Unfortunately, to my considerable disappointment, we have failed so far to make any direct connection through our family tree. However, my father took the precaution of christening me Charles as a tribute to the great man — in anticipation of just such a discovery.' Vignoles spread his hands apart in lieu of any further explanation. 'But sadly, we have no time to discuss the great railway engineers at this moment. We have a considerable amount to both discuss — and do.'

An hour later, a huge pot of tea and a meagre pile of sandwiches brought by W.P.C. Jane Benson from the station refreshment room before them, and the air fuggy with cigarette and pipe smoke, the four officers finally allowed themselves a few much-needed minutes to relax.

It had been a long session, with revelations on both sides. Early on, Vignoles had swept up the little cards on the shedmaster's desk, flipped them over and written the names of the various players in this bizarre and complex case, as well as all of the known key events, such as the arson attack on the goods' train, the printing press at Water Street, the unfortunate corpse in the coal. To the surprise of Vignoles and Trinder, the box of stolen detonators reported by Saunders appeared to join the puzzle. Bainbridge explained that just such a box had been discovered lying outside the Anderson shelter where the unfortunate young man had been found bound and gagged. They soon put aside this revelation, however, feeling that its theft and discovery appeared to add little to their understanding of an already puzzlingly, complex case.

'We need food. I don't know about you, but I am half starved. Despite the fact that vital time is passing, we need sustenance to keep our brains working. Tuck in, gentlemen.' Vignoles, meanwhile, glanced over to the array of cards laid out on the desk whilst he selected a tired-looking ham sandwich and took a hefty bite. 'I need to try and get a view of the whole picture.'

'It's a darned puzzle, that's for sure, Vignoles. We had no plausible explanation for why this Jenny McIntyre was abducted this morning, and now I just feel more confused.' Bainbridge gulped down some tea. 'I still think the key somehow lies with these two McIntyre girls. What with the elder one, Violet, being seen near the crime scene of the dead man, um, Jimmy what's-his-name.' He started to devour his second sandwich, pausing mid-bite to look at Vignoles. 'How reliable do you think the witness is?'

'Hard to say, as he's only a lad. But the sheer detail of his other observations, and his extraordinary story, which tallies with that of the Howerth lad, make me inclined to trust him. His story also places a vast quantity of money in the same shelter that the young man was trussed up in. This money has to be the same counterfeit stuff we have been trying to track down.'

'Seems to me that this was their storage point. Maybe the gang were disturbed when they came to collect it? Things then got out of hand?' Trinder's sandwich was polished off in three bites and he was wiping his mouth as he spoke.

'That's my way of thinking as well, sergeant, but then why was Violet near the crime scene? And why did Jimmy Cresswell end up dead? I want to speak with Violet urgently, as I think this Prenton character was there at the same time as Violet and Cresswell.'

'Prenton was the loan shark you met with?'

'Correct, Dobson.'

'I seem to remember you said he rode a motorbike.' Dobson had eaten a sandwich in even less time than Trinder, and was looking through his notes whilst brushing crumbs from his jacket. 'With a sidecar?'

'Yes, that's correct.'

'There's just such a combination parked up at the side near the McIntyres' place. I had a scout around earlier, and noticed it. Got boots and over trousers and the likes all stored in the sidecar, under a tarpaulin.'

'Good work. Well, that really puts Prenton in the frame. He could have had dealings with the McIntyre girls, maybe even roped them into earning a little extra.' Trinder stood up and walked over to the desk, stopping in front of it, moving the card with Prenton's name closer to the two bearing the McIntyre's names. 'So it is possible that Prenton was collecting the money last night, and is involved in whatever it was that happened, and now, I think he has the young girl.'

'But why?'

'I just don't know, Dobson.' Trinder shrugged his shoulders.

'We need to interview Violet. Urgently. When you spoke to her, Bainbridge, you were naturally unaware of all this. Only that she was the sister of an abductee. Where is she now?'

'At her shop premises. I agree. I should like you both to visit the crime scene and ask her to explain herself.' Bainbridge took a deep draught of tea. 'Don't you think it's a bit rum, the younger girl spending a night with her fancy man, alone?'

'He was only helping her decorate the back parlour.'

'So her sister says. Alone? One thing leads to another, Sergeant Trinder. I tell you, if my sister had done the same, our father would given that lad such a hiding he wouldn't know what'd hit him.'

'With respect, sir, I can't quite see that has much bearing on the case?' It was Sergeant Dobson speaking.

'Maybe, maybe not. Having said that, almost anything could have a bearing on this tangled mess.' Bainbridge spoke the last part more softly, whilst looking into his teacup as if the leaves would reveal the answer. 'Whatever, I still think there's something not quite "right" about these McIntyres.' Bainbridge furrowed his brow.

Vignoles stood up. 'We must move on, I am fearful that we are losing valuable time as we speak. Sergeant,' he looked at Trinder, 'make a call to Blencowe and find out what the latest word is on the Leicester chaps moving in on the Water Street premises. They might squeeze something out of them. I also want to lock down the Channel ports, and all ferry boats to Ireland. Get descriptions of the fugitives telegraphed to the port authorities, and advise all bureaux de change to be on the alert for large exchanges of five-pound notes into foreign currencies. Green and Blencowe can arrange all this. And stand all railway police — up and down the line — at high alert. My orders.'

'So they are bolting abroad?' Bainbridge looked quizzically at Vignoles.

'The passports make me think so. What worries me is the girl. She's going to attract attention. They will have to … well, get rid of her, at some point. Or use her as a bargaining tool for safe passage.'

'Either way, she's in mortal danger.' Trinder looked grim as he lifted the handset and started to dial.

＊　＊　＊　＊

'I've already explained to you. All I did was borrow fifty pounds from him. Oh, how could I have been so stupid?' Violet blew her nose, then took a couple of deep breaths and composed herself. 'Look, I admit it. I began to have my doubts.'

'About the legality of the money?'

'Yes, inspector, about the money. I challenged this Mr Prenton, and he was pretty decent about the whole thing and convinced me it was all OK.'

'So you proceeded to spend the counterfeit money?'

'Well, I thought it was real.'

'You just said you had doubts.'

'Well, I, what I meant was, I had doubts at first and then I didn't; after he reassured me.'

'No, I don't understand. You said you went to the locomotive yard on impulse, because you saw him and wanted to challenge him — again — about the illegal money? But this was after you talked with him in your shop?'

'No. Well, yes. I suppose it was.' Violet dabbed at the corner of one of her eyes. 'I changed how I felt, again. Put like that, it does sound pretty foolish, I agree. I can see that I am not coming out of this looking very good, am I? When I saw him there in the yard, the way he was acting, he just looked so —'

'What?' Bainbridge interrupted her.

'Suspicious, a bit crazy, even. I just knew he was up to no good. That the money was not real — and I wanted to tell him so. Once and for all. But then I couldn't find him, it started to rain, the coal tower covered me in dust, and then he can running towards me.'

'Why was he running?' Vignoles asked the question quietly.

'I don't know. Then he pushed me, and spoke very roughly towards me in a most unkind manner, and ran off.'

'Hmm. I don't need to remind you that you have committed a serious — a very serious offence indeed. One carrying the possibility of imprisonment.' Bainbridge's voice was clipped and cold.

Violet nodded silently.

'Easy, inspector, go easy. There are more important issues at stake here.' Vignoles spoke softly and waved a hand towards the young inspector.

'D.I. Vignoles, Miss McIntyre has admitted to securing goods and services in exchange for counterfeit money. This is not a small matter,' Bainbridge looked at Vignoles. 'Worse still, she has chosen not to report the matter to the proper authorities. I fear a dim view will be taken of that fact by the judiciary.'

'On another day, that may be so. But we are in danger here of getting sidelined. We have at least established that whilst Miss McIntyre has an unfortunate link to the gang, it is nothing more than through happenstance. Frankly I don't much care about the fifty pounds right now.'

Bainbridge was about to reply, but stopped himself. He chewed his lower lip in thought as silence fell in the room. 'You're right, Vignoles. I'm getting pulled off course.' Bainbridge coloured slightly around the collar, 'Yes, indeed, we need to get back on the trail of that missing million-or-whatever pounds. Good Lord! Imagine the turmoil it would cause to the financial markets if all that illegal money flooded into the system? The stock exchange would be in turmoil. It would put this poor, starving country right back under.'

'What?' Violet stood up and faced Bainbridge. 'What are you saying? You're worried about a bag of worthless paper? My Jenny's missing, my poor, darling Jenny has been taken away, and all you stupid, silly men can think about is paper money and the stupid stock exchange. I cannot believe this. When are you going to look for her? When are you even going to start?' Her eyes flashed around the room, challenging each in turn. 'All you do is talk, talk, talk!' Her tears had dried up, replaced by a strong, burning intensity that was uncomfortable to receive, and each man was forced to look away.

It was Vignoles who broke the silence. 'I understand your frustration, Miss McIntyre. I share your frustration. Unfortunately we really must take time asking questions and appearing to prevaricate, but only by so doing have we any chance of understanding what has happened and then plan a strategy for action.' He gave a wan smile at Violet and then a reproving glance at Bainbridge that stopped him from reacting to Violet's outburst.

'But we've got to do something: look what they did to poor Tom.'

'Agreed. And in fact a lot is already happening. Sergeant Trinder here has already alerted all port authorities to prevent them escaping by ferry boat —'

'— By boat! Oh, but where?'

'We suspect that they intend to try and bolt over to the continent, but, as I said, we have initiated moves to prevent this. And Inspector Bainbridge has had his men combing the area since dawn. Is that not so, inspector?'

'Oh yes! Absolutely. We're sure that they're local chaps who've taken her, so if they are lying low in the area they won't get far, mark my words!' Bainbridge still retained some of the edginess he had betrayed moments earlier, but he had felt the full force of Violet's anger, and was grateful for Vignoles's conciliatory words. To further help the young detective, a distraction was caused by the hurried approach of one of his men, who then forgot to remove his helmet as he entered the back kitchen of the McIntyre's shop. His looming presence effectively ended the discussion. 'Helmet!' Dobson snapped the command at the bobby, who rather foolishly reached up with both hands for the offending article before quickly removing it.

'Sorry, sir.'

'Well? What is it, man? Don't just stand there.'

'I found this, sir, I think it's significant.' He held out a red headscarf, which he had pulled from his uniform jacket pocket.

'Oh my! It's Jenny's. I gave it to her about two Christmases ago.' Violet reached out and touched one corner, gently caressing the fine cotton. 'I can detect her perfume on it.' She looked at the faces gathered close around her. 'It's hers, for sure.'

'I found it high on the railway embankment, back there,' the officer indicated with his other hand the approximate direction. 'The interesting thing was this: it was kind of pushed into the wet earth in a few places. Look, here's the mud staining. As if it had been deliberately placed there, by fingers pushing it into the ground. And then nearby, there are signs of feet, of people climbing, and I should say, sliding as well, as they scrambled up the bank.'

'And it has some flecks of white paint on it as well.'

'What was she thinking of, using this to paint in?' Violet's face was a mixture of concern and indignation.

'I'm glad she did, she left us a sign! Show us where this was.' Vignoles was out of the back door almost immediately, everyone else following, including Violet.

'Miss McIntyre, I really think you should wait here.'

'Why? I can't just sit here and wait. It's my girl who's missing. You've just lost your precious money!' And with that she pushed past Sergeant Trinder and strode purposefully after Vignoles.

They were soon climbing awkwardly up the side of the railway embankment, finding the route just as steep and treacherous as the fugitives had the night before. Other signs of their flight had been inadvertently left behind in the form of fresh gashes in the turf, cut by boots and shoes, and damp grass flattened smooth in places, all caused by more than the policeman who had rescued the scarf. Vignoles stood with one knee bent and the other leg at full stretch, as he sought to keep his balance, rapidly surveying the evidence. He looked up to the top of the embankment: 'So, they climbed on to the running tracks. It looks like they chose the railway as their means of escape.'

'Let's get up there and see what jumps out at us.' Sergeant Trinder took another step higher, 'Here, Miss McIntyre, let me help.' He smiled at her as he extended his arm. 'Please?' Violet had just slipped in much the same way as Jenny had done a few hours earlier, her hands gripping at the cold, wet grass to stay her fall. She had a determined look on her face, and wanted to refuse the sergeant, but having regained an upright position that was anything but dignified, she could feel one of her feet starting to slide again from under her. She looked at the sergeant's hand, then to his face and his smile. She felt desperately in need of a friend at that moment, so full-to-bursting was she with pent-up emotion, and so accepted this small gesture. Once the sergeant had helped haul her up alongside the fence, she quickly let go of his hand and insisted that she could climb between the wires unaided.

They were soon looking into the platelayers' hut, Vignoles being the first to enter, treading carefully and looking intently at the floor. 'Look: matches, cigarette butts — all fresh.'

'They were here last night. Damnation! So close and they evaded us.' Bainbridge threw up his hands in despair. 'If it had not been for the blasted fog we might have seen this scarf much earlier.'

'But full marks to your officer for finding it and correctly interpreting the evidence. We can only wonder why they chose to hole up here. But right now, that and every other puzzle about this case can wait. We've got a full-scale manhunt on our hands. A woman-hunt, I should say.' He glanced at Violet, then at Bainbridge as he spoke. 'We have to rescue that young woman at any cost. Alive! If it means we lose the gang and the money, and they sail to the continent, so be it. They won't get far. Interpol will soon be on to them.'

'So Jenny was here? Last night? And all the time I was just a few hundred yards away. Ugh, what a filthy hovel. Oh, I will never forgive myself.' Violet looked around the cramped little hut, hardly more than a glorified garden shed, one wall lined with heavy tools for working on the railway track. 'Why did they take her?' She narrowed her eyes and looked at Vignoles. 'You find the men who took her, inspector, you find them! Get my daughter back to me.'

The room fell silent, and Violet's eyes slowly widened. She stared defiantly at Vignoles, but her face coloured a deep rose and then, just as suddenly, drained to a dreadful white. All eyes were upon Violet. The silence in the room was almost palpable. She slowly raised one hand to her throat and gently rested it there. Her eyes brimming with tears, but she was determined by force of willpower not to look away, though waves of shame and humiliation were coursing through her veins.

Vignoles looked at her and nodded slowly. 'So Jenny McIntyre is not actually your sister? She is your daughter?'

'Yes.' Violet finally looked away, staring at the grubby rough wooden floorboards, tears now running silently down her cheeks.

'And her father?'

She shrugged. 'He's not here looking for her, is he? I am.' Violet spoke softly, conscious that her words were having a profound effect on the men gathered around her.

'What did I say, Vignoles? I told you there was something not quite right about these two girls!' Bainbridge didn't look at Violet as he spoke, his voice almost triumphant.

'Indeed, that was most observant.' Vignoles glanced at Bainbridge with a look that fell short of disdain, but only by a fraction, then he returned his gaze towards Violet, his eyes gentle. 'It's good to understand the relationship.' He nodded slowly. 'I can see that you care deeply, and of course that is why you are standing here now.' Bainbridge made a snorting noise that might have been a cough. Vignoles continued to observe Violet for a few more moments, then pulled himself upright, and in a strong, confident tone, addressed everyone. 'OK. Gather round. We need ideas, and we need them quickly. We believe they stayed here for a while. For how long? Well, we don't know that. But sometime during last night, in thick fog, three men and a woman took a train away from here. So which train? How did they get on board? How will they remain undetected? And how can we intercept the train?' He looked around at the faces etched with concentration in the dim, soft light inside the hut.

'They could halt a train easily with fog detonators. They took some from that box by all accounts. It was wide open with many missing.'

'Spot on, Trinder. But what train?'

'A passenger makes sense, as it would be relatively easy to climb into a carriage and blend in with the others.' Bainbridge looked at Vignoles.

'Hmm. There's always the chance of being rumbled by a ticket inspector. But surely Jenny would find a way to raise the alarm, seated amongst other travellers? It would be a very high-risk strategy.' It was Trinder who answered. Violet noticed that he used her daughter's name, and spoke the word kindly.

'Yes, I take your point; but then how?' Bainbridge looked puzzled.

'Goods' train, Bainbridge. Not in the wagons themselves of course, it would be far too slow to force the doors open and then if it were stuffed full, they would never get aboard. But what about the guard's van?' Vignoles was gesturing with his hands.

'So they could well have incapacitated a guard. We could have a train under the control of these maniacs.' Bainbridge was looking quickly from one face to the other.

'Quite so, inspector, but remember two of these men are experienced railwaymen. It would pose little problem to act the part, and with low visibility, no one would see the swap.' Trinder grinned ruefully.

'That will do me as a working plan; so, now, which train are they on?' Vignoles was stroking his chin in thought, 'But hang on a minute, we should ask the signalman. Box three is close by. They record every train movement, so we can at least see what went past last night and have an idea of what we are up against.' And without waiting for the others, Vignoles stepped outside into the gentle, liquid sunshine that was slowly burning off the night fog, now reduced to no more than a gentle mistiness.

As he walked towards the signal box he watched a long passenger train pass through Woodford station and slowly advance towards him, pulled by a magnificent, old locomotive. It was a real throwback to the Edwardian age: graced with sweeping curves and a rounded dome that had prompted some comic to say that these same shapes brought Lillie Langtry, the music hall entertainer, to mind and the name had stuck. But this poor Lillie was wheezing and coughing her way towards him, hopelessly overladen with at least ten coaches in varying states of dilapidation. The windows were steamed up with condensation and he glimpsed pale, wan faces peering through arcs swept clear by a sleeve on the sweaty glass. No doubt a few of the bored passengers would have found entertainment at the faintly comical sight of a motley group of people, some uniformed, running beside the track like a scene from a film of the Keystone Cops.

Vignoles climbed the wooden steps and walked into the signal cabin, briefly knocking as he did so. A feeling of relief swept through him as he saw Laura Green pulling and pushing the levers into place. He lifted his hat and spoke quickly but quietly, conscious that he must not create alarm, although he felt sure that the confident Miss Green would take it all in her stride.

'Sorry to barge in unannounced. No time for introductions,' Vignoles waved vaguely towards Violet and Sergeant Trinder, who were already following him in close behind, 'and I'm afraid no time for explanations. All you need to know, Miss Green, is that we are working with the local constabulary on an investigation into number of very serious matters. An abduction, an assault,' he paused, 'and a murder. Here, in Woodford. I need your full co-operation, please.'

Laura raised an eyebrow but, apart from a sharp intake of breath, she looked as though this were a perfectly normal announcement. She wiped her brow with the back of her sleeve, and then readjusted her cap, setting it back on her head and nodding very slightly as she absorbed the information. 'Okey dokey, detective inspector. And all this happened under our noses, I suppose? Not that I could have seen much until the last hour or so, what with this fog. What can I do to help? Oh, hang on.' She quickly answered a tinkling bell with a few short rings, then pulled four levers into place. After she had completed the actions, she wiped the shining bright levers with the ever-present rag, and turned again to face Vignoles and the expanding crowd of people shuffling into the box. 'Fire away!'

'We need to know what traffic passed here since about midnight last night. And your best judgement of where each train might have got to along the line, by now.'

'The first part is easy: look, here's the log book, talking of which …' Laura quickly made a one-line entry about the passenger train that had just wheezed its way past as Vignoles had arrived. 'I came on at six am, but here is everything that passed during the night. As you can see, it was not so very much. It being a Sunday night, combined with the dense fog, messed everything up. Look, you can see how late everything was running.'

'How much disruption are we talking about?'

'A lot, inspector. Visibility was down to just yards in some places. Most trains are experiencing five, six, maybe eight hour, delays.'

'That long?' Sergeant Trinder looked at Laura intently.

'Oh yes. We will often shunt many freight trains out of the way and try to get the passengers through first, and other priorities like the mail, but after a while it all bottlenecks up. I'm not sure exactly what will come through next, despite the fog clearing. I have to listen carefully for the bell-codes, to work out what is coming along next. Everything is just so out of place.'

Vignoles was reading the entries in the logbook, tapping the page with his fingers. 'What do you think, sergeant? North or south?' He pointed to a number of possible entries.

'I'm not sure why, but I favour south, down to London. Perhaps it's just what I might have done in their shoes. It would be easier to get lost in the crowd down there, and there are more options to the coast. There are three or four which seem good choices here.' Trinder was copying down the details of every train movement and its reporting number, editing out the light engine movements and short-distance workings. 'We need to get a fix on each of these trains, find out exactly where they are right now.'

Laura leaned over the desk and read the entries being pointed out by Trinder. 'I can put some telephone calls through, we can soon get them located. Take this one. They were already three hours late into Woodford. It's my guess that it won't have got to its destination (which is over on Great Western territory) and it shan't do so until tomorrow is my guess. They might be parked up in a siding along the way. They'll take the engine off and send another down later.'

'Really?' Vignoles was looking at big, round clock on the wall, and mentally counting backwards. 'I think we are in with a chance, Trinder. We have the London stations and the ports on alert, and on top of that, I think our gang won't even have reached that far yet. We shall be ready for them. We need to get descriptions of the men to all the signal boxes up and down the line, get the signalmen on the look-out for any suspicious activity. I am pretty confident that they are sitting cooped up in a siding somewhere, and pretty darned frustrated, hungry and impatient as well. Just the right conditions to flush them out of hiding.'

'Do you really think you can find them? Can you be sure that they haven't already taken Jenny overseas?' Violet spoke quietly, looking intently at the detective.

'We will get them. They are making mistakes. Events are spinning out of their control as each hour goes by.'

'But won't that just make them get angrier? More dangerous?' Violet was looking first at Vignoles then across at Trinder, trying to read their thoughts.

'That of course is the flip side. And we will have to handle them pretty carefully. And —' he paused before continuing, '— we don't yet know if they are armed. That would put an unwelcome spin on things.'

'Armed? Good God, who said anything about that?' it was Bainbridge, who was now standing in the doorway, unwilling to step forward into the already uncomfortably-full signal cabin.

'I think it could be a possibility. If they have a hostage, then they probably have a gun. They could be bluffing of course, but Rollo is an experienced ex-serviceman and he could handle a gun, I am sure.'

'I agree inspector, we should assume that they are armed.' Trinder smiled grimly.

'I shall put a call into Blencowe back at the office, it's time we prepared ourselves to meet force with equal force, if needs be.' Vignoles glanced at Violet, who looked ashen. 'Whilst we await any word back from down the line, we'll stay here on standby. Blencowe can bring firearms with him.' Vignoles felt the weight of his own pistol, tucked deep inside his coat. 'Bainbridge? Have your vehicles on standby also, so we can be ready to follow up any leads.'

Bainbridge looked thoughtful. 'Are you sure that it is really necessary to carry arms? And I was not aware railway police could carry arms?'

'Since the General Strike in '26, we can take whatever measures are required to keep the transport system running. That includes carrying guns. However, in this case, I am less concerned about the running of the railway and more in the safe return of this young woman.'

'And you are, ah hum, trained in the use of firearms?'

'Yes we are, we all take a course once every few years. But what you should know is that Lucy Lansdowne is a crack shot. She beat everyone on the range, scoring top marks. Put a few noses out of joint too, I can tell you. Some men took it rather badly. Apparently she's a member of a gun club, been shooting since she was tiny. Was a junior representative for Great Britain in 1939.' Vignoles grinned at Bainbridge. 'May I use your telephone, Miss Green?'

'Yes, I see. Well, that is good news at least. This is all becoming rather serious.' Bainbridge was nodding slowly, as Vignoles started to dial. He pulled himself up straight and visibly puffed his chest out. 'Well, we have not been exactly inactive ourselves. I have stood every man onto full alert, and they are at this moment moving into key positions up and down the running lines through the county. The chief constable is talking about bringing in the army to throw a cordon on some of the bigger stations to check everything that goes through.'

'Good work!' Vignoles was cupping the receiver to his ear, waiting to be connected to Blencowe. 'Once I have this matter in hand, I think all we can realistically do now is find some food. And wait.'

Chapter Twenty-Seven

'SKYLINER'
Charles Burnett & his Orchestra

The guard's van was now catching the sun broadside and, whilst it was far from hot outside, the small, claustrophobic interior was overheating. The stove was glowing, providing the only means to make food or tea and so whilst its heat was now unwelcome, it was also a vital necessity. The last lump of coal had been used an hour ago and the embers were just beginning to cool; the thought of a night trapped in the van without heat was preying on their minds.

Everyone was tired, fractious and very hungry. The doors at both ends were propped open to create a through draft, with Peter crouched close to one, and Ken at the other, keeping watch. Rollo was sitting on one of the benches that lined the walls, his legs stretched out straight before him. Jenny had attempted to bandage his face using supplies raided from the meagre First Aid box. She wondered why she had bothered, but a combination of acute boredom, her innate discomfort at seeing a fellow human in pain and perhaps a feeling that she might receive some mercy in return for her own kindness, prompted the action. Rollo had grunted something that might have passed as an acknowledgement of thanks for her actions, but now he just stared morosely ahead of him, nervously twitching one of his feet.

Jenny was sitting against the opposite wall and alternated between staring at his constantly moving foot, watching it move side to side, over and over again, until her eyes would be drawn again, down to the dark, purple-brown stain that filled most of the floor space. She was transfixed by this outrageously livid stain, and had watched as it slowly changed from blood red to a dark chocolate brown, her eyes tracing the shape of the blood, seeking always to try and identify what the shape looked like, as if she were playing some sick parlour game. She was now convinced that it looked like the outline of Australia. This was her attempt to mask the awful reality that this stain was the symbol of a man's last moments of life.

The guard was dead. That had become immediately apparent to everyone. He had lain in the centre of the floor, sightlessly staring at the cream-painted ceiling and the bullet hole beside the oil lamp that hung from the centre. He had remained there for what seemed like hours, though it was in all probability far less than this. No one wanted to touch him and, what made it seem even more disturbing to Jenny, no one even mentioned him. It was as if there was in fact no one lying in the centre of the floor at all. It was as if he was a figment of her imagination alone. He was a ghost which only she could see.

Jenny found this denial increasingly alarming, and eventually plucked up the courage to challenge Peter, asking him what they intended to do about the dead man. Peter just stared at her for a long time, unblinking, as if he were struggling to comprehend a foreign language. Eventually he mumbled a reply that she 'should not worry herself about that'. The train had continued ever more slowly down the line until its progress was interrupted yet again by a long pause on a lonely stretch of track. At this point Peter and Ken, without any discussion, took the corpse and lugged him out of the back end of the van, amidst much huffing, puffing and grunting. Rollo kept his beady eye on Jenny, the Luger ready by his hand. The men were gone some time, but when they climbed back aboard, they made no comment except that Peter nodded to Rollo. Silence then fell.

The train had finally continued its painfully-slow journey but eventually had been shunted off the running lines into a siding. The battle against the fog and the backlog of trains blocking the line was clearly lost. A long and interminable period of inactivity descended in which no one seemed able to summon the will to take decisive action. Rollo looked tired and ill, and fell asleep for a few hours. Peter seemed withdrawn and depressed, spending long periods staring out of the van into the ever-thinning fog, but what exactly he was watching and waiting for was unclear. Ken was also silent, lost in thought, sucking upon his pipe, his brow furrowed.

Birdsong now filled the noonday air, as the sun warmed the surrounding hedgerows, but this peace was shattered by a sudden, distant sound of the locomotive at the far end of the train, blasting steam from its safety vales in a gushing roar. A short crow on the whistle followed the metallic clank of the coupling chains swinging loose. Both Rollo and Peter sat up and looked around.

'They're taking the engine off,' said Ken, suddenly breaking the silence, 'one of us is going to have to speak to the crew. They'll be offering the guard a lift to the next shed, I expect.' Ken was filling his pipe, and talking as if this was a normal afternoon's work.

'Don't even think about taking the lift.' Rollo winced with the effort of talking.

'But it'll look mighty queer, staying with the train. They'll consider it a bit odd to want to stay here.'

'Maybe they will, but we've got to stick together. Anyway, don't fool yourself into thinking you'll be all right back there. Remember, you're in too deep to go back now. Make up some story. Spin them some tale, but get yourself back on here.' Peter stared at Ken. Looking intently at him, clearly assessing whether he was going to do a runner.

'Oh, that sounds easy enough, but what if I know them?' We've got no idea who they are. Hopefully foreigners, but if they're Woodford or Annesley men I'm scuppered. They know I'm no guard.'

Silence fell as the men took in the truth of what the old driver was saying.

'Assuming we can get shut of the engine and its crew, then what? How long do you think it will be before we get back on the move?' Peter was biting his lower lip.

'Could be a few hours; could be tomorrow. I'm not sure what goods we have here, but nothing perishable is my guess. That makes us low down on the list of priorities. We could be marooned here.'

'But that's no good; we need to get on the move. The police will find Jimmy before long, and they will certainly know about her.'

'Exactly, Peter!'

'What the hell are we going to do? Rollo's not fit for anything, and now we've got no engine, no food, and the bloody police on our tail. They'll soon track us down.'

'You're right, of course, they'll track us down. Sooner the better.' Rollo pushed himself into a more upright position. 'Listen,' he winced, 'we're stuck here, OK? And we need transport to a ferry port. Well, the police can help us get that. We hole up here and wait for them. When they get here, we use Jenny as the bargaining tool: she'll buy us a car and safe passage.' The effort of speaking caused Rollo to close his eyes and bring one hand to the side of his face.

'Are you out of your mind?' Ken stared at Rollo, 'Wait for the police to find us? It's insane. That whack on the jaw has done more harm than we thought.' He shook his head in disbelief.

'Blimey, that's one bold strategy, Rollo, I'll give you that much.

I'm not convinced though. We'd do better to get out of here and cut across country, find a car and hotwire it.'

'I agree, Peter. That's what we do.' Ken drew upon his pipe. 'Heck, they're whistling up the bloody wind down there.' He walked out onto the veranda of the van and leaned out, looking down the length of the train at the engine that was whistling angrily. He waved his green flag in acknowledgement then watched as the engine eased forwards. A few moments later he saw it reverse down the main line and advance towards him with surprising speed. 'Oh well, here goes. Now keep yer blinkin' heads down, OK?' and then he leaned on the low side panel of the veranda and waited for the locomotive to draw level, pipe in his mouth, trying to strike a note of nonchalance. The engine hissed to a halt and the driver, face blackened and the whites of his eyes tinged with red from tiredness and smoke, leaned out of the cab window, calling across to Ken.

'Hop on! We're sent back to Woodford. We've not got enough coal and water to continue. Anyway, we're fair done in.'

'Thanks, lads, but I'll stay with the train, you know how it is.'

'Are you crackers? You must've been on for hours. It ain't going anywhere. Get on here and we'll go and get some food and some kip.'

'Well, I'd rather not.'

'Jesus. You're a bit flippin' keen, aren't you? Get on the engine, man!'

Ken could see the face of the fireman, dishevelled and even blacker than the driver's, his head shaking in disbelief. 'I'd really rather stick with the train. Duty and all that,' he tailed off. His heart was heavy and depressed. He couldn't say any more. Woodford Halse was now forever lost to him. It was no longer a place of comfort, friendship and rest.

'Please yourself, then. I'm off to get a bloody hot bath and some fish and chips. I'm not waiting around here any longer. Enjoy your wait.' With that, the engine hissed and puffed away, accelerating sharply now it was freed of its heavy load. Ken watched it diminish until he could only just hear the rhythmic pulse of its exhaust gently reverberating across the fields. He turned and entered the van and sat down heavily on one of the benches.

'Well, that went OK.' Peter was dragging heavily upon a cigarette. 'We should think about making a move now, before a relief engine is sent down.' Ken nodded silently in agreement. He looked old and tired, his shoulders sagging.

'Excuse me, but if you're thinking to drag me across the countryside, I need food and drink first. And that silly gun doesn't make any difference to how I feel.' It was Jenny speaking, causing the others to stare at her in surprise.

'We didn't ask for your opinion!' Rollo spat the words out.

'No, you didn't. But you're going to get it, anyway. I need to eat something. We all do. That's a fact. Whatever you lot think you're doing, we can't do anything unless we eat. You can wave that stupid gun around as much as you like but I'm so hungry, I really don't care. So why not get outside and see what is on this train? It could be full of food.' She looked at each man in turn. 'Look, I'm not going to run off, am I? Where can I go to with you lot after me?' silence fell. 'I'm being practical.'

'You do have a point. I'm desperately hungry as well. I can't even think straight.' Ken rubbed his hands over his face and sighed deeply.

Peter stared at Jenny with a look of bewilderment, then looked at Ken. 'OK. I agree. Come on then, let's get cracking.' He stood up, and selected a long-handled sledgehammer from the many tools fastened to the sides of the van. The three of them then climbed down onto the ballast, Rollo had said nothing throughout, but made no effort to prevent them, and just lay slumped back against the van wall.

It was good to get moving, and the three were momentarily linked together in the shared pleasure of feeling their arms and legs working and took in deep draughts of fresh country air. They walked along the train looking up at the little cards slotted into the spring-loaded holders that described the contents. 'Bingo! We hit the jackpot.' Ken momentarily cheered up. 'Here, Peter, bring that hammer and get this one open.'

The padlock was high up the side of the van and Peter needed to stretch his arms out fully to land a hit upon it. Three or four times he struck a glancing blow that failed to have much impact, and he started to breathe heavily; but finally the wood splintered and the lock came away. The heavy door was pulled open amid much grinding and squealing of stiff runners, to reveal a wagon completely filled with boxes, all stamped with the unmistakable symbols of the U.S.A. Marshall Plan.

There were boxes labelled 'margarine' and others with tins of 'cooking oil', but their eyes were caught by 'baked beans', 'tinned mackerel' and 'rice pudding'. Peter was soon standing on the edge of the open doorway and pulled out a box, dropping it with a deep metallic thud to the ground, closely followed by another. The boxes spilled open, revealing tins of produce. A third box he ripped open whilst standing on the edge of the wagon, and turned, smiling to Ken and Jenny: 'Look! More apricot jam than I've ever seen!' He held up a large metal tin with a garish picture of the fruit. 'Oh boy, I've not had this much jam in years.'

'I think this'll do you more good.' Ken was extracting some cans of baked beans. 'These'll keep us alive, at least. Come on, grab a few and let's get on.'

'Phew. We could make a fortune selling this stuff.' Peter dropped down onto the gravel, a big can of jam under each arm.

'But we still need water. I'm so thirsty. There must be a stream or something near here.' Jenny was holding a can of fish in each hand, but scouring the fields behind the train.

'Fancy the task, eh? I bet you do.' Peter leered at Jenny, 'I tell you what, though: you've got some spirit, I'll give you that. But you aren't going anywhere on your own. Get back up there, and see if you can open these.'

'But we do need water. Even with your silly gun, you still need to drink. So are you going to find some?' Jenny stood defiantly and stared at him. Peter chewed his lip, one eye twitching slightly. 'Well? Or are you just going to live on jam?' She turned away contemptuously and started to walk towards the guard's van, then stopped. 'Look. We're all in this mess together now. We need to work together if we're going to get out of it. I can also see that your friend is in trouble, and the old man is losing the will to carry on. So if you have any hope of avoiding hanging from a rope, I suggest you start thinking clearly and we all help each other. So, either you, the old man, or I, go for water.'

Peter looked at Jenny, and then glanced away. The afternoon sun was raking underneath the wagons, sending long shadows across the gravel ballast and illuminating their legs with a warm, golden light. The fields seemed to shimmer with a rich glow, the overarching sky now a pale blue. There was a profound stillness in the air, as if it was holding its breath. Peter sighed, and wearily looked back at Jenny. 'You're right. Christ knows why Rollo dragged you into all this. You shouldn't even be here. It's bloody stupid.'

'And don't I know it. Well, I am here. And apparently I'm your ticket to freedom.' She spoke sarcastically, with a lightness of voice that clearly was at odds with her real feelings. 'So I suggest you keep your "ticket" alive and well, eh?'

Peter, however, was no longer listening to what Jenny was saying; instead he cocked his head and squinted with concentration. He held up his hand. 'Shhh! Can you hear it? Where is that coming from?' He searched the fields anxiously. 'Oh no, that's just what we need!'

Jenny had turned and looked in the same direction and now she too, could clearly hear the deep throaty roar of a tractor. It was coming over the crest of the gently-rolling hill opposite, towing a large trailer that looked to be carrying at least seven or eight persons in it. They were seated, holding various long-handled tools upright, like the lances of ancient knights. Jenny smiled to herself. Help might be nearer at hand than she had dared hope for.

'Quick — get back on board!' Peter looked back at the open wagon and its contents spilling out on the trackside, calculated for a few moments, then jumped back onto the open doorway and started to heave the heavy door closed. It ground its way a couple of feet, but then stuck fast. He looked back over towards the tractor, which was moving relentlessly closer. He could now almost distinguish the various persons in the trailer and could see that the driver was wearing a brightly coloured headscarf that glowed vividly in the afternoon sunshine. They were Land Army girls.

The tractor had now stopped, the engine ticking over with regular beats, like the panting of a fierce dog. He could hear shouts, and saw that the driver was waving towards him. Another woman was standing up in the trailer, shielding her eyes from the dazzling sun and staring towards the train. They had been rumbled.

Peter dropped down to the ground and ran to the guard's van, hauling himself up on to the nearest veranda.

'They've seen us?' Rollo was alert to the threat.

'Yes, worst luck. There must be nearly ten of them.'

'Damn!' Rollo leaned at the open doorway and watched the tractor, which was advancing towards them again, although cautiously now. The women in their raggle-taggle clothes, headscarves and floppy, boy-scoutish hats could be seen straining to look at the silhouette of the goods' train.

'They'll see the open door and the boxes. I couldn't draw it fully closed.'

'What are we going to do? They'll think we're looters.' Ken was at the other end of the van, his eyes wide with concern. 'Can we bluff our way out?'

'And say what?' Peter was watching the women closely. The tractor and trailer was now heading towards a gate leading into the field adjacent to the train. 'We don't have much time. I think they saw me and the girl.'

'A warning shot. Keep them at bay.' Rollo was leaning heavily against the doorjamb, checking the cartridge on the pistol.

'No. How will that help? We can't shoot our way out. Let me try to reassure them.'

'And how're you going to do that, Ken?' Rollo was sweating hard, his face livid and red. 'What are you going to say? Boxes of stuff scattered on the ground and the wagon door forced? We can't take a chance of them getting too close, with so many we could in trouble. We've got to keep them at bay.'

'This is crazy. I thought you wanted us to be discovered? A bunch of Land Girls or the police? I'd rather take my chances with this lot.'

'The police have influence. They can give us a safe passage out.' Rollo lurched through the open door, resting his elbows upon the edge of the veranda wall and steadied himself to take aim. He was breathing hard, beads of sweat forming on his brow.

'No. This is stupid, Rollo. Stop!'

Rollo squeezed the trigger as Ken started to run towards him. There was a sharp 'crack' and a slight puff of smoke as he fired a shot. After a slight delay, the tinkle of broken glass could be heard as one of headlights on the tractor exploded. 'I've not lost my touch anyway.' He turned to give a lopsided grin, and then wiped his brow. Ken stopped in his tracks and stared back in dismay.

The tractor had stopped and two of the land girls could clearly be seen looking at the shattered headlamp. An arm was pointed towards the guard's van and an animated exchange seemed to be taking place. Suddenly the tractor lurched forward and accelerated fast down the hill, dipping behind a veil of trees and a thick hedge. It was clear that they had realised that they were under attack.

'They've taken cover. But surely they will send someone back to raise the alarm?' Ken had turned and walked away from Rollo and was now crouched low, peering over the opposite veranda wall.

'I guess so. Well, let them.' Rollo was squinting down the gun barrel.

'Jesus, Rollo, I don't get this. You've really buggered everything up now. We're in a right bloody hole.' Peter was leaning against the low wall of the veranda just behind Ken and glaring at Rollo. 'And if we hadn't listened to you,' he spat the words out at Jenny, 'we might never have been rumbled either.'

She shrugged her shoulders and pulled a face. 'What do I care?' She was growing more confident, or perhaps losing the will to worry about her predicament. 'But since we're just going to sit here and wait for the cavalry to arrive we may as well eat something. Yes? Have you got anything to open this with?' She smiled coolly at Peter.

'Oh, what the hell.' He reached into his jacket pocket and slid a small pocket-knife along the floor towards Jenny. 'But don't even think about doing anything stupid with that.'

Jenny pulled a face. 'Don't worry, I'll leave the stupid things to you lot.' She grasped the knife, pulled out the can-opening tool, then started to work on a can of beans.

Rollo, meanwhile, was watching the hedgerow carefully. The tractor engine was idling, but otherwise everything was still. He thought he detected a few small movements behind the hedge at one point, but it was too dense to see clearly. An uneasy calm surrounded them, but they knew that they were being watched.

'So what now, Rollo?' Peter had taken his pistol out of his pocket, had tipped the shells into his lap, and was now inspecting it, checking the barrel was clear and then carefully replacing the shells. Jenny noticed that he had a small box containing more beside him on the floor. 'We can't just sit here, can we? And we need water. But with that lot watching, we can't hope to find any. And it's going to be hard to escape this van until at least nightfall.'

'Just wait. When the police get here, we'll let 'em know she's 'ere. I lasted longer than this in the desert without water. A few more hours won't hurt.' Rollo's words were becoming slurred as he found it hard to move his broken jaw. He sounded drunk, but his eyes were bright. 'Just watch out in case they try and get any closer.' He turned back to contemplating the hedgerow. The engine note of the tractor had changed, a plume of dirty, black exhaust appeared in a cloud and then the tractor roared past the gate, its trailer bouncing behind, two women crouched down, clinging on as it sped behind the hedgerow and away towards the far corner of the field.

'They're going for help. I reckon as they'll cut up the far side of the field and keep well out of our range. And I think they've left some of them behind.' Ken was nodding to himself as he spoke. 'They're keeping a watch on us. We should give ourselves up, it's the right time to do it. This situation is becoming a kind of madness. We can't get out of this now.'

Rollo just grinned at him: 'Yes. I'm sorry to hear you talk like that. I thought that was more Fancy Dan's style. But suit yourself, Kenno; you can walk over there if you want. Take your chances with a bunch of Land Girls with pitchforks, but just watch your back as you walk away from here, eh?' His smile was unpleasant and his eyes seemed to have a feverish quality.

Ken stared back at him. 'Jesus. You've really lost it, Rollo. You've gone too far.' He shook his head and fell silent for a few moments, fighting to control his emotions. When he spoke again it was with a calmer tone to his voice. 'Look, Mickey, you need a doctor for your jaw. It's stopping you from thinking straight. I can understand that. It's too late now for all this.' Ken waved his hand around the van interior. 'We can't run any more.' He reached for his unlit pipe and jammed it into his mouth. 'And how long before they find the guard? For all we know they've found him already. What then?'

No one spoke for a while, but the smell of beans being warmed on the stove filled the air. It was a homely smell, transporting each of them back to a time that was but a day or so ago, but now seemed a lifetime away.

✻ ✻ ✻ ✻

Vignoles pulled the Rover to a halt and sat behind the wheel for a few moments, taking in the view ahead. Before him he could see the train of box-vans sitting in a siding beside the main running tracks. The guard's van chimney was pouring out a curl of filthy black smoke that was hanging in the still, early-evening air. He could also see that one of the vans had its door partially open. But apart from these two clues the scene before him looked completely still and devoid of life. He knew that that was far from the case, though. Hidden in the fields around the siding were some of the Land Army who had raised the alarm, a truckload of army squaddies brought in from a nearby camp, and some of Bainbridge's men. Thin layers of mist were gathering in the fields, hanging like gossamer sheets above the damp grass and collecting against the hedgerows and drainage ditches at the bottom of the hill.

He got out of the car, as did Sergeant Trinder, W.P.C. Lansdowne and Violet McIntyre. Vignoles remained unhappy that she was accompanying them, for they already knew that the gang were armed and had fired at least one shot, and an accurate one at that. But Violet had been so insistent, even threatening to find a vehicle and drive herself there, that he relented. It convinced himself that it was probably safer that she was under their jurisdiction and remained in their sight, rather than acting like a loose cannon.

Bainbridge got out of his car, which had pulled up behind at that moment, together with his sergeant, and two brutish-looking constables. Vignoles had left W.P.C. Benson and P.C. Blencowe — who had driven the Rover down from Leicester — at Woodford, manning the temporary command centre they had set up in Saunders's shed office.

Vignoles spoke to Lansdowne: 'All OK?'

'I took them apart and cleaned them on the drive down and they are serviceable, at least. But how accurate and over what distance, I wouldn't like to say. Ideally, I could do with a few practice rounds to check the accuracy.' She was inspecting the rather ancient, Spanish-built pistol as she spoke.

'I'm not aware these have ever been used in anger. Or even used at all, come to think of it.' Vignoles dubiously felt the weight and grip of another pistol but then handed it to Trinder. 'I prefer to use my own. OK, are we all set? Sergeant?'

'Yes, I'm ready.' Trinder was looking suspiciously at the gun but, after first checking that the safety catch was on, slipped it into his coat pocket. Vignoles walked over to Bainbridge.

'We need to work our way around to a position of cover, roughly opposite the van — down there,' he indicated towards the hedgerow that the tractor driven by the Land Army had taken refuge behind. 'A second party needs to work its way around the train taking the long route around the front end, to avoid being sighted. They should then take up position at the far side of the running tracks. That way we have both sides covered.'

'I have men stationed there already.'

'Good, I shall send Lansdowne to join them. Her sharp-shooting abilities will be better served with the sun behind her back. I suggest Sergeant Dobson accompanies her.'

'Look, Vignoles, are you really sure she's up to the job?' Bainbridge spoke quietly, hoping that the W.P.C. would not hear.

'I am. Completely.' He nodded to Lansdowne as he was speaking, and she started to walk towards the front of the train with the tall figure of Sergeant Dobson beside her. They cut across a field, keeping low as they advanced towards the line of wagons. 'We don't do anything until we are sure everyone is in place. Where did you place the army boys?'

'They threw a cordon around the whole area, about half a mile or so back. I instructed them to just hold the line and avoid firing a shot unless absolutely essential. But look, Vignoles, are you sure about this? You carrying firearms, and all that? A couple of sharp-shooters from the army would be far better, surely?'

'We're on railway property, and we take control of what happens. That also means we take responsibility for any use of firearms. And remember, I shall do all I can to avoid it. On top of that, Lansdowne is crack shot. We would be lucky to find a better. Those army lads are hardly out of basic training. I wouldn't fancy their chances of hitting a cow's arse with a banjo, to be honest.' He grinned at Bainbridge, who laughed, relieving the mounting tension. 'But as I have said before, getting Jenny McIntyre back safe and sound is the aim.' He glanced at Violet, who had remained silent throughout, her gaze fixed upon the train. 'I will let the gang cut and run if so be it. Let no one forget that. I hope negotiation will sort all this out. The game really is up for them.'

'I just hope they see it that way.' Bainbridge looked down at the goods' train. 'OK, shall we take up our positions?'

＊　＊　＊　＊

As the sun sank below the horizon, there was now a chill in the air, laced with the dampness of low-lying mist, as Jenny McIntyre attempted to warm some food on the stove. But the coals were little more than dying embers that only glowed when she blew on them, but created no flame nor heat. Taking little notice of the men crouched in each doorway, she searched around the van for something to burn, and managed to assemble an oily jacket, a length of equally oily rope, a tattered, red guard's flag and other oddments. She commenced stuffing the rope into the little stove and watched with satisfaction as it flared and spat wildly as the oil caught fire. The flames roared up the narrow, metal chimney, pouring a dense black smoke into the evening air.

She then looked at the leather holdall that had sat, ever-present but ignored, in the corner. Apparently this was the reason for this crazy escapade, but now it just sat there, useless and unloved. She unzipped the bag to reveal the neat bundles of banknotes. 'We could burn this. It's all fake, isn't it?'

'What is? Hey — what are you doing with that?' Peter looked away from the fields outside and glared at Jenny, who was clutching a bundle of notes and holding them aloft.

'This money. It's just useless paper, isn't it? It's not real. Or so you told me, and you can't use it, especially not now. What are you going to do with it now?' She stared down at the money, feeling herself becoming transfixed by its captivating appeal, even though she knew it to be worthless.

'You can't burn that!'

'Why not, Pete? Come to think of it, she might be right to burn it. It's brought us no bloody good.' Ken laughed, 'Hey, but you know nothing about fires, girl. It won't be much use in the stove: the ash will just clog up the fire. Ach, what the hell, stuff a bundle in on top of that rope. But no more, it'll just smother the flames. We could do with some warmth in here.' Ken shivered, though whether from the cold, Jenny was unsure.

Peter looked at Ken, then shrugged his shoulders. 'Burning money now? Oh, do what you like. I've got my stash of the real stuff. And there's plenty enough in the bag.' He looked away and then started to laugh, a sound that was startling and incongruous in the tense atmosphere. 'It's funny really, burning money to stay warm. Now that is rich. Ha ha, warming our hands on burning fivers. Yeah, go on girl! Burn the bloody stuff, why not?'

Jenny needed no further encouragement; she pulled the holdall closer to the iron door of the stove and picked up a bundle of notes, placing it on the burning rope. The fire was almost instantly quenched, as Ken had told her it would be, and started to smoke profusely. She looked around, her brow furrowed with concentration, and then picked up a conical metal can that was streaked with rivulets of oil. It was stoppered with a cork attached by a small chain to the neck. She moved it from side to side and felt that it was nearly full. Uncorking it, she then sloshed some of the lamp oil into the stove and a brilliant red light glowed around the interior as the flames flared up. Jenny smiled to herself and glanced around, but the men were apparently concentrating on something that they had noticed outside. They looked tense and were watching with renewed concentration. Rollo, who had fallen increasingly silent at the opposite end, was now crouching with the Luger raised and ready to take aim. His face was pale and waxy, with beads of sweat forming on his brow. Jenny knew that he was using all his energy to maintain his concentration. This was her chance to strike back.

She made as if to place the can of oil on the floor, but whilst keeping her eyes on Rollo and her back turned to the others, allowed the oil to spill over the bundles of money, thoroughly drenching them. She then let more oil flood onto the floorboards, lying the can on its side as the liquid spread away from her across to the far side of the van. She then picked up the grimy cotton drill jacket and allowed it to soak up more oil. The stove was roaring wildly and the heat was becoming uncomfortable. The bruise on her cheek where Rollo had struck her was throbbing painfully. She touched it with her fingers, then narrowed her eyes in determination. Ken and Peter were talking quickly and quietly behind her. They had seen someone approaching the train and all their attention was now outside. This was her chance.

As Jenny stoked the little stove, Vignoles and Trinder had field glasses trained on the guard's van. They could just make out two, possibly three, figures crouched low and still in the doorways at each end. Dusk was falling and their vision was dropping off significantly, hampered further by a thick, oily smoke from the stovepipe chimney.

Vignoles was ready to make his first move. He planned to advance forward under the cover of the encroaching darkness and then hail the occupants, hoping to enter into some kind of dialogue and negotiation. So far, there had been no attempt by the gang to engage or communicate, a fact that he had found curious. As each hour passed, the net had tightened around the train and there was now no means of escape. However, the gang also held Jenny McIntyre hostage, and Vignoles was sure that they would try to use her as a means to buy their escape. Certainly he knew that whilst the gang was holed up inside with Jenny captive, he and his officers could make no serious attempt to storm the van. So negotiation was their only option.

Together with Trinder, Bainbridge and two police constables, they walked slowly towards the low bushes of hawthorn that edged the field. They crouched low, near a gap in the hedge formed by a narrow, weed-choked culvert that led to a small, brick-arched tunnel under the railway line. There was a strange, flickering red glow inside the guard's van, as if they were stoking up the fire. Vignoles and Bainbridge exchanged puzzled glances. Vignoles then gave a short blast on his whistle. It carried clearly on the still evening air. It was a signal to W.P.C. Lansdowne, and the officers with her, to stand ready. It also served, he hoped, to draw the attention of the people inside the guard's van. 'Can you see any movement?'

'No ... but wait! Yes, there's movement there, I can just make out a shape against the sky. I think there are two at this end, maybe one at the other, but I can't be sure of that.' Trinder was speaking in a whisper. The men stared intently at the van.

'What is going on inside? Why so much blasted smoke coming out of the chimney? It stinks to high heaven.' Bainbridge tapped Vignoles arm to draw attention.

'I'm not sure. Maybe they're cold? OK, I'll try to open up negotiations.' Vignoles stood up, still largely hidden by the hawthorn, spread his arms wide to show that he was not holding a weapon, though he could feel the weight of his pistol concealed in his coat pocket, and prepared to hail the fugitives.

But, at that very moment, there was a bright red-and-yellow flash that illuminated the small windows of the guard's van with a blinding light that left little dancing rectangles of colour on the eyes of those watching. There was the deep, resonant sound of an explosion of heat and flame, followed by the tinkle of glass as the side window on the guard's van shattered. Flames and boiling smoke poured out of the tiny aperture, licking the painted wooden sides. There were shouts and, in the bright light, two men could be seen standing with arms flung across their eyes, backing away from the van interior, followed by a running figure of a woman who briefly cried out then stumbled to the floor. Flames appeared in the doorway, followed by dense, black smoke that rolled out and smothered them.

'That's Jenny. Come on!' Vignoles gave three sharp blasts on his whistle and started to run forwards, his gun now in his hand. He was aware of Trinder sprinting quickly past him, making a curving run around the back of the train. Two of the men on the van exchanged a few shouts and then disappeared from view, as did Jenny. The van was now burning furiously and filling the air with the choking fumes of burning oil. Vignoles was close to the wheels of the van, and could hear someone coughing on the far side of the vehicle. He reached for his pocket-handkerchief and held it to his nose and mouth. He looked around, frantically trying to locate the fourth person on board, but he could see no movement and hear only the crackling of the fire. Vignoles crouched low and peered underneath the railway wagons into the gloom gathering at track level but could see nothing except the legs of Sergeant Trinder. He could not locate any of the escaping fugitives.

He made his way around to the rear of the train just as three figures dropped to the ground and started running away from him, already three or four wagon-lengths down the train. The air was filled by the acrid smell of burning wood and paint and Vignoles could feel the searing heat of the flames on his back. Clouds of dirty smoke billowed down and around the train, folding into great, grubby balls and obscuring his view of the running figures. He looked around and saw W.P.C. Lansdowne, accompanied by a number of uniformed officers, on the far side of the running tracks, well clear of the smoke. Someone blew a whistle. Trinder was standing some way in advance of Vignoles, legs slightly apart, holding his pistol with both hands and trying to find a target.

'Hold your fire, sergeant. Jenny is with them. It's too smoky and dim to be sure of not hitting her. We need to get closer.' The two men sprinted forwards.

'Stop! Police!' Trinder's voice boomed out clear and loud.

'Get back — or we'll shoot her! Don't come closer!' The group had stopped and turned to face them, alerted by the whistle and the sound of their feet crunching on the ground. A bullet pinged into the ballast near Trinder, who promptly threw himself face down onto the ground, his hat rolling to one side. Vignoles flattened himself against a wagon. He could see Prenton waving a silver pistol towards them, his other arm around the waist of Jenny. His extended arm was sweeping rapidly from side to side, trying to cover both Trinder and Vignoles.

'Sergeant, hold your fire.' Vignoles spread his arms out wide and stepped away from the wagon, his pistol clearly pointing to the sky. 'Don't do anything foolish. You are surrounded. We have armed police officers and the army all around you. There is nowhere to escape. Just put the weapon down, and put your hands up.' Vignoles shouted as loudly as he could. In reply, another bullet fizzed through the air.

'I'll shoot her if you come any closer!'

'And what good will that do you?' Vignoles tried to keep his voice clear and calm, his mind trying to recall how well Trinder had fared on the shooting range. If he was to rely upon the accuracy of his sergeant's shooting, it was an important point. He seemed to remember that his sergeant had flunked the course, described as showing much enthusiasm, but little aptitude. Vignoles glanced briefly across the running tracks and thought he could just make out the crouching shape of Lansdowne. He would have to put his trust in her. 'There is no escape. Don't make matters worse by doing anything foolish. Just put the gun down, and let the girl go. We can talk about this.'

Peter pointed the gun at Vignoles, but despite the increasing gloom and drifts of smoke, Vignoles could see that he was indecisive and agitated, his head moving from side to side, trying to assess the situation. The other, a much older man, moved a few steps away from Peter and Jenny, his eyes wide with alarm, and fixated upon the gun in Peter's hand.

'Let the girl go. She is nothing to do with this. If you hurt her, do you really think you will walk away from here? You are surrounded by armed officers.' Vignoles took slow, measured steps forward, his arms stretched wide open, and beads of sweat forming on his brow around his hatband. As Vignoles advanced he could hear that a train was approaching from behind him, its exhaust ricocheting across the misty fields in rhythmic beats that seemed to amplify his own pounding heartbeat.

The roof of the burning wagon behind him suddenly collapsed in a crackling roar and the bright-yellow light of the flames illuminated the group standing before Vignoles. He saw his own dancing shadow stretching out, rippling over the stone ballast and almost meeting with the group of three. Peter stared at Vignoles, his little silver pistol reflecting the flickering flames, his tongue again flicking around his mouth like a snake. Vignoles, in turn, halted his advance. He could see that Jenny was hurt, probably burnt by the explosion and now clearly in pain and close to fainting; her head was lying loosely to one side and her eyes were partially closed. The man's shirt she was wearing was scorched and smoke-blackened.

'It's all up, Peter. You know it is. We're all washed up now.' The older man was speaking to Prenton. 'Let her go, she's hurt. She can't help us now.' And with that he suddenly turned and started to walk towards Vignoles.

'Get back here, you idiot! Ken, get back here!'

'Stop where you are! Put your hands up or we'll shoot!' Vignoles tried to shout above the sound of the approaching train, but Ken was still advancing. There was a brief flash of light to his right coming from some way across the running tracks, and then the sound of a gun followed. The advancing figure spun around on the spot, his left arm clutching at his right shoulder, knees crumpling at the same time. Ken staggered, then collapsed into a sitting position against the wheel of a wagon. At the same moment, as if on cue, Jenny collapsed, her legs buckling under her. Prenton, with one arm outstretched holding the pistol, was unable to support all her weight and was pulled off balance, releasing the dead weight of Jenny just in time to stop himself being also pulled to the ground. In trying to regain his balance, his gun arm lifted high into the night sky as he staggered two steps back, away from Jenny. At that same moment the advancing train was almost upon them, whistling frantically. The engine was protesting loudly as the driver attempted to slow down and clouds of exhaust steam wrapped themselves around Vignoles and Trinder. Before his vision was totally obscured, however, Vignoles saw Prenton leap backwards as two rapid shots rang out. Trinder was now sprinting past Vignoles, who followed him close behind. The huge bulk of the locomotive was moving in parallel beside him, the deafening noise reverberating off the stationary wagons and roaring in his ears. Trinder had reached Ken, who was nursing a gunshot wound to his upper arm and repeatedly shouting: 'Don't shoot! Don't shoot!'

'Stay where you are, and we won't. Now, shut up!' Trinder barked at the wounded man, then continued towards Prenton and Jenny. Prenton was lying on his back, groaning, his hands clutched to his groin, groaning and coughing for breath at the same time. Jenny was, to the surprise and relief of the two approaching officers, standing close to Prenton. With her dishevelled hair, paint-spattered trousers, scorched white shirt and the small silver pistol in her outstretched hands, she looked like some kind of pirate. Vignoles even managed a smile as he approached. Trinder, without hesitating, pounced upon Prenton, rolling him onto his side and forcing his hands behind his back and into handcuffs. Prenton was coughing and sputtering wildly, his face red with the effort. 'Is there anyone else? Answer me! On the train: is there anyone else.' Trinder was holding his face close to Prenton's ear. 'Is it just you two?'

Whilst Trinder tried to get Prenton to reply, Vignoles pocketed his own gun and put his arm around Jenny, gently removing the pistol from her grasp. 'Are you very badly hurt? I thought you had fainted.'

'I'm fine, really I am.' She looked at him, eyes wide and fierce, her face smudged with grime. 'I just made out I fainted, then kicked and punched him in the stomach and in … where it hurts.' She giggled, but more from shock than mirth. 'It was time to get my own back.' She started to cry soundlessly, tears streaking her face.

'There's another one — Rollo — and he's armed!' Trinder was looking at Vignoles, then immediately turned away again to look along the line of parked wagons. The heavy goods' train continued to rumble and clatter past them, filling their ears with a noise that made it hard to think clearly. Vignoles glanced behind him and saw Bainbridge and a number of uniformed officers closing in on them.

'Jenny — they will look after you — we must find the other man.'

'Do! He's the one you want. But be careful. He's dangerous.'

'Don't worry.' With that, Vignoles retrieved his own gun and started to move along the line of stationary wagons, thinking that that was the best, if not only, place of concealment for Rollo. It was almost fully dark now, though the roaring fire of the burning guard's van provided some welcome illumination, but its effect was rapidly diminishing as they moved further away.

Trinder was moving quickly forwards, bent low, trying to peer beneath the wagons. Vignoles squinted along the corridor formed by the stationary train to his left and the still-moving one to his right. Suddenly, his eye was caught by a sudden movement, perhaps that of a figure darting across the gap between the two trains. It was a long way ahead, so he was not absolutely sure of what he had seen, but sensed that this was Rollo, and if so, then he was attempting to board the moving train. The train had now slowed to little more than the speed of a jogging run as Vignoles started to keep pace beside it. The guard's van was adjacent to him, so he reached up for the handrails and mounted the low running board. The guard was above him, leaning out and watching the proceedings unfold. Vignoles called up to him. 'Police! We need to stop this train! There's an armed man aboard. Keep yourself back!' With that, Vignoles looked back along the train towards the locomotive.

Trinder had seen Vignoles climb aboard and was running beside the train, making ready to jump aboard as well.

'I think Rollo is on the train, riding between the wagons. If he doesn't kill himself first, we need to get this train stopped.'

'Wilco.' Trinder swung himself up onto the rear of the guard's van. 'Can you signal to the driver?' he asked the guard.

'I can try, but he's slowing her down, anyway.' The guard was waving a red lamp towards the engine whilst he was speaking.

'OK, but duck inside now, this devil has a gun,' Trinder advised, whilst leaning out of the opposite side to Vignoles. The train continued to move forwards into the night as they left the bright glow of the fire and the groups of police gathered around Jenny and the two apprehended men behind them. Vignoles was aware that they were inexorably departing the cordon laid down by the army and the welcome back-up of their fellow officers and in particular, the accuracy of Lucy Lansdowne's aim.

He knew that the train would soon come to a halt, but at what point would Rollo jump off and disappear into the dark, mist-layered fields that lay around them? He and Trinder would be hard pressed to track him down unaided. He felt frustrated that they might lose their quarry at the last hurdle, but allowed a moment of satisfaction that they had saved Jenny McIntyre's life. The train was now almost stationary, crawling forwards at walking pace towards a red light in the distance. The signal box had been alerted and set the distant signal to danger. Now Rollo would have little choice but to abandon his short-lived escape route, but the impenetrable dark was rendering it impossible for Vignoles to see very much. He climbed onto the front veranda of the guard's van and called to his sergeant: 'Can you see anything at all? I'm as good as blind here with all the engine steam.'

'Not a bleedin' sausage! Dammit!' Trinder joined Vignoles on the open veranda. 'What next?'

'Right now, our options are few. If he's already jumped off, we haven't a chance, but hopefully he might be caught in the army cordon.' Vignoles was leaning out and staring intently along the train.

'Trying to hunt him down in the dark in these fields and woods? A needle in a haystack comes to mind.' Trinder did the same and looked across the rails into the fields beyond. 'Too many places to hide. But if we use all the civvies and army lads, we could flush him out by morning. Especially if they use dogs.'

'Agreed. When we halt we had better check that he has not stayed on board, and at least make the train safe.' As Vignoles was speaking there was the sound of a gunshot, then the train lurched forwards, the wagons bumping into each other violently like a line of dominoes as the locomotive suddenly started to accelerate. The wheels were slipping under the engine as a volcano of fire and smoke jetted out of the chimney. The men in the guard's van were thrown off balance as they received the full juddering force of the wagons shunting together.

'He's accelerating? He's crazy … listen! He'll ruin that engine, acting up like that!' The guard was back on his feet and looking along the train at the blaze of smoke and steam ahead. The locomotive wheels were alternating between slipping wildly and pulling the train forward in ugly, aggressive jerks.

'That's Rollo! He fired a shot. He's making them move off. He must be on the engine.' Vignoles looked at Trinder.

'He's forcing them to move on at gunpoint?'

'No engineman would ever deliberately accelerate towards a danger signal.' The guard looked angry. 'It goes against all the rules in the book. But listen to the way he's thrashing that engine. It's bloody madness, if they keep this up he'll wreck the engine.'

'Or break the couplings and lose us. I think Rollo knows exactly what he's doing. He wants them to break free of the train, and lose us.' Another vicious jolt along the train was accompanied by a loud sequence of metallic bangs as the buffers clanged into each other, running like a ripple along the train. Vignoles, despite holding on tight, and half-expecting the jolt, was still thrown to the ground, the guard likewise. Trinder was leaning over side of the van, clinging on with all his might.

The train had accelerated noticeably but the locomotive seemed to be making only intermittent progress, alternating between lurching forwards and spinning its wheels on the damp, greasy rails. There was another violent sequence of jolts and crashes, then suddenly the train was rolling along calmly, whilst the locomotive spun its wheels faster and faster, the plume of smoke now towering high above the train, flickering with flashes of red as the fire was thrown out of the chimney.

'She's gone! We've broken loose, but the engine's lost! He can't stop that wheel spin.' Trinder was watching the disaster unfold. 'Hold on! We're in for an almighty smash now.'

The locomotive had hurled itself forward a hundred yards in advance of the greater part of the heavy goods' train which it had broken free of, but now its link motion was disintegrating in a sequence of sickening bangs and searing metallic squeals, the engine was shaking and rocking as it now skidded along the rails, its wheels locked together tight. The driver had shut off the steam, but it still careered forward, making a sound like a thousand nails being dragged down a blackboard, sparks flying from the rails and the metal tyres glowing red hot. The engine stopped like a dead weight as the goods train, now free of the engine, continued its course towards it.

The two collided in a terrific crash and splintering of wood, and rending of metal. Three or four wagons left the track and twisted themselves across the track before literally bursting their sides and spilling their contents into the air. The noise was deafening, but increased as the engine's tender also skewed off the track and commenced to rip the wooden sleepers to shreds and pull one of the running rails from its fastenings as huge lumps of coal tumbled into the cab, spewed over the trackside and rolled down the grassy bank. After what seemed an age, but was probably less than a minute, the whole wreck came to a halt. The engine was hissing wildly as steam issued from all around it. A sequence of groans, cracks and ticking noises were the last sounds, before all fell silent.

Vignoles lay on the floor of the guard's van, rubbed his elbow and gently felt the back of his head. There was something warm and wet there and, whilst it was too dark to be sure, as he touched his tongue to his fingers he tasted iron, and knew it was blood. It ached, but as he was aware of the ache he thought that this might be a good sign. His eyes felt heavy as if with sleep, but he had to make himself move. 'Anyone hurt?'

'I think my arm could be broken,' Trinder replied quietly.

'Nothing broken I think, unlike my train. Ouch, but maybe I've done my knee and ankle in.' The guard was crumpled into the far corner of his van, looking like a rag doll.

Vignoles started to tentatively move, feeling his body ache and complain, his muscles refusing to obey, his eyes feeling heavy with sleep. He managed to get himself up onto one elbow, then stopped. He could hear the distant sound of police whistles and the crunch of booted feet running over gravel. 'The cavalry are on their way!' He heard his voice as if it were coming from a great distance. He smiled, and suddenly felt sleep overwhelm him. His eyes were so heavy. He just had to sleep. But he had a job to do: he must apprehend Rollo, make the train safe. But maybe the cavalry could do that? Yes, he could let them do that now.

He slipped into unconsciousness.

Chapter Twenty-Eight

'WHEN THE LIGHTS GO ON AGAIN, ALL OVER THE WORLD'
Vaughan Monroe & his Orchestra

Edward and Simon were sitting on the bench normally used by Mary and Margi to prepare the oil lamps. The sun on their backs was warm and pleasing, the aroma of paraffin oil, creosote, steam coal and the hot, intangible, almost animal pungency of steam locomotives filled the windless air. A midday peace had fallen upon the normally frantic locomotive depot, whilst stands of smoke rose from the chimneys of the dozen or so engines in steam. The fizzle of steam punctuated by just the occasional clang or a shout disturbed the air, but otherwise all was still. Even the coal tower was at rest. It shimmered in the haze like a grotesque cenotaph, a permanent and unavoidable reminder of a recent death, yet softened now by the welcome sunshine; it was already starting to lose its menace.

The women, unusually, were nowhere to be seen, but as the bench caught the direct sun and also afforded a grandstand view of the recently wrecked locomotive, the two lads eagerly snapped it up. They sipped their tea and looked across the yard to where the battered engine had been brought to rest a few days earlier. The eight small driving wheels were shorn of all connecting rods, the cab was buckled and misshapen, whilst the tender was crumpled and twisted as if made of tinplate. Fresh, shiny gashes, metallic wounds cut into the sombre black of the unwashed engine, spoke of the ferocity of the smash. A rope had been tied to the front buffers and then strung around the engine in a loose and ineffectual cordon, propped up by lengths of kindling and two up-ended brooms, their handles driven into the grey morass of the yard surface.

'I can't believe anyone survived that.'

'Lucky that the crew managed to jump clear, but that Rollo fellow didn't; he was crushed between the tender and the first wagon. Not much left of him, so I've heard.'

'Yeah. He lost both his legs.' Simon drank some tea.

'Nah, they said it was his head.'

'What?'

'Chopped clean off!'

'Jesus! Who told you that?'

'Piggy did, straight up, no kidding! He said they were looking for it for a good hour, 'cos it rolled into a ditch.' Edward poured more tea into his enamelled cup and slurped some down, enjoying the effect his words had on Simon.

'No, he's having you on. You know how he likes to pull your leg.' Simon looked back at the engine, 'Come on, would a head really roll?'

'Well, they always say "heads will roll".'

'Yeah. Suppose you're right there. Cor, who'd have thought it? What a way to go.'

'Do you think the company's going to press charges on the driver? For wrecking the engine?' Edward frowned as he stared at the twisted cab.

'Seems a rotten trick to do that. He was at gun point and ordered to pass a red light, but instead of maybe running into another train and killing others, he chose to wreck his own engine, risking only himself, the fireman and the guard.'

'And the policemen.'

'Yeah, but he didn't know that they were on board, Eddie.'

'True. Well I'm glad the crew survived. It's weird, Simon. I was talking with that Rollo and Driver Price just days ago, and now one's dead, and the other's been shot and in prison.'

'Custody. He goes to prison later.'

'Right. Custody.' Edward paused. 'Strange word that, a bit like "custard".'

They sat in silence for a few moments.

'Si? Do you think we're kind of responsible for all this? I mean, if we hadn't taken the money, this might not have happened.'

'We couldn't know it would end like this.'

'No, but remember when you said we had to "make things happen", and then we did. We made this happen!'

'Oh, blame me! Thanks a bunch, Eddie!'

'No. I don't mean it like that. We both did what we did. I was part of it, I took the bag, remember?' Edward looked across at his friend, who returned the look, and then grinned.

'Yeah. And how brilliant that was! Just the most exciting thing ever. You've got to admit it.'

'Apart from hiding in the ash pits when they chased us.' Edward's mood also lifted, and he smiled at the memory. 'Hey, but I wonder how the policemen are doing? They're still in hospital apparently.'

'I wonder? Do you think we're going to have to give evidence? I don't fancy the idea of going to court. As much because Mum and Dad are really not seeing anything good in what we did, despite doing my best to …' Simon paused as he looked for the words, '… to put the very best light on our part in solving this crime.' He pulled a rueful face.

'I know exactly what you mean. I really think Dad was going to take a belt to me.' Edward shook his head. 'OK, it's all bluff with him. But he made his point well enough.'

'Maybe that nice Detective Vignoles will speak up for us? Put in a good word about all we did to help?'

Edward nodded. 'I wouldn't say no to that right now.' He looked away, and then suddenly exclaimed, 'Hello, there's Margi and Mary. Not seen them around all day. Hey! Over here!' Edward waved his free hand at the two women, who were walking slowly out of the gloom of the engine shed into the brilliant sun. Mary was looking at a magazine as she walked, occasionally jabbing a finger onto something on one of the pages. Both women looked anxious and agitated.

'Hello lads. Enjoying the sun, are you?' Mary smiled, but it lacked her usual, full-on warmth. 'The two young detectives, taking it easy, eh? Tiring work solving crime mysteries.' Her voice sounded weary, despite her attempt at levity.

'What's up? You two look a bit in the dumps.' Simon slipped off the bench and stood up to face them, Edward following likewise.

'Oh, it's nothing.' Mary paused and after hearing how unconvincing her voice sounded, corrected herself, 'Well, yes, I suppose we are. We've had some pretty rough news, to be honest.' Mary sighed, but still tried to retain her smile.

'Now, surprises I don't mind. It's shocks I can't stand! Oh yes, and have we had a shock. Guess what?' Margi waved the magazine in the air, and pointed at the open page, 'The wonderful London and North Eastern Railway, have, in the kindness of their hearts, announced that they are ending all war work for women, outside of clerical grades, with immediate effect.' Margi stared at Edward and Simon, who were struggling to take in what she had just said.

'We're sacked is what Margi is saying. End of the week. Sacked through the pages of the company magazine, can you believe? Not even a personal letter.'

'Not so much as a thank you very much.'

'But that's dreadful. That can't be right.' Edward reached for the magazine and started to read the official letter printed on a full page of the magazine.

'They can't just sack you! The union would never allow it.' Simon was shaking his head.

'No? You've got a lot to learn about the ways of the world, young man. The N.U.R. couldn't wait to get shut of us. We're just a ... a nuisance, that's all. The union never really wanted us here in the first place, so they won't speak up for us women, mark my words!' Mary took a deep breath. She looked as if she were tempted to use stronger language, but stopped herself. Edward handed the magazine back to Margi.

'I'm sorry, it's not your fault and we shouldn't be beastly to you. We knew well enough that this would come one day soon. The war's over, and we're expected to stand down.' Mary attempted another wan smile.

'It's just the way they've gone about it. It makes you a bit sick at heart.' Margi looked at the ground.

'But, but we need you here. We've not enough cleaners by a long chalk. It's got to be a mistake.' Edward looked genuinely shocked.

'Maybe. I suppose there's always a faint hope that they will see sense. We shall know soon enough.' Margi looked up and smiled for the first time, 'It's sweet of you to care, more than some of them will. The union reps in particular.' She shook her head, the ends of her pale blue headscarf shaking on the nape of her neck. 'I'm not sure how I'm going to be able to get used to not working on the railways. We moan about it, what with the long hours and the dirt, but we love it here, really.'

'But what will you do?'

'Dunno, Simon. I can't stick the idea of typing in an office. The Land Army is still recruiting, so maybe we'll join them?'

Edward and Simon stood and looked at the two women, unsure of what to say. The stillness in the yard seemed to intensify. Margi's anger had changed into sadness as she looked around the yard at the locomotives warming in the sun, her eyes shining wet, but then rallied herself. 'Hey, Eddie, but you're on your own now. I can't embarrass you helping to shovel coal. Ha! That was just so funny. At least you won't get ribbed by the men for having a woman on your footplate!' Margi threw the magazine into a nearby coal bucket and mimed shovelling coal. 'But you'll be all right.' Margi winked. 'Eh, chin up lads. Anyone would have thought it was you two who'd just lost your jobs!'

'Oh, to hell with it all. Enough of this talk.' Mary looked over at the wooden bench. 'Is there any more tea in that billycan, because if not, I fancy a brew. What d'you say, lads?'

* * * *

Whilst Woodford Halse stewed quietly in the unexpected heat, Detective Inspector Vignoles was stewing in his own way on top of a hospital bed, wearing a dressing gown, a bandage wrapped ostentatiously around his head and with a pile of books lying on either side of him. A dissembled newspaper was falling, a page at a time, to the floor, whilst he, much to the fury of matron, filled his pipe. He needed a pipe, hospital rules or no hospital rules. Either he had his pipe, or they sent him home. He had already opened the window wide to let in some much-needed fresh air from the gloriously sunny day outside and was now forcing himself to stay in bed as ordered, despite feeling perfectly all right in body and mind. Correction, his mind was in principle unaffected by the heavy blow he had taken when the train had crashed, but the last twenty minutes of listening to Chief Superintendent Badger had seriously threatened a relapse.

Yes, chief superintendent, of course he could appreciate that the planned V.I.P. visit had been somewhat ruined by the enforced hospitalisation of his two most senior officers. Yes, he also appreciated just how regrettable it was that the police Rover had been all but abandoned beside a remote railway siding in Buckinghamshire when it was due to be bringing Sir Anthony Prazen-Beagle to Leicester. He agreed that it was terribly embarrassing that, once it had been retrieved, it was found to be not only empty of petrol but all the petrol coupons for the next few months had been used up on one journey. No, sir, with respect, it was not a wild goose chase, but I can fully appreciate the immense difficulties this must have caused you, trying to find more petrol coupons.

Vignoles started to smile to himself. Upon reflection, now the self-important little man had left the room, it was actually really quite amusing. The thought of Badger sniffing around all his colleagues, desperately calling in any favour he could dream up, in exchange for coupons, was worth a verbal mauling from him any day. He took a long drag on his pipe, and enjoyed the aroma as it blotted out the smell of disinfectant and atrocious food permeating the hospital. He looked at the azure-blue sky outside and hoped that it would stay fine until at least tomorrow, when Anna would come to collect him and free him from this enforced imprisonment. Then hopefully they could sit outside in their garden for an hour or two and enjoy the sun. He leaned across the bed and inhaled the scent of the roses beside the bed that she had placed there soon after he had been admitted.

His mood lifted another notch a few moments later when there came a light knock, and Sergeant Trinder popped his head around the door. 'How's the patient today?' He grinned. 'I passed the Badger on the way in.' He raised a questioning eyebrow.

'Oh, hello. Don't worry about Badger, he moaned about everything that he could think of, in particular how dammed inconvenient it had been with us both in hospital, and almost completely forgot to mention how pleased he was that we sorted out the Water Street gang, let alone the excellent part W.P.C. Lansdowne played in it all. But I reminded him in the nick of time.' Vignoles grinned in return, 'But come in, come in, John.'

Trinder walked into the room with a slight limp, his right arm in plaster and a sling, and then turned to make way for Violet McIntyre, who was carrying a vase filled with wild flowers. 'Miss McIntyre, what a pleasant surprise.' Vignoles started to get out of bed.

'Oh, your poor head. No, no, don't get up, I insist, stay where you are!'

'It's nothing, Miss McIntyre, I really shouldn't even be here, it's quite preposterous to keep me cooped up like this, but the doctor absolutely insists. I can escape tomorrow, thank God.'

'Quite right too, you've had a terrible blow to the head. You need to take it easy. You cannot be too careful.'

'That's what Anna said.'

'Now you stay where you are, and let me put these somewhere. They're just picked from the fields around Woodford, I am afraid,' she glanced at the vase full of roses, 'and a little wilted by the sun.' She smiled at Vignoles as she placed them on the windowsill.

'They are lovely. I can dream of the open countryside and not this horrid little room.'

'I am afraid Jenny could not be spared by Mrs Walsh, but she absolutely insists that you let her know when you are next calling in for a cup of tea at Woodford.'

'Of course. That shall be at the top of my list as soon as I can get out of here. How is she anyway? I hope not feeling too awful after her experience? Was she badly burnt?'

'She's really doing fine. She frazzled her hair rather, but otherwise is fine and bearing up well. She's a tougher than you might think. I suppose we have the Blitz to thank for that.'

'I was saying to Violet on the way here, what a clever move it was to look as though she was fainting and fall from Prenton's grasp. Sheer genius.' Trinder looked away from Vignoles and gave Violet a warm smile that was immediately returned.

'Indeed it was. Jennifer is a brave girl, and that piece of clever deception allowed Lansdowne to put in a shot and wing him. Though if I understand the situation correctly, it was her two — let's say well-aimed — punches that really floored him.' Vignoles took a puff on his pipe.

Violet flushed. 'Yes, well frankly it was the least he deserved, under the circumstances.'

'I couldn't agree more. But really, what a delightful surprise. It was most kind of you to come and visit. You really didn't need to.'

'I most certainly did, after all you have done for Jenny, for us both. We simply cannot ever repay your kindness and bravery. Were you dreadfully badly hurt?'

'Oh no, just a bump on the head and a few bruises. Sergeant Trinder got a far worse deal, if you ask me.'

Violet looked across at the sergeant and gave him another warm smile. 'Well, I think you both deserve a medal for bravery, I really do. I hope you are going to get some kind of recognition for what you did.'

'I am not expecting anything, we were just doing our job, but your kind words and the safety of your ... your daughter, was quite reward enough. Wouldn't you agree, sergeant?'

'Hear hear! The look of relief on your face when I saw you and Jenny together that night was a picture, I must say.' Violet blushed slightly at Trinder's words. 'Perhaps I should not repeat this, inspector,' Trinder spoke in an exaggerated stage whisper, 'but I got a kiss on the cheek before they carted me off in the ambulance.'

'You promised you wouldn't mention that again. Really.'

'What? And I was out cold and missed out? I was robbed.'
Vignoles laughed.

'It was absolutely nothing, inspector. I cannot see why John
— I mean, the sergeant — had to repeat it. I was just a bit shaken
up by all that had happened, and what with the sense of relief in
getting Jenny back, well, I ...' Violet stopped, her cheeks glowing.
She changed the subject rapidly. 'But tell me, what happened to the
men who took Jenny? The sergeant,' she stressed the name, 'refused
to tell me, saying was a classified police matter, or something like
that.'

'Did he, now? I don't think there is any harm in you knowing
how things stand at present. Prenton — that's almost certainly not
his real name, but it will do for now — and Price are in custody.
Both, I understand, are handcuffed to their hospital beds with the
civvies standing guard on them day and night.'

'How beastly.'

'Indeed, but then it is no less than what they deserve. If you
start taking hostages and shooting people, you cannot expect a
comfortable time of it. It's my guess that Price will get the lighter of
the sentences. This Prenton fellow is pretty adamant that he did not
kill the poor guard who fell into the coal at Woodford, nor did he
shoot the other one found at the trackside, someway along the line
out of Woodford. Thrown off the train no doubt.'

'To think these people had my Jenny.'

'Agreed. Ballistic tests will probably confirm that it was
Michael Rollo's gun that killed the train guard, and if Prenton gets
a good lawyer he might just swing the jury his way. Of course they
are both guilty to varying degrees of abduction, assault, destroying
railway property, dealing in counterfeit money ... I could go on.'

'And the one who crashed the train? This Rollo. He was killed,
wasn't he?'

'Yes, he died instantly, it seems. Rollo forced the driver, at
gunpoint, to make the train accelerate rapidly, hoping to lose the
wagons carrying us by breaking the coupling chains. His intention I
suppose was to break through the police and army cordon. Put some
distance between himself and us. It was a hopeless and desperate
plan. The driver was never going to agree to such an outrageous
demand, and so deliberately did what was demanded of him, but in
such a manner that he might throw Rollo off the train, or even wreck
the engine. He succeeded in doing both spectacularly well.'

'Rollo was crushed between the locomotive tender and the following wagon.' Trinder spoke quietly.

'Oh, how horrible. But I cannot say I feel any real sense of remorse about that. I'm sorry if that seems a bit unfeeling of me. He struck Jenny, and he threatened to kill her. But that is still an awful end.'

'The courts would have demanded that he was hanged, so I suppose we could say that it saved a long and drawn-out process. Perhaps it was kinder in the long run.' Vignoles also spoke quietly.

'He got what he deserved. And,' Trinder glanced at Violet, 'I'm not sorry if I sound harsh, he couldn't expect to carry on like that, and not reap what he sowed.' Trinder spread his one free hand in a gesture of acceptance.

'Yes. I suppose you could be right. And what of the engine crew?' Violet looked at Vignoles, then back to Trinder, who answered her.

'They will both make a full recovery, but the driver was badly hurt. He was scalded and suffered various broken bones as he threw himself off the engine, whilst the fireman sustained a broken ankle. They were both braver men than myself.'

Violet smiled again at Trinder, then looked out of the window and shook her head gently. 'I just don't understand why they did all this.'

'Money, Miss McIntyre. The desire for money would seem to be the starting and the finishing point in their reasoning.' Vignoles was gesturing with his pipe. 'These times are hard, sometimes desperate, and desperate people do all manner of things that ordinarily they would never do. One of those desperate things is that they try to get money by any means they can, thinking that this will solve all their problems ...' Vignoles tailed off, seeing the colour rise again around Violet's neck, and the way she dropped her eyes to her hands clutched together in her lap. 'Forgive me Miss McIntyre. That was thoughtless of me.'

'No. No, you are quite correct. I also found myself, innocently I like to believe, doing things I would never have dreamt I could have done. Money, or the lack of it, also dragged me, and worst of all, Jenny, into this awful mess.' She looked at Vignoles, her eyes brimming with tears. 'Have you heard if, if charges will be brought against me for the money that I borrowed?' She stopped abruptly, 'The counterfeit money, I should say, that I borrowed and, er, spent.' Violet glanced at Trinder, and then returned her gaze to Vignoles.

'That is a matter for Detective Inspector Bainbridge, for it lies outside of our jurisdiction. However, he has bigger fish to fry right now, if you will excuse an indelicate expression, for he is trying to pick up all the loose ends of this case which deals with far graver matters, so I feel sure that once the sergeant and I have sat down with him and looked at the full scale of the investigation, he will agree that your involvement was purely innocent and accidental. Many others will have found themselves, unknowingly, passing on counterfeit money as genuine. And you and Jenny have certainly suffered more than enough as a result of this grubby affair.'

'Thank you. I do hope so.'

'The strange thing about this case is, that whilst I most definitely condemn their actions, I am not convinced that these men were really so very bad. They were misguided; they made foolish errors of judgement and then found themselves in an increasingly tighter spot. Eventually they could only think of fighting their way out. They ended up killing, which is of course indefensible; but I think more by accident than by design. Once they had resorted to violence and kidnapping then it was always going to end in tragedy. Such a terrible waste.'

A silence briefly fell in the room. Violet took a breath, composed herself and then smiled, 'But inspector. What about the two lads; Edward and Simon? I have heard all kinds of stories around the village. It's quite buzzing with talk. I don't suppose anything has happened in Woodford Halse like this, since goodness knows how long. It seems they had a part to play in solving the crime? Is that really so?'

'Ah yes, Edward the baker's son, and his friend Simon. Why yes, their careful detective work gave us some vitally important information. They were extremely useful to us and I shall, in due course, be recommending them for a small award in recognition of their services.'

'I think that would be a lovely gesture.' Violet looked at her wristwatch and stood up, smoothing her neatly-tailored dress as she did so. 'Forgive me, I really must dash. I have to pay a call on my mother now, then hurry back to the shop.'

Vignoles stood up and extended his hand, 'Of course. Take care. Thank you for the visit.'

'My pleasure. Get well soon.' Violet turned as if she was about to leave the room but hesitated a moment near the door.

'Violet?' he hesitated briefly, 'As we agreed?' Trinder spoke softly.

'Oh yes; as agreed. Goodbye.' Violet left hurriedly, her cheeks flushed pink.

'What?' Trinder extended his free hand in mock disbelief in response to Vignoles's knowing smile.

'"Violet", "John"? I see all the formalities have been quickly dispensed with.'

'Well, it's a drag all this "sergeant" this and "Miss" that.'

'Friendlier?'

'Much friendlier.' He gave Vignoles a shrug.

'So for how long was I knocked out? An hour; or was it a week? You two seem to be getting along famously well. Have I missed something?'

'No, no, it's nothing. Really.' Vignoles however, held his questioning look, forcing Trinder to continue. 'Violet and Jenny came to see us both; but you were still sleeping, and so we talked about this and that, the weather, you know how it is? And then we got onto music. Found we had a lot in common. She's a big Artie Shaw fan, you know, not to mention Geraldo. And then I discovered she has not been to a concert in more years than you can imagine, and I suggested maybe one day we could ...'

'But John, I am really pleased.'

'About what? That she likes Artie Shaw?'

'Oh, don't be coy, John. She's a lovely and — dare I say it — a fine-looking woman. I would be dancing around the room if I was you.'

'Well, funnily enough, I was just going to mention that I might be doing just that — dancing.' Vignoles raised a quzzical eyebrow in response. 'The arrangement you heard us discuss —'

'Yes? I'm all ears.'

'is that I have just bought the two of us a pair of tickets to see The Modernaires at the De Monfort Hall this Friday night. And I don't mind admitting that I am rather looking forward to it.'

~ THE END ~

Smoke Gets in Your Eyes is the first book in the Inspector Vignoles series. Here is the prologue to the second, The Murder of Crows...

Prologue
A MURDER OF CROWS
January 1947

The murder of crows had feathers blacker than the mouth of Catesby Tunnel.

They were perched along the looping garland of telegraph wires running parallel to the railway tracks, hopping and flapping from one wire to another, making croaking and cracking noises that rattled around the deep, but otherwise silent, railway cutting. The land lay still. The wind had finally dropped, leaving undisturbed the fresh snow caught upon the black-etched lines of the tree branches, and only the birds' movements sent showers of fine powder from the sagging wires to the drifts below.

The crows watched and waited, impatiently flapping a wing or making small jumps along the wires as they looked for any chance of food: searching for a small rodent stopped dead by the cold far from its cosy nest, or a rabbit, chilled and starved to the bone, its last hope of food buried beneath impenetrable layers of snow, now crouched into a furry ball, eyelids drooping as merciful sleep lulled it away from life in this frozen land, soon to become the crows' next meal.

Snow had fallen, snow on snow.

Two emboldened jackdaws were strutting confidently around the railway tracks, turning their heads in jerky movements to fix their sapphire-blue eyes on the ground, pecking speculatively at any small object welded by ice to the hoary sleepers. Wires squealed as they pulled a signal into action, fighting against the deep frost caked upon the little pulley wheels that carried the wires from the distant signal box. The yellow-and-black signal arm groaned and pointed its twin metal fingers skywards. A deep rumble started to resonate through the frozen ground, the wooden sleepers quivering slightly under the feet of the jackdaws as the rails raised a fragile, glassy, ringing sound. The tunnel mouth exhaled a blast of air that smelt of wet loam and sulphur as the sound of a panting beast became clearer. Huffing and hissing, with fast-measured beats that ricocheted and roared around the tunnel walls, it drew closer. The jackdaws, without even a glance at the tunnel, flapped slowly into the air with long, easy wing-beats and curved across the dimming sky towards the skeletal trees in the fields above the cutting.

The crows, taking this as their lead, leaped into the air like so many pieces of burnt paper swirling above a bonfire as the snorting iron horse thundered out of the tunnel, whistle blowing in a wavering, mournful blast that carried far across the iron-hard land.

The locomotive was streaming steam and its pounding motion was wrapped in clouds of white that swirled around the trailing carriages, dipping and diving between the bogies until finally the last shreds were torn into tiny fragments and melted away into the air. The engine was a rich, apple green, startlingly fresh against the white of the snow, and rimed in frost where the steel was not warmed by the roaring fire in its belly. The smoke clouds collecting around the cab were flashing in reds and oranges as the barely-visible fireman shovelled more coal into the open firebox, looking for all the world like a devil stoking the fires of hell. The driver leant out of the cab window, cap pulled tight down over his forehead, squinting at the signal arm, flecks of snow stinging his eyes and cheeks.

The train rattled past, a fine spray of snow swirling briefly around the rails before the land settled back into its frozen stillness. One by one, the crows circled above the railway cutting, watching the train stream past like a tiny model, then glided back down onto the telegraph wires, eager to see if the passing train had shed any crumb of food or disturbed some small creature from its lair. The piercing eyes of the jackdaws drew them in still closer; a ragged black vanguard, swooping and curving in graceful patterns just feet above the rails then, flapping and stalling their flight, they dropped down upon their long legs into the powdery snow. A chorus of excited cracks and croaks started up from the watching crows, like a sinister audience urging the jackdaws on.

Their luck was in.

The Inspector Vignoles series comprises

Smoke Gets In Your Eyes
The Murder of Crows
The Torn Curtain
The Marylebone Murders

'Stephen Done has originated the new literary genre of "Post-war Austerity Gothic".' *Liverpool Daily Post*

'Amongst the best books I have read in recent years.' *Steve Master*

'What a page turner! An atmospheric and gripping story.' *Sian Harrington*

'All of the characters and settings ring true - you really feel that you are transported back in time, on the footplate of a war-weary steam locomotive.' *Dave Baker*

'Very well plotted.' *Tony Boullemier*

'Absolutely riveting.' *British Railway Modelling*

'Exciting and fast-moving. Each move is meticulously told and there is a pace to the story that keeps one wanting to turn the pages.' *Main Line*

✳ ✳ ✳

Each book is priced at £8.99. They are available from any high street or on-line bookshop or by direct mail order (plus £2.75 P & P, total £11.74). Please make cheques payable to Stephen Done.

5 Richmond Street,
New Brighton, Wirral
CH45 2LE

To pay by credit card, visit our website: www.hastingspress.co.uk

If you have any queries please telephone 01424 442142 or email hastings.press@gmail.com *The Marylebone Murders* will be published in late 2010.